PRAISE FOR

BRIGHT EYES

"FLAWLESS . . . lots of action and intrigue and puzzles and sex and blood, all the good stuff so necessary for a good serial killer story."
—*Vero Beach Press-Journal*

"EXCELLENT . . . a wonderful protagonist, and a surprising conclusion."
—*Booklist*

"SUSPENSEFUL."
—*Publishers Weekly*

"More than the usual case of cops and killers."
—*Affaire de Coeur*

THE ANGEL'S CRIME

Preston A. Pairo III

AN ONYX BOOK

ONYX
Published by the Penguin Group
Penguin Putnam Inc., 375 Hudson Street,
New York, New York 10014, U.S.A.
Penguin Books Ltd, 27 Wrights Lane,
London W8 5TZ, England
Penguin Books Australia Ltd, Ringwood,
Victoria, Australia
Penguin Books Canada Ltd, 10 Alcorn Avenue,
Toronto, Ontario, Canada M4V 3B2
Penguin Books (N.Z.) Ltd, 182-190 Wairau Road,
Auckland 10, New Zealand

Penguin Books Ltd, Registered Offices:
Harmondsworth, Middlesex, England

First published by Onyx, an imprint of Dutton Signet,
a member of Penguin Putnam Inc.

First Printing, April, 1998
10 9 8 7 6 5 4 3 2 1

Printed in the United States of America

PUBLISHER'S NOTE
This is a work of fiction. Names, characters, places, and incidents either are the product of the author's imagination or are used fictitiously, and any resemblance to actual persons, living or dead, events, or locales is entirely coincidental.

To my parents and Moira, once again,
for all their support;
and Anges Birnbaum for being
a fine agent;
and Laura Anne Gilman
for her savvy editorial guidance.

1

The Angel landed shortly after midnight, carrying a small satchel with a drawstring top. The bag was crudely stitched with thick wool thread and appeared in need of swift delivery if the Angel's pace was any indication.

On a starry March night, the air was cold with winter's last storm of the season. A canvas of clean snow painted the rolling hillside: one hundred acres of grazing field interspersed with pockets of woodlands.

The Angel blended with the land, making for thin shadow. His footprints pressed fast impressions as he crossed powdery snow, carrying the satchel forward to the small farmhouse nestled in the gentle pitch of the valley.

The restored two-story home was built into the easy slope of a hillside, protected from north winds. Not far uphill from the wooden house, exposed to free-flowing currents of air, a windmill turned slowly in the cold breeze, wood planks creaking from ice frozen in its veins.

It was very late and yet a light was on upstairs in the house, silhouetting a figure seated by the window. Someone was looking outside, not at the snow, but searching for explanations. He didn't see the Angel.

* * *

The trial had been long and stressful. The jury had returned its verdict less then seven hours earlier, after two days of deliberations and a near mistrial.

Terry Moore had been a trial attorney for ten years; he was experienced in law, good at it, but not inured to its traumas. His pulse remained elevated. His blood pressure, borderline high anyway at age thirty-three, was over the edge now. He felt his pulse beating in his stomach and saw it throbbing in his vision. Trials did that to him.

He used to have a wife, but lawyering ended that marriage. His grandfather, also a lawyer, had warned the law was a demanding mistress. A sadistic lover. Maybe so—at least the sadistic part.

Terry lived alone now, in the farmhouse on land still held by his grandfather's estate. The grazing fields were leased to a man who raised steer. "Excellent beefsteaks," the farmer always bragged. "Best in the States."

Terry watched the beautiful animals raised on expensive feed and saw them slaughtered. The farmer brought steaks to cook on Terry's grill. Blood-red meat charred on the outside, left red inside. Terry was always in denial that what he was eating had been the animal he'd admired grazing on green grass. Terry was in denial about many things, but not tonight. Tonight he was painfully aware of reality.

A man, Raymond Jarvis, forty-seven, a farmer himself, had been indicted by a grand jury for the murder of Colleen Baker. Colleen was seventeen when she disappeared one night last July after working her summer job at an ice cream parlor on the highway.

Witnesses put Jarvis's truck in the shopping center parking lot about the time the store closed. Jarvis had a thing for high school girls. Blonds. Pretty. Tall. He liked them with long, straight hair, and straight teeth. Straight hips, too. Not too curvy for Jarvis. Breasts were okay, but not too big. He liked them with "nice titties"; so testified Jarvis's cellmate at trial, adding that Ray liked enough size to hold on with his rough hands while he sodomized them.

My God. My God! Terry Moore suddenly jumped up out of the chair he'd positioned by the window. He was haunted by Raymond Jarvis. The trial. Colleen Baker.

He paced by the window. No longer looking outside, Terry Moore didn't see the Angel crossing the lawn, going to the side of the house, the covered access to the basement: concrete steps beneath a pair of metal hatch doors.

Terry never locked the hatch. He wasn't paranoid about locking doors, either. Other lawyers in the office said he had a death wish. So many crazies in the world. Crazies like Raymond Jarvis.

The girl who testified at trial, Susanna Lavetik, sixteen, was blond like Colleen Baker. She had straight hair, straight teeth, straight hips. Susanna shook on the witness stand, crying, struggling to recount the time Raymond Jarvis accosted her in a shopping mall parking lot.

Jarvis followed her out to her car. Jarvis was in his truck, the old red one she said looked like an antique. The engine made a rumbling sound, as though threatening to quit any minute. Jarvis drove by her once. He smiled at her, giving her "the creeps" by winking.

He had a hat on. A baseball cap with a logo from a farm feed company. The hat hid his eyes, but Susanna said she could feel him looking at her. Very scary.

She hurried to her car. No one else was around except a couple on the other side of the lot.

Susanna wished she'd left the mall sooner and hadn't stayed to hang out with her friends. She should have been home an hour earlier . . .

At that point in her testimony, she'd looked for her parents in the gallery and burst into tears, telling them she was so sorry. Her father started crying, too. Her mother was shaking.

Susanna's eyes streamed with tears. Terry Moore had patiently asked her to continue. He'd stood there firmly but patiently, pretending the whole process wasn't tearing him up inside. That his heart wasn't pounding. He ignored the rage he felt, having to focus for the courtroom. Get the evidence in. Keep logical. Organized. Present the case.

Susanna had been unable to speak for three minutes. Then, head low, hiding her face, she recounted how Raymond Jarvis's red truck pulled up beside her. He got out. A tall, rangy, skinny man with a leathery face creased with age and overexposure to sun. Raymond Jarvis grabbed her hair with one hand and clamped his other hand around her mouth. He smothered her scream with a hand that smelled strongly of onions.

Strong hands. "So strong," Susanna whimpered quietly, "so strong." Susanna sobbed painfully, as though Raymond Jarvis weren't seated at the defense table but were attacking her again, tearing at her with those hands that smelled of onions.

Again, Terry Moore had to prompt her to continue.

Susanna said he held her hair and pulled her off her feet. He banged her head against the door of his truck. Once, twice, then she blacked out. The next thing she remembered was waking up in an abandoned barn. She was naked, shivering on a pile of wet, decaying straw smeared with mud. There was a terrible sharp pain in her head—a worse feeling between her legs.

"Do you mean your vagina?" Terry Moore had to ask.

"Yes . . . yes . . . my . . ." Susanna couldn't say it—that her vagina felt as though it had been torn open. Couldn't say that in front of fifty people in the courtroom. And her sobbing father. Her mother looking as though in shock.

Susanna struggled desperately to continue her testimony as Terry Moore tried to establish rape. Defense counsel objected when Terry's questions became leading, but Susanna was falling apart on the stand. Her head was down and her hands clutched her face so it was difficult to hear her speak.

Susanna cried loudly, "Please, please, let me go home." She'd begged that of Raymond Jarvis, and begged it again of Terry Moore.

The judge convened a recess. Susanna Lavetik never returned to the stand. She'd been fragile before trial in the nonconfrontational atmosphere of the prosecutor's office. Her therapist had been there with her. Susanna believed she'd be able to testify against the man who'd knocked her unconscious, abducted her, and raped her. But despite all the counseling, all the rehearsals in the prosecutor's office, it was too much for Susanna. She couldn't take the stand, couldn't grant Raymond Jarvis his constitutional right to confront his accusers. His crimes against her proved too horrific to recount.

When Susanna couldn't return to the stand, the State's case against Raymond Jarvis for the murder of Colleen Baker began to fall apart. Susanna's testimony was to have established a pattern of criminal activity: Raymond

Jarvis's dangerous sexual proclivity for young blond girls.

The State needed that because it didn't have Colleen Baker's body. Jarvis, with a record of similar assaults in his native Georgia, seemed to have decided not to chance leaving live witnesses to testify anymore. Colleen Baker had disappeared. So had Leslie Henryton after her.

When Susanna couldn't continue, Terry Moore called a new witness to the stand: the owner of the ice cream store where Colleen worked. He testified that Jarvis came into the store a couple of times. Colleen talked to him. She was very friendly that way, would talk to anyone. But she did later tell the owner she was uncomfortable working nights any more, because the man in the red truck made her feel scared. Not because of anything he'd done. No. Just the way he looked at her. The way he smiled. And his hands—they were so ugly and smelled so bad. Onions, the owner said. Jarvis would come into the store stinking of the onions his hands had spent all day digging out of fertile soil. The smell was even on the dollar bills he passed over the counter. A smell so bad other customers would leave the store. And Jarvis never seemed to notice.

Onions. Stinking of onions.

Terry Moore knew he'd never be able to eat onions again. Never be able to see or smell an onion and not think of Raymond Jarvis. Especially after Raymond Jarvis was acquitted of the murder of Colleen Baker.

The jury found him not guilty. And now Jarvis was out. He was free, having posted bail on the Susanna Lavetik case the judge wouldn't revoke even after the Colleen Baker indictment. Raymond Jarvis was free. Because the State couldn't produce Colleen Baker's body, and defense counsel, so slick, had painted Colleen as a free spirit, inferring she may have run away, not been murdered.

The State didn't give the jury enough evidence. It gave its members reasonable doubt instead, and now Terry Moore was left with the horrible thought of another girl having hands stinking of onions pressed to her mouth, and it seized him with rage.

The first he saw of the Angel was a presence of whiteness. A motion detected in a corner of his vision. He turned and saw the figure standing in the darkened hallway outside his bedroom. The figure in white seemed to emit its own light.

Terry stopped. Stared. Strangely, he was not afraid. As though a soothing benevolence radiated from the figure he now saw was a man—though Terry was unable to determine his age or see his face.

The man was no more than five-seven or eight, medium build, dressed in white: a thick wool sweater, heavy pants, and pale hiking boots. He was holding a satchel.

The man spoke in a calm, almost lyrical voice. "Fear not." His tone resonated strength and understanding.

Terry Moore felt weak and disoriented. This was not possible. He shivered as hairs raised along the back of his neck. He did not believe he consciously decided to kneel but that it was a reflex, as though something he always had hoped to be true *was* true. A hope, a belief he'd long since given up on.

The man said again, "Fear not." He seemed so much taller now that Terry was kneeling. The man paused, then: "You tried the case too soon. It wasn't ready for trial. You were too eager." Not scolding, but teaching. "You should have waited. Let the police work longer to find the girl's body. Raymond Jarvis is not that smart. He made a mistake that would have led you to her, but you needed to be patient, to uncover that mistake."

"I know, but—"

"You let others make decisions for you. Others decided the case must be tried quickly because of public outcry and demands for justice. Yet those who decided that the case must be tried—your superiors—they left the responsibility of conviction upon *you*. And now put this suffering upon you. That Raymond Jarvis has gone free and it is because of you."

Terry Moore didn't question how this man knew so much. He didn't want to question. He wanted to believe. He entire adult life had been spent searching for answers. Trying to re-create the past through twisted, sometimes illogical rules of evidence. Rules left open to misguided interpretation that often fell victim to the blinded light of justification.

The man dressed in white said, "Please pray with me."

Terry Moore hesitated, feeling a tug toward reality by the gravity of logic.

And yet when the man said, "Close your eyes, pray with me," Terry Moore closed his eyes. He clamped them shut because he so desperately needed an answer for what had happened today, and if this was some madman who'd broken into his house to torture him further, then perhaps this was what he deserved for Raymond Jarvis going free.

"Dear Lord," the man began, and Terry Moore repeated, "Dear Lord . . ."

Because the case had been brought to trial too quickly.

". . . give me strength to carry on in an imperfect system . . ."

Because Terry Moore had been caught up in the manipulation of the man who ran his office. Had let his ego be stroked by the challenge to take a weak case to trial—a murder charge without a body, and scant circumstantial evidence—Terry's boss telling him if anyone could do it, he could do it.

". . . to treat fairly my adversaries, with respect, and without malice, for they too are bound in webs of imperfection . . ."

Because Terry had a vendetta against the lawyer Raymond Jarvis hired. A man not unlike the devil, whom Terry Moore had sought to banish from the halls of justice, and Terry Moore had failed.

". . . to have faith in myself to bring to justice those who are deserving of punishment, and to have faith that even those who escape conviction will ultimately be sentenced for their crimes."

Slowly, Terry Moore repeated the man's prayer. ". . . to have faith that even those who escape conviction will ultimately be sentenced for their crimes." Having spoken that, he waited, but no more words were offered. No amen.

Terry Moore opened his eyes. The man in white was gone.

The satchel that had been in the man's hands was now on the floor. Terry rose slowly from his knees. He felt lightheaded and unsteady, unsure of what had happened.

He picked up the satchel and unbound the crude rope that tied it shut. Even before he looked inside, he smelled onions. And when he saw what was contained within, he dropped the bag and screamed.

Hands that smelled of onions flopped out of the bag onto the floor. Raymond Jarvis's hands. Sawed off from his arms. Drained of blood. Drained of life. Drained of evil. Raymond Jarvis would molest no more young girls with those hands.

The Angel had seen to that.

2

It was beautiful here, no doubt about that. Jimmy Griffin renewed that opinion every day as he jogged across the dual-lane road and stepped onto the salt-stained boardwalk that bridged a narrow line of sea grape. He descended a dozen wood steps until his Avia running shoes landed in soft, beige sand.

At the threshold of dawn, Griffin started running along the beach.

The air was pleasant and warm and full of sweet tropical smells. Juno Beach, Florida—a kiss thrown from the tip of Florida's Gold Coast. North of the rampant growth spiraling from Miami to Palm Beach, and south of the tedious dull of coastal-rural Jupiter, Juno Beach was present-day heaven.

There wasn't a fee at beach parking lots like down in Boca Raton. Highways were blissfully empty. You could fish on the beach without hooking a tourist, buy stamps at the post office without waiting in long lines, sit on the porch without hearing sirens, and get a smile from an unhassled grocery clerk at Publix.

Trouble was, the devil was lurking offshore, tail concealed by the sharp tailoring of expensive suits: land developers, time-share salesmen, and advance men from real estate investment trusts looking for sites to plop down a new super center anchored by a Best Buy, Wal-Mart, or mega-screen movie theater.

But Juno Beach *was* a thousand miles from Baltimore. For Jimmy Griffin, not only a thousand miles but almost ten months from Baltimore. Sometimes it seemed like enough distance, enough time. Sometimes . . .

Griffin's entire life had been spent in Baltimore. Thirty-four years. Born and raised in the city. A kid during the civil rights riots that erupted after Martin Luther King, Jr., was shot dead. An era when Griffin's father, a Baltimore cop, had been beating heads with a night stick while on duty, and been a mean drunk at home when he wasn't.

Griffin had become a cop himself—a good one. He'd married his high school sweetheart. Saw his father through a stroke, bad debts with bookies, and into alcohol recovery. Griffin started law school at night. Finally, after so much struggle, life seemed to come together. Then it all fell apart. Ripped apart.

Griffin couldn't pinpoint where it started going wrong, there were so many possibilities. The job. His marriage. Two men dead by his hand.

Sometimes, even in Juno Beach, Griffin didn't sleep well. Some nights he couldn't go more than two hours without coming to abruptly. Terrible dreams awakened him, and yet, once conscious, he usually couldn't remember them. The images were like a specter darting around in his subconscious, haunting him.

There was one harrowing image that stuck with him, a recurring nightmare so powerful he began to fear it was a premonition. Over and over, he dreamed of lost children screaming for parents they couldn't find.

And so he ran.

That morning, Griffin did two miles north along the

beach to another set of wood steps that took him up to the highway. There was hardly any traffic at that early hour, so he ran in the street instead of on the sidewalk on the way back. Keeping up a good pace, he did six-minute miles, returning to the house two hundred yards off the beach that had been home for the last three months.

The cottage had pink stucco walls, a white barrel-tile roof, and furniture from a discount place where you could point to a decorated room and they'd deliver the whole package within seventy-two hours. Mostly it was laminate furniture for snowbirds who bought places for the winter and needed to set up residence in a hurry.

Griffin was housesitting for the couple who owned the cottage while they went north for the spring and summer. He stayed rent-free and was paid $200 a month to keep the little yard in shape, which was easy, taking about twenty minutes every ten days to mow the lawn, and a little extra time to pull palm fronds out of rain gutters now and again. He felt guilty taking the money and put it toward minor improvements, sanding and repainting the porch and having the carpet cleaned.

He didn't need the money. His severance pay from the city attorney's office in Baltimore would have been enough to live on for a few years, plus a small pension—a grand a month—and his expenses and tastes were minimal.

Griffin's life appeared simple and pleasant. Every couple of weeks, Liz flew in from Atlanta, where she worked as a reporter for a national tabloid newspaper. They'd met in Baltimore when Liz was there on assignment, beginning a relationship without ever defining if they were just friends, lovers, or more.

There was also Janice, whom Griffin had just recently

met in Florida, and who was unlike anyone he'd ever had feelings for or thought he could have feelings for.

All in all, there was enough here with which to start a new life, but Griffin didn't know how. He didn't know what he was supposed to do. He'd been a cop for so long, an investigator for the prosecutor's office after that. A husband. A father. And then suddenly, without warning, he was none of that.

The first months in Florida had been spent recuperating, trying to get over Baltimore. He'd lived with his parents over in Fort Myers, and enjoyed seeing his folks both doing so well now. Griffin had pretended he liked golf, getting up at dawn to play eighteen, riding in carts with his father and his retired cronies. Six months of that had been enough, so he'd come to the east coast to look around and lucked into this housesitting.

Griffin thought he'd be able to sleep if he was somewhere closer to the ocean, where he could hear the waves. But his soul—that's what he'd decided it was—was tortured. He was not at peace.

He even tried something he'd never done since childhood, which was to go to church. At first he went with Janice. Other times he'd go alone, and it didn't matter which denomination, didn't matter as to the particular secular meaning. He was searching quietly, almost desperately for solace.

He stopped going to church when he began to feel like a trespasser and a hypocrite. A sinner. He'd killed two men back in Baltimore, one in cold blood. Church wasn't a place for someone like him.

After his run, he showered and drank a breakfast health concoction—powders and milk tossed into the blender with ice. He was at the gymnasium by ten, a little hole-in-the-wall place tucked around the side of a failing shopping plaza. It was a no-frills gym, no socializing or aerobics classes, strictly free weights.

Griffin's purpose was to expend energy. If the running and lifting didn't exhaust him, he'd swim the ocean, having befriended lifeguards to keep them from whistling him in when he voyaged into deep waters cut with riptide.

His body was responding. What had always been a strong, athletic frame was turning even harder, defined and powerful without evolving into that subhuman bulge of muscles and veins sought by serious lifters who spent more time in the mirror than in reality.

The physical strain had become like a mantra. It drained him of the energy that stirred his restlessness. It was an outlet. Yet, at the same time, he began to wonder if there was some other reason for getting into this kind of shape at a time most men his age were settling into desk jobs and starting to blame their wives for shrinking their jeans in the wash when the waist got snug.

Griffin also found himself back in courthouses. Sitting in the gallery, watching trials. Maybe he did it because it was the only life he'd ever known. Maybe it was a barometer to see if he really did want to complete the application he'd received from Florida State University to transfer University of Baltimore credits and finish law school. In two years, he could be on the other side of the rail again, back at the trial table, not as a cop or assisting a prosecutor but as a lawyer.

Friday afternoon, in the North Palm Beach courthouse on PGA Boulevard, the criminal docket listed defendants and the charges they faced. Griffin read it, remembered it—sort of a game—so he could sit inside and play *Match The Perp With The Crime*.

It wouldn't be a bad TV game show. Cheap, reality

TV. Have contestants stand before a big blow-up screen of misdemeanants and felons sitting in court among lawyers, witnesses, and cops, and the idea was first to find the defendants, then guess what crime they'd been charged with.

Griffin would have to disqualify himself from participating. It wouldn't be fair. He was too good at it, too experienced. Be it Baltimore or Palm Beach, the clothes were different, but the faces and body language were the same.

The lawyers were the same, too. Some adopted hard, rigid stances and appeared indignant, ready to fight on their toes. Others were more laid back, quietly cocky, working angles on the prosecutor. Some wielded case law while others had a knack for making truths seem like lies and vice versa once they got someone on the stand.

Friday afternoon the game was made more complex by sheer numbers. The docket was heavy. The bailiff tried to coax folks lining the walls to squeeze into bench rows that were already full of nasty-looking people.

The sitters were Griffin's first clue as to defendants. Defendants almost always sat. They ambled into court, gave a lazy nod to their attorney, a ballsy yeah-hey-you-workitout-whatever motion of head and shoulders, figuring they were screwed no matter what, grabbed up in some system that wasn't even logical much less fair. Defendants who weren't even bright enough to work up a good lie sauntered onto the witness stand, forgot all their lawyer had prepped them with, and proceeded to become indignant with the "bogus" process. Almost as an afterthought, they offered a lame story and went to jail.

Most of them were like that, especially the ones who

got busted because they needed money for drugs, not because they were intent on a life of thievery. But when you had a $100-a-day habit and a minimum wage job—hell, hon, do the math—there weren't enough hours in the day to get along once they took out taxes and garnishment money owed on that used Nissan the smiling salesman instant-financed you with no money down.

The defendants who were sitting weren't going to give you much trouble. They were going to take theirs sitting down. It was the ones who stood with their attorney, the ones who wanted to work the edge, the angle, who wanted to get out, *they* were the hustlers you worried about.

Griffin saw one Friday afternoon. He was in his late twenties, white, not a big guy, but the kind of medium-build scrapper who'd blow his paycheck on Jack Daniels, get all wound up, and make dispatch send three cops to get the cuffs on him. He had on a suit that hadn't been worn much since its lapel size had gone out of style—maybe worn only for court appearances.

Griffin knew the guy's name and what he was charged with, not because he'd seen him before but because of how the guy mean-stared at a woman seated across the courtroom, attacking her with his eyes.

The woman was in her early twenties, reed-thin, with dark hair hanging unwashed and uncombed over the shoulders of a faded logo T-shirt. She sat in the second row behind the prosecutor's table, near the police in the first row.

When the prosecutor talked to her and glanced back at the man standing next to his lawyer, referring to him, the woman wouldn't turn around to look. She seemed too scared to look.

And the perp knew to glance away when the prosecutor gestured toward him.

Griffin read the prosecutor's lips when he asked the woman, "Is that him?"

The woman nodded without ever looking. She knew he was back there. She could feel him.

Drew Millundra. That would be the guy's name. Griffin knew. On the docket sheet in the hall, the charges listed across from Drew Millundra's name were Stalking and Telephone Abuse.

Griffin took a seat in the gallery. He waited for the prosecutor to finish talking to the line of attorneys, cops, and witnesses for the afternoon docket. He waited for the judge to come on the bench. He waited for Drew Millundra's case to be called. And he wondered if this was what Janice might refer to as a sign.

That's how she explained what he was going through right now—Janice, the woman he'd met in the Christian bookstore and was seeing now and then. She was young, pretty, unblemished, and naive—lots of things Griffin wasn't. He felt peaceful with her but at the same time confused by their differences.

Janice told Griffin he needed to have faith. Even if he was unsure as to his beliefs, he had to have faith. And through faith he would get a sign about what he was supposed to do. What did she say it was? His calling.

But could something as potentially ugly and mean as Drew Millundra staring at the woman he was accused of stalking be a sign?

Maybe.

3

Once court began, Drew Millundra sat next to his attorney, five rows back on the left side of the courtroom—the defense side of the courtroom. Millundra propped himself at an angle from which he could glare across the aisle at the young woman who was afraid of him.

She sat rigidly in her seat, never looking back, keeping her head turned slightly to the right as though feeling Millundra's hot stare and not wanting to show him even the side of her face.

Millundra whispered occasional comments to his lawyer, who mostly nodded, sometimes took notes on their quick, whispered exchanges.

Griffin suspected Millundra had a bit of a sixth sense about being watched. As soon as someone was about to look at him, he took his stare away from the girl.

Millundra sat with a posture of concern. That suit and fresh haircut were supposed to keep him from looking like a stalker—create the impression the crime didn't fit the person.

Griffin had seen it thousands of times. Guys who spent their nights crawling in and out of busted-in basement windows looking for anything they could fence to buy crack—guys he'd arrested with grime-stained clothes, greasy hair, and long, dirty fingernails—showed up showered and shaved for court.

They wanted to make it seem as though the only unrespectable part of them was the crime with which they'd been charged, doing that so they could walk out of court through the same door they walked in. Guys like that wanted to pay their fine, start a bullshit spell of probation, sit through some Narcotics Anonymous classes, and get back on the street. They were the ones who knew how to torque the system—give a little turn, a little nudge, make those scales of justice tip ever so kindly in their direction.

Pierced earrings disappeared for court. Ponytails got cut. Big gold necklaces, pagers, and cell phones were left at home. Dress 'em up and take 'em out for a little vaudeville act in court. Here's a scumbag: now you see him . . . Poof! Shower, shave, wardrobe. Now you don't.

The ones who showed up contrite, pretending to be sorry, faking blinded eyes as though having "seen the light"—they were the ones to watch. They wanted to get out so they could do it again. They didn't like jail any more than they liked the laws jails were meant to enforce. They knew not to swagger up to the defense table or say, "Huh?" to the judge.

They knew, as Drew Millundra knew, when your case was called, you looked a little scared and really, really sorry. Misunderstood. You nodded obediently like a good dog, because that's how you got another chance, and another chance, and another. As long as your rap sheet wasn't too nasty or violent, you could turn the entrance to the courthouse into a revolving door. In-out, in-out, in-out. Pay the lawyer, pay your fine, like throwing change in the toll baskets on the Florida Turnpike.

Drew Millundra was "court smart." He anticipated when the cop in the front row, the one Griffin assumed had arrested him, was going to glance back toward him. The cop never saw Drew Millundra other than with his head lowered, as if he might be praying. And as soon as the cop turned forward, Millundra was staring at the girl again. A hungry stare. An I'm-gonna-get-you stare.

Millundra was good. He was white, had probably made it through high school, and had enough control over himself to massage the system. He was in front of a white judge, white prosecutor, and a hard-luck-looking white girl was his victim. He'd walk. Drew Millundra was on the revolving door plan today. Griffin knew it. He didn't have to stay to hear the case to make sure, but he did anyway. In case he was losing his touch. In case Florida pulled a surprise on him and did something Baltimore wouldn't.

When Millundra's case was called, he walked penitently toward the defense table, too "ashamed" to look up or speak up until his attorney urged him to repeat his name and address more clearly for the record. Millundra pulled himself together for that. Quite the actor.

His victim shook her head in the second row, still too scared to look at him, but she knew this was an act.

Millundra took a plea to one count of phone misuse, to wit: repeated calls intended to harass, frighten, or embarrass. The stalking charge was nol-prossed—dismissed—because the prosecution witness who saw Millundra outside the victim's trailer had not appeared in court.

The victim, Angie Hanes, told the prosecutor her friend, the witness, had moved back to Jacksonville and didn't want to testify. And Angie had never seen Millundra outside her trailer with her own eyes, she knew only that *someone* had been out there, tapping on her windows in the middle of the night, probably the same person who'd broken into her trailer and ripped the curtains off the bathroom window. But no, she couldn't say it was Millundra for sure.

Millundra's attorney explained to the judge how it was all a mistake. "Judge, Mr. Millundra met Ms. Hanes at the club where she works and he thought there was the possibility of a relationship between them. He gave her a ride home one night, and Ms. Hanes gave him her phone number but didn't return his calls. He left a few messages on her machine and, when he didn't hear from her, made the mistaken judgment to call and swear at her. He did call her terrible names. He did accuse her of using him for a ride home and of lying that she'd like to go out with him . . ."

Angie Hanes shook her head and trembled slightly.

". . . but that was all. Mr. Millundra has never been back to Ms. Hanes's trailer, has never followed her in his car, and has no intention of ever contacting her again. He was upset because he'd thought she was attracted to him—realizing she wasn't, he made a mistake by calling her. I would note that there haven't been—and the prosecutor and Ms. Haines can confirm this—any instances of phone calls since Mr. Millundra was arrested on this charge."

"What about people outside the trailer?" Judge Brenner asked, looking over wire frame glasses at the prosecutor. "Or break-ins?"

The prosecutor leaned back across the rail and spoke in private to the arresting officer, then reported to the judge: "No other incidents at Ms. Haines's trailer, and a peeping tom was arrested outside another trailer a few weeks after Ms. Hanes was having problems."

"This other man who was arrested, the peeping tom, has he been convicted or did he confess to breaking into Ms. Hanes's trailer or spying on her? What I'm getting at is, do we know he was the one who broke into Ms. Hanes's trailer and not Mr. Millundra here?"

The prosecutor said, "Not my case, Judge. I don't know." He turned again toward the cop. "Officer Weller?"

"Trial's coming up next month, Judge, but I'm not sure of any confession. I didn't handle the arrest."

"All right." Judge Brenner glanced at Millundra, whose head was tilted down in a studied pose of feigned shame. "So this is guilty to one count of phone misuse, recommendation of probation. We have a record on Mr. Millundra?"

"DWI in Pensacola five years ago, judge," the prosecutor reported. "We don't have an FBI record, but defense counsel advises his client has no priors."

"That right?" Brenner asked.

"Mr. Millundra, is that correct?" his lawyer asked him.

"Just the DWI," Millundra said quietly. "I stay away from trouble."

In the gallery, Jimmy Griffin whispered, "Bullshit."

The judge said, "No agreement as to a fine?"

"Court's discretion."

"Let's make it five hundred dollars. Maybe Mr. Millundra won't have so much extra gasoline money to give people rides home. And Mr. Millundra, you're going on two years' probation, and I'm making it unsupervised, but a condition is you stay away from Ms. Hanes. Even if she moves into the apartment, house, condo—whatever—next to you, you move out. Got it? This poor girl's shaking over there. She's afraid of you because you're a lot bigger than she is."

"I'm sorry." Millundra kept his voice quiet and unthreatening. "I know it was dumb. It won't happen again." He began to pivot toward Angie but stopped short of facing her. He glanced sheepishly, eyes angled to the floor, no hungry look now, just a pitiful-me expression, offering, "I'm sorry. I didn't mean anything bad by it. I'm sorry."

Judge Brenner spoke the terms of probation he noted on the disposition sheet. "No more phone calls, Mr. Millundra. And you stay away from her. I'm not even going to name a distance, except that if you're close enough for her to see you, you're too close. She lives in Lake Worth, you're way down in Davie. Maybe you should stay down there, Mr. Millundra. Let Broward County worry about you."

"Yes, sir."

So polite, contrite, misunderstood. So full of shit.

Angie Hanes stayed in the courtroom until Millundra and his lawyer exited, the stalker and his esquire off to the clerk's office to pay a slap-on-the-wrist fine and fill out some probation papers.

Angie sat in the second row as though numb. She stared straight ahead, looking as if she might cry.

Griffin didn't blame her. The uniform cop who'd talked to Angie before court said he was sorry, said he'd drive by to check on her. Angie nodded but didn't look reassured.

After a couple of minutes, she angrily grabbed her floppy pocketbook and hurried from the courtroom, walking hard steps that turned to a run by the time she reached the double exit doors. She rushed through the building and outside to the parking lot, digging into her pocketbook on the way to her car.

She unlocked her little blue Cressida that had a rusty license plate holder and lots of body damage, threw in her pocketbook, threw in herself, and got out of there. Driving between grassy islands planted with palm trees, turning onto PGA Boulevard, speeding toward I-95.

Griffin hoped she didn't get herself killed on 95, but Angie was probably more worried about what Drew Millundra was planning for her, the way he'd eaten her up with his eyes. Visual maniacal desire.

Millundra emerged from the North Palm Beach courthouse into the sunny afternoon kicking and scratching, grinning it up with his lawyer, who suddenly didn't seem all that interested in hanging around. The lawyer'd been paid, his show was over, and Millundra really wasn't the kind of guy the lawyer wanted to know . . . at least not until he got busted again.

Millundra waved a hearty farewell to his counselor and started down the row of parked cars toward his late-model black Camaro angle-parked across two spaces to keep from getting door-dinged. About thirty feet from his car, he first saw Griffin.

Griffin leaned against the bumper of a Nissan Altima, a car the cottage's owners kept at the house and said he was more than welcome to use. Griffin appeared to be enjoying the weather, soaking it up.

Millundra became wary. He probably pegged Griffin as a cop, as if there was an aura that survived even after Griffin had been off the job for ten months. Millundra assumed a tough posture, belligerent, no charges pending against him now. He was out.

Griffin smiled, casual friendly, said, "See ya around."

Millundra said, "Uh-huh," got in his Camaro, gave

the engine a roaring stomp, and peeled wheels out of there.

Griffin opened the Altima's glove box and retrieved the road map he needed less and less as he became familiar with Palm Beach County. He wanted to check the distance to Lake Worth, estimate how long it would take him to get there tonight.

4

There was a message from Janice on Griffin's answering machine at the cottage. Her clear voice was like a pleasant hymn: "Jimmy, hi, it's Janice, but you know that don't you? Just calling—see how you're doing. Haven't seen you in a couple days . . . miss you. And I don't know, I'm working at the bookstore tonight, but after, if you want, we could rent a movie. I could drive over. Or you could come down here. And if not a movie, whatever, pancakes at Denny's, something like that. Anyway, call me tonight at the store? Hope you're good. 'Bye."

She made Griffin smile. It was like getting a call from a cute girl in your seventh grade class. There was an awkwardness about Janice's rapport with him, with men in general. There was an attraction but also a hesitation she tried to play off with cheery, sometimes nervous chatter. From what she'd told him about herself so far, Janice and her sisters had been raised in a sheltered environment by very protective, devoutly religious parents. No smoking, drugs, alcohol, no sex out of marriage, and nine o'clock curfews.

She'd graduated from a Baptist college. Now twenty-five and finally out from her parents' shadow, Janice was trying to figure out who she was, and what she believed, including whether what her parents had preached as evil truly was.

For Griffin, being raised in an atmosphere of brutal reality, his father being a cop, it was difficult to identify with Janice's thought process. Still, he liked and respected her a great deal. Her presence glowed about him like an antidote. Janice was very un-Liz.

Griffin no sooner thought about Liz than the phone rang, and it *was* Liz. Long distance from Atlanta. The rigors and noise of tabloid *America Exposed* offices in the background. No hello from Liz, but right into it: "How does multiple homicide sound to you? Multiple *family* homicide. The Straight A Killer. I got a name for him already—I'm so *goddamned* good at this. I'm a pro!" Liz was high on work. "This's a hot story. Very hot. I want you on it with me."

Griffin enjoyed Liz's wild energy as much as Janice's peaceful innocence. He carried the phone onto the porch. "Hello to you, too."

"Screw hello, Jimmy, I've known you too long. There's a ticket for you at the airport. Tomorrow a.m. Do your little sun-up run on the beach and bust balls down to West Palm."

"Liz—I'm no reporter."

"You're not anything these days except fit and desirable. All that working out you're doing, I get turned on just thinking about you. But that's not enough. You spend much more at-ease time in that cottage you're gonna get a membership app from the AARP."

"We've been through it, Liz. You're the reporter. I'm the cop."

"Not all that different, and actually my job's better. I get to write the story and put my spin on the end. You arrest someone and your entire work product goes into the hands of slick defense lawyers and incompetent judges—did I mention there's a potential kidnapping in this story, too? And that the kid's on the run. Cops can't find him or his girlfriend. And did I mention the girlfriend's father . . . no, I guess I didn't, guess that wouldn't be of any interest to you. You wouldn't want to work this story with me. Nah."

"I'm dealing with something down here, Liz. I could be busy for a few days."

"Oh . . ." That surprised her. "Okay." She hesitated. "Is it . . . ? Never mind—none of my business."

"No, it's not Janice. You know she's just a friend."

"You don't have to explain. You've got no commitment to me." Liz always told him that, and Griffin echoed the sentiment for her as well, but neither of them ever sounded that committed about *not* being committed. As though it were just a coincidence that Liz, who'd been quite liberal in her dating habits, hadn't seen—hadn't slept with—anyone but Griffin for ten months.

"Come on, Liz, we agreed, none of this talk on the phone." Meaning relationship talk. "Only in person."

"Okay . . . so what's this thing—this whatever you're dealing with?"

"I'll tell you about it once I know what's happening." He didn't want to give her any details over the phone, didn't want her worrying. He probably shouldn't have mentioned it at all.

"Once what's happening?"

He needed a white lie to change the subject. "I don't want to jinx it."

"Jinx it? Is this a job offer? The paper will match any offer you get, Jimmy. You know they want you, and you're foolish not to jump on while you've still got some billable notoriety. You're the cop who got Bright Eyes, for God's sake. And you don't have to do any writing, just investigation. Like this story I've got breaking. You and me. We get the kid's tail, we find him, that's big headlines. Major big. Your worth goes up even more." She was pitching him like selling a story to the editors. "Take this one freelance. I can get you ten grand, then thirty, maybe fifty if we snag the kid before the cops. You run him down and I do the story. The paper covers all your expenses, and you're a grocery-store-checkout-line hero again."

"I never did it to get my name in the papers." On the cottage porch, looking at the calm, turquoise sea, Griffin felt the past antagonizing him.

"I know. So don't do it to get your name in the paper now. Do it for the money."

"I don't need the money."

"Everybody needs—all right, forget the money. Do it because maybe you and I, we might catch this kid before he kills someone else. Do it for that."

Griffin didn't respond.

Liz's rapid speech patter slowed, quieted, asking, "Do it for me?"

And Griffin found himself nodding, but Liz wasn't standing there beside him. She was on the phone. She couldn't see the nod, only heard his reply: "Can I think about it?"

"Not for long. This story's red hot *right now*. By the time I get there, the cops could have him."

"When do you leave?"

"Two hours."

"Where's this happening?"

"That's a surprise. You'll see when you get your ticket. Not *if* you get the ticket. *When.*"

"Okay," he conceded. "When I get the ticket."

"Soon." Realizing she said that a little forcefully, Liz tempered, "Please." Then, emotions getting the better of her: "I miss you a lot."

"I miss you, too. Wish you were here."

Their conversation became quiet. Liz reminded, "We've talked about that, too."

"Yeah." Griffin sighed, taking in a deep breath of ocean air and letting it out. "You've got a plane to catch."

"Bags to pack."

"Be careful."

"I will be . . . see you there?"

Griffin was nodding again. "All right . . . sure, why not. See you there. It's some kid you're after, right? That's what you said?"

"Seventeen years old. Honor student. Gifted and talented."

"Who'd he kill?"

"For starters, his father and sister."

"Seventeen . . . unreal." Griffin pretended to be shocked, because that's what people expected, but nothing shocked him anymore. He knew it should have, but it didn't. That was part of what was wrong. "Seventeen . . ." He considered the implications practically, like a doctor operating on a teenager with cancer: not saddened by the age factor but evaluating how age impacted the case. "Seventeen. A kid. Something got inside his head and set him off. He'll be disorganized, so the cops won't know where to look for him at first. He'll be unpredictable, but he'll make a mistake. Like a runaway case, but there's motivation not to get caught. Still, he'll run out of money. He might make it three or four days. You say he's got a girlfriend?"

"She's either with him, hiding from him, or dead and no one's found the body yet."

"If she's with him, she'll take off in a day or two. She'll get scared. She'll tell the cops where her boyfriend is."

"Or if *we* find her, she tells us." There was a smile in Liz's voice. "You're liking this, aren't you?"

Griffin nodded again. "See you soon."

"Fantastic. Your ticket's for tomorrow morning, but if that doesn't work out, take the next available flight. It's an unrestricted ticket. First class, even."

"Okay."

"Looking forward to it. 'Bye until then."

Griffin switched off the phone. He sat down and put his feet up. The restless energy that had made it a habit to churn inside him suddenly had a focus point. Two points, actually: Drew Millundra and Liz's story.

He couldn't sit still. So he changed and did a quick mile on the beach, finishing with a sprint. Back at the cottage, sunset's light glowed through the circle window set in the kitchen ceiling peak. He mixed up a higher-calorie dinner version of his breakfast blender drink, more carbohydrates. He took it into the bathroom and drank most between his shower and shave, finishing it while getting into jeans and a T-shirt. A change of clothes went into a nylon Avia-logo bag.

He drove the borrowed Altima to a video store and rented a movie he figured Janice would like, something light and breezy, doing that now in case there wasn't time to pick it up later.

Back outside, the final purple-orange colors of dusk sprayed across the horizon.

Griffin got on I–95 headed south toward Lake Worth.

5

Griffin turned into the trailer park around nine-thirty. It wasn't a bad place, but like anywhere the rent was low, the riffraff weren't priced out.

The entrance was marked by a palm tree with dead fronds clinging to branches that still had some green life left in them. A ground-level flood lamp shone orange light up the rough tree trunk.

The driveway was a single lane, which changed from macadam to crushed rock just beyond the entrance and looped toward the back of the park like a narrow lasso. Every hundred yards, a vapor streetlamp cast a green glow.

Larger aluminum trailers were propped on concrete blocks. Smaller ones had wheels and trailer hitches, ready to be pulled out at a moment's notice. It was a real mixed-bag place. Some lots were well if tastelessly tended, adorned with plastic statues and flower boxes; others were overgrown and cluttered with debris.

The Altima's tires crunched slowly over rock road. Griffin kept an eye out for Millundra's black Camaro while checking numbers on mailboxes and front doors.

Some trailers didn't have any identification at all; some proudly boasted resident's names and personalized signs, one announcing WE WORKED OUR WHOLE LIFE

FOR THIS. Griffin wasn't sure if that was sarcasm or celebration.

He continued slowly toward the rear portion of the park, looking for Angie Hanes's address, which he'd culled from—simple enough—the phone book. A. HANES 63 PALMETTOPK. CIR. FT WRTH.

There it was. One of the tiniest tin cans in the whole place, shaped like a big bullet sliced in half. Silver side walls were rounded at the roof edge. Windows were narrow rectangles with torn flaps of screens falling out.

Angie's inside lights were off. A bug-repelling yellow porch light was on, but it wasn't doing much of a job at keeping away bugs. Griffin doubted that Angie's having her lights out would trick Drew Millundra into thinking she wasn't home.

Griffin continued on, wanting a feel for the area, not just Angie's lot. He followed the driveway loop back toward the entrance, now and again spying someone looking out an opened window. A few people, mostly retirees, sat outside on aluminum folding chairs.

It wouldn't do well for him to drive through repeatedly. Someone might get suspicious. He was going to have to find a place to park and wait.

Drew Millundra *couldn't* wait—wait to see the expression on that bitch Angie's face. Maybe she figured his being arrested and having to appear in court had scared him off. That he wouldn't want any more of that trouble. Yeah, right. Ohhh, so scary. Some fat cops, skinny four-eyed prosecutor, a judge who tried to sound mean, but big deal. Like he hadn't been in jail before. Lots of places. Lots of times. Kentucky. 'Bama. Louisiana. Under a host of fake names. Mister Alias, they should call him. Fingerprints on file under different names, but who was going to run his prints on some minor charge? Find out he was the same guy who'd beat up women in four—no, five—different states?

Women were the same most everywhere. They just downright pissed him off. Hard to say why exactly—they just did. Like Angie. He gave her a ride home in the rain, wanted to get a little friendly with her—like it was something she'd never done before—and she wasn't interested. No, not once she got what she wanted out of him: got that ride home. Same deal as when she waited tables and got her tip. See ya. Wouldn't give someone who'd passed her a fiver the time of day once they paid their check. Like her smile was worth five bucks. Get real, Angie baby.

Millundra smiled as he carried a bottle of Jack Daniels by its neck and banged it on the counter. Asked the clerk, "Whaddayou lookin' at?"

"You smilin' like you havin' a good time. I'm jus' glad you happy, man, tha's all. Glas for yo bidness."

"Yeah, well, good for you." He pointed behind the counter. "Gimme a pack of smokes. Marlboro hard pack."

The clerk turned toward the cigarette shelves. Running his finger along the carton edges, looking, "Marlboro hard side . . . hard side. Here we go."

"And one of them disposable lighters."

"Uh-huh." The clerk snagged one off the display.

"And some lighter fluid."

"Can't refill these," the clerk said of the lighter.

"No shit. Maybe I want something else to catch fire."

"Then this'll do the trick." The clerk put a yellow two-ounce tin of lighter fluid next to the Jack, Marlboros, and Bic lighter. "That it?"

"Gimme a lotto ticket."

"You feelin' lucky?"

"Oh, yeah. I'm feelin' real, *real* lucky."

Griffin sat in the Altima across Military Trail from the trailer park, watching the entrance. A fast-food place had gone out of business on the site, leaving a vacant lot, For Sale sign, and clumps of grass growing through broken sections of tarred parking pad.

Griffin wasn't thrilled with his vantage point, which, as far as Angie's trailer was concerned, wasn't any vantage point at all. He couldn't see her trailer from here but hadn't been satisfied with any place inside the park; it wasn't that there were that many lights or people, but he needed to minimize his chances of being seen. It wouldn't be good for Angie to see him either—no sense having her scared any more than she already was. So he was staking out the entrance: the only way in or out. Millundra would have to drive by to get to Angie's.

This was assuming he'd be driving the Camaro, but he probably would. Griffin knew plenty of guys like Millundra. They had some street instincts, could manage not to get caught staring at their victim in court, but basically their brains were so small their concentration barely foresaw the next ten minutes. And despite wholesale stupidity, they were arrogant. They focused only on the crime, not the total circumstances. They went on flash impulse, looking straight ahead. Like in the courtroom earlier: Millundra made sure the cop and prosecutor never saw his gonna-get-you glare at Angie, but he never once turned around to see if someone might be watching him from *behind*.

But guys like that were also easily distracted. Millundra could *think* about Angie but end up in a barroom argument that would turn into a fight. He'd get arrested again, locked up, do five months, and not get back to terrorizing Angie until he was out. But he'd be here eventually. Or wherever Angie moved next. She could be married and have two kids, living in Duluth, and Millundra, who couldn't find a job on a bet, would find Angie and menace her *and* her family.

That judge did the world a disservice letting Millundra walk today. Griffin shook his head. Judges didn't get it. They didn't get it at all. Not even the ones who considered themselves hangin' judges. They'd get fooled at the other end of the spectrum and put away some guy for ten years who had about zero chance of committing another crime, so that by the time the guy got his release—his family, job, and life shot to hell—he'd have no option *but* commit another crime.

What a system. What a disaster.

"Glad I'm out of it," Griffin muttered. "Glad that part of my life's over." And then he wondered if it *was* over, just what was he doing sitting here? How would he define it?

He didn't really want to think about it, because if he did, he'd have to confess what was happening inside him. How a strong desire—an almost fatherly urge—had swelled inside him today seeing Angie Hanes in that courtroom. She needed to be protected, but the courts, the police weren't going to protect her. And she couldn't protect herself very well against someone like Millundra. So Griffin was here. To protect her.

Drew Millundra said, "Ah, shit," when a branch hit him in the head. Hadn't seen the damned branch. Damned, damned branch. He'd fixed his path on the vapor lamp for direction, trying to make his way through the overgrowth without falling into the drainage ditch. Which was why he didn't see the low tree limb. "Dammit!" Branch whacked him right on the forehead so hard Millundra almost lost his grip on the bottle of Jack Daniels. Close one. 'Cause if he lost that, what would he and Angie have for cocktails?

He rubbed his head and glared at the tree like it had hit him on purpose. He squirted some lighter fluid around its base, snarling, "Drink that up. Hope it poisons ya." He turned back toward his route through the grass.

The area was a lot more tangled with weeds than four months ago when he'd come through on his last visit to Angie. To his left, the same chain-link fence enclosed a used-car lot, but razor wire now ran along the top. Millundra listened for the dog that had come barking at him last time. That snarling German shepherd had charged the fence and barked until Millundra peed on him. No dog tonight. Maybe the razor wire was taking Fido's place.

Millundra stayed along the fence, away from the drainage ditch, watching for tree limbs now, too. He used that amber pole light like a sailor navigating by the southern cross. The amber lamp was just about in line with Angie's trailer.

He started singing a song about Angie, the one that went "Angie, baby" over and over, but that was all he could remember, except there was some other song that sounded a little like it. How'd that go? *Oh, Angie, how you came and you something and you something else.* No, hell, that was Mandy. Barry Manilow for chrissakes. Was it Little Angie? *You've got so much love, Little Angie?* No, that was Jeannie. Little Jeannie. Which got him thinking about *I Dream of Jeannie.* Now there was a good show. Watching that as a kid and getting a prepuberty hard-on over Barbara what's her name in that slinky outfit. TV was good back then. Not any more. All these wimpy shows about geeky baby boomers. Bunch of crap. Millundra figured if he ran one of those networks, he'd get TV back in business. Start up that *I Dream of Jeannie* again, for one thing.

He wondered if Angie liked *I Dream of Jeannie*. He'd have to ask her. Assuming she wasn't doing so much screaming he'd have to put a gag in her mouth.

Sitting in the car, waiting, Griffin found himself thinking about Cassie. How he used to be Cassie's father, and held her at night in the small second bedroom of their Baltimore home. He'd felt so comforted by her. He missed her so much.

All of a sudden, Griffin felt as if he might cry. These spells came on without warning. No specific reminder triggered this needful ache, there was just a sudden hole hollowed through him that left him feeling empty. He rested his hands on the steering wheel and laid his head on his arms. He missed Cassie so much. He hadn't planned on being a father. Hadn't been sure he'd be good at it. Then Carla had gotten pregnant and Cassie was born and he was overwhelmed with love for her. Even when he and Carla had problems, Cassie was so wonderful. She'd become his entire life. And then she was gone, taken from him.

What would happen to Cassie? How would she grow up? Would she turn out to be someone like Angie Hanes? Have to worry about lowlifes like Drew Millundra sniffing after her? What was going to—

Griffin sat up, alerted by a car pulling into Angie Hanes's trailer park. A Palm Beach sheriff's car.

Griffin got a glimpse of the driver: it was the officer who'd been in court today, the one who promised Angie he'd stop by. And here he was, making sure Angie was okay.

Millundra said, "I" and drew the letter. "Love" Millundra drew a heart with lighter fluid on the hood of Angie's car. Then spelled and spoke, "A . . . N . . ." A moron in a spelling bee. "G . . . I . . . E. Angie." He tossed the lighter-fluid can into the brush. "I love Angie. That's so sweet of me."

He fished the Bic lighter out of his pocket, about to light his belated valentine, when headlights shone over the stone road. A car approached along the oval-shaped circle.

Millundra ducked behind Angie's car, peeking around the rear bumper. "Cop." He pivoted completely out of view, plopping down on his butt. "Goddammit."

Headlights shone across the front of Angie's trailer. The cop making the turn. Stopping. Flicking on a door mount floodlight and shining it around Angie's lot, throwing long shadows of the trailer and car back toward the drainage ditch. Light reflected off the silver bottom of the lighter-fluid can in the grass, but that was just another piece of trash. The light moved on, panning to the other side of Angie's trailer.

Millundra sat still, smiling. Lazy-assed cop wasn't getting out of the car. But Millundra jumped when he heard a door open. He flinched and scurried toward the rear bumper, further from sight.

"You okay?" Man's voice. The cop.

Millundra was face down on the ground, looking under the car, seeing the cop lean over to talk out the passenger window.

"I'm okay." Angie.

She *was* home. He knew it. Keeping those lights out to fool him. Hah.

"Keep to doors locked."

"I will."

Millundra said, "Duh. No shit. Keep the doors locked." Like that was going to do any good.

"And you see any signs of him," the cop called, "you hit nine-one-one."

Christ, that's right, Millundra remembered. The phone line. Cut the phone line. He was so damned excited about this, he'd almost forgotten. And even with the wire snips in his pocket, digging into his hip like a reminder.

"Take care now." The cop drove off.

Angie closed the door. Locked it.

Millundra waited until the police car was out of sight, passing the time humming one of those Angie songs in his head. Then he stood, brushed himself off, and toed quietly to the junction box that wired the phone line into Angie's trailer. Keeping his footsteps to the grass, not crunching rocks, not wanting to let her know he was there *juuuust yet*.

Millundra squatted beside the junction box. He set down the bottle of Jack, that fine Tennessee whiskey—or was it Kentucky? Who cared? It went down warm and swirled his spirit.

He pulled the wire snips from his pocket. Felt down for the phone wire coming up from the ground pipe. Pretty tight fit. He moved aside, needing to get his shadow out of what little light there was. Moving a little more to the side. Wondering, how come that light wasn't—?

Something hard struck the back of Millundra's head. An explosion of light blew up in his brain. Millundra thinking, *Jesus Chr—* when the bottle smashed over his head. Broken glass and cool liquid ran over his face, burning his eyes. Millundra about to let out a hellacious yelp when a foot stomped his mouth, broke teeth, broke his jaw.

Agony rifled through him. God. Goddamn. What was happening? Where's this coming from?

Someone was standing on his face and now kicking his ribs. He could feel them breaking. Close to blacking out. In so much pain around his head and mouth he only sensed his ribs cracking, didn't actually feel pain from them.

Tasting his own blood. Choking on it as it went down his throat.

Angie? Was she doing this to him? The bitch. He'd kill her. He'd cut her up, set her on fire, put her out in the drainage ditch and wait for alligators to come along and eat her. That's what he'd do.

The foot came off his mouth, but he couldn't close his jaws. Like they were unhinged. He rolled face down, spitting blood. In so much pain, but he'd get up. He'd force off the dizziness. He'd get to his feet. Fight back.

Millundra slowly drew onto his hands and knees. Hurting so bad. But he'd get even. He'd get whoever was doing this to him.

And then the light appeared before his eyes. He squinted and turned away. A lighter. Dammit? *His* lighter. Someone flicking it in his face, waving the butane flame around.

Some guy saying, "You know, my father used to tell me shit doesn't burn. Whaddayou think about that, Drew? You think shit burns? *You* think *you'll* burn?"

Millundra stared into the flame with demonic eyes, blood and drool oozing from his mouth.

"You're soaked in whiskey, Drew. Think you'll burn?"

The flame waved closer to his face.

Through the twisted knots of pain sticking through his head, Millundra heard the man's tone, and he didn't sound at all like some cop or judge you could put on a good act for. Something in this guy's voice . . . something dangerous. The blood in Millundra's mouth suddenly felt cold. He started shivering. This guy was going to kill him. He tried to say, "No," but his useless jaw, the uncontrollable tongue . . . A groan, "Unh-unh," struggled from his throat, a sound that came up with blood and spit.

The light flicked out. Millundra's vision remained imprinted with white flashes he tried to blink away. And when the light blindness wouldn't fade, he closed his eyes and waited to die. Waited for this man to kill him.

Griffin changed clothes in the car, stuffing his jeans and shirt into the athletic bag and throwing it into a dumpster. He wondered if being around Janice would make him feel innocent tonight. He wondered if somehow she'd be able to tell what he'd done. As though her purity were a litmus strip and could react at his presence.

Griffin also couldn't help thinking about his father. How, when Griffin was a kid, his father would come home in his police uniform, talking about working over suspects with his nightstick. Griffin would ask why he'd done that, and Charlie Griffin would talk to him with wicked beer and bourbon breath and say, "So they get the message. They gotta get the message."

Slamming the trunk shut, Griffin figured Drew Millundra got the message. Griffin wondered if he should feel remorseful about having delivered that message, because he didn't. So maybe that was the sign Janice said God would send him. The sense of—hell, admit it—satisfaction going through him right now. But was that the kind of sign God might send?

It was after midnight when the Angel worked on his sermon.

"Your prayers are being answered," he wrote. "The wickedness of those who have cheated and lied, maneuvering clever escapes through loopholes of the legal system, are receiving their due reproach. Their crimes no longer go unpunished. Justice is no longer diverted.

"Some important trials are coming up this week. Henry Marcett for the murder of his wife in St. Louis. Tyron Lenora for shooting a policeman in Queens, New York. Albert Braxton for the rape of a nineteen-year-old girl in Foley, Alabama.

"Please pray to guide the lawyers and police who will prosecute these cases, and pray, too, for the judges and juries who will decide them. Let their discretion and judgment be fair, just, and true to their souls. Pray that the devil be barred from the courtroom. Pray so that God will once again be able to hear us.

"Pray so that punishment is swift and decisive, and that the guilty do not go free."

6

Griffin slept surprisingly well. Deeply.

It wasn't until he sensed a stirring against him that he awakened. For a moment, he thought he was back in the rowhouse-converted-condominium in Baltimore. That he'd fallen asleep with Cassie cradled in his lap, because it had been this kind of sleep he'd enjoyed holding his daughter. Peaceful and secure.

But that's not where he was. He was in Janice's apartment. He'd fallen asleep on the sofa, with Janice beside him. That happened sometimes. Now Janice would be waking him up to say he had to go home.

It was okay for him to stay late, but if he was still there when the sun rose, it meant he'd spent the night with her.

Only tonight . . .

Janice was beside him, sitting tentatively on the edge of the sofa, wearing a long-sleeved T-shirt and jeans without socks. Her hand was stroking him . . . his penis . . . through his pants. Her fingertips tentatively traced the contour of his erection. Very unsure.

She saw he was awake and their eyes met in the darkness. Her hand stopped, pulled away. They looked at one another without speaking, then she touched him again. Janice whispered, "Show me how . . . ?"

Griffin gently took her hand away.

Thinking he was rejecting or scolding her, Janice curled into a ball on the floor at the foot of the sofa. "I'm so sorry . . . It's wrong. I know."

Griffin lay beside her, hugging her, conscious of his posture so his erection wouldn't press against her. "It's okay. Don't cry."

She was so innocent. So unlike him.

"I don't know what I'm doing. It's dirty. I'm sorry."

"No, no . . . it's okay."

"I've never done that before. Touched anyone there." She wanted him to know that.

"It doesn't matter."

"Yes. It does. It's not right. The Bible says—"

"Janice, look . . . I don't know what the Bible says. Sometimes I'm so far off that page—"

"No. No, you're not. You're a good man. You're the best man I've ever known."

"You don't know me that well."

"I feel it in you, Jimmy. I feel goodness radiating from you." She turned her face toward him. "You're a good, good man." Her eyes looked at him clearly, even in the darkest of light. Janice was so pretty, so pure and unadulterated. Her complexion was smooth as honeyed milk. Her face was softly framed by golden-pecan hair she washed every day and set in curlers. "It's just that I know . . . I know men have certain needs. I know you've been with other women . . . like Liz . . . who can do things about that. And I think . . . I've *been* thinking about it. That maybe it's not so wrong—it could be okay . . . just to do *something* . . . about your needs."

Griffin smiled fondly. "That's what that was?"

"I woke up and saw . . . and . . . you were like that for a while. I could see your . . . that you were . . . like that.

Hard. And it looked uncomfortable. So I wanted—*want*—to do something to make you comfortable." She shivered slightly.

Griffin held her in his arms. "No. We don't do that."

"You won't want to keep seeing me if I don't. Not when you could be with someone like Liz."

"That's not true. I like being with you just how it is right now." He squeezed her firmly. "Because of how you make me feel. Just the way we are right now. There doesn't have to be any more than—"

"I'm in love with you." She confessed that suddenly, and closed her eyes after the words were spoken, fearful of his reaction. That Griffin didn't love her. "You're the best man I've ever known."

Griffin held her tighter.

"I love you so much."

"Don't."

"Why? Because you don't love me?"

He buried his face into the sweet smell of her hair that cascaded around her neck.

Janice said, "Maybe you'd love me if I did—"

He tightened his hug. "What does the Bible say about killing?"

"What?"

"About killing," he insisted, afraid of his question as much as the answer. "What does the Bible say about that?"

"It's wrong."

"That's right. It's a commandment: Thou shalt not kill."

"Yes?"

"I've killed two people, Janice. I shot them. When I was a cop—"

"Killed them?" She was startled but not afraid.

"Yes."

"But . . . but were they criminals?" She asked because she didn't know; he'd never told her this.

"Does that matter? What they were? Who they were? Or just that I killed them?"

"I . . . I don't know. If they were trying to kill you . . ."

"Is that what the Bible says?"

"I don't know." Janice was confused, and about more than the awkward, foreign temptation that had seized her upon finding Griffin with an erection while he slept.

"I don't know either. Sometimes I feel absolutely no remorse about having done it, and other times I'm scared to death I'm going to hell. Like there's two of me. One that wants to be passive, innocent—to be like you—and another part of me that knows if someone came in here right now looking to hurt you, I'd do it again. I'd kill them like the other two. And I'd do it without hesitating."

"To protect me."

"Yes. Because nothing bad should happen to you. You need to be protected."

She took his face in her hands and looked at him with those crystal-clear eyes, a look of astonishment on her face. Not fear or shock. Whispering in amazement, "And to guard the innocent, the angel was sent, to ward off evil that was devil spent."

It was all so simple, the way Janice explained it. He was a guardian angel whose sins would be forgiven. It could all be washed away.

It was all so simple. All he had to do was believe. That's all it took.

In the morning, Janice drove him to his cottage and

helped him pack. She took him to the airport in her little convertible. She was beaming, seeing even more in Griffin than had caused her to fall in love with him in the first place. Assuring him a sign would direct him away from the confusion that had become his life. And maybe he'd already gotten that sign, had already been given his mission, and was merely yet to understand it.

Janice wasn't even jealous of Liz now, even with Griffin on his way to meet Liz to help her on a story. Janice said, "She needs you. You're her guardian angel, too, just like you're mine." It all made sense to Janice.

Griffin appreciated the pure simplicity that there was reason for every event of humankind, because there was comfort in explanation, and in faith. But he didn't buy into it. It seemed too convenient, too easy, and he knew from experience that life was anything but easy.

Griffin considered this on the drive to the airport, and also found himself thinking how Janice had stroked his erection through his pants. Months of a platonic relationship and all of a sudden this: he could still feel the gentle, tentative touch of her hand, and it was making him hard again.

He shifted in the passenger seat, not wanting Janice to know. And here she was talking about him being a guardian angel.

She parked the car and walked him into the terminal. They were arm in arm, and Griffin wondered if the urge stirring inside him had been there all along and he'd suppressed it because of the eight-year age difference, because of her innocence, because she deserved someone better. Someone who went to church and who believed as she believed. Someone who had faith, not endless questions about life's meaning and its ultimate toll.

Griffin felt guilty for his prurient thoughts. He'd had his arm around Janice numerous times in the past but always as a friend. Now he was conscious of the curves of her slender body. He felt the line of her bra stretched across her back and imagined unsnapping it, feeling her bare, smooth skin, hands straying to the firmness of her small breasts. Cupping them. Sucking her nipples.

Less than two hours into these sexual thoughts about Janice, Griffin believed he was being punished for them. Because at the airline counter, he got the ticket Liz's newspaper had bought for him. He stared at it.

The ticket agent asked if anything was wrong.

Janice gasped quietly. Perhaps it *was* a sign—at the very least a test.

The ticket was to Baltimore. Griffin was going back to Baltimore. Where he'd killed two men. Where his life had been torn apart. Where his sins had been cast like stones on a smooth river, and the ripples of repercussion were yet to calm.

7

The killings started Thursday night. Before Griffin ever knew of Angie Hanes and Drew Millundra. They happened hundreds of miles away from Florida. Many state lines away. They started with a high school student.

Randy Arminger was rigged, baby. Oh yeah. Rigged and ready. Checking his gear one last time.

Three o'clock in the morning. Time. Yeah. This was *the* time. The CD player strapped to his belt told him so. Phil Collins singing about moments waited for all his life. Volume turned way up. Cranking.

The time Randy Arminger had been waiting for all his life was now. Seventeen years old. An eternity. Stuck in this house. This family. This insanity. This society where mediocrity was so readily accepted and genius so misunderstood. Randy was tired of playing by their rules. By everyone else's rules, when all he wanted was no rules. He had bumper stickers all over the walls of his room exclaiming in big, block letters: NO RULES.

"No rules." Randy saying that as he checked out his gear again. "No rules." Believing it.

Besides the CD player, Randy had a portable police scanner wired in to that same earplug headset: originally

Randy's freshman science project at Centennial High, what had been fashioned to pick up air traffic control was now a little further over on the bandwidth and there were the cops. Police band.

Cops. Randy hated cops. They enforced the old rules. But there were no rules. NO RULES.

A triple lithium battery pack on his belt ran the scanner, the CD player, and an 8mm video cassette recorder. Another pet project. Palm-sized video recorder into which was wired a tiny video camera; the wire ran inside his shirt, up the back of his neck, around his ear, to the camera sewn into the cupped bill of his surfer-logo baseball cap.

Randy got the idea from the *Letterman Show,* Dave getting Rupert G. to wear that gizmo and act like a lunatic on the street, embarrass people. Dave knew all about NO RULES. Dave broke all the rules. No respect for his bosses, told them to shove it, called them pin-heads, said they didn't know what they were doing. Dave was right about that. Dave knew NO RULES. Randy loved Dave.

Randy was a lean and fit kid. Good-looking. Thick, dark, curly hair. Beautiful dark eyes and long eye-lashes. Six-two and still growing. One hundred eighty pounds. Narrow hips and broad shoulders. Hands like a pianist's. Girls loved his hands even more than they loved his hair.

Randy was into girls almost as much as computers, math, and science. He'd even managed to score with some of the college girls in the advanced courses he took at Hopkins. Randy was only in the eleventh grade and hitting on Hopkins chicks, conniving two of them into some threesome action with him.

Some chicks would do anything for a little of the synthetic designer drug Randy produced on blotter paper. His idea of a high-tech study aid—you'd be revving all night long. A drug to open the brain and let information flow in. Randy called the stuff Cram, and used it the night before exams. Was on a little of it now, because he needed that edge tonight. He'd need about ten, twelve hours, then he could crash for a while.

Because tonight the rules came down. Because the life he'd been living was on the verge of a snag. All because of that dumb-ass teacher. Cynical bastard. Something about him. He and Randy never clicked, even though other teachers loved Randy. And why shouldn't they? He made them look good, like their bogus teaching methods were turning out one of the country's brightest high school students. But not Mitzner. Mitzner was not fooled. Well, give him credit for that. But too bad. Too bad for Mitzner, because tonight the rules came down.

Randy wasn't into school that much anymore anyway. He'd miss the convenient playground for his scams, but it was all too easy. And too many rules.

Like all the rules his father had, thinking he had to be a hard-ass disciplinarian since the divorce. Anal-retentive Dad, always worried about Randy doing drugs but never bright enough to catch him. Dad was okay in the computer lab, but in real life, fuhgeddaboudit. And once Dad found out what Mr. Mitzner was going to call him about . . . well, best to fire a preemptive strike. That was Randy's thinking.

He'd come too far, done too much to fail now. Besides, it really was the moment he'd been waiting for all his life—just coming a little sooner than he'd planned. But part of the plan had always been to be on standby alert, ready to book at a moment's notice.

So here he was up and running. Cool. He hefted

the Halliburton case—portable computers inside—and headed down the hall.

He crossed the architectural-marvel catwalk section of hallway that appeared to be suspended over the huge open foyer and curved double staircase. Dad's bedroom was at the other end of the house.

Dad's door was closed, but look at that, light on. Dad was probably working on the computer, getting a middle-of-the-night idea for debugging a program, or maybe cruising the Net.

Randy knocked on the door—tap-tap-tap—with the silencer screwed into the barrel of the 9mm Glock. A weapon bought right there in the pride-and-joy Centennial High parking lot from a school buddy who had connections in the city. An even swap for an eight-by-eleven sheet of Cram.

Behind the door, Dad's swivel chair squeaked. Dad stood. Footsteps toward the door.

Randy stepped back.

The doorknob turned. The door opened.

Stoop-shouldered Robert Arminger, his thinning hair tousled, wore striped pajamas, moccasin slippers, and wire-frame glasses. He squinted into the darkened foyer, saw a shape the size of his son but not the details of him. Saw the bright flash of light but didn't hear anything, wasn't sure what that was. Hearing his son swear, "Shit!" Randy's father didn't realize a bullet had just missed his head.

Then another flash, and a hot explosion hit dead center in his chest. Robert Arminger was knocked onto his back, landing hard on white carpet, gasping for breath as his son stood over him, pointed the 9mm Glock at his forehead, used the lenses of his glasses for targets, and fired two more times. Bullseye number one. Bullseye number two.

Which left ten more bullets for sister. More than enough for that twelve-year-old-pain-in-the-ass princess.

Sometimes, Scott Haskins wondered how he'd gotten here. How he'd come to a point in life when he couldn't imagine feeling more helpless or impotent.

He'd started work for Westinghouse right out of college, twenty-one years ago, on the promise of a good career with a thriving company. It *had* looked to be a good, solid base, and Scott Haskins dreamed of a nice house for his new wife and their soon-to-be family—married not eighteen months when Darlene got pregnant, and they were thrilled.

Scott Jr. was born, then Holly two years later. Great kids. Cute. Smart. Scott and Darlene were on top of the world. Probably never going to be rich, but that was okay. Westinghouse was treating Scott well, rewarding him with promotions and raises.

When the kids were in their early teens, the Haskinses stretched their budget and moved from a near suburb of Baltimore to Howard County. There was a real land move on, and it was becoming *the* county to live in—*the* Maryland hot spot, more D.C.-oriented than Baltimore-based.

Scott and Darlene signed a contract for a modern-style house just outside of Columbia, the planned city getting national raves as a liberal multicultural community where businesses and communities thrived.

It was a nice big house. Grandiose, considering their upbringing. Their parents were very impressed, so were their friends. Scott must be doing very well. Very well.

And he was . . . until Westinghouse started the layoffs. Hacking names off the payroll with the compassion of butchers cleaving fat from cuts of beef. The pink-slip parade sent thousands into the unemployment line, leaving behind horrible morale as survivors fearful of losing their jobs worked longer and harder just to stay employed, and no one asked for a raise.

Scott Haskins worked long hours, well into the night. He was no longer able to spend time with his kids, and it was a time his kids needed him. Other kids in the area seemed to run wild, no parental supervision, driving expensive cars, stealing, doing drugs, and their parents seemed oblivious, more insulted than concerned at their children being accused, refusing to believe *their kids* could be in trouble.

Scott Jr. got caught in the thick of it. The night he was on PCP was the worst; Scott and Darlene thought he was going to die from the overdose, but he pulled through. A horrible night in the emergency room.

Then Holly turned fourteen and it was as though someone had thrown a switch inside her. The music she listened to started getting louder and more violent. Holly abandoned a closet of stylish outfits for black clothes and clompy unbuckled army boots. She got her body pierced all over and started getting into fights at school.

Holly came home one day fired up about being on the wrestling team. But wrestling was a boy's sport. "No shit, Sherlock, and it's discrimination"—Holly talked to her parents like that. Darlene left the room crying. Scott tried to keep his calm, his composure, maybe he should have smacked her, but God's truth, he was scared of her. He'd had to pull her off her mother one time when Holly started hitting her, and the effort had winded him and made his chest hurt. He thought he was having a heart attack.

Holly was a strong girl, about twenty-five pounds overweight at five-four, a big-boned girl with wide hips, a fleshy stomach, and big, pendulous breasts. Her size was deceiving as to how quick and strong she was.

So maybe she'd be a good wrestler. Maybe that would spell her anger and aggression. Scott took time off from work and talked to the school and the Board of Education, and Holly was allowed on the wrestling team. It was horrible. Boys pawed all over her body, grabbing her breasts and between her legs, but Holly didn't back down. She'd fight back, sometimes winning. But it was such a spectacle that the coach cut her from the team.

Holly was livid. She trashed the locker room, breaking windows, going so completely out of control that Scott had her institutionalized. She missed the rest of her sophomore year, time spent instead in Sheppard Pratt. There was some improvement—some through counseling, other progress through medication. She was considered manic-depressive and also had sociopathic tendencies. But she could be treated.

Suddenly Scott got laid off from Westinghouse. One of those pink slips finally found his name, and his health benefits eventually expired.

They couldn't afford to keep Holly in Sheppard Pratt without health care. So Holly came home, and it was like having a time bomb in the house.

Darlene was a nervous wreck, because even during the quiet periods, when Holly would seem almost normal for a few weeks, there was kinetic tension waiting for the next disaster. Like last summer when Darlene found Holly sunbathing topless on the deck in full view of the neighbors. Not only that, but Holly had gotten a barracuda tattooed on her left breast and her right nipple had been pierced and was stuck with a hoop earring. Responding to her mother's shock by demanding, "What? What? What're you looking at?"

Holly openly and frequently declared her parents losers. Her father had no job. Her mother was working a retail job at the mall just like kids Holly's age. "And you want me to listen to what you say?" Holly demanded of them. "Your advice's really done good by you."

Thursday night, Scott was unable to sleep. And look at the time. Almost four in the morning. Lying in bed five hours now.

Darlene nudged him. "Scott?"

"I'm awake."

"I hear something."

"What?" He listened, but his hearing wasn't as good as it used to be.

"I don't hear it now. But it sounded like something in Holly's room. Something squeaking."

Scott exhaled frustration and felt his pulse increase, anxious about another confrontation with his daughter. He pushed his legs out of bed and stood. Unlocked the bedroom door and looked down the hall, said dejectedly, "Her light's on." His footsteps carried him forward, dreading this. Scared to death of what she might be up to at five in the morning.

Always scared to death about something now, it seemed. Because there was a lot to be scared of.

8

"Are you filming this?" Holly Haskins was on top of Randy Arminger, her oversized T-shirt pulled up to her waist, her slick, warm sex engulfing Randy's stiff shaft. Asking slyly, "Is that why you want the light on?"

Holly saw all the gizmos hooked to Randy's unbuckled belt, Randy's pants opened, Joe Boxers tugged down under his tight scrotum.

Holly fingered the slender wires that ran under Randy's shirt and came out at his collar: one set for the earphones he kept plugged in, listening to White Zombie and the police scanner while they screwed; the other wire connecting to the pencil-thick device taped to his baseball cap, a tiny lens at the end. Holly confirming, "This the camera?"

Randy, into the feel of being inside her, moaned, "Yeah." His hips moved, thrusting his shaft in time to the music, making the mattress squeak.

"Video?"

"Yeah."

"Cool." Holly pulled her T-shirt over her head, twirled it, tossed it across the room where it caught on the doorknob. She raked her hands through her black hair, spiking it up. She grabbed her breasts, rough with them, pulling one nipple hard like the stark girls in X-rated videos. Giving a little tug to the hoop pierced through her other nipple. Pain was a turn-on for Holly. Good thing, she always thought, because her life was so full of pain. Everything hurt.

She hated everything, everyone, except Randy. Randy was slick. Her first lover, and she wanted him all the time. Was getting bold about it. Giving him a key to her house, telling him anytime he wanted to come over—middle of the night—come on over and make her feel good.

Randy felt good now, too, moving his erection inside her as Holly pushed down around him.

Holly winced with pleasured pain. Smiled. "If my father saw me doing this . . ." Broader smile. ". . . it'd kill him."

"Yeah," Randy groaned. "Oh, yeah!"

Holly asking, "You going to come?"

"Yeah. Move like that. Move your pussy."

A knock on Holly's door—Scott Haskins called to his daughter, "Holly?"

Holly grinned, whispered, "Oh, shit, it's him," then toward the door, she sang innocently, "Yeah, Dad?"

"You all right?"

"Oh, yeah." Holly moved wildly on top of Randy, the mattress really squeaking. "I'm feeling *great*!"

"What's going on?" Scott started to turn the knob—it was unlocked—but he didn't open the door.

"Nothing's going on, Dad."

The bed squeaked loudly. Headboard butted the wall.

Randy grunted, "I'm gonna come."

"Whose voice was that?"

Holly shouted, "Nobody, Dad!" Then, whispered to

Randy, big sexy smile, shaking her heavy tits, "Come on, baby. Come! Come in me!"

Scott Haskins made a decision in the hallway. He opened the door to his daughter's room, and was gripped by pure shock seeing his daughter having sex with a boy. Scott froze, then started to yell, "My God—"

Randy Arminger, erection stroking inside Holly, yanked his hand out from beneath the covers and fired three quiet shots through the muffled barrel of the 9mm Glock. Hitting Scott Haskins, spinning him around and dropping him face down in the hall, bleeding horribly.

Holly screamed, "Cool! So cool!"

Randy moved inside her, groaning, "Yeah, baby. Coming now! Right now!" Ejaculating inside her.

Holly felt his warmth surge inside her. She loved how flushed his face got when he came.

Holly's mother screamed from the other end of the hall.

Holly pulled off Randy's spent shaft and ran out of the bedroom. Yelling at her screaming mother, "Shut up, shut up, SHUT UP!" Her feet landed hard near her father's head, Randy's semen running out of her. As her mother screamed, Holly screamed and charged down the hall.

She threw herself at her mother, a flying tackle that took Darlene Haskins off her feet. Darlene was unable to breathe even before her daughter's hands clutched her throat.

By the time Darlene Haskins was dead, Randy Arminger had his pants zipped up. He came out of Holly's room, nudging Scott Haskins with his hiking boot, making sure he was dead. Sure was.

Randy came down the hall where Holly was putting makeup on her mother's face—Holly's kind of makeup.

Lots of black and dark blue around the eyes, but she was having trouble when her mother's eyelids stayed open, staring in horror.

Randy said, "You gotta put pennies on them, babe. Like in the old Westerns."

"Shit!" Holly got impatient and smeared eyeliner all over her mother's face, around her mouth, then threw the container across the room.

Randy smacked her heavy ass, said, "Get dressed. We're on a timetable."

The Angel twitched. He was asleep, but he was dreaming. That vivid image again. That devils were invading heaven.

Just before 5:00 A.M., Randy pulled his father's shiny new Volvo into the parking lot and snapped off the lights, coasted to an empty space at the end of the court.

The cul-de-sac was lined with new townhomes, less than two years old. Houses full of just-marrieds and young families starting out.

Randy checked windows fashioned with ready-made curtains or blinds. "Damn. Got some lights on. Goddamn people get up early."

"We gotta do it. Gotta." Having just heard Randy's plan, Holly was into it.

Randy's palms lightly drummed his thighs to the music pumped into his ears. He'd been here numerous times, planning, but never quite this close to sun-up.

Holly had him a little off schedule. He'd just figured on picking her up and coming here. But the sex was so good with her. And then her parents had to be dealt with. He was off schedule by almost an hour. He was tempted to abort this part of the plan.

Holly urged, "Come on, Ran, it'll be such juice."

He grinned. "It *will* be cool." Deciding to do it. "We need to be quick. Twenty minutes, tops."

"Let's go."

Randy gave Holly the spray can of paint, and they were out of the car, sprinting down the back of the townhouse row once out of sight of the street.

The end townhouse had a side walkout. The basement door was inset with a glass window. Randy worked quickly. A diamond tip cutter made clean work of the glass with minimum noise. A suction cup kept the circle cut of glass from falling to the ground and breaking. Randy spun the round section of glass into the woods like a Frisbee.

"So cool," Holly squealed excitedly. "So cool."

Randy reached in, unlocked the door, and they were inside the cool, dark basement. Randy secured the glass cutter and drew the Glock.

Holly followed Randy up the steps. No light showed under the bottom of the door. No one was up for breakfast yet in the Mitzner household.

Randy's steady hand touched the doorknob, turned it. He peeked into the kitchen. Dark except for a nightlight in a wall plug behind the counter and the digital timer of a coffee machine.

Randy eased into the kitchen. Stopped. Checked his belt.

Holly whispering, "What?"

Randy tapped the video cassette. "Forget to swap tapes. Might run out before it's done." He kissed Holly. "You used up tape. Sexy."

She rubbed against him. "More where that came from."

He felt her breasts through her T-shirt. Holly lifted

her top, baring her tits. Randy gave them each a kiss, then went back to business.

He nodded toward carpeted stairs leading to the second floor. "Bedroom's in that back corner." Pointing to that direction with the gun. "Baby's room's there." Front right corner.

Holly nodded. She was wired. This was so cool.

Randy started up to the second floor. Had the gun aimed ahead of him. Anything came in his path, he'd shoot it.

Near the top of the stairs, he tilted forward for a quick glimpse down the short hall. Clear. He pulled back, nodding to Holly. She had the spray can of paint ready.

Randy mouthed, "Here we go."

Holly nodded.

Twenty feet to the bedroom door. All doors open. Randy stepped lightly across the carpet. Holly was just as silent behind him.

Randy edged to the master bedroom. He plugged the CD headsets into his ears. White Zombie. Violent sounds matching his mood. But the Cram had him focused. Keyed in.

Beside the master bedroom door, he could see into the baby's room. The infant—six months and three days—was sleeping.

Randy knew the kid's birthday, a big announcement at school. Mr. Mitzner's wife had a baby girl! Big wup. In a couple seconds, Mr. Mitzner's wife was gonna be having a cow . . . when she saw them.

Randy glanced into the master bedroom, which was dark, but not pitch black. Easy enough to see. Mitzner and his wife asleep. Mitzner in pajamas—fruity-looking things. Randy should have figured.

Mitzner was on his back like he might snore, but he had one of those breathing strips across his nose.

His wife was on her side, facing the door, wearing some smock top designed for nursing mothers.

Randy glanced back at Holly. She nodded. They eased quietly in.

Randy went to the foot of the bed, his step squeaking a floorboard.

Mr. Mitzner's breathing pattern changed, a pause, then slightly quicker.

Randy moved toward his teacher's side of the bed.

Holly stopped in front of Mrs. Mitzner, the can of spray paint aimed for her face.

Randy aimed the gun for Mitzner, the cool tip of the silencer almost on his cheek, moving closer, closer, brushing lightly.

Mitzner stirred, but didn't come awake.

Randy placed the muzzle flush to his cheek and poked him, calling quietly, "Billy . . . Bill . . . Bill Mitzner."

Mitzner jumped, suddenly awake. "Jesus Christ!" He saw an intruder's figure, maybe made out the gun, and started to jump up when Randy's left hand smashed into his nose and knocked him back.

Mitzner groaned in pain.

Randy flicked on the nightstand light. Get some wattage on this scene for the videotape.

Mitzner's nose was bleeding through his hands.

Alice Mitzner awakened, and as soon as she opened her eyes, Holly sprayed paint into her face. She screamed.

Randy grabbed his teacher's hair and pulled him out of bed. As Mitzner tumbled face down on the floor, Randy seethed, "You've messed with the wrong fella this time, jerk-off. You don't mess with *my* life."

Mitzner was dazed from being hit. He'd heard his wife's screams, but now, through some kind of struggle, her cries were muffled.

Holly had a pillow pinned over Alice Mitzner's face and used a school-taught wrestling hold to render her defenseless.

William Mitzner groaned, "What do you want? Who are you?" In full surrender mode.

Randy turned him over. "It's me, Bill. Your prize student. Randy."

William Mitzner's muscles trembled with fear, looking down the barrel of the handgun aimed at his face.

Mr. and Mrs. Mitzner's baby was crying when Randy and Holly stepped into the hall.

Holly, her hands and T-shirt smeared with spray paint, pointed to the baby's room. "What about the kid?"

Randy closed his eyes and aimed the Glock into the baby's room. He fired out the end of his clip—only four shots left now.

The slugs popped quietly from the silenced barrel, and, once fired, the baby kept crying.

Randy shrugged, "The baby lives."

9

From the window seat, Griffin looked down at the Chesapeake Bay. The jet's shadow glided across deep-blue water, briefly shading a few of the hundreds of sailboats that skimmed the placid sea. Inlets from marinas along the shores of Annapolis were busy with pleasure craft, boaters making the most of a sunny June day. The eastbound span of the Bay Bridge was crowded with day-trippers and weekenders heading to the beach.

As the plane descended toward BWI, banking away from the bay's scenic vista, Griffin's eyes focused beyond trees that were bright green with the leaves of a new season, and he saw downtown Baltimore. His jaw tensed, and he heard himself say, "Why am I here?"

"Hey, handsome, Glad you made it." Liz met him at the head of the jetway with a big lover's hug and kiss. Liz's hand strayed across Griffin's butt, giving a very quick squeeze.

Griffin managed a smile through a web of anxiety, asking Liz what he'd asked himself earlier, "Why am I here?"

"To be with me. Work with me." Liz was keyed up, having stayed awake most of the night faxing, modeming, and FedExing material to Atlanta to meet *America*

Exposed's weekly deadline. Very wound up on the story and expectations of being with Griffin.

Liz picked up her ever-present oversized saddle bag and put her arm around Griffin, spiriting him toward the airport hub. She wore acid-washed jeans and a faded yellow tennis shirt—casual, cool slouch attire. A quick-to-get-out-the-door look that went with her latest in an ever-changing array of hairstyles. Liz currently was a mostly natural brunette with henna highlights, a short, tapered cut with bangs swept to the side.

Griffin muttered, "You said this was going to be a surprise."

"You weren't surprised?"

"Surprises are supposed to be good."

"Ah, like your birthday present?" A few months ago, Liz had flown in unannounced on Griffin's birthday, staked out the beach for his early morning run, and been lounging there topless when Griffin jogged past. Liz McKinley liked bold.

She was a few years older than Griffin, never married and much traveled. Her naturally slender frame was picking up a little extra weight, but nothing Liz bothered with, figuring when her body dictated it was time to start dressing more conservatively, that's what she'd do. Meanwhile, she outfitted herself casually hip by day, sometimes shifting to sexy, even raunchy, by night. Liz was a staunch believer in balancing work and play, which was easy for her to do.

Her responsibilities were few, owing time and duty mainly to herself and her employer, a tabloid paper she liked working for just fine, especially since the pay was very nice, her expense account unquestioned, and they let her freelance for wire services on the side.

She was as much an equal to Griffin as he had ever

known. In ways, Liz was a lot like him. The field was level and few secrets remained between them for very long.

Liz asked, "How've you been sleeping?"

"About the same."

"I called you last night—there wasn't any answer."

"I went down to Lake Worth."

"That 'whatever' it was you were working on?"

"Yeah."

"Down there with Janice?"

"No."

"D'you see her last night?"

Griffin's second of hesitation gave him away.

Liz said, "I see . . . should I be jealous?" She kept her smile, but there was some trepidation behind it, looking up at Griffin.

"She and I aren't like you and I."

"But—should I be jealous?"

"No."

"Would *you* be jealous if *I* spent last night with another man like you spent it with Janice?"

"No," he answered without thinking that might not be entirely truthful.

"Okay . . ." Liz seemed to contemplate another question, but opted to drop it. "So we'll leave it at that."

"Thank God." Griffin made it sound as though she was being foolish.

Liz tightened her hold on him. "You know, every time I'm away from you, I miss you more."

"I miss you, too." That wasn't a lie, not even close, although statements of that sort often lay awkwardly around them, as though their feelings for one another were like jigsaw pieces they couldn't quite figure how to make fit.

Holding hands, they went down the escalator to baggage claim, and when Liz started tugging Griffin past the turnstiles, he said, "I've got a suitcase."

"It won't be out for fifteen minutes yet. Lemme show you something. Story's out in the parking lot. Latest chapter."

Liz steered him through the automatic doors, hustling across the cab lane, coming out from under cover to mild sunshine and low humidity. A very un-Maryland day.

Heading toward the concrete multi-levels of short-term parking, Liz filled Griffin in on Randy Arminger. "He's still on the loose. The girlfriend, too. And they're a real team. Arminger's a straight-A genius. Perfect SAT scores. Four-oh GPA. Taking advanced placement courses *and* college courses at Hopkins, and he's just a junior. He's got a week and a half left of his junior year—not that he's ever going back to school—at least not out of stripes or a straightjacket. The girl, she's a real whip. Holly Haskins. With Arminger in school. Long record of trouble for Holly. She's already been institutionalized. History of violence."

"So he *didn't* kidnap her? You weren't sure about that."

"That's what I tried to call you about last night. Kidnapping's out. She's in it with him. And looking to be right up to speed." Liz walked Griffin through a planted area of wild grasses, a Tribute to the Chesapeake garden between the terminal and parking garage.

"Arminger killed his parents, you said?"

Liz clarified, "Father and sister. Parents are divorced. Mother lives out of state."

"Any fix on a motive?"

"You mean besides insanity?" Liz shook her head.

"Who knows. You know how they talk about biological changes happening faster to kids? Girls get their periods sooner. Boys hit puberty earlier. I think depravity and wickedness is looking to join the list. Arminger isn't just killing people, he's relishing it. And the girl's the same way. They're into it."

Griffin felt his neck tighten. "Just like last time," he said, feeling the past swell inside him. "Like Bright Eyes."

"Worse." Liz wanted to put distance between Griffin's past and present, differentiate them. She needed him looking ahead, not behind him. So if it took making Arminger and Holly Haskins greater purveyors of evil to accomplish her task, so be it. Just get him focused.

They entered an enclosed stairwell, going down.

Liz's voice echoed off poured-concrete walls. "Arminger shot his father through the eyes. And shot his thirteen-year-old sister in bed—probably waking her up before he did it, to make sure she *knew* he was going to kill her. He put the gun right to her forehead and pulled the trigger. Then he spray-painted her face red and painted the word *Angel* across her bed and body."

"Angel?"

"A-N-G-E-L."

Griffin thought about Janice calling him her guardian angel, saying that he was Liz's angel, too. "Anybody know what Angel refers to?"

"Not besides the obvious guesses. And I can't say I'm impressed with the local homicide detectives. The word *experienced* doesn't come to mind. Nor does *skillful, observant,* or *insightful.*" Liz opened the door.

They were on the lower garage level, a section of which was completely underground. The air was dank and sour-smelling. Very few parked cars were near the stairwell, but there was a lot of activity in the far corner.

Yellow police tape strung off the area. Squad cars from Howard and Anne Arundel counties, and the Maryland state police. A rollback tow-truck was being directed toward a cream-colored Volvo.

Liz said, "Arminger's father's car. They found it here a couple hours ago."

"The kid flew out of town?"

"That's what the cops're checking. Little jurisdictional scrape at present. State police look to want to take it over, and FBI's been around, figuring if Arminger's on a plane he's in federal jurisdiction even if he doesn't cross a state line."

"Should be easy enough to find out what flight they were on. Two teenagers traveling alone."

"I've got a charge card standing by, ready to pay for airfare wherever the chase takes us."

"Out of Baltimore would be nice."

"You're just saying that. You know you love it here."

Griffin glared at her.

"Kidding—just kidding. A little levity amidst the bloodshed." Liz opened her shoulder bag and pulled out her camera—auto-focus motor-driven Canon. She focused on the Volvo being drawn onto the rollback, talking while the motor-drive whirled. "Girlfriend's—Holly's—parents were also murdered. The father was shot. Mother was strangled."

"Jesus . . ."

Liz put her camera back in her bag. "They didn't stop there. Last night—Friday? Yeah, Friday." Traveling and weird hours tended to make Liz lose track of the days. "A guy comes home from work and hears a baby crying next door. People named Mitzner live there. The baby keeps wailing, so the neighbor went to see what was wrong. No one answered the front door, so he checked around back and the place had been broken into. The couple was killed, Jimmy. Husband, one of Arminger's teachers, was shot, wife was strangled. And she had red paint all over her face and in her mouth, and there was a message sprayed on the wall. It said: 'Hey Angel, how about this?' "

Griffin frowned. "He's showing off?"

"Kids call it goofing. But whatever the word, the only thing for sure besides Arminger having a taste for killing is he doesn't care about getting caught, or maybe I should say isn't trying to conceal he's the one doing it. His fingerprints are over everything."

"How the hell does a—you said he's seventeen?"

"Uh-huh."

"Straight-A student?"

"Gifted and talented. No run-ins with the law, and he's lived in the same county since he was ten. Cops'd never heard of him connected with anything."

"So how the hell does a kid that age go this crazy this fast?"

"That's my story. Beneath all the hype and headlines, that's the real issue. And it's going to play big. The paper's running a campaign piece by a quack psychiatrist: Can This Happen To Your Child? It's marvelous marketing to play on parental fears."

"Try not to remind me who's paying for me to be here."

Griffin and Liz viewed her employer in markedly different light. Liz didn't see any harm in sensationalism, and trusted readers were smart enough to separate soap-opera reporting from hard news. Griffin worried about the modern-day craving for quick fragments of information—that disjointed and badly informed messages were being haphazardly bandied about in the media, and people were believing, too busy and tired to question tabloids and radio talk-show supposition. It was news à la hedonism. It it feels good, believe it.

Liz said, "You'll love Monday's edition. Big head: 'Straight-A Killer and Nuthouse Girlfriend Go On Kill Spree.' Subhead: 'Who Is the Angel?' Sidebar: 'Bright Eyes Detective Jimmy Griffin Joins Kidhunt for *America Exposed*.' "

"Great."

"We're getting mileage out of you. Gotta move those papers." Liz snapped her fingers—snap-snap-snap—selling imaginary papers.

Across the parking garage, the rollback was pulling away with the impounded Volvo. Remaining police milled about, very concerned, almost edgy.

Liz asked, "You know any of them?"

"No." Griffin didn't see a familiar face but could read their expressions. "They've got nothing. No leads. They've got no idea where this kid's gone."

"So let's get there first."

"School out for summer up here?"

"Not for another two weeks. Making up winter snow days."

"Where's the kid's school?"

"Howard County. About half an hour from here."

"That's where we start."

"I'm a step ahead of you."

10

Liz drove a rented Toyota Camry, taking I–95 to the Howard County line and exiting on Route 175, a suburban highway. Saturday traffic was steady with folks using a day off to hit the super centers on Snowden River Parkway and Dobbin Road.

Liz pointed to a Marriott Courtyard as they breezed by it. "Our hotel."

"Nice enough." Griffin made mental note of where they were, somewhat familiar with the area from when he lived half an hour east in Baltimore City.

Before they were married, Griffin and Carla used to take drives out this way, stopping at Sewell's Orchard for Red Haven peaches in springtime and Golden Delicious apples in the autumn. Now Sewell's remained in name only as a housing development; the peach and apple trees had been uprooted for building lots.

As the land had become consumed by suburban sprawl, Griffin and his wife's sojourns turned less pastoral, making a habit of trips to the mall when first married but hardly at all once Carla started battling depression.

Griffin tried not to think about it, but it was coming back in waves. Impressions from the past were still strong enough to color more immediate concerns.

Liz saw him frowning, asked, "What?"

He shook his head, but Liz guessed the problem. She knew him.

"Everybody's got a past, Jimmy. Sadness. Pain."

"Yeah . . ."

Liz braked for a light. The car idled quietly. "Are you going to try to see her?"

"Carla?"

"I was thinking more about Cassie."

"I don't think that's . . ." He stared out the side window. "Probably not."

"You could call. When's the last time you talked to Carla?"

"Not since the house settled. She asked where she should send the check for my half."

"I still think that was a peace offering—that *she* called and not her lawyer."

"I wouldn't knew what to say to her that wouldn't start a fight." He took a deep breath. "I'm not going to see her."

"What about Cassie?"

He shook his head. "Too painful. And what's the point, really?"

"Does it matter that—?"

"Yes," Griffin cut her off, knowing this question, because they'd been there before.

"You're making a mistake, Jimmy," Liz said, but she didn't press the issue. Griffin's ex-wife had cheated on him and broken his heart, but what was even worse was how it tore Cassie away from him. His daughter . . . but only for nine months.

The light turned green. The exit onto Route 29 was just ahead, so Liz shifted lanes.

They didn't talk for a while, until Griffin changed the

subject. Their conversations were like that. Serious issues were dealt with like walking on thin ice: a quick, cautious venture that left them eager to get back to land where the footing was safer.

Griffin, focusing his attention on the present, not the past, said, "Assuming we find this kid before anyone else does, before the police, what do we do?"

"Get a big-time story. Big scoop. Exclusive. The reason people will buy copies of *America Exposed* and not the competition."

"A story?"

"That's what we do. We're a reporting team. We investigate, we observe, we write. We're not cops. We can't arrest anyone."

"Going to take some serious getting used to."

Liz pulled into the parking lot of Centennial High School, where she'd spent a great deal of time the day before, covertly interviewing students before the principal, Sam Reese, ordered her off the property.

She'd spoken to about fifty kids in all, trying to get a lead on Randy Arminger and having some success.

There were few cars in the lot on Saturday: a handful of nondescript clunkers were outshined by two baby Mercedes E-class sedans, a BMW, and a Corvette.

Glancing around, Liz said, "Doesn't look like my girls are here."

"Your girls?"

"Uh-huh." Liz stopped at the outdoor basketball court, where six boys dressed in slack homeboy regalia played unimpressive three on three. Pointing to them, Liz said, "But, the guys are here. Right on schedule. Every Saturday afternoon. Basketball."

Envisioning NBA heros, the kids cut awkward moves

to the basket and launched ugly shots, trash-talking one another—shouts of "In yo' face," trying to sound intimidating and coming off cartoonish. A boombox set on the macadam thumped bass-heavy Gangsta Rap. Four white and two Asian kids, with double-income-producing professional parents, imagined they were black and bad.

Griffin leaned an elbow out the window and watched them. "When I was in high school, we came out here to play in a basketball tournament. Not right here, I don't think, but somewhere around here." Griffin looked for a familiar landmark without success. "They had a guy, Leroy Scott . . . he could really light it up. Only way I could try and stop him was foul. I was out of the game by half time. I think we lost by about thirty."

Liz liked it when Griffin recalled a fond memory of growing up; so much of Griffin's youth had been racked with pain. Sports had been one of his few outlets, a place to go and forget himself for a while. By concentrating on the game, he could run himself ragged so he was exhausted enough to block out all the rest.

Liz reached into her black saddle bag and pulled out last year's Centennial High yearbook. She showed Griffin a bookmarked page. "Here you go. Centennial High Computer Club. Randy Arminger, president."

The photo had been taken in a room of computer stations. Long-haired Arminger was seated on a table—big smile—while eleven other kids sat in chairs or stood behind the table. Arminger was clearly king.

"Computers," Liz said, "aren't just for geeks anymore. Some of these fellas actually get out for some fresh air."

Griffin checked faces in the computer club photograph against those of the basketball players. He made matches of three.

On the outdoor court, one of the kids hit a three-pointer, banking it violently, unartfully off the backboard. He set about rapping, "To de bank, to de bank, take it to de bank!"

Liz unfolded a back issue of a county newspaper across the steering wheel. She read a section she'd highlighted. " 'While real estate prices in the rest of the county increased at an average of three percent last year, properties in the Centennial school district shot up a startling fifteen percent. Proximity to one of the state's premiere public high schools continues to spark demand.' " Liz reached for another section of paper. "And this is from last summer: 'Angry residents decried the school board's decision to redistrict a portion of Dorsey Hall, thereby moving approximately seventy-five students from the popular but potentially overcrowded Centennial High School, and sending them to Wilde Lake. A proponent of the plan dismissed the parents' complaints as racist. Wilde Lake High School has one of the county's larger black populations.' "

Griffin asked, "What's this have to do with Randy Arminger?"

"Maybe nothing, but it has a lot to do with people I've talked to around here. This school's commonly referred to as a country club, and this big-time reputation is something people don't want smudged. There's been reluctance to talk about two of their students running amuck. When I went door to door in neighborhoods around here, looking for high-school-age kids, their parents didn't want them to talk to me—like it would scar their academic record if they admitted knowing anything about Arminger."

"Bizarre attitude." Griffin opened the door and sauntered over to the kids who were playacting black. He settled into a little playacting himself, putting on a casual exterior, smiling but not appearing too friendly.

One by one, the kids took notice of him and stopped their game to strike a quick what's-this-shit posture, backed up by their Gangsta Rap.

. . . whippin' out my piece and the cop goes dowwwwnnnnn . . .

A kid with thick hair—not one from the computer club photo—offered a casual "Whussup?" along with an MTV gesture of greeting, half waving, half pointing at Griffin.

Beyond the basketball court, the school's athletic fields backed to farmland. Housing developments were scattered across distant rolling hills. The air smelled fresh.

"You fine young gentlemen into what goes on around here?"

The kids were suspicious, but mostly up to their would-be bravado image, saying, "Yeah," "Uh-huh," "Depends on what goes on." The ones who didn't talk nodded. One of the talkers dribbled the basketball.

"I'm looking for a guy goes to school here. Randy. You know Randy?"

"Randy who?"

"Randy Arminger."

"Yeah, sure," one kid answered, eager to fit the hip.

But another boy nudged him, muttered, "Shit, man, shuddup, shuddup."

Mr. MTV Dribbler said, "*You* a cop?" And again there was the half-pointing gesture, a loose arm thrusting a hand turned sideways.

"Used to be."

"So what're you now?"

"You ever hear of a newspaper *America Exposed*? They sell it in the grocery store. It's a tabloid."

"Yeah-yeah. My grandmama reads it."

"That's who I work for, and we're looking to find Randy Arminger—"

"Whaddayou wanna do that for?" One boy appeared puzzled.

The dribbler said, "He wiped out his old man and sister, dumbfuck."

"Wiped them out?"

"Yeah. Where you been? Randy killed 'em. Shot 'em dead. Chittity-chittity-bang-bang," he half-rapped.

"What?" One boy, a handsome kid with dark, curly hair, was stunned.

Apparently the news, not having broken to the public until the afternoon before, hadn't circulated through the entire school population as of Saturday morning.

The kids started to open up, talking fast among themselves, transferring energy from basketball to conversation. They spoke what they perceived as street lingo, although it was a struggle to keep the diction rough-edged. Griffin suspected they were mostly yes-ma'am and yes-sir at home, and honor students in class. They had clear eyes, white teeth, and mostly unblemished complexions.

The curly-headed boy appeared dazed. "I've been working on a program for independent study . . . I didn't know anything about it . . . I didn't know . . . He killed his father?"

"He and Holly Haskins."

A kid with black shorts hemmed below his knee said, "You know she was on the wrestling team for a while. I swear—one time—she tried to smother me with those big-cow tits."

They all laughed, except the boy with curly hair: Paul Demmis, the member of the computer club who was seated beside Randy in the picture. Randy's hand had been resting on Demmis's shoulder.

"She did, man, I'm serious. Came down right on my face. Whomp!" He placed his hands over his mouth and nose. "I couldn't breathe."

"Only action you've gotten your whole life."

Paul Demmis muttered, "I can't believe Randy did this . . ."

The dribbler said to Griffin, "You want to interview us?"

"Maybe," Griffin answered, watching Demmis. "Any of you know Randy? Or who his friends are? Who he hangs with?"

"I'm tight with him," the cool dribbler reported.

The other kids mocked him.

"He don't even know your name, dipshit."

"Ow, yeah, like blood brothers!"

"Shuddup, assholes." Then, confessing, but no less cool, to Griffin: "So we're not best friends, but we've been around the computer lab together. He showed me some programs he'd downloaded off the Web."

"You guys into computers?"

"Oh, yeah. You?"

"Nah, I'm a dinosaur."

Paul Demmis ran a hand through his hair, looking troubled.

Dribbler said, "Randy's very into computers—super into them. I'm into them, yeah. But Randy's up here." He raised his hand above his head. "He's above the rim. Way, way above. He's so far up he could dunk with his feet."

"He does know computers," one of the Asian computer club members said. His name was Henry Assan. Wiping his glasses, he said, "Randy knows a *dangerous* lot about computers. Dangerous lot."

"Like hacking?" Griffin said, wondering if that was still the term for breaking into someone else's system. He'd worked on the prosecution of a few computer crimes while in the city attorney's office downtown.

Sixteen-year-old Henry Assan put his glasses back on and blinked his eyes into focus, looking up at Griffin. "Randy might snoop where he doesn't belong on line, but he doesn't tamper. I've watched him a couple times. Once he eased onto a network and in the process of surfing around found a virus the sys-ops didn't seem to know was there; Randy disinfected it. If he hadn't done that, their system would have crashed. It was a nasty strain. Randy's brilliant. Pure and simple." There was envy in the boy's voice.

The boys' fantasy land was fading, revealing their true personas as prosperous, intelligent students.

Griffin felt briefly intimidated, beginning to estimate just how much these kids knew that he didn't, and that their knowledge wasn't about current sports stars or alternative music but information being used as the backbone of a new global economy.

"Randy's the best," the boy with the baggy shorts concurred. "No one else is even close, except maybe Paul." He gestured to the boy with curly hair.

"And sure not like that Leanna Landy," Dribbler cut in.

"Bitch," two boys said simultaneously.

"Who's Leanna Landy?"

The dribbler answered: "Leanna and Randy have been odds-on-favorites to be class valedictorian since midterms last year. The only two left with four-ohs."

"Straight A's," Griffin confirmed.

"Yeah, only Leanna's a real bitch."

"Super bitch."

Considering a theory, Griffin asked, "She wouldn't happen to have a nickname Angel, would she?"

"Angel? No way."

"Not that I've heard."

"You know anyone named Angel? Anyone Randy would call Angel?"

A few nahs and shakes of head. Dribbler added, "But it *sure* wouldn't be Leanna, because word is she's the one who ratted Randy out to Mr. Mitzner."

"Ratted him out about what?" Griffin asked.

The kids glanced to one another uneasily—unspoken communication that resulted in eventual shrugs of compliance. A silent vote authorizing the dribbler to say:

"Randy wasn't only good with computers. He was fantastic in chemistry."

"Above the rim?" Griffin asked.

"In the fucking clouds."

Griffin hoped Paul Demmis would add something to the conversation, but he remained quiet.

Henry Assan, again appearing envious, said, "Randy invented his own drug. He called it Cram—to be used for cramming for a test. You could stay up all night and be super sharp all the next day. It's amazing stuff, but not like being wired on caffeine pills. There's no racing pulse or jitters. It just puts you there. Right on it. Like a new part of your brain is being accessed."

Sang, another computer club member, agreed. "Like formatting a new and bigger hard drive."

"Just like. And you're on this incredible edge. Not high, but clear."

Sang said, "Focused."

"I Crammed every calc test and nailed it. Boom-boom-boom. Perfect scores. Unreal. And I'm not kidding, the last SAT session, Randy set up some of us with Cram and we annihilated our past scores. Three of us right here," he pointed around the group at the other two computer club members, "Paul, Sang, me—our scores will get us a look-see by Ivy League schools."

Sang said, "It's like having your brain in turbo drive. Sometimes you know the answer, but it just doesn't come. It's there, but you can't find it."

"Hidden file."

"Yeah . . . and Cram takes you to it."

Griffin asked, "Randy made this stuff?"

Henry said, "Invented *and* manufactured."

"What's it look like?"

"On blotter paper. A square about this big," he measured a half-inch, "with Einstein's face on it, gets you through a whole night before and day of finals."

"Do a lot of people know about this?"

"Not for sure. Word's around. Rumor. But nothing official."

"Official?"

"No faculty knew until Mr. Mitzner last week. Somehow he got a sample."

Sang swore, "Fuckin' Leanna, man. And there goes the Cram."

Henry said, "You don't know for sure it was her."

"The way she was grinnin' the end of last week? It was her."

Griffin asked, "So what happens if you get busted on drugs around here?"

"Zero tolerance," Sang answered. "It's an automatic expulsion. You can't get back in the school. Same as carrying a weapon on school grounds."

"So Mr. Mitzner was about to bust Randy?"

Dribbler said, "Not going to happen now, though."

"That's cold," Sang snapped.

"Man fucked with Randy," Dribbler defended.

"You're nuts."

Griffin asked, "So where's Randy now?"

No one had an answer.

Griffin said, "I'm not looking to bust him."

Shrugs, denials. The dribbler bounced the ball. The well was turning off, maybe had pipelined too much already, but it was hard not to talk about your hero.

"What about his close friends?"

Two boys glanced at Paul Demmis, but Paul remained quiet.

Henry Assan offered, "Randy was away from school a lot. He took classes at Hopkins."

"Any teachers he was close to?"

"Maybe Mr. Wester. Chem teacher. He's pretty cool."

"How about Randy's mother—you know where she lives?"

"South, I think. Carolinas?" Assan looked at his friends for confirmation.

The group was becoming restless.

Griffin knew not to push it. "Guys—I appreciate the help. I'm staying at the Marriott Courtyard. Name's Jim Griffin. Griffin," he repeated. "If you think of anything else . . . want to get your name in the paper . . . call me, okay?" He waited until Paul Demmis glanced at him—their eyes meeting for only a second before Demmis turned away. It was enough. Griffin recognized the look.

He walked back to the car where Liz was completing some covert transaction with two teenage girls pulled alongside her in a blue BMW. The girls laughed, announcing, "Off to the mall," before peeling Daddy's wheels across the parking lot.

Griffin got into the Camry and shut the door. He nodded toward the oversized Tyvek envelope on Liz's lap. "What've you got?"

"Computer-generated proof pages from this year's about-to-go-to-press yearbook. Cost me a hundred bucks. This is *definitely* a high-rent district." Liz flipped through some pages, asking Griffin, "How'd you do with the Un-Harlem Globetrotters?"

"They talked about Arminger like an idol, but no one claims to know where he is. I've got some hope on the little guy with curly hair. Demmis. He's got the look of someone who needs to talk about what he knows. Like he knows something good." Griffin watched the kids mill about, debating whether to play more hoops or call it a day. "I'm registered in the Marriott under my own name, aren't I? In case one of them calls?"

"We've got separate rooms. Adjoining, but separate. The one in your name would be for work. The one in my name for play."

Griffin smiled.

Liz had the back-issue yearbooks opened again. Randy Arminger's freshman picture was bookmarked. "Good-looking kid. Looked seventeen when he was fourteen."

Griffin studied the small picture. Arminger had a neat haircut, easy smile, and brilliant eyes. A vivacious look about him. Energetic. Griffin wondered if that's how Cram made you glow. Two and a half years ago, there hadn't been the slightest expression of disturbance about Arminger. He was just another kid.

"He does look older than his age—which means if he kept maturing at that rate, he's not going to alert attention as some teenager traveling alone. He could have hopped on a plane at BWI, just another college kid headed home for the summer."

"Maybe *he* could," Liz said, "but check out Holly Haskins."

Liz turned forward two pages and ran her finger along the alphabetical list of names in the column, finding *Haskins, Holly,* then locating her picture. "Color me troubled."

Holly's round face was cocked to the side, her mouth forming more smirk than smile, eyes looking as though about to roll in impatience at how stupid the whole thing was. You could almost put an insolent voice to the picture and imagine the photographer barely had time to snap the photograph before she gave him the finger. Her hair was a messy rake, spiked and moussed.

"Poster child for tubal ligation and vasectomy. You'd want to have both procedures to make damned sure you'd never end up with a kid like this." Liz handed Griffin the yearbooks and reached for the flip phone in her bag. "We've got to get you one of these," she said, dialing out.

"Yeah, that's me. Mr. High Tech."

Into the phone, Liz said, "Mitch Thompson, please." Covering the mouthpiece, she whispered to Griffin, "I bought myself a mole in the state police. Two hundred bucks a day buys me instant Kidhunt updates."

"Nice to know there's still corruption in law enforcement."

Liz motioned for Griffin to keep quiet, then, her voice sounding all smiles, said: "Mitch. Liz McKinley. Any news on Arminger?"

11

Mitch Thompson, ten-year veteran of the Maryland State Police and recently hired mole for Liz McKinley, sat behind his desk in the department's Pikesville headquarters. Mitch was having a good time because his superiors were sweating. Superiors holding jobs that should have been his.

The way Mitch saw it, he was the wrong color and sex to advance in his chosen career field, being white and male, so since he couldn't get ahead, he took great and perverse pleasure in hoping those promoted over him failed. And when opportunity arose, Mitch didn't mind helping them fail and absolutely loved publicizing their failure whenever possible.

The big scandal about the lack of evidence-vault security? Mitch had a hand in exposing that. Leaking sexually explicit photographs one of the captains kept in his office desk? Mitch. Anonymously calling the *Sunpapers* about a superior officer's stepson being investigated for gang activities in D.C.? Mitch was all over that one.

It surprised Mitch how easily it came to him, snitching on fellow officers. To think how loyal and dedicated he'd been his first eight years on the job. Officer of the Month. Public liaison. Had never even thought of himself as racist until the black guys started getting moved up over him. But he was even getting over that to some extent. By gad, these days, he was snitching on fellow cops no matter what color they were. So maybe he wasn't a racist after all.

And now there was a seventeen-year-old kid and his girlfriend on a kill spree, and Captain Dennick had been all over wanting the state police to take the case, smelling an easy victory, only now Captain Dennick's Arrid Extra Dry was struggling. The kids were gone. Vanished.

"No news," Thompson gleefully advised Liz via phone. His feet were on his desk, strong hand brushing the whiffle cut of his brown hair. Thompson was a compact, strong-jawed man of forty-one. He had a trim waist around which he cinched his belt an extra tight notch. "We've impounded the car left at the airport, torn it apart, and there's bunches of fingerprints, Arminger's and Haskins's, traces of the red spray paint, but nothing else. No compass point as to where they are now. And the airport interviews are coming up empty. No one remembers them. No flights booked in their names, although there was one Arminger, but it wasn't the kid. Then again, Friday's a very busy airport day, so if you're gonna pick a time to blend in, Friday morning or afternoon rush would be it. So now Dennick's sending guys over to the MARC station a couple miles away to see if Arminger and Haskins got on a train. He's also planning to interview *all* the teachers at Arminger's school. The principal didn't want police around the building Friday, but that was before a dead teacher was found. That changes things. We've got guys working overtime pulling teacher unlisted phone numbers and paying visits. It's a circus!" Thompson laughed. "A zoo."

Liz told him to try not to have too much fun.

White light shone through the skylights as the Angel redrafted his sermon. He thought he'd been finished, then he read the news.

Hey Angel, how about this?

Multiple murders. The boy on a rampage killing his father and sister, his girlfriend's parents, his teacher and the teacher's wife. The Angel tried to remain calm, because you could not fight the devil with emotion. The devil preyed on emotion, took it in his hands and twisted until rage boiled over and sin filled the flesh.

The boy was taunting him, because the boy did not believe. The Angel had tried to persuade him, but the boy was so disdainful, claiming religion was nothing more than rules dressed in secular pomp and circumstance. The boy believed in chaos, not rules. The boy didn't believe in righteousness and good. He believed in science but failed to see how God's miracle encompassed science and technology, revealing its vast secrets so man could thrive and evolve.

The Angel had tried to educate him, but the boy was used to being smarter than his teachers. Perhaps that had been the Angel's mistake. He shouldn't have established himself as a teacher but an equal.

Now the Angel was left tortured by the thought he could have prevented this . . . but there was so much to do and the Angel was tiring. He was not a young man anymore. He was still strong, but he needed more time to rejuvenate himself.

And last week had been so stressful, tracking down the man who'd killed a young mother and her little girl in the car accident. The man had been convicted of automobile manslaughter but served only two months in jail. And was no sooner out of jail than he was drinking again. So Thursday night the man's car had gone off the bridge with the man, drunk, inside. The man was still conscious as water had filled the vehicle, slowly taking it to the river's depths. The man being given enough time to realize he was being punished for his sins.

"It is important," the Angel wrote in his sermon, "that punishment is no longer merely left to one's faith that the afterlife will reward good and condemn bad. As the light from our collective faith dims, it is important to see punishment take place in the here and now. We must be assured that our time on earth is not wasted or without definition. Which is why your prayers are so important. Your prayers need to be loud and strong, to send out the message that we have not abandoned God, and that our voice is not to be consumed by sin and depravity and lawlessness.

"We must pray for Randy Arminger to seek redemption, and pray for our law enforcement officers to have the acumen, resources, and perseverance to capture Randy Arminger before he commits further acts of evil.

"Hear my sermon, Randy Arminger. Feel the power of prayer as it closes in around you, as it draws you from your malefic ways. You have always chosen to disregard and disrespect God, but to thus flaunt your lack of belief so savagely is a transgression for which you must and will be punished. You seem confident that God does not exist, but your confidence is unfounded. Prayer will prove you wrong."

The Angel's hands were weary as he composed that final line. His spirit was heavy. Because as strong as he cast faith into his sermons, the Angel feared Randy

Arminger could be right. The Angel feared God was dying.

The dreams were his sign. The Angel repeatedly dreamt that he was walking on clouds through white rooms, rooms that should not be empty but were; and the air was thick from the heady, sickening smell of all the fresh blood splattered across the walls. The devil's men had stolen into heaven and were committing slaughter. And the blood upon the walls was the blood of angels.

Liz and Griffin ate lunch at a shopping center restaurant called Shannon's on Route 40. Great shrimp salad sandwiches. Then they worked the phones, Griffin dropping quarters in a pay phone outside the restaurant while Liz used the car phone. Each doing a lot of shrugging and shaking of heads. Trying the roster of unlisted phone numbers for Centennial High teachers Mitch Thompson had dictated over the phone—Liz getting her $200 worth today from Thompson.

But no teachers were answering the phone. Just message machines and endless dial tones.

Then Liz got a strike. Griffin saw her talking, taking notes while he listened to a little kid's message on his parent's answering machine.

Liz hung up and called over to him. "Got one. Come on, let's go."

Griffin hung up and jogged to the car, only to find Liz reaching into her bag, her wallet, handing him two singles.

"Honey, sweetie," using the pretend voice she thought made her sound like a wife. "Get me a yogurt, would you?" Gesturing to the I Can't Believe It's Yogurt store behind him. "A cone. Something fruit-flavored."

Ever since Liz had started cutting back on the gin, her sweet tooth was in overdrive.

Minutes later, Liz was licking a raspberry–key lime swirl, driving the Camry with one hand, heading out I–70 at seventy-five mph toward the less-populated western end of the county. "Nancy Marler," she said. "English teacher." Pointing to the yearbook. "Page thirty. Sounds very mad."

"About what?" Griffin asked, flipping to the page.

"Something she doesn't want to discuss over the phone."

Griffin found the teacher's picture, tried to focus on it, but suddenly the past snapped back at him.

He was reminded about the last time he and Liz had been on this road together. Last summer. The day he'd learned his wife had been unfaithful to him. A day he'd tried to block from his mind but relived every day.

How he'd seen the door being opened, a man he trusted standing there, shirtless. His wife in a sexy Victoria's Secret's outfit. Griffin feeling as though he were going insane.

He'd never been the same since that day, another landmark incident that took a big hunk out of him, left him torn and tattered.

And now, he was here again, where it all had gone so terribly wrong.

He tensely snapped his head to the side as though physically struck by memories.

Liz looked over, her expression asking what was wrong.

Griffin said, "Thinking too much. I'm okay." But his heart was pounding. He could still feel how the scratches had burned his face when his wife slapped him that day, Carla defending the man she was having an affair with. Forsaking Griffin. The beginning of a long, downward spiral—a dive he couldn't seem to pull out of.

He'd lost himself and had started running, living on instinct. All the while feeling as though being pulled into something over which he had little if any control. That something was looming out there waiting for him. Some demon.

12

Liz said, "This's her," seeing a woman sitting on the concrete steps of an older split-foyer home that still had its original mustard-colored siding.

Griffin checked the Centennial High yearbook, confirmed, "Nancy Marler. English."

Liz turned onto the gravel driveway off rural Route 97 and had to immediately hit the brakes when a barking Yorkie darted over from a neighboring yard. The Yorkie came suicidally close to being mashed into a dachshund under her tires.

Nancy Marler moved quickly to shoo the dog, clapping her hands and scolding, "Georgie, go home. Go home!"

Georgie zoomed circles around her and kept barking.

Nancy Marler warned, "You're going to get a squirting." She reached for a length of garden hose connected to a bib beside the carport, and the dog took off running, hurdling a low row of scotch pine seedlings planted along the property line. He resumed his noise-making from beyond range of the nozzle.

"Annoying dog," Nancy commented, as Liz and Griffin got out of the car, "but smart." She set down the hose and wiped her hand on the hip of her shorts, introducing herself over incessant barking. "Hi. Nancy

Marler. And that," gesturing to the dog, "is Georgie. Our neighbor's dog, although you wouldn't know it from the amount of time he spends here. I don't even know why they bother to have a dog. He'd rather get fussed at here than ignored over there, I guess."

Georgie was barking and inching his way closer, until Nancy feigned going for the hose, which sent him on scampering retreat.

"Like a bad kid," she complained.

In her early thirties, plain and fresh-scrubbed, Nancy Marler looked like someone who could read bedtime stories to children and change her voice for all the different parts.

She wore a discount-store outfit with a floppy-collared polo shirt left untucked over matching shorts to hide her thickening middle.

Liz said, "I appreciate your meeting us. I'm Liz McKinley. This is James Griffin. Here's my card." Liz produced a glossy *America Exposed* business card that listed the many ways to contact her—Atlanta-local phone/fax, e-mail, toll-free phone, pager, cellphone, plus temporary local numbers attached to the back of the card by label.

Griffin spotted a man's face at an upstairs window, the man watching suspiciously but pulling back from view when Griffin waved.

"My husband," Nancy said. "He told me not to say anything, to do what I was told. He said let the union handle it. But no one's going to do anything. They never do. Why don't we go 'round the side. Georgie will stop barking if he can't see us."

Liz and Griffin followed her across green grass. Their trespass sent purple martins scrambling to flight from a green and white birdhouse. The birds took wing soaring and calling.

Nancy Marler stood against a panoramic backdrop of distant blue hills. The area was a high point. Small houses built along the dual-lane road backed to a gradual slope that ventured to a valley of rolling farmland. The western half of the county still maintained an agrarian image; development was approaching, but more slowly than for the region caught in the ever-widening corridor between D.C. and Baltimore.

Liz, starting friendly conversation by flattering her interviewee, said, "You look young to be a high school teacher. I'd figure you more for the little ones."

"I'd rather be elementary-ed, but it's so tough getting a teaching job in this county that when a friend recommended me to the principal at Centennial, I realized it would be foolish not to take the job."

"Have you been there long?"

"Only two years. This is my second year."

Liz said, "You don't sound enthused. Centennial's supposed to be *the* school from all we've heard."

Nancy shook her head. "Maybe it's because I've gotten older. Or maybe it's high school kids—I've never taught them before. Before I took this job, I'd been away from teaching for five years—we had two kids, but once they were old enough I decided it was time to go back to work. Now I'm not so sure it was the right decision. I think a lot changed in the time I was away. The parents and the kids are different. It's very competitive, very stressful."

Liz took her compact recorder from her bag, "Can I turn this on?"

Nancy thought for a brief second, then nodded. "Sure, why not?"

Liz said, "You were talking about the classroom being competitive and stressful."

"The whole way the country is changing is having negative impact on the schools. In the same classroom I've got kids who drive to school in BMWs and kids whose parents have been laid off and are about to have their home foreclosed. It's left the kids with this all-or-nothing approach. They're not optimistic about the future. They think when they grow up you're either going to have it all or lose it all. And these kids are determined to have it all right now. Most of them, anyway. I'm afraid for these kids, I really am. Their self-esteem is so fragile, like balloons afraid the tiniest pin-prick could burst their bubble. It's unhealthy."

Liz asked, "Is Randy Arminger that kind of kid?"

"No. He's not like that at all. Randy Arminger is probably one of the smartest students in the country, but he's also the most arrogant, and he *is* a manipulator. There are certain students who can get away with just about anything. They're given wide liberties. They hook school or get into carousing or roughhousing and the tendency is to look the other way. Like they used to do for athletes, and maybe still do in other schools—I don't know. But at Centennial, the superior student is our star. That student's the one we hold up for other schools to admire. And until a few days ago, Randy Arminger was that prize. He was a sophomore my first year at the school—last year—and other teachers were jealous because I had him in my English lit class."

Nancy looked over her shoulder again, and Griffin began to wonder if they were around the side of the house to be away from the Yorkie's view or that of Nancy's husband. There were no windows on the north wall of the house.

"At first, I'll admit, I was very impressed. He acted more like a college student than a sixteen-year-old. He looked and acted much older than that. Very sophisticated. You could have told me he was twenty and I'd have believed it. He was studious, attentive, very verbal, well-behaved, charismatic—the kind of student you sometimes find yourself so drawn to you start teaching just to him. As though you're blocking out all the other students in the class—they're not even in focus—and you concentrate on Randy." She formed a tunnel shape with her hands and gestured forward. "You teach to him because he's such a pleasure *to* teach.

"English tends to be a subject other students sleepwalk through—even the good students. They're so much more math- and science-oriented now. So when someone like Randy seems to be hanging on your every word, it's . . . well, it's very flattering." Nancy Marler couldn't keep from blushing.

Liz asked, "So what happened to change your mind about Randy . . . assuming you have?"

"My opinion of Randy most definitely changed." Nancy's voice quieted. "About two months into the year, he started flirting with me. It was innocent at first. Typical schoolboy crush. He sent me flowers for my birthday, and at Christmas, and for Valentine's Day. But he also sent something else on Valentine's Day. Although he denied it.

"I went out to my car after school and there was a beautifully wrapped box on the passenger seat, and inside was . . . it was a very sexy piece of lingerie." Nancy blushed again, and as she looked aside, the breeze blew hair away from her face. "There was also a note." She crossed her arms, looking at Griffin, then Liz.

"And the note—it was very pretty, computer-generated artwork in color—said, 'Can I see you wear this?' "

"That's bold," Liz remarked.

"But he didn't sign it?" Griffin assumed.

"No, but I know it was Randy. Because the next day I asked him to stay after class, and he looked . . . I'm not sure, I guess I'd call it . . . expectant, and then I told him while I was flattered by his present, it really wasn't proper, and he had to understand he couldn't give me something like that and certainly couldn't send me a note like that."

"What did he say?"

"He looked confused, and puzzled. Or pretended to be. He said he was sorry, but he thought I liked flowers."

"Because he *had* sent you flowers," Liz said.

"Yes. You see? It was a simple plan he had. But devious. That's how his mind works. He always has an out. And not just any excuse or lie, it's thought out. Like a chess game. Before he does something today, he's already thought five or ten moves ahead. Not that he can't think under pressure, but usually he doesn't have to."

"So maybe it was just a teenage fantasy," Griffin suggested. "And he was embarrassed to be caught at it."

"No. He didn't show it, but he was angry. I could feel it brewing inside him. The very next day something else was put in my car. I stopped at the grocery store on the way home, and when I came out there was an envelope in my car. There was a card inside, more computer-generated art. On the front it said, 'Since you won't wear it for me,' and on the inside there was a picture of a woman wearing that exact same piece of lingerie he'd given me. Except this woman was in a very explicit pose, and my face had been superimposed over hers. Underneath the picture was printed, 'Since you won't wear it for me, I'll just have to dream about you like this.' "

Nancy's fingers tightened on her arms. "It shook me up." She took another peek over her shoulder toward the house. "I didn't tell my husband, because he'd have gone crazy. I did report it to the principal the next morning."

"Sam Reese?" Liz asked, wondering if last year's principal had been retained.

"Yes. I told him I wanted Randy removed from my class, that I wanted him disciplined and that I wanted to report the matter to the police."

"So what happened?"

"He said I was overreacting."

"You showed him the notes?"

"No. I was too embarrassed."

Liz said, "Did he move Randy out of your class?"

She shook her head. "He said he'd monitor the situation."

"What about filing a report with the police?"

"I didn't because I realized they'd want to see the notes—and the picture with my face put on it. I was too embarrassed. And I've wondered since if Randy knew that's what I'd do. That I wouldn't take action against him, not only because I couldn't prove that he'd left the lingerie and notes, but because of how humiliating it would be for me to have to show someone that photograph he'd created. Or even show the lingerie. He knew me well enough to guess that. He knows how people can be manipulated."

Griffin asked, "Did Arminger do anything else?"

"He sent me flowers for Easter—tulips—and no matter how cold I tried to be towards him, he never changed. He stayed as friendly and active and attentive in class as ever."

"Maybe he wasn't the one," Liz said.

"No. In his perverse way, I'm sure he enjoyed every minute of my class for the rest of that year. He enjoyed the fact that he'd upset and frustrated me and was getting away with it. And he was smart enough not to do anything else that might get him caught. And I wasn't the only person he targeted. There've been other disturbing events, but again," she sighed, "nothing any one could prove. And, maybe I'm paranoid, but I can't help think it was Randy. Frightening messages get into teacher e-mail. One teacher resigned very suddenly a few months ago and the rumor is he was being blackmailed. And worst of all, according to one of my students, her friend was raped at a school dance. She was blindfolded and gagged, and taken to a room somewhere in the school where a very bright light was shone on her—she thought she heard the sounds of someone putting videotape in a camera to film her being assaulted. It was all so well planned."

Griffin said, "Did the police come up with anything on that?"

"The girl never told the police. That's why her friend was confiding in me. She wanted to know if she should try to talk her friend into going to the police."

Liz suggested, "You're sure it was the 'friend' she was talking about, and it didn't happen to her?"

Nancy Marler's mouth tightened. "I guess it could have been she. I asked, and she said it was her friend, but she was crying. My God, she was only fourteen years old." Her voice was intense but quiet, enraged. "And now the school is telling us not to talk to anyone about Randy Arminger or what happened to Bill

Mitzner. Sam Reese is going to play spin doctor to keep his precious school from being tarnished! He's put a gag order on us, making it very clear our jobs could be at stake. He reminded me my allegations about Randy Arminger were never proven. He's afraid this is going to come back and hurt him. And it's not right. It's absolutely not right!"

Liz said, "I'd like to talk to the girl who was raped. And any other teacher or student who thinks they were targeted by Arminger."

Nancy Marler's anger had made her slightly short of breath. She drew air deeply through her mouth, exhaling, "I don't know."

Griffin asked, "Who were his friends? Or the Haskins girl's friends? Who might they stay with to hide?"

"A friend's house! He wouldn't do anything that easy. Look at what he's done!" she pleaded. "How many people he killed in one night. Do you think he did this without a plan? Without thinking ten steps ahead? Didn't you hear what I told you about him? He's smart. He's a smart, calculating, dangerous boy. He doesn't care about other people or their feelings. I pity the girl with him. I'm sure he doesn't care about her. He's just using her for something. Because that's what he does. He's a manipulator. He uses people. And he gets away with it. He always gets away with it. Look at what's happening now. He's murdered a teacher and he's got the principal telling us not to talk about it. Someone who might know more about him than I do might be kept quiet because we don't want to reveal all the dirty little secrets our school—every school—keeps from getting out. All the fights, the drugs."

Without sounding accusatory, Griffin said, "There's a

big difference between Arminger sneaking intimidating notes into a car and doing what he's doing now."

"Tell me that after he's caught." As though somehow Randy was going to get away with this, too.

13

Back in the car, Liz said to Griffin, "I think he broke her heart."

"Who broke whose heart?" He turned to face Liz, having been staring out the window, thinking about Randy Arminger, his image of the boy changing rapidly.

Liz's throaty voice carried over warm air blowing through opened windows. "Randy Arminger broke Nancy Marler's heart. I think something about what happened with her and Randy Arminger, even though it became scary, it tapped something inside her. Call it her dark side. This small yet powerful lobe of her brain—maybe not even her brain—some part of her was flattered getting that lingerie from him. And some little wicked part of her fantasized about doing just what Arminger suggested in that note."

"No way."

"Tell me we all don't have tiny little voices of debauchery inside us, Griff. Hell, all I've whispered to you in the heat of the moment doesn't come close to revealing the whole spectrum of hedonism whirling between my ears."

"Then I can't wait to hear more."

"You never will, because some of what I think about might send you screaming from the room. But what I'm saying is I think this kid saw something in Nancy Marler, and he exploited it for his own pleasure. Look at the scenario: she'd been out of teaching for five years. Had two kids. Been home playing mother. Living with *that* husband? Did you get a look at him peeking out the window? He looked like Boo Radley's illegitimate son. Some tradesman type, probably hasn't read a book in his life, and she's an English lit teacher. She's probably from a small town—you hear the West Virginia in her voice?—and when she was younger, her husband probably looked good to her, maybe someone she played teacher to. Maybe the men in her family never went to school but worked hard at steady jobs, and that's what her down-home image of a husband is. So she marries this guy and now he's in the pipefitter's local, sitting around waiting for the phone to ring with the next union job, and she's stuck home with him for five years of childrearing. All of a sudden he's not so thrilling any more, especially when his subscription to *Penthouse* gets more attention than she does."

Griffin enjoyed Liz's fanciful take on people, a part of her profession, comparable to the way he matched defendant to charge on the criminal docket.

"So," Liz continued, "Nancy takes this job at Status High, and here's this smart, good-looking student with a crush on her. Nancy's a little innocent, a little naive—she's been a small-town girl, a steady Kmart shopper, she's thirty-something with two little kids and not exactly your hard-beach-body type. Enter this handsome kid who acts like she's hot stuff. Tell me that didn't do something for her. That her ego didn't rise in the thermometer that day."

"Sure—he had a crush on her."

"Uh-uh. More than that. I think she's right. I think he

manipulated her for fun. His idea of fun. He flattered and deferred to her, then he scared her—on purpose. I sure don't think he expected her to go along, play lingerie model for him. No way in this world. I think he knew he was going to scare her, and he wanted to scare her. I think he got a sadistic kick from it." Liz shivered. "Pretty devious for a seventeen-year-old—sixteen at the time."

"We've got to forget he's seventeen. Assume he knows a whole helluva lot more than that." Griffin stretched, feeling the need for exercise after being cooped up in the plane all morning and the car all afternoon.

The highway was open and empty ahead of them. Traffic was sparse in the western half of the county as the afternoon wore on into evening.

Griffin watched out the window, saw golfers on a course that paralleled the highway, and was briefly reminded of his father and his cronies hacking around eighteen, cheating like mad behind one another's backs. Griffin hadn't told his parents he was coming back to Baltimore because it would have been too upsetting for them; not only had Griffin lost a daughter, but they'd lost their only grandchild.

He thought back to when he was seventeen: the intense arguments he'd gotten into with his father. Yet no matter how loud and nasty those shouting matches had become, Charlie Griffin's drunken screams carrying through opened windows to the street, it was unthinkable that they could have resorted to the sort of violence Randy Arminger acted out upon his father.

Sadly, Randy Arminger wasn't the first seventeen-year-old to shoot a parent and a sibling, nor the first to kill a girlfriend's parents, not even the first to murder a teacher. But while individually the murders could be classified as acts of impulse, put together in such coordinated fashion they amounted to a well-planned crime.

Yet as effectively and brutally as Randy carried out the killings, what was even more disturbing—if that were possible—was that he made no attempt to commit these murders covertly. If Randy had, as alleged, mentally tortured Nancy Marler, he'd done it stealthily and gotten away without being caught. These killings, the spray-painted messages referring to someone named Angel, were of an entirely different structure. No attempt had been made to look for another suspect. Randy's fingerprints were everywhere. The same gun was used in all three killings.

Arminger *had* to realize the evidence would point to him. Didn't he care? What Griffin had learned about Arminger so far didn't leave the impression of someone who wanted to be caught, subconsciously or not. Probably the little son of a bitch considered himself so brilliant he thought he could leave behind a trail of blood and bodies and not be found. Which meant his escape route was likely as well-conceived as the murders.

Griffin's head tilted upright with realization. "He didn't get on a plane." Griffin reached into Liz's saddle bag. He rummaged around for the cellphone and handed it to her. "Call your mole at the state police. Ask if they checked car rental agencies."

Liz took the phone but didn't dial out. "Rental car?"

"He only went to the airport to make it *look* as if he got on a plane. He rented a car and is making the police waste time checking airlines. Two birds, one stone. There's at least five major rental-car operations at the airport."

"Why rent a car when he *has* a car?"

"Exactly what he wants the police to think. But Arminger didn't get on a plane and he didn't trek a couple of miles to the Amtrak station. Assuming he didn't ditch the gun he used and has it with him, he's not going to risk carrying it on the plane, and he would be wary of raising suspicion if he checks it in his luggage and his bag gets x-rayed. Plus, he wouldn't want to be confined like that. He's up in the air for a couple of hours, even on a train from BWI to D.C. or Wilmington, there's a chance the police find out what he's done sooner than he's planned, maybe figure out where he's going, and are waiting for him when he gets there. No plane. No train. He's in a car. He'd take the chance driving because he stays in control."

"With every cop in the state looking for him? If he gets a speeding ticket, he's busted."

"How long between the time of the last killing—the teacher and his wife—and the time the police found out about *any* of the killings and started looking for him?"

"I don't know for sure—three, four hours at least."

"So what if by the time the police *start* looking for him, he's already driven where he wants to be? He's eliminated most of the risk. Besides, consider this: he's changed his looks." Griffin went through two back-issue yearbooks and page proofs of the upcoming volume. Arminger's pictures. "Freshman year, a normal haircut. Next year, longer. This year, it's on his shoulders. All this thick dark hair—what if he gets a military cut? He might not fool anyone who knows him, but everyone's looking for a seventeen-year-old with long, dark hair."

"Still, his license?"

Griffin was shaking his head. "He's probably got a

phony. New name. New age. Old enough to get a rental car."

"Major car agencies want you to be twenty-five. He looks old for his age, but twenty-five?"

"Who's going to check?"

"The rental agent."

"Unless he didn't go to any counter. He could have picked the car up express. Hertz Number One Club. Avis Wizard. National's got Emerald something. You make the reservation by phone, set up an account in advance with a credit card, and go right to the car. There's no rental agent at any counter. No papers to fill out."

"But there's always a guard in the rental car lot, or someone who checks your paperwork on the way out."

"Right. Checks the *paperwork*. He's going to match the name on the rental agreement with a name on the driver's license. That's it."

"But if he sees some kid driving? And the girl? No way she looks old enough to be out without a note from her parents."

"Assume Arminger knows that. So she's not with him when he picks up the car. All Arminger has to worry about is that he gets by the guard. Tell me you think he didn't figure a way to do all that."

Liz dialed Mitch Thompson, who told her that every rental car agency at or near the airport had been contacted, and no rentals were made in the name of Arminger or Haskins.

Liz echoed this to Griffin, who replied, "But did they check records or *show* Arminger's picture?"

Liz relayed the question.

Mitch Thompson started laughing. "Hey, great,

another potential screw-up. They only ran the records. No photo check. Oh, boy I'm loving this."

Over Thompson's glee, Griffin said to Liz, "Tell your buddy to suggest they show Arminger's picture to all the rental lot guards who were working Friday morning. And have them create a composite of Arminger with short hair. Tell him to put it in a memo and maybe he'll get an attaboy."

Into the phone, Liz said, "Hold on, Mitch," then covered the mouthpiece, asking Griffin, "Why don't we do that ourselves? I want to find this kid first, Grif, *before* the cops."

"Tell him," Griffin insisted.

Liz scowled but forwarded Griffin's advice to Mitch Thompson, then hung up. But she wasn't happy about it.

Griffin asked, "What'd he say? Is he going to do it?"

Liz replied curtly, "As soon as he calls some friends at the newspapers—yeah."

"Great." Griffin smirked. "Everyone's got their own agenda."

Liz bristled at Griffin's having told her what to do, and was a little upset with herself that she'd done it. She wasn't an order-taker as a matter of course. "Look," Liz got firm, laying down some rules, "it's a coup to come up with a piece of information before anyone else. Before the police, before the other papers. It means I'm doing my job better than them. So if I find some old guy who worked night guard at a rental car company, and he I.D.'s Randy Arminger as having driven off in a late model this or that under the fake name of Bob Smith, I'm ahead. I'm the story everyone else's chasing." She looked over at him. "This is *reporting*, Jimmy. Not cop work. It's a different frame of mind."

He understood her point. "Sorry . . . you're right. But

if it's any help, I don't think I.D.ing the car's going to get the cops to Arminger any faster. That car's probably already dropped and Arminger's moved on."

"Still . . ."

"Okay. It won't happen again."

Liz watched the road, pretending to be madder than she was just to make her point. She did love him, but this was business. Her business. After a couple miles, she reached over and touched his leg. Most of the edge was gone from her voice. "Worst-case scenario, the cops find him before us because of your idea, I'll write the story so it's clear they wouldn't have snagged him without your input. I can make that work."

"Good." Not that he felt a need to apologize for suggesting a tactic that might help the police find Arminger before Liz, especially if they found him before he killed someone else.

After a moment, Liz proposed, "So where is he, Jimmy? Where's Randy Arminger?"

"I don't know, but wherever he is, I'm getting this bad feeling there's more to it than what's happened already."

Carl Nicholson and his bud Jacob were both fifteen. They didn't know Randy Arminger, but they were finding out about him. Students at Howard High, they heard rumors Friday night while hanging around at Long Reach Village Center.

Now, Saturday, back at Long Reach, nothing else to do, they were talking about it again. A friend of theirs, Bobby, who'd been expelled from school back in November for sporting a piece at a basketball game, asked, "You ladies hear? Some Centennial brat blew away his old man."

Jacob, who'd been buzzing over twenty-four hours

from hits of crack purchased in home room the day before, hopped up from the curb. "Yeah, man, yeah. We heard." Jacob pointed his finger. "I could do that too. Hey, Pop. Bangadabangadabangada." Laughing. "The asshole comes over for our 'Sunday visit.' " Jacob drew quotes in the air. "I greet him at the door with a rod."

"Uh-huh," Bobby said, unimpressed, "then tell him how your mother been blowin' her manfriend in the room 'cross the hall from you *all night*. How she all night long on his longshlong dong."

Jacob jumped-stepped toward Bobby, screaming, "Shuddup, man. You shuddup!" Drawing back to punch Bobby, who didn't flinch.

Bobby slouched on the hood of a parked car. "What, little white girl? Whatchoo gonna do? You gonna hit me?" Bobby always calling them ladies or girls, because Jacob and Carl came from middle-class families that owned houses in the county. Bobby was a city export, living with his mother in some Title This or Title That section, builders having to promise the county they'd put up subsidized apartments on Parcel A to get profitable zoning decisions on Parcel B.

Jacob's fist turned to a pointing finger. "I bust you, man! I bust you, you don't quit about my mother!"

"Settle down, little girl. Settle you skinny ass down." Bobby spoke with a sly smile. He liked hanging with Jacob and Carl. They said some funny shit sometimes, and were good entree to parties where white girls hung out. Bobby especially liked those parties where Momsy and Dadsy were home, smiling, telling everyone this was a substance-free party, and putting on that extra big smile seeing Bobby's jet-black face come into their lily-white home with all the farmhouse sort of knickknacks hanging on the wall. Bobby put a little pressure check on their liberal philosophies once he was in their finished basement with pool table, fake Tiffany lamp, and their daughter and all her cute friends.

Bobby laughed at Jacob, who couldn't seem to stand still, shaking his arms and hopping in place. "Lookit this little dancin' girl. Little girl, you got ants in yo panties?" Asking Carl, "What with him?"

Carl shrugged. Carl didn't say a whole lot. He was—as always—just along for the ride. He felt a little uncomfortable around Bobby, how Bobby was always smiling but could turn nasty in a second and the rage would fly out. Carl was pretty sure Bobby was going to end up in jail one day, and he figured Bobby knew that, too. This was all the relative calm before the storm.

Bobby leaned back over the hood of the car, swiveling his thick neck when a car horn blared at him.

A voice shouted, "Bobby Ray, you faggot." The shouter drove a sported-up Nissan Maxima, six-year-old model shined so bright-black it reflected sunlight with enough strength to blind. It had a spoiler, license plate holder shaped like a length of gold chain, and vanity tags: ON IT. King sized bass thumping rap from serious speakers shook the whole damned car.

Bobby rolled slowly to a standing position, called to the guy in the Nissan, "Cleavon muthahfuckah! You early, man,"

"Checkin' things out. Spied a ride cross the way." Cleavon, shades tipped down his nose, raised a long, spidery arm out the window and pointed over the roof of the Nissan. "Over at the hotel. Four-wheel drive. Emrald green. Brand muth-ah-fuck-inspank-in' new."

Bobby Ray pushed off the car he'd been lounging on. "We on it." He started toward the Nissan as Cleavon reached into the back seat to sling open the door. Bobby

Ray turned a half circle and walked backward a few strides, saying, "You girls comin'?"

Jacob, hopping, hopping, dying for an invite, said, "Yeah, yeah." He started running toward the Maxima.

Carl stayed on the curb. He wished Jacob hadn't become such a doper. They used to just hang around, watch TV, play video games, and pickup basketball. Now none of that had enough "edge" for Jacob. Had "no teeth." Carl had no idea where Jacob came up with that line. He asked him about it once and Jacob said, "You know, no teeth, like an old geezer." Jacob said "no teeth" a lot around Bobby Ray, or "teeth" if something would be a kick, trying to get Bobby Ray to adopt the expression, but Bobby Ray just laughed at him. Sometimes Bobby Ray called him, Teeth, when he wasn't calling him girl or lady.

"Carl," Jacob yelled from the back seat of the Nissan. "Come on, man, what're you waitin for?" Jacob jerked his head to the rap music, looking like an idiot.

Carl pulled himself off the curb and sauntered toward the car. What the hell. Nothing else to do.

At the Marriott Courtyard, Liz unlocked the door and Griffin followed her inside, suitcase in hand.

Liz had one of two adjoining rooms set up as her on-the-road office. Her laptop computer on the desk was equipped with a fax/modem and portable printer. "I'm going to upload some last minute changes to my story." She checked her watch: six o'clock. "I'll need about an hour. Then shower, dinner? Sound good? There's a couple of decent places to eat around here."

"Sure. I'll take a run."

"There's an indoor pool and weight room. Scouted it out for you." Liz settled behind the desk.

"Too nice out—I'll run."

"Okay." The blue glow of her computer screen shone across her. She pushed back her hair, said, "Sorry again about before. Snapping at you."

"Ancient history."

She smiled, said, "Damn."

"What?"

"We got that resolved too soon, didn't even get in any good makeup sex."

"So pick a fight with me about something over dinner."

"We can only hope."

Griffin took his suitcase into the adjoining room and unpacked. He changed into a sleeveless T-shirt, shorts, white socks, and Avia cross-trainers, gave Liz a "See ya," that barely raised her head from her work, and headed out the door.

Griffin went down two levels of stairs to the parking lot, was stretching in the warmth of early-evening sun, when he heard a man shout:

"Hey, goddammit. Get outta my car!"

14

A middle-aged man in suit pants and a shirt ran toward a green Jeep Cherokee.

The Jeep backed fast out of a parking space and mashed the side of a parked car.

The man shouted, “Stop!” He reached for the driver’s door handle, raised a fist to bang the window, when:

Pop! Pop! Pop!

Bright flashes of light. Holes cracked through the driver’s side window.

Shots fired. One went through the man, spun him around, dropped him to the street.

Someone in the background screamed.

The Jeep’s engine wound out, accelerating. Smoke ground off spinning wheels as the dark vehicle sped forward.

Griffin ran into its path—trying to make the Jeep swerve and run into something—to hijack the hijackers.

The driver laid on the horn, coming right at him.

A bright flash. Pop! A hole cracked through the windshield. Someone inside firing at Griffin.

Griffin dove left, flesh scraping gravel, and rolled behind parked cars.

The Jeep veered toward him, clipping the bumpers of three cars like dominoes, slamming vehicles into one another, squeezing Griffin between and half under two cars.

Griffin swore, "Goddammit," struggling to get out and hearing the moans of the man who'd been shot.

The Jeep was backing up.

A black voice screamed, "Getouttheway, *out-the-way*. I'm gonna shoot dat muthahfuckah!" More shots fired—*pop-pop-pop*—small caliber, .22. Aiming for Griffin but hitting metal.

Griffin crawled out from between cars as the Jeep peeled out and roared for the exit. The vehicle sped down a U-shaped driveway that doubled back toward the street.

Griffin got to his feet and ran down a grassy incline, looking to cut the Jeep off or at the very least get a clear look at who was inside. See their faces.

A window was lowered but not fast enough for the shooter. A round fired through glass sent a slug into the green grass behind Griffin.

Griffin saw the shooter: black kid leaning over another kid scrunched down in the seat, a face Griffin couldn't see. Another kid in the front seat screamed, looking scared.

The Jeep sped into the intersection against the light, horn blaring. A sports car braked and swerved. A van got nailed in the left rear and was spun into a head-on collision with a pickup truck. A horrible, fast explosion of twisting metal and breaking glass threw a young father into the constraint of a shoulder harness; the small heads of his two kids in the back seat jerked violently.

More tires screeched as other vehicles tried to avoid the accident.

The Jeep was going too fast to make the turn and rode up onto the curb. Its tires turfed grass and got stuck.

Griffin sprinted hard toward the stolen vehicle as its rear door opened. A kid—white, tall, athletic—bailed out.

A black kid—the shooter?—yelled from inside the Jeep: "Getbackinthecar, man. Get in."

The white kid got up, but the driver wanted out of there. The Jeep's spinning wheels found traction and sent the big vehicle off the grass, churning up sod. It bumped onto the street, wheels smoking, fishtailing. The opened rear door swung wildly.

The kid who'd bailed was left behind. He saw Griffin coming for him, and turned and ran.

The kid was fast. Crossing a clearing, he hurdled a low guardrail into a shopping center parking lot. He stayed away from the sidewalk, where people stared.

Griffin yelled, "Grab him!"

No one was fast enough—or wanted—to react. Stunned parents pulled toddlers closer to them. What was happening?

The running kid made the end of the strip center and turned the corner, heading across an open field of uncut grass, trying to make the woods.

Griffin closed in. A rush surged through his body, sensing the impact.

The kid glanced back, wide-eyed with fear. A kid. Just a kid.

Griffin launched himself forward and hit him hard, and for a second they were both in the air. The kid cried out, landing hard with Griffin on top of him, grabbing his wrist and jerking his arm behind his back.

The kid struggled until Griffin pushed his face hard into the ground. "What the hell's the matter with you?"

The kid continued to kick and squirm, so Griffin

jerked sharply on his thumb, dislocating it. The boy screamed in pain.

"Shut up, you goddamned baby. What's your name?"

When the boy hesitated, Griffin grabbed another finger and jerked it back, ready to snap it.

"Carl Nicholson," the kid grunted. "Carl Nicholson."

"Carl, I'm Jim Griffin, and I'd like to know what the hell you and your buddies had in mind today. Huh?" He put pressure against Carl's middle knuckle, making it clear he had the strength to make his fingers look like a pile of sticks.

"I didn't know Bobby had a gun! Honest to God. Honest. It was a joyride."

"Well, this is pretty joyous, ain't it, Carl?"

"You're hurting me."

"Not really. This can't hurt that much. Tough guy like you."

Carl Nicholson winced.

Griffin looked over his shoulder. Some guy was starting across the field but not in too big of a hurry. Great, just what Griffen needed now—help. Where was this guy five minutes ago? Griffin leaned over the kid. "What's Bobby's last name?"

"I don't—" He screamed when Griffin snapped his finger out of joint, and grabbed another finger.

"There's a bullshit- and time-limit here, Carl! Now tell me the name of everyone in that car." Griffin glanced back at the man coming toward them.

Carl's scream seemed to stop the man. He shouted to Griffin, "Are you all right?"

Griffin yelled back, "Just get the police."

"What about the one you've got?"

Carl was wailing.

Griffin mumbled, "The one I've got . . . ?" Then shouted, "What about him?"

"Is he hurt?"

"Who gives a rat's ass! Get the police."

The man turned back toward the shopping center as sirens sounded from the distance.

Griffin told Carl, "You believe that? Guy's asking if you're all right."

Carl shouted, "I'm not! You hurt me!"

"I think you hurt yourself jumping out of that Jeep is what I think. Now I want the names of everyone else in that car. No bullshit!" He seized another finger, ready to twist it.

"No, no, no!"

"Start talking, Carl!"

"Bobby Ray," he gasped, "he had the gun. Cleavon something." Wincing when Griffin started to turn his finger slowly, about to pull it out of joint like turning the handle of a vise. "*Jesus!* I swear, I don't know his last name. Friend of Bobby's. He was the driver."

"Keep talking."

"Jacob Ericsson. Jacob lives down the street from me. Ericsson. Okay, okay?"

"Yeah. Beautiful." Griffin stood and pulled the boy to his feet. "Let's go get you a medal."

Liz hadn't heard the shots, but there was a commotion in the hall. People yelling about a man being shot.

She'd run out, frantic. Worried it might have been Griffin. In the parking lot, seeing people huddled over a body on the ground. A man rushing over saying he was a doctor. Liz seeing the injured man's shoes: dress shoes. Not Griffin's. Where was he?

Two people pointed across the street to the shopping center. Saying one of the carjackers had jumped out.

And there had been Griffin. On a dead sprint after him. Two figures running hard, the kind of pace most people couldn't sustain for a hundred yards.

Liz gasping, "Oh my God. Oh, God!" Afraid the joyrider might have a gun, Liz starting to run herself, then she saw the accident just over the hill.

Kids were crying. Traffic was at a stop. Dozens of people were out of their cars. Pedestrian first aid was being administered to a man taken from a pickup truck who had so much blood all over him. A man sat outside a van, cradling an unconscious child in his arms as voices screamed for ambulances and the police.

Liz ran back inside the hotel, but someone was already on the pay phone calling 911.

Liz felt helpless. She didn't know what to do because she'd never been this close to this kind of trauma. She always got there well after the fact, after people who knew how to deal with this were on the scene. That's when Liz would capture everything through her camera.

So that's what she'd decided to do. Legs weak with anxiety, she went up the stairs, got her Canon, and photographed the scene. She focused in tight on faces: the father's blank stare, his mouth mumbling reassurance to the child in his arms; another little boy still inside the van, safe in his car seat, screaming. There was broken glass all around him, but the little boy wasn't cut.

The police arrived. Ambulances. Quick response time and lots of personnel. Witnesses pointed in the direction where the Jeep had taken off. Others pointed where Griffin had disappeared behind the building.

Two squad cars headed in that direction when Griffin

reappeared holding the joyrider's arm behind his back as if he might twist it off. The joyrider wasn't so much on his feet as Griffin was keeping him upright.

A truck driver who'd witnessed the whole accident shouted, "He got the son of a bitch! Goddamn little punk. I'm gonna tear the shit out of him." The driver ran to his truck and came out with a crowbar. The melee had almost caused him to jackknife his rig and he was going to take it out on the kid when two cops held him back.

Liz saw how young the boy was. Fifteen? Sixteen? Lanky, strong-looking. But just a boy.

The truck driver yelled as the cops held him back, "Somebody oughta lock you up and throw away the fucking key!"

Carl didn't hear, trapped in his own pain.

The restrained truck driver yelled to Griffin, "You shoulda beat the shit out of him. The punk!"

People were applauding.

Jesus. It was almost a riot. People cheered as Griffin turned the kid over to the police, thinking they were seeing a rarity. That someone had committed a crime and actually been caught. It was as though they were starved for it—some symbol of justice.

The truck driver wasn't the only one shouting Griffin should have hurt the boy. That he should have killed him.

Liz ran through one roll of film and into another, unsnapping a canister attached to the neck strap and winding it in, fingers trembling. Telling herself, Breathe, Liz, breath.

Griffin stood amidst the cops—his former brethren. Liz moved closer, overhearing Griffin give them a license plate number, description and names of the shooter, driver, one other passenger in the Jeep.

The cops reacted quickly, getting descriptions over the radio. One of them knew Griffin, shook his hand and slapped his shoulder before introducing him to others. Solemn handshakes passed quickly around.

A photographer from the local paper circled the scene, taking pictures.

Liz heard a couple of younger officers on the side; one gestured to Griffin, saying, "Christ, you know who that is? Former city cop. He's the one who killed Bright Eyes last summer. He's the reason all those crooked city lawyer bastards are doing time."

Griffin and Liz sat at a table for two by the window, a square pizza between them, two square slices on their plates.

Liz said, "This isn't so swift." Maybe nothing would have tasted very good just then.

"No, it's not." Griffin pushed his plate away and drank iced tea.

Behind them, a jazz ensemble set up in an alcove played too loudly.

Liz said, "They're not so swift, either."

Griffin took out his wallet, put a twenty on the table, and said, "Come on, let's go."

"Get a receipt. Expense account."

Griffin gestured at the lousy trio. "And listen to more of that off-key crap? It's not worth it." Griffin helped Liz from her chair, then picked her oversized black bag from the floor and handed it to her. They went outside arm in arm.

It was a warm Saturday night. Almost summer. Kids drove into the lot of the multiplex theater next door for the nine-thirty show amidst a lot of yelling and hooting.

Griffin stopped and watched them grab-ass one

another. He said to Liz, "You notice they don't go on dates any more. There's fifty kids over there and not one couple. Three guys and three girls. Three guys, four girls. Two girls, one guy."

"You see a lot of that these days," Liz said. She had both arms around Griffin and her head against his shoulder. She tried not to think he'd been shot at a couple hours ago, and that he didn't seem to care, had barely noticed.

Griffin said, "I don't think they feel safe."

"They're kids," Liz said. "They're at that indestructible age. Immortal."

"I don't think that comes with childhood anymore. They travel in groups because it's safer. They might not even realize it. They're scared. Even if they don't think about it."

"I don't know . . . except I know *I* don't feel that safe anymore. It's out of my mind sometimes, but never for long. It's the way things are now, Grif. What're you going to do?"

"What're you going to do?" he echoed. "Exactly."

More cars of teenagers pulled into the lot.

"Saturday night," Griffin remarked, "and there's not even a line at the movies. People stay home and wait until it comes out on video. Watch it in the living room where the group sitting behind you isn't going to talk, crunch popcorn too loud, or pull a gun."

His comments reminded Liz of a recent issue of *America Exposed*. "I don't know if you saw it, but we published this statistic last month that in nineteen sixty there were three policemen for every one incident of violent crime. By nineteen ninety, incidents of violent crime outnumbered police two to one."

"Yeah, statisticians. You gotta love 'em. People who never have solutions getting paid for analysis."

"The idea is that we need more police. But where do more police come from?" Liz proposed. "Where's the money? Country's broke. We're hip-deep in red."

"Ink *and* blood." Griffin watched the teenagers, shadows of innocence lost running through the night. Last weekend, one of those kids could have been Carl Nicholson or Randy Arminger. And look where Carl and Randy were this week. Griffin asked, "Where'd Arminger live?"

"Fifteen minutes from here."

"I want to see."

15

The road wound like a gentle brook through woods and open areas. Massive custom-built homes were set back off the street on private five-to-seven-acre parcels of land. Architectural styles ranged from conservative two-story colonial to modern monstrosity.

There was even one ostentatious pink house, lit up like a fairy godmother's summer place, cedar shake roof shingles resembling pieces of gingerbread as snack for a giant.

The singing of frogs carried from man-contoured lowlands planted with marsh grass.

"I guess Arminger felt deprived living here," Griffin said sarcastically. "And there was no alternative to blasting his way out of the ghetto. Look at these things. What do these people do for money?"

"I don't know," Liz said, looking from one side of the street to the other, one house more spectacular than the next. "Dad's probably an orthopedist. Mom's a dermatologist. Bringing home about half a mil between them." Liz drove slowly as a tour guide. Coming to a bend, she said, "Arminger's is up here on the right."

"What'd his father do?"

"Computer programming. He founded a software company that specialized in three-D applications. He was apparently a pretty smart guy—in computers and business—because when the military backed off on interest in using his software to enhance satellite photos with three-D images, Arminger switched over to the medical field. He got bought out by a French pharmaceutical company that thinks his program can revolutionize nonsurgical evaluations of tumors."

"Amazing."

"Yes, it is . . . and so is this: Arminger's house."

The beautiful Tudor featured multiple roof pitches that blended in perfect visual harmony. Every precise exterior detail reflected careful thought and planning, creating an effect that was intricate yet simple. The elevation incorporated wood, stone, brick, stucco as though painting a canvas with building materials. A home of vision built for a man with great vision, only Mr. Arminger had failed to recognize the fault lines within his own family and now it was all for naught.

Griffin said, "Car in the driveway."

A white late-model American four-door was parked where the driveway curved toward a side-entry garage.

"Cops?" Liz guessed, braking to a stop. "Staking out the house?"

"Figures they'd be here somewhere." Griffin looked over his shoulder. "But I doubt the kid's going to walk in the front door with what could be an unmarked car sitting there."

"You don't think it's him, do you? Arminger? Could be that's the rental you've got him driving."

"Wait. Someone around the side of the house. Left side."

"See him," Liz said.

A white-haired man who looked to be in his mid-fifties emerged from shadow into light cast from fixtures in the roof eaves. He sauntered slowly along the flagstone walk beside free-form plantings of ivy and arborvitae, stopping briefly to consider something on the ground. He pushed the toe of his shoe where copper downspouting fed buried drainpipe designed to carry water from the foundation, but his interest in that particular spot was distracted when he looked toward the street.

"And he sees us," Griffin said.

"What do I do?" Liz asked. She eased her foot from the brake and the car drifted forward.

"Wait here." Griffin got out and started down the driveway.

The man looked directly at Griffin, examining him benevolently. He showed no signs of concern or suspicion, as though this was his house and Griffin a friendly salesman with whom he wouldn't mind speaking.

The man wore a blue and white striped seersucker suit. The french cuffs of his white shirt showed a precise two inches from his jacket sleeve. He looked like an advertisement from the old *Life* magazines Griffin's father used to keep in the basement. All that was missing was the martini glass.

He smoked a cigarette that sent a distinct, fragrant aroma into the warm night air, more like expensive pipe or cigar tobacco.

His face was full and somewhat cherubic, and his smooth, unwrinkled skin was flushed. He appeared overweight, but his stomach was still less in breadth than his chest. He carried himself well, his stride quite fluid as he met Griffin beside a lamppost positioned in another garden of ivy.

"Good evening." His voice was clear and calm, and it gave Griffin the immediate impression of a mannered and educated academic. He extended his smooth hand. "Ravlite," he said, just that single name, then added: "FBI." His grip was strong, shaking Griffin's hand.

"FBI?" Griffin questioned.

Ravlite placed his cigarette in his mouth and reached inside his jacket to produce his badge.

Griffin asked, "What's the FBI doing here? This a fed case?"

Ravlite put away his shield. He took a calm, hedonistic puff of what Griffin now saw was an unfiltered, hand-rolled cigarette. Ravlite exhaled slowly and considered the clear night sky. Vision focused skyward, he asked, "And what might you be?"

What, not *who* was Ravlite's question, which Griffin found to be interesting phrasing. Griffin liked him. The man's easy manner was very un-federal agent, most of whom tended to be rigid as stone beyond their own circle.

"Ah, you smiled," Ravlite said, voice brightening as he smiled himself. "I've said something that has meaning to you."

"No. You just don't sound much like FBI."

"You've known other agents?"

"Plenty."

"When you used to be a cop."

The easy style had caught Griffin off guard; Ravlite knew more than he was letting on.

"You were a city cop." He snuffed out the last inch of his cigarette under the toe of his polished Johnston Murphys. Giving away inches in height, he looked clearly into Griffin's eyes. "I know who you are. And I know why you're here. But do you?"

"What the hell does that mean?"

Ravlite smiled. "*America Exposed* is one of my

favorite papers—I love the tabloids. I saw you at BWI this morning with Elizabeth McKinley. Is that her in the car?" Ravlite glanced toward the street.

"You know Liz?"

"Just her writing. She's very good. Insightful."

"I'm helping her investigate this story."

Ravlite thought about that. "Would you like to come inside the house? Look around?"

Ravlite opened the front door into the opulent foyer. A sparkling chandelier was suspended from a twenty-foot ceiling. The double winding staircase ascended gracefully to the second floor walkway. The—

My God! Liz gagged and clutched her mouth and nose. The smell!

The house stank of violent death. Harsh and pungent remnants of blood, tissue, bodily fluids, and excrement. And it was much worse as they followed Ravlite up the left side of the double staircase.

Liz pulled a handkerchief from her bag and held it to her face, fighting the urge to vomit. The air was vindictive, as though wanting to punish every breath taken until the horror of death was rinsed from its walls and expunged from its carpet.

Ravlite said, "The bodies have been taken out, but the killings were messy, especially the girl's. We're hoping someone from the family will call a clean-up company to take care of things, but no luck so far. There don't seem to be any relatives in state." Ravlite glanced back. "Did you know there's a local company that specializes in disinfecting crime scenes? They were written up in *People* magazine, and talked about franchising. Imagine that. Business must be good."

Ravlite's hand slid along the polished railing as he

neared the floating walkway that connected the north and south wings of the house. "By the way, in your articles, Ms. McKinley, please make sure you refer to me as an 'anonymous law enforcement source.' I don't want to get suspended for failing to secure a crime scene. Not that it wasn't already contaminated by the local police before we ever got here."

Griffin asked, "How so?"

"The first officers on the scene—local county—went through here like young bulls escaped from their pen. Even though the bodies were already cool, they thought the shooter was still on the premises and left nothing untouched looking for him. Not that it matters much. Randy wants everyone to know he's done this." At the top of the stairs, Ravlite turned right. "Randy's room is down this way. Claire—that was his sister—her room's opposite Randy's."

"You sound like you know him."

"Getting to," Ravlite replied.

Liz struggled to pull her camera from her saddle bag while keeping the handkerchief to her mouth and nose. Her words partly smothered, she asked, "All right to take pictures?"

"Help yourself."

Ravlite pointed to the rooms they passed. His coat sleeves slid up his arms to reveal starched french cuffs and gold cuff links. "Two guest rooms. Guest bath. Feel free to look around, but not much in there. Well-decorated if the coordinated Waverly look appeals to you as it did to my ex-wife—at eighty dollars a yard."

Griffin said, "Has the FBI taken over this case?"

"Assisting."

"But you're watching the house."

"Actually, no. The county police have charge of that aspect of the case."

"So where are they?"

"I sent him on an errand for me."

"Arminger's not coming back here," Griffin stated.

"No. Of course not."

At the room at the end of the hall, Ravlite reached inside and flipped a dimmer switch on full, turning up six recessed ceiling lights, announcing without malice or sarcasm, "Home of the boy wonder."

The room was large and stark, twenty by twenty, with ten-foot ceilings and cherry hardwood floors. Walls painted midnight blue were stamped with bumper stickers preaching NO RULES in neon colors. Black curtains blocked off three windows on the front wall and one on the side; the fabric was fixed to the wall with masking tape so no light seeped in along the edges, as though Arminger had been developing film.

A king-sized bed was positioned dead center in the room, and a dark red comforter was neatly fitted atop it as though to pass West Point muster.

Griffin immediately felt a strange presence, as though the insanity that dwelled here had been actively brewed and its presence lingered like the smell of death that now draped the house.

Liz stuffed her handkerchief in her shirt pocket and held her breath, snapping pictures as quickly as her camera flash would recycle.

Ravlite directed their visual tour of the room while remaining out of Liz's viewfinder. "He worked here, at this desk."

A large, elaborate sectional of black laminate had cubbyholes and shelves stacked full of computer reference manuals, two printers, switch boxes, stereo speakers, numerous joysticks, a scanner, and other computer peripherals Griffin didn't recognize. Rectangles of dust-free sections on the desk top revealed the former location of now missing objects, what Griffin assumed were computers.

Ravlite said, "You've got three phone cables, formerly connected to as many computers. All portables. They're gone, and we assume Randy's got them with him."

Ravlite moved to the walk-in closet, opening double doors. "For an anarchist, Randy dresses well. Ralph Lauren. Hugo Boss. He likes the fancy name tag. A couple suits in here are worth a month's salary at minimum wage."

"*Is* he an anarchist?" Griffin asked.

"Most definitely."

Liz's flash took longer to recycle in the closet, having to send out brighter light to get a good exposure.

"Randy, as you can tell," Ravlite said, backing out of the closet to the bedroom, "does not like rules. Or so he thinks."

Liz photographed dozens of NO RULES bumper stickers slapped across dark blue walls, some attached to black out curtains as well.

"What Randy's really saying is that he doesn't like other peoples' rules. His own rules . . . methods . . . *pleasures* . . . those he likes a lot."

Griffin considered electronic equipment on a second, smaller desk against the front wall. "Was he pirating videotapes?"

"Possibly. That's a high-speed copier. The other is a videotape editing machine."

There was also a thirty-five-inch stereo television, hifi

VCR, laserdisc player, and Boston Acoustics shelf speakers.

"Little dusty," Griffin noted.

"Yesterday's technology. Randy's gone eight millimeter. See here." Ravlite picked up a connector that still had one umbilical end hooked to the VCR, but the other end was unplugged. "This is probably for a portable camera, which I assume Randy has with him."

Griffin thought back to what one of the basketball kids had told him earlier. That there was a reason Randy had killed his father and sister. That supposition seemed to gain some merit in light of the organization of Randy's crime. It wasn't any quick task to pack up three computers—not the kind of thing done on the verge of homicidal impulse.

Liz ran out a roll of film, said, "I'm going outside to reload," and hurried down the hall.

Griffin walked around the bed, considering the dark blue walls, finding the color a peculiar choice but surprised it wasn't more depressing. It felt, in fact, oddly peaceful. "So why did he kill them?"

"Everything he does, he does for pleasure. Keep that in mind. Everything is for pleasure. Everything." Ravlite stressed that as though it was a lesson. "You're going to have to pervert your mind if you want to catch Randy Arminger."

"You've looked for hiding places, stash boxes?"

"Randy doesn't have anything to hide that isn't digital. Any notes, correspondence, books are all on computer or stashed on the Internet."

"I'm not much into computers myself."

"Randy is."

Griffin followed him out of the big closet. "What about drugs?"

"What about them?"

Griffin wondered if mentioning Arminger's own-made Cram to Ravlite might reduce Liz's chances of a scoop on that subject. "Did Arminger do drugs?"

"Yes. Sure. He's in high school, isn't he?"

"Right."

Ravlite left Randy's room and crossed the hall to Claire's room. He opened the door and turned on the light.

In a same size room as Randy's, the death smell was strong. The bed had been stripped of blood and excrement-smeared sheets, but the smell remained, as did stains that had soaked through sheets into the mattress: dark red blood dried near the French Provincial headboard, and a darker blood and feces stain near the center attracted a pair of buzzing flies.

The walls were papered in a paisley print of seafoam, pink, and white, with expensive lace window treatments and pleated pink shades. The word ANGEL was spray-painted in red across the wall and lowered shades, tentacles of paint running down from individual letters as though they were veins severed by the sharp twist of a knife.

Ravlite stood to the side of the bed. "After Randy killed his father, he came in here, stood here. His sister was asleep and he woke her, or perhaps she was woken by his opening the door. She was awake, at any rate, when he put the gun within a few inches of her head and shot her. And after he did that, he took off her pajama bottoms and raped her with what the medical examiner is terming a large, blunt object, but since nothing was found here, my guess would be he used his fist."

Ravlite said that to shock Griffin and it worked, horror hitting Griffin a moment ahead of rage and with greater combustion than he'd felt in Florida with Drew Millundra. It was more like what he'd felt last summer chasing another killer.

Coming into the room, Liz saw the change overcome Griffin's expression and his posture. She recognized the tension and intensity coursing through him. In a dark but powerful way, this part of him excited her, because she believed Griffin had a rare and unique ability to take a situation into his hands that was grotesque and unjust and avenge it. Many angry and frustrated people recognized how justice had become snarled into twisted knots of insanity and illogic, yet so few could unbend those knots with their will. It was why she wanted him on this story.

Ravlite studied Griffin's reaction, too, had been studying him from the beginning, and was intrigued. Ravlite asked, "Enough here?" His hand was on the light switch.

Still watching Griffin, Liz replied, "Let me get a couple of shots."

Griffin wasn't looking at her, because it was as though he weren't there. Right then. He was out there, wherever Randy Arminger was, wanting him. Wherever that place might be. And yet his voice was perfectly calm, asking Ravlite, "Where was the father killed?"

Ravlite led him to the master bedroom.

The room was massive and masculine, decorated in dark greens and pale brown. Occupying the total floor space above the three-car garage, the master bedroom was sectioned into separate areas for sleep, reading, and work. A computer was fitted into a custom-built rolltop desk. The computer was on.

A second hallway off the back part of the room led into a marble bath with Jacuzzi and sauna.

Griffin stood beside the stains of Robert Arminger's death, which had dried hard into carpet fibers, trying to envision the murders. "He shoots his father first; why doesn't the girl hear the gunshots? Why's she still in bed when Arminger goes in?"

"Randy did a lot of shooting, but no one reported hearing gunshots. Not here, not at the Haskinses' or the Mitzners'. No one reported hearing anything. The same gun was used in all three locations, so I assume he's fitted it with a suppressor. The silencer keeps Claire from hearing him murder his father. Randy missed with one shot . . ." Ravlite gestured to a hole in the wall: ". . . hit with one shot, and once his father was on the ground, stood about here and shot him once through each lens of his eyeglasses. There were shards of glass in his father's eyes."

"Where's Mrs. Arminger?"

"Myrtle Beach, South Carolina. She has a new husband, the club pro—a golfer. At first she was going to fly up for her daughter's body, now she's changed her mind and is having the body sent down there. Her house is being watched—so is she."

"You think Arminger might want to kill her, too?"

"Always possible, but unlikely. Randy and his father had an antagonistic relationship. His father was very cold and demanding, and very sparse with a compliment. Randy's mother was just the opposite. She fawned over him. In her eyes, Randy was perfect. He could do no wrong. She's the one who bought him all those expensive clothes, because despite the wealth that came lately to Randy's father, he was extremely frugal. This house was his only extravagance, which I'm sure he justified as an investment. Meanwhile, Randy's mother shipped him gifts on a regular basis. We've tracked

Federal Express records back five years, since his parents divorced. A steady stream of gifts. And she treated the girl the same way. She referred to them as her little angels."

"Angels again," Griffin commented.

"How's that?" Ravlite's ears perked up.

"Nothing—how's Randy's mother reacting to the news of all this?"

"She says there's some mistake. That it's impossible Randy could have done this. She's sure someone else did the killing and has kidnapped Randy."

"Is that possible?"

"No."

Liz came in from Claire's room, no longer holding the handkerchief quite as tightly to her face. She breathed without it a few times, snapping shots of Robert Arminger's taped outline on the floor. "You're free to wander the rest of the house," Ravlite invited. He slipped off his jacket and sat down in front of the computer, watching typed messages appear on the screen. Each communication usually no more than a paragraph. Then a pause. Then a response. Pause. Counter-response.

On the screen appeared: YOU CANNOT TELL ME THERE IS NO GOD. GOD'S WORKS ARE ALL AROUND US, EVERY MOMENT OF EVERY DAY. THE OCEANS, THE SKIES, THE SUNSET.

Griffin asked, "What is this?"

"Conversation over the Internet. Chat, is the official term."

"Two people talking? They've never heard of a telephone?"

Liz said, "Forgive nineteenth-century man, for he knows not of what he speaks."

"It could be two people," Ravlite explained, "or a

thousand. Consider chat on the Internet like a huge town meeting or a party line, where anyone with a computer, modem, and some software can communicate in as complete or partial anonymity as they want. There are tens of thousands of Chat rooms where people can log on and contribute or just listen. It's an electronic playground for broadcasting your opinions or playing voyeur while others chat. And besides what your Internet server charges you to connect, it's free. You could be in Prague and I could be sitting right here, and we could 'chat' all night at zero cost."

"So this bedroom is a chat room?"

"Not really. The chat room is in cyberspace."

"Not really a room, is what you're saying."

"It doesn't have walls. It's more like an ubiquitous space. It's here, there, everywhere, nowhere. The Internet exists, but you can't really touch it. You can be *there,* but you're also *here*. This chat we're watching could be maintained by a computer in the house across the street, or New York, or Alaska, or Italy. Anywhere there's access to a phone. And the people chatting could be sitting at computers in their home, their office, or on a boat in the middle of the ocean if they can link up to a satellite."

Griffin said, "This is how you spend your time looking for Randy Arminger?"

Suddenly, the screen was filled with rapidly appearing blocks of letters, like a stock market ticker shifted into manic turbodrive: THERE IS NO GOD. IF THERE EVER WAS, GOD IS DEAD. GOD IS DEAD. GOD IS DEAD. GODISDEADGODISDEADGODISDEAD GODISDEADGODISDEADGODISDEAD.GODISDEAD GODISDEADGODISDEADGODISDEADGODISDEAD GODISDEADGODISDEADGODISDEAD.GODISDEAD

GODIDDEADGODISDEADGODISDEADGODISDEAD GODISDEADGODISDEADGODISDEAD.

Ravlite said, "Yes, this is how I spend my time looking for Randy Arminger." He pointed to the screen, and a ray of light caught his gold cuff line. "And there he is."

"Where?"

Liz peered at the screen.

"Right there."

Liz understood. She pulled her tape recorder from her saddlebag and dictated the chat room's Internet addresses to microcassette.

A language foreign to Griffin: *backslash, www, dot com, http.* Griffin pointed at the screen and demanded of Ravlite, "That's Randy Arminger?"

"That's right."

"So where the hell is he?"

"Here . . . there . . . everywhere . . . nowhere."

16

"Angel, Angel, Angel . . . you're such a chickenshit hypocrite." Randy Arminger had three computers in front of him, but only one was set up to go online.

Randy was online now waiting for the Angel to reappear on the Net. "You're awfully scared for an Angel. Where'd you run to? Huh? Where are you, little fella? Here until a little while ago, and now, whaddayawhaddaya say. Where'dya where'dya go?"

Randy and the Angel first met on the Web and kept meeting there, debating religion, faith, morality, and God. The Angel maintained a home page, The Angel Pages, from which he preached his version of the gospel to an electronic congregation.

It was The Angel Pages that quickly filled Randy with animosity and rage.

Randy was a disciple of numbers, facts, mathematics, and science. He lived in an intellectual world where there was only one right answer to a question. One answer! The right answer. The answer Randy *always* knew or could figure out.

The Angel lived in a universe defined only by faith and God. Definition by a lack of proper definition. Bullshit, bullshit, bullshit, in Randy's point of view.

And the Angel was dead wrong about all that. There was no God. If there ever had been, God was dead now. And Randy wasn't just going to argue his theory, he was going to *prove* it. Which, Randy knew, was scaring the pious piss out of the Angel.

He waited a few more minutes, but still no Angel, so Randy got up from the dining room table and stretched. The sliding glass doors were open, and warm, humid air came in along with the sound of the ocean. Randy was at the beach. Ocean City, Maryland.

He was in town for Senior Week. Time of the June Bug. When graduating seniors celebrated the end of high school in rowdy fashion at the mid-Atlantic resort.

Being a junior, Randy was at the beach a year early, but he always had been ahead of the rest of his class, especially Leanna Landy. They could have had a real battle for class valedictorian next year. Two 4.0 students waging the GPA wars. Those loser teachers would have been all tangled in their panties about that. So weren't they going to be disappointed when neither Randy nor Leanna were in school next year. But Randy was getting ahead of himself.

Leanna wasn't on his syllabus quite yet. She was supposed to come to the beach to stay with friends Monday night. And there were other events scheduled before then.

Randy stood at the sliding glass door, five floors above the beach. All the lights were out in the expensive condo except for the computer screen and the red diodes of the CD player/scanner/microphone combination wired to his belt. Randy plugged into White Zombie again, loving how their music crashed in his brain.

Some parents worried this kind of music motivated illicit behavior. Wronga-wronga-wronga. Talk about misconstruing an entire generation. It wasn't the music that motivated, it was the world these fine young adults had been thrown into that caused stress reactions. The music was merely a soundtrack, an echo of the senseless world and the people who ruled it. The Rulers.

Rulers when there were no rules. What an oxymoron. But they didn't see it. Which was why Randy was going to show them. Was showing them already. The newspapers were impressed. The cops, enforcers of the rules, looking very, very poor. Poor Mr. Po-lice. How does a seventeen-year-old murder his father and sister, then go to his girlfriend's house, kill her parents, *then* go to his teacher's house, kill him and his wife, and escape? How? How? How?

How shocking! they said.

Everyone shocked not just that he'd done it but that no one could find him. Where's Randy? Not going to be as easy to find as that little Waldo character. Little doofus in a dunce cap hiding among a thousand other images of mediocrity.

How fitting that Waldo's inventor had become rich and famous. Where else but this country was complete and total mediocrity so well rewarded? Where else was every little pissant kid in some gifted and talented program? Come on, now. Those little spoiled-brat-swooned-over-by-mom-and-dad morons? Gifted and talented? It was a ruse. A political gem figured out by school-board officials. What parent can complain about a school system that thinks their worthless little kid is gifted and talented?

And the parents? These pseudo-psychoanalyzing-every-nook-and-cranny, whining, greedy, selfish, Volvo-BMW-driving, mutual-fund-investing baby-booming idiots! Dolts! An entire generation out there thinking their precious little children were some immaculately conceived prizes, while they were really no more than biological miscreants. Sperm-egg-baby. Wow, wasn't that amazing. A miracle. A Godsend. Put blinders on those baby boomers and they would widen their horizons, for God's sake. Whining, spineless consumers. Tell them anything was good for their precious children and they'd third-mortgage the house to buy it.

Those same stooges were reading the newspaper, gasping how Randy had killed so many people. And how could he disappear? As if that wasn't the easiest thing in the world—for someone like Randy.

The police checked Randy's friends' houses—oh, puh-lease, as though he'd have been dumb enough to go there. That was almost insulting.

The airlines had no record of him, nor did the rental car companies, or those bozos at Amtrak who couldn't keep a Christmas garden train on the track. Go-go Greyhound had no record of Randy. Nobody knew where he was. Because he *wasn't* anymore.

Randy Arminger had disappeared, body vanishing as easily as his electronic impressions out on the Net. And now Randy had reappeared in Ocean City.

A new look. A new identity. And all so easily accomplished.

Holly, for all her faults, was damned fine with scissors. She wanted to be a hair stylist, and had practiced on lots of wacko friends she'd made during that funny-farm stint in Sheppard Pratt. Randy warned her he didn't want any of that goofy shaved-head garbage, he needed a real haircut, like a young stockbroker's. And Holly had come through, trimming his thick long-grown locks Wall Street neat.

With his new haircut and a change into one of the

conservative suits his mother had bought for him, he looked the age shown on his new license: twenty-five, which was pushing it a little, but the fact that he'd been shaving for two years already helped. That little five o'clock shadow, plus rings under the eyes from being up the entire night before: by the time Randy got on the Hertz bus at BWI Friday morning at eight-thirty, travel bag over his shoulder, he'd blended right in with the other young-turk businessmen flying in for the day.

The Hertz bus dropped him right at his rental car—a white Grand Am—and the trunk was up, key in the ignition, rental contract on the seat, ready to go. Randy drove to the guard kiosk at the Hertz exit—the guard looking like he'd been up all night, too—and showed the man his contract and phony South Carolina license—new name, Joseph Cotton—and off he went.

From Hertz to the airport garage where he'd left the Volvo and Holly. Holly was waiting obediently in the trunk, but she was weird like that, liked cramped dark places, liked the idea of being abused and mistreated. It actually turned her on. Which Randy knew how to exploit.

From the airport, they were off, picking up Route 97 to Route 50, across the Chesapeake Bay Bridge onto Maryland's eastern shore. Past the outlet malls. Flat, flat land. Farmland. Soy beans and corn spreading toward marshy fingers that stroked salty waters feeding the Atlantic Ocean. A few old, small towns along the way: Easton, Cambridge, and Salisbury, home of the infamous Frank Perdue and his empire of big-breasted chickens.

Thirty-five minutes beyond Salisbury was Ocean City, a narrow dune developed into crowded resort island. The tourist season just beginning to warm up with the weather. Condos, hotels, cottages, and beach houses packed hip to hip like sunbathers on the sand. Ocean City was truly a small city, drawing crowds from D.C., Baltimore, Philadelphia, New York, and beyond. All at outrageous prices for what you got, but money was of little consequence to Randy, for while he had very little cash, he had the resources of a millionaire.

These days, money was a lot like how some Dark Ages people insisted on thinking about God. People still believed in paper money—currency—even though it had very little in the way of an existence. The twenty-dollar bill passed for an OC-logo sweatshirt on the boardwalk or lobster dinner at Phillips's was no more than a vague promise that somewhere behind that folding green stood some government authority claiming cash was a valid way to settle a debt.

But most financial transactions never needed currency. Promises "coined" in dollars passed along electronic networks between banks, businesses, governments. Figures moved from computer system to computer system based on the theory that bolstering someone's electronic statement of account were real dollars to pay.

Well, Randy had lots of electronic dollars. Lots and lots and lots.

Randy was in Ocean City renting a $2,000-a-week three-bedroom condo right smack dab on the beach, driving a rental car, even getting carry-out from the Popeye's drive-thru, and hadn't needed a single greenback. Nary uno dollero. He just had a credit card issued to a fictitious person Randy had invented years ago: Joseph Cotton, who had a $10,000 credit limit with five separate financial institutions.

And that was just Mr. Cotton. Randy had dozens of

other identities complete with driver's licenses, credit cards, and passports. All created with information and materials appropriated with a computer, a phone line, and some really cool know-how. Meeting folks on the Net or the street willing to trade stolen driver's license blanks or guns fitted with silencers for some Cram was as risky as it ever got. That was Randy's total exposure.

So here he was, standing by the opened sliding glass door, thinking about the Angel—wanting a meeting with the Angel so he could show him once and for all there was no God. No God and no rules. Randy was going to spread the word through that electronic preacher phony, on his way to showing the world. Civilization was held together by a moral glue that had no basis in science, and once that glue melted away, it would all crumble. It would *all* come undone.

Randy took a few deep breaths of that wonderful ocean air, then locked the door and went back to the spare bedroom where the lights were on bright, including an extra halogen lamp he'd brought in from the living room and had turned up full.

Holly heard him open the door and jerked her head toward the sound. She whimpered. Holly's round, fleshy body was stripped naked, tied to the bed, blindfolded and gagged, waiting for her big moment.

17

Back at the Marriott Courtyard, Griffin leaned over Liz at the desk, watching her work the laptop computer.

Liz had already pulled her e-mail off the *America Exposed* network—scanning notes from her editors about the story changes she'd uploaded hours ago—and now she was accessing the Internet through *America Exposed*'s direct Weblink.

On the Web, Liz returned to the chat room where Ravlite had located Randy Arminger, Arminger having failed to offer additional conversation after posting his five-minute-long message: GOD IS DEAD.

Griffin asked, "Is he back?"

"Hard to say," Liz said, reading conversation.

The chat room was now home to a tamer discussion of religion.

"MStanton at symbol aol period com?" Griffin pronounced one participant's chat room moniker.

"You say it: M Stanton at a-o-l dot com. Computer talk."

"Which means absolutely nothing to me."

"The first part, to the left of the "at" symbol—M Stanton—that's the person's alias, their 'handle' it was called in CB radio days. It's the name the person goes by on the Net. In this case, someone probably with the last name of Stanton and the first initial M. The at-symbol shows where they can be reached on the net. In this case, M Stanton connects through a server called A-O-L, short for America On Line. The 'period,' what's referred to as 'dot,' separates further definition of the type of server you're accessing. Most addresses end in c-o-m, n-e-t, e-d-u."

"So where does the M-Stanton-at-aol-dot-com live?"

"Who knows? America On Line has offices in northern Virginia, but M Stanton could be dialing into AOL from anywhere there's a phone, and from any kind of phone that can handle a data signal."

"He—or she—could be in a car on a cell phone?"

"Right."

"Incredible—and frightening."

"That's just the tip of the proverbial iceberg," Liz said, preparing to post a note. "You're on the Net, you're here, there, everywhere . . ."

"Nowhere," Griffin chimed in, quoting Ravlite. He stood upright. "I knew there was a reason I didn't like these damned things. Technology—another means to put more distance between people. No one will have to leave the house anymore. They'll work from home, shop from home. It won't matter how polluted the air gets or that the rivers have turned to factory-regurgitated slime. No one will notice until one day their tap water runs brown and they'll run to their computer for an answer and the thing'll plaster a big fat message on the screen. It'll say: Gotcha, sucker."

"The paranoia of the computer illiterate." Liz smiled.

They'd had this discussion before.

"In the depression there was talk of a chicken in every pot, now Bill Gates wants a computer in everyone's house. Goddamned computers aren't the answer, Liz. They're a placebo."

"Well, it might not be our answer. But it's got a definite shot at being a tool. Come here and watch this."

He leaned over her shoulder again. "Okay. Come on, wow me. Make Randy Arminger appear on the screen."

"I just might." Liz had typed a brief message on the screen:

RANDY ARMINGER: MY NAME IS ELIZABETH MCKINLEY AND I'M A REPORTER FOR AMERICA EXPOSED, YOU KNOW, THAT TABLOID IN THE GROCERY STORES YOU PRETEND NOT TO READ WHILE YOU'RE WAITING AT THE CHECKOUT LINE. I'M REPORTING THE MURDERS. I'M CALLING YOU THE STRAIGHT-A KILLER. DOES THAT SOUND OKAY TO YOU? I HOPE SO. I'D REALLY, REALLY LOVE TO HAVE YOUR STORY FROM YOU. LIZMCK@AMEXED.NET.

Griffin read the message post, said, "And?"

Liz hit a command key. Something inside the computer made a quiet clicking sound. Liz said, "It's out there."

"Out where?"

Liz's fingertip touched the screen causing a pop of static electricity. "There. Plus," Liz exited and disconnected, "by tomorrow morning, our *America Exposed* home page will have an entire section on the Straight-A Killer, compete with e-mail address and eight-hundred number for people to call in tips on Randy sightings. There's also going to be a special Randy-only e-mail address that lets Randy and Randy only leave a message."

"And how does the home page know it's Randy?"

"There are three passwords he's got to answer. His latest verbal and math SAT scores, the name of his teacher he sent lingerie to for Valentine's Day, and the name of his favorite blotter-paper drug. No one besides Randy should know the answer to all three questions."

"You think he'll respond?"

"He's not trying to hide what he's doing, Griff. He's right out there. And he's got a message. God is dead, God is dead, God is dead, over and over again. I'm offering him a forum with a few million readers, all of whom are going to read this disturbed kid's message and let me tell them he's the devil incarnate!" Liz raised her voice like a tailgate preacher's. "He's a hungry fish, and this is good bait. I'm going to sell *so many* papers it'll make us sick."

"But are we going to *find* him this way?" Griffin asked. "Really find him? Not out there, but here?" Griffin gestured with his hands as though grabbing the air and wanting something for his grip to close around.

"I hope so."

Liz took a shower, wanting to rinse the smell of Arminger's house out of her hair.

She turned the water on hard and hot and let it rain around her. She felt herself changing. Aging. Emotionally more than physically. Was it Griffin doing that to her?

The first time she'd met him, phase one of the Bright Eyes case, Griffin had been a hard-edged cop. Liz was a free-spirited and, by her own definition, wild-fucking (and loving it) reporter. Living all around the country. Postcard places. Vegas. Phoenix. Miami.

No attachments. Lots of guys. She'd had a ball, and always put aside those empty feelings that sometimes came to her when she thought about what she might be missing by not having a family and being married.

Asking herself why marry, because the doctors told her she'd never have a family, at least not one of her own. She could adopt . . .

God . . . that didn't seem like that long ago, but it was getting to be, wasn't it? Time had hurtled by like a frantic wind, and Liz had been all too happy to ride it out. Drinking. Smoking. Nights spent in such blissful, passionate embraces she could have lit up an entire city.

She was still living that way when she came across Griffin again last summer, ten months ago. OL' BRIGHT EYES IS BACK, that had been Liz's headline. Another grabber to sell papers. And the papers had sold.

Griffin had been in the center of the story, only it was different between them. An initial attraction years ago had survived, and Liz was really pulled to him. She'd tried to seduce him, but Griffin had been married and was determinedly faithful despite his wife's infidelity. That bitch Carla. Liz hated her, and with good reason.

Griffin had good reason to hate his estranged wife, too, but Liz knew he didn't. He couldn't bring himself to, even as badly hurt as she'd left him, as badly hurt as he was still.

Griffin wasn't over her, the marriage, or, especially, the little girl.

Liz squeezed another glob of hotel shampoo into her palm and washed her hair again, so preoccupied she wasn't sure if she'd done this two or three times already. But the water felt so good, and Griffin was going to feel even better.

When they were reunited after being apart a few weeks, she always had the urge to take him right to bed, and it seemed as if he was on that edge, too. Only neither one of them was quite ready to admit how much they meant to one another, so there were always a few hours of wonderful tension, as though they were just friends, not lovers. And then the day wore on and the inhibitions came down. And then it was nighttime.

18

Randy had been going at it all night. Brain-wired on Cram, working at the computers on the dining room table. He hardly moved a muscle beyond fingers striking the keyboard and clicking the mouse. He was so tuned-in it was as if he were inside the computers—part of the flash bursts of electricity that created information, stored it, changed it, saved it. He was creating a masterpiece.

Randy was so focused he didn't even realize the sun was rising over the ocean, a beautiful pink light spreading across the horizon as though stroked by a soft brush of watercolor. The ocean was coming to life from murky darkness to pale orange reflections of dawn.

Randy didn't feel the warmth of the sun over his shoulder, and he barely noticed the glare it cast across his computer screens. He was too busy at work. The CD-ROM drive spun White Zombie, hard-cracking music he coordinated with images on the computer screens. Editing. Creating. Such a work of beauty.

Randy was thrilled with the final result. He played it over and over while the music pumped into his head through the earphones. His concentration was so clear he could follow calls for the Ocean City police picked up by the scanner that also fed his earphones. His brain was multi-tasking, not restricted to one lane of thought at a time. Fixed on this project but keeping an ear out for the law—not that he expected it to be looking for him beyond the routine description all cop houses would get. Still, he listened in just in case.

Mostly he was focused on this project. It was huge. Mega-huge.

The most powerful of his three portable computers, what Randy considered his on-the-road mainframe, displayed a sudden image of a cuckoo clock: an animated bird sounding a cartoon alarm.

Wow-wow-wow. Where did the night go? Look at the time. Hey. Daylight. Cool. Time flew on Cram.

Randy was super-awake and ready to ride again. Because hey-hey-hey, check the clock. Sunday morning! Almost time for church! Don't want to keep the preacher waiting.

Griffin came back from a morning run and found Liz at her computer.

She was naked.

"Nice sight," he said, kissing her.

"Sweaty," she said, tasting him on her lips.

Griffin took off his T-shirt and wiped his face, checked out what Liz had up on the screen. "Arminger get your message?"

"Hard to say, but no reply so far."

"Any phone calls for me?"

"You expecting someone?"

"That kid I talked to yesterday at the basketball court, Paul Demmis. I had a little hope riding on him. He knows something. I can read it in him. He hadn't heard about Randy's spree until yesterday, and it seemed to hit him pretty hard."

"It's a shocking revelation. One of your friends, maybe one of your heroes, turns homicidal maniac."

"Maybe I should try to call Demmis, get to him alone."

"Alone?" Liz shot him a look of concern.

"Just to talk," Griffin assured. Notwithstanding yesterday's forceful coercion of names from the joyrider, Griffin's police techniques had never been like his father's—then again, Griffin wasn't acting as a law enforcement officer yesterday; he'd just been a concerned citizen.

"Well," Liz pointed to the phone, "at least we're not falling behind in the race. Just talked to my mole at state police and they've got nothing new."

Griffin's gaze strayed, drawn to Liz's body. He brushed aside hair and kissed her neck, his blood pumping from the run, his cock starting to get hard. "It felt good last night." His hands went onto her breasts.

"Yeah . . . my calves are killing me," Liz sighed. "Always a good sign." She shut off the computer and stood, putting her arms around Griffin and not caring that he was sweaty. She stroked his chest and arms. He was so powerful from all the weight training, his stomach hard and rippled. Her hand slipped inside his running shorts, fondling him. "Seemed like you slept okay for a little while last night. Think the first dream I woke you out of was around five."

"Same damned thing."

"Children crying?"

"And nobody to take care of them. Freaky."

Liz took her hand off his erection, leaving him sticking hard in the flimsy shorts. Standing back, she admired, "Like that look."

"Like yours too."

Liz couldn't believe she blushed a little bit, actually feeling a touch self-conscious at being naked in front of him in the daylight. All the guys she'd pranced around with bare-assed over the years—the one-night and more serious lovers—and here she was in her mid-thirties, blushing. "Take your shower and let's have breakfast."

The Angel held a nondenominational religious service on his Internet home page—The Angel Pages—every Sunday morning at 8:30 A.M. EST, and repeated the fifteen-to-twenty-minute electronic liturgy every hour on the hour until 12:30 P.M. EST.

The remainder of Sunday, The Angel Pages didn't exhibit the same fare as the other days of the week—no comments on news events, surveys of pending criminal trials, or examples of how evil deeds had been punished. Sunday was a day for rest, contemplation, family, and prayer.

From approximately 12:50 P.M. EST Sunday until 9:00 A.M. EST Monday morning, The Angel Pages displayed a single message, a single thought, pale red letters on white background. The Angel's planned message for this Sunday was:

PRAY THAT THOSE WHO DO NOT SEE THE ERROR OF THEIR WAYS WILL DISCOVER GOD BEFORE CAUSING HARM TO OTHERS, AND PRAY THAT THOSE WHOSE ERRANT WAYS HAVE CAUSED HARM MEET SWIFT AND MEANINGFUL CHANCE FOR REDEMPTION.

That message was more muted than that which the Angel was set to deliver in his morning service.

Last night, his online communications with Randy Arminger had been provoking, maddening. For it was clear Randy Arminger was no longer intent on religious debate about the existence of God. Randy Arminger had turned venomous, murderous. His debate had escaped the rational confines of thought and turned into an insane physical display, a testing of Randy's theory that evil deeds were not punished.

That it you were smart enough, rich enough, had a slick enough lawyer or quick enough brain, you would slip from the grasp of retribution. And there was no payment for sin.

Randy's message would be believed by some . . . perhaps many. All the work the Angel had done over the years, slowly returning people to faith like putting drops of water in a bucket, and Randy Arminger was kicking the bucket's sides.

Randy did not see value in faith—the inner security that God has created and maintains an orderly universe, and that reward or punishment would be meted out as deserved. Randy Arminger was selling an easy evil, the death of God, because there were so few signs around with which to magnetize faith.

The brilliance of the constellations that had bedazzled ancient man now stood explained by science. The magic of flight had been reduced to a formula. So much that had seemed explained by nothing short of divine intervention was now simple mathematics. Less and less was unexplained, and that so much remained a mystery still did not intensify faith, because a pattern had been established. Today's miracle was taken for granted tomorrow. Disease was no longer a plague from God but virulent toxicology. The examples were unending of man undoing what had once been God's domain.

So the simple proof of God, the least common denominator that could be found, was to show how the most basic tenet of good and evil was still strongly enforced.

That good was rewarded and evil punished. And not in the hereafter but in the here and now.

That was the Angel's theory, and he was making people believe again. His examples of punishment gave comfort and closure to those who had suffered an evil that was yet to be condemned. He showed that prayers *were* still answered, especially when prayers were raised in harmony, hundreds, thousands of people praying for a common goal.

There were prayers on The Angel Pages. And there was church on the Internet: a place so many attributed to science, overlooking the presence of God.

People put faith in the tasks performed by a computer, unseen tasks taking place in a realm of electronic charges. Yes, I have typed a prayer on my computer. There it is on the screen. I can see it. And now I save it, and the image is no longer on the screen. So where is it? It's kept somewhere else. A place called memory, altered into bits of information stored in binary code. Not even looking like letters anymore, not kept in a place where the eye can see them, but contained on bits of silicon the size of an oregano flake shaken from a jar. And while those pieces of silicon could be examined in microscopic detail, the letters of my prayer would not be visible. They are to re-emerge only through the electronic mapways of a computer. And just as God is unseen, so, too, is the science—the faith—that what is stored in memory on silicon will be brought back to view for the human eye. The computer, perhaps the most un-Godlike creation in the world, was actually very much like God.

And yet people like Randy Arminger placed much faith in silicon and little faith in God.

The Angel, tired though he was, had to change that. He had to show how wrong Randy Arminger was.

That was the topic of Sunday's sermon, but when the Angel sat in front of his computer, preparing to begin his service, to deliver his message, there was a message waiting for him. It appeared suddenly, inexplicably. It said:

TODAY'S GUEST BIBLE-BELTER: RANDY ARMINGER.

How had that gotten there? The Angel turned around, expecting to see that Arminger had somehow found his home and broken in, was here waiting for him.

The image on the screen changed.

LET'S SEE IF WE CAN PISS OFF GOD TODAY, SHALL WE?

The Angel expected to see his keyboard being pressed by a ghost like an old-time player piano, but the keyboard was still. More letters appeared on the screen. Letters being placed on The Angel Pages and broadcast over the Internet worldwide.

LET'S DO SOMETHING REALLY, REALLY NASTY. REALLY EVIL. OHBOYOHBOYOHBOY!

The Angel began typing commands, trying to clear Randy's invasion from the screen, but his system had been disabled. Infected. Somehow . . . the text file! Randy had sent a file to The Angel Pages by modem, and the Angel had scanned it for a computer virus, but Randy had outsmarted the virus protection. He had infected the Angel's computer. Randy was *inside* the computer now.

The Angel's heart palpitated with fear. He began to sweat. Just as in his nightmares, devils had broken into heaven.

In his dreams, there was blood on the walls. Blood everywhere. Dripping, bright red, oozing. The sickening smell. And the light in the room was fading. No longer bright light but wearing dim. God's energy fading.

The Angel Pages went black and, for a moment, the Angel's fear was met by a glimmer of hope, then the screen filled with a new image. My God! No!

Liz said, "Hey, look, you made the paper." Seated across from Griffin in a booth at Bob Evans, she folded the local section and turned it around for him to see, pointing. " 'Bystander Chases, Catches Juvenile Car Thief.' "

A two-column-wide photo of Griffin bringing the boy across the field was laid out beside pictures of the wreck at the intersection.

"Not a bad picture," Liz commented. "Think I'll save it."

"Please . . ." Griffin scanned the article. "Looks like everyone's okay. Treated and released. Minor injuries. The man who was shot's still in Shock Trauma, but in good condition. Jeep was found abandoned five miles away. Remaining suspects at large, but police assure they have been identified and will be caught."

"Sounds like the one you grabbed ratted out his buddies. There's a small miracle. Don't they usually claim they don't know anybody else's name? It's always some guy they just met."

"Uh-huh." Griffin considered the overcooked waffle on his plate, wishing it tasted better than it did: like baked flour-and-water glue with thick, flavorless syrup. He missed his protein-carbo blender breakfast. This waffle looked like a lot of dead calories that would leave him feeling groggy in about two hours.

Liz, on the other hand, spent so much time on the road, she'd acquired a taste for minimal meals. This morning she spread cream cheese on her toasted bagel, ready to put grape jelly on top of that.

The restaurant was in a mini-restaurant park less than five minutes from their hotel. The after-church crowd created a bit of a wait at the entrance, dressed in lightweight summer suits and dresses. Kids looked starched into expensive outfits with clip-on ties and polished shoes, and wanting out of them.

Griffin had forgotten what a racially balanced community this was, the customers almost equally black and white. Dressing the same, driving the same better-than-average cars, even speaking about the same—a dialect that, to Griffin, didn't sound to carry any accent at all, though people born and raised above the Pennsylvania line would have considered it a southern inflection.

Griffin watched the kids in line, tugging their parents' arms, their expressions beseeching, Let's go, let's go, wanting either to get some food or go home. Kids already seated drew pictures with restaurant crayons or played a peg-jumping game on a triangular block of wood. A little blond-headed girl went stomping determinedly toward the bathrooms, muttering, "Wheh awe my stupid bwothahs?"

Liz chewed her bagel and watched Griffin. He wasn't saying anything, just watching the kids. Liz said, "Why don't you take the car downtown and see her? Don't even call. That way Carla . . ." Liz almost called her "the bitch." ". . . won't say anything to make you change your mind. Just show up on her doorstep, tell her you want to see Cassie—you don't want to rehash up the past—and spend some time with her."

Griffin shook his head.

"Why the hell not?"

"I've got no right."

"Oh, come on, Jimmy." Liz leaned forward to keep her voice from carrying to little ears at nearby tables. "That's bullshit. You're the only father that little girl's ever—"

"Liz—"

"No. Uh-uh. Not now. Not here. That I've-got-no-right stuff doesn't play all that well when you're a thousand miles away. Here, it's empty."

"I need to let it go . . . let *her* go."

"The last time you saw her, Carla came to the house with a cop and took her. Carla and that bastard Mickey Blane lied and got some judge to sign an order that you were a danger to Carla and Cassie, and they took her. And you never fought back."

"Fought back with *what*, Liz? I'm not the girl's real father. Why won't you let me try to forget about it . . . put it behind me?"

"Because you'll never be able to do that." She reached into her saddle bag, digging past her flip phone, microcassette recorder, and notepads. She retrieved the rental car keys and tossed them onto the table, keys sliding over Formica, past a plate of lousy waffles.

Griffin caught them before they landed in his lap.

"Go. Right now. Take the car and go downtown."

"I was going to try and talk to the Demmis kid this morning."

"So you'll talk to him this afternoon."

Griffin looked at the keys cupped in his palms, then met Liz's eyes. "How're you going to get back to the motel?"

"I'll walk," she replied briskly, wanting him to think she was angry with him and was going to be angrier if he didn't do this. "I'll get a cab, Jimmy. I'll manage. Get out of here. Go!" People were starting to look. Liz nudged him under the table. "I'll make a scene if you don't. Go. Get!"

He could only think of reasons *not* to do this, because that's what always came to mind. But he nodded, said, "Okay." He squeezed his hand around the keys and slid out of the booth.

Yesterday he'd been shot at, almost run down by a group of wild boys stealing a car, and hadn't felt much fear. Now he was scared to death: going to see his estranged wife and the fourteen-month-old girl he'd spent three blissful months believing was his daughter.

Across the Angel's computer screen and onto the Internet, onto the Angel Pages came Randy Arminger's image.

A flash of Randy standing in front of a mirror, baseball cap on, all sorts of devices hooked to his belt, headphones wired into his ears. Randy saying: "No rules."

CUT TO BLACK.

CUT TO: Randy. Flash image of him. Same as before. "No rules." An image that repeated like a record needle stuck in a groove, image and soundtrack quick blipping: "No rules—No rules—No rules."

Music blared. Horrendous, violent sounds. Screaming guitars. Wailing voices. Exploding drums.

RANDY'S POV: Randy going down the hall. A closed door at the end.

QUICK CUT: The door opens. Randy's father standing there. Surprised.

Randy's arm lifts into the frame. Holding a gun. A blast of light.

His father is stunned, but not hit. Randy misaimed.

But the next shot hits his father. Knocks him down.

QUICK CUT: Robert Arminger bleeding on the floor.

CLOSE-UP: The frames of Robert Arminger's glasses as they rest on his face.

SUPER SLO-MO: A bullet pierces the lens, cracks it, little shards flying, the bullet exploding into Robert Arminger's eyeball.

The Angel screamed in horror.

The sick, insane boy had videotaped the murder, had edited it into an MTV-style video, and was broadcasting it. He was proud of it!

"My God!" the Angel shrieked, his face red with rage. "God, give me strength. Give me strength!" Screaming as he grabbed the electric cord and pulled it from the wall.

The computer went dead, its light fading. The modem disconnected the phone line. The Angel Pages went blank on the Internet, invaded, assaulted, attacked by Randy Arminger like the devils who'd sneaked into heaven to kill angels and leave their blood on the walls.

The Angel screamed with outrage.

As soon as he stepped off the elevator, Griffin heard crying. It came from the end of the hall—the fifteenth floor of the high-rise where his estranged wife moved after she'd left him. A newly renovated building with plushly carpeted halls and high ceilings.

The sound of crying carried down the hall. Griffin walked faster toward it, breaking into a run. Cassie crying. The little girl whose room he used to sleep in, caring for her through the night after he and Carla stopped sleeping together.

Cassie was not a crier. Hadn't been. He'd never heard her cry like this, not even that horrible night of high fever when he was afraid she might die. So small and frail and sick.

Griffin knocked on the front door and called over the baby's cries. "Carla. Carla!" Rapping harder. "Carla! It's Jimmy. What's wrong with Cassie?" Knocking again. "Carla!"

Alerted by the noise, a neighbor opened his door, a slender man in his mid-forties, wearing jeans with an ironed pleat and a pink button-down shirt. Concerned and annoyed. "She's been crying off and on all night. Since I got home at three."

"Three?" Griffin tried the doorknob, but it was locked. He rapped harder. Hearing only Cassie's wailing, no sounds of Carla inside.

"It sounds so pathetic," the man said.

"Is there a building manager?" Griffin demanded urgently. "A super? Someone with a key."

"No. These are condos. There's a maintenance group that does cleaning, but only—"

"Neighbors? Was she friends with anyone who might have a key?"

"I don't think so. She kept pretty much to—"

Griffin kicked at the door with his foot.

"What are you doing?"

"Breaking the goddamned door down!" He kicked it harder. "Breaking . . ." The sole of his foot drove the deadbolt against wood molding. ". . . the goddamned . . ." Feeling it start to give ". . . door . . ." Almost through it. Hard, strong kick, turning his body sideways, making rigid contact with his heel. Wood splintering, pieces flying. ". . . down—" A hunk of worthless security chain snapped back against the wall.

Griffin rushed inside. "Carla!"

All the curtains were closed. No lights on. It was warm inside and the air smelled stale.

"Carla!"

Newspapers and magazines were scattered about the living room floor, not as if the place had been ransacked, just left in disarray.

The neighbor followed Griffin inside. A kitchen trash can had attracted roaches and they scurried for cover when the neighbor turned on a light. The kitchen sink was clogged with gray, slimy water. "This is awful!"

Griffin yelled, "Carla, where the hell are you!" Going down the dark hall, hearing Cassie crying.

The first room. Door open. Curtains closed. Griffin going in. A nightlight was plugged into the wall. Cassie stood in her crib. Standing! Look at how big she'd gotten. Howling. Tears streaming down her face.

As Griffin reached for her, emotion swelled through him, the love he'd felt for this little girl from the moment she was born. It was there as strongly as when he'd last seen her. Nothing had changed about that. Even all her mother's lies and deceitful behavior couldn't diminish the love that soared through him. Such intensity as he picked her up and her small arms clutched around him, as though she hadn't forgotten who he was. Could she remember? Had she missed him?

Her diaper was soaked. Her face felt warm. Griffin held her close against him, getting his shirt wet from her. So heavy. So big. Carrying her from the room, "It's okay, honey. It's okay." Her screams sounded so pained.

Griffin went toward the second bedroom. "Carla! Carla! *Carla*!"

His ex-wife was on the bed.

"Help me!" Griffin yelled back to the living room. "Come here! Come here!"

The neighbor ran down the hall. He saw Carla. "Oh, dear Lord!"

"Hold her!" Griffin handing him Cassie. "You know how to hold a baby?"

"Yes."

"Hold her."

"Oh, she's wet—oh, well, hell, now so am I."

"Call nine-one-one. We need an ambulance!"

"Where's a phone?"

"Fucking find one." Griffin felt his ex-wife's neck for a pulse. Her skin was cool.

Carla was sprawled across the king-size bed, wearing a sheer nightgown, the kind of thing she used to order from Victoria's Secret when they were married but wore only for her boyfriend, not Griffin. An opened bottle of pills and warm glass of water was on her bed stand.

"Is she alive?"

"Call nine-nine-one!" Griffin yelled, and started CPR.

19

Griffin paced the hospital's foyer. He felt trapped inside himself, what was happening. His heart beat hard and fast, not seeming to pause at all between beats.

And then the doctor came out. An emergency room physician. A dark-skinned Indian woman with thick black hair. "Mr. Griffin?"

The Angel knew what had to be done. It was time to face the unseen devil. First to find that devil. Root him out. Punish him.

Randy Arminger was a brilliant, evil, insane boy. But he was also foolish to believe he could flout faith in his vile and repulsive way.

The Angel did not spread word of punishment meted out justly to those who had otherwise escaped condemnation by prayer alone. Prayer did not create magic or acts of fate. Prayer resonated to give strength to those capable of performing deeds others were too weak or scared or corrupt to effect. Prayer gave strength to the Angel so the Angel could act. Prayer was the spiritual and physical fuel that had allowed the Angel to right so many wrongs. Prayer provided guidance like a beacon of white light cutting through darkness, assisting the Angel in planning, execution, and escape. So that the

Angel could wage his wars without injury, without hindrance.

And so, calmed by prayer after the morning's invasion by the devil, a revitalized Angel sat before his computer and switched it on. Knowing the devil would be there, lingering inside. Dormant until the fire of electricity sparked him back to life.

The computer ran through its initializing sequence, but the usual operating system screen did not appear. The devil appeared. His words. Randy Arminger's message, created, maintained, and functioning via a Randy Arminger programmed "bot": a robotic string of commands capable of learning, teaching, destroying.

Randy had sent a bot into the Angel's computer over the Internet, traveling unseen through the digital ether and burying itself in the Angel's system.

The message on the screen said: HEY, ANGEL. WHERE YA BEEN?

A flashing cursor prompted the Angel for an answer.

The Angel held his hands above the keyboard, hesitating, as though the devil's own viselike grip were about to seize his wrists.

The screen displayed a new message: HELLOOOOOO? ANY ANGEL HOME? AS THEY SAY IN BALTIMORE—MAKE THAT BAWLMER—WHERE YOU'Z BEEN AT, HON?

The Angel checked to make sure the phone line remained disconnected from his modem. To make sure Randy had not been able to dial into him right now. The phone *was* disconnected. Randy wasn't outside phoning in. Randy was inside the Angel's computer.

The Angel's fingers lightly touched the keys, not typing but touching. Waiting. But there was no diabolic response from the computer. The Angel exhaled. He typed: I'VE BEEN PRAYING.

The screen immediately displayed: OH, YEAH-YEAH, RIGHT. I SHOULD HAVE FIGURED. WELL, A LOT OF GOOD THAT DOES. PRAYING. JUST WEARS OUT THE KNEES OF YOUR PANTS. BUT WE'VE TALKED ABOUT ALL THIS BEFORE—

The Angel began to type, but the screen didn't display his words. The computer began to beep, the screen displayed:

HEY, YOU WANT TO WAIT UNTIL I'M FINISHED. DON'T INTERRUPT!

The Angel had been reduced to the role of Randy's subordinate. If he wanted to communicate with Randy, it was going to be by Randy's rules.

The computer, processing commands imbedded in Randy's bot, displayed:

NOW, LIKE I WAS SAYING BEFORE I WAS SO RUUUUDELY INTERRUPTED. BUT WE'VE TALKED ABOUT ALL THIS BEFORE ON LINE . . .

Randy's program had instructed the computer to go back to the beginning of the last sentence it was displaying if any key input interruption came from the host computer, and to reprint that last line, as if restating a sentence, then to add:

. . . AND WHERE HAS IT GOTTEN US, HUH? I MEAN IT'S JUST SO MUCH DEBATE. THEORY. LET'S GET RIGHT DOWN TO IT, SHALL WE? LET'S DEAL IN MATTERS OF PROOF. I'M COMMITTING ALL KINDS OF SIN, AM I NOT? AND IT'S EARLY YET, ONLY, WELL, LET'S CHECK THE CLOCK.

A digital timer appeared in the upper right-hand corner of the screen, tracking time to thousandths of a second.

CLOCK SAYS IT'S BEEN SIXTY-ONE HOURS, SEVEN MINUTES—MAKE THAT EIGHT MINUTES NOW—SINCE

Dad got a bullet in each eye. And I haven't felt a single feather of punishment. I know, I know, like I said, it's early yet, but no one seems to know where I am. And as brilliant as those doughnut-eating cops looked on the news the other night. Well, who knows, maybe they'll get lucky . . . but I doubt it. The point of all this is that I'm going to give you the rare opportunity to stop evil before it happens. Doesn't that sound like one of those bad cartoon commercials they'd show during the after-school hour on tv? Just Say No to Evil. And wear a button to school with a picture of two people doing it doggy-sytle in the center of a circle with a line drawn through it. A Stop Sodomy campaign. Look, there's a sermon for you. No charge. But, again, I digress. I was talking about letting you stop evil and bad deeds. Would murder qualify? I'm never sure. It seems like such fun, it can't possibly be bad—a sin. Oh, but that's right, all the fun stuff IS bad. That boring stuff like prayer's how we're supposed to pass the time. Yawwwwwnnnnnnnn. Yah, whew, well, I almost fell asleep.

The Angel felt heat churning inside him, boiling into rage.

Let me put it to you like this, Angel-o. Angelo, I like that. New, from chef boy-ar-dee. Angelos, with or without meat sauce! How about Alphabet Angelos. Kids, can you spell LET'S FUCK! Here, let momma show you. No, let's not. Let's talk about you and me. Let's talk about putting all this religious bull-shit to the test. Here's the deal. I'm going to kill someone real

SOON. AND I'M GOING TO GIVE YOU THE CHANCE TO STOP ME. YOU LIKE THAT? ANSWER YES OR NO. Y IS FOR YES. N IS FOR NO.

The Angel quickly, angrily struck the "Y" key.

GOOD. NOW PLUG IN YOUR GODDAMNED MODEM, YOU GODDAMNED CHICKENSHIT WORTHLESS PIOUS SON OF A BITCH, AND LET'S GET TO IT. I'LL BE IN TOUCH IN A FEW HOURS. ONLINE. BY THE WAY, IF YOU DON'T PLUG IN YOUR MODEM, ALL THE INFORMATION STORED IN YOUR COMPUTER IS GOING TO BE EATEN ALIVE. YOU'LL NEVER SEE IT AGAIN. AND THAT LAST BACKUP YOU MADE THREE NIGHTS AGO? IT WON'T SAVE YOU. I LEFT A LITTLE PRESENT IN THERE FOR YOU, TOO. IN FACT, YOU'LL FIND THE BACKUP DISKS ARE COMPLETELY EMPTY. SEE? YOU'RE FUCKING WITH THE WRONG HOMBRE, BUDDY! AND SO YOU PAY!

The screen flickered, Randy's programmed images disappearing. The Angel's operating system came online as though all was normal. And yet the devil was there in the silicon, lurking, waiting.

The Angel's instinct was to unplug the computer and abandon its infected programs. He could access his home page by another computer, but Randy would not be ignored. Randy would be a constant thumping fist on his door. Black winds of evil swirling soot in the air.

It was only fear, a lack of resilience and weakening of faith, that inspired the Angel's instinct, and that instinct had to be defeated, as he had defeated the many other internal compulsions that once threatened to destroy his life.

The computer would remain turned on. The Angel reconnected the modem. He would wait for the boy to make new contact. And until then, he knelt before the desk he had built with his own hands, his carpentry skills having turned proficient over time. On his knees, washed in a pale blue glow from the computer screen, the Angel prayed.

Griffin hugged Liz hard, gasping, "She's okay. Cassie's okay." His eyes teared and he wiped them on the shoulder of Liz's shirt.

Liz stroked his back. She'd never seen him like this. Griffin was actually shaking. "Come on, let's sit down." She led him to an upholstered bench against the wall. Rays of sunlight shone through skylights and painted oblong rectangles on the carpet at their feet.

Griffin's breathing was rapid, as though on the verge of hyperventilating. He sat forward, elbows braced on his knees, head hanging down as Liz's hand rubbed circles across his strong back. "Sorry about this," he apologized.

"Don't be silly."

"It's so strange . . . she was just crying . . . screaming . . . and she felt warm . . . I thought she had a fever. I don't know why it made me so afraid for her, but it did. It was like the dream. Just like the *damned* dream. Kids crying and no one there to help them."

"But you were there."

"I might not have been."

"But you were."

Griffin took deep breaths.

A doctor came by, paused, considered Griffin, then looked at Liz.

She said, "He's fine. Thanks." But Liz wasn't so sure that was entirely true. This was the hospital where Bright Eyes killed a girl the summer before. The place where Liz and Griffin had been reunited. In a way, it was the beginning of the events that had tried to destroy

Griffin's life. He was struggling so hard against the past, and now the present was making that battle even harder.

"Jimmy . . ." she whispered to his ear, starting to tell him she loved him, but maybe this was the wrong time. ". . . it'll be okay. It will all be okay."

"Carla's dead."

"I know, honey, I know."

"Why did she do it? Why the hell'd she kill herself?"

Because she's a mixed-up, confused, heartless bitch, Liz wanted to say but didn't. "I don't know."

"James Griffin?" a woman asked from fifteen feet away.

Griffin raised his head, vision blurred by tears. He squinted from the sunshine shining through the skylights and saw the woman wearing an expensive summer-white suit over a lightweight blouse, fine tailoring slimming her heavy-set figure.

She came toward him, extending a smooth hand, her fingernails polished coral pink. A big diamond wedding band on her ring finger. "I'm Dr. Marrisett. I'm your wife's psychiatrist. I'm so sorry." She was a pretty woman in her late thirties, but not the psychiatrist Carla had been seeing before separating from Griffin.

"What the hell happened?" Griffin couldn't keep accusation out of his voice. He'd had enough of pychiatrists and therapists—and all their bullshit—during the years Carla was supposed to be getting better and was screwing his best friend behind his back. Everyone lying to him.

Dr. Marrisett pulled over a heavy chair, sliding its oak-railed legs across the carpet. She sat forward on the cushioned edge of the seat, hands folded. "Over the past few months, Carla's depression intensified. She was in a deep depressive phase and not responding to medication that had helped in the past. She was suicidal during the last two weeks of December and into January but seemed to recover from that. She blamed it on the holidays, that it was the first time she'd been alone during Christmas. She missed you a great deal."

Liz said, "Oh, come on. After what *she* did, she misses *him*!"

Dr. Marrisett's voice maintained that therapist calm that drove Griffin crazy, talking about such emotionally charged issues as though reciting directions to the airport. "Carla suffered a great deal of guilt because of what she'd done. She was full of regret."

Liz said, "Good."

"She wanted to love you, and I believe she did love you, Mr. Griffin—she knew that she *should* love you, but she could never escape her feelings for Mickey Blane. Even though she knew their relationship was very wrong, even after all the pain it caused at different times in their history, she kept going back to him."

Hearing his former best friend's name was like taking a knife. Griffin's jaw clenched. Fucking Mickey Blane. The rich boy. Screwing his wife.

"She couldn't stop."

Liz said, "Not that she tried."

"She did," Dr. Marrisett asserted calmly, "just not very successfully, not with the strength necessary to stay away from him. It was a very powerful, very dangerous attraction, and it wasn't until the past few months that Carla realized how Mickey Blane had used her. That their relationship would never be more than a sexual one. That he didn't love her. It was then she began to realize just what she'd done to you, Mr. Griffin. One session in my office she cried for the entire hour, just repeating over and over, 'What have I done to him, what have I done?' And soon after, she swung into a brief manic phase where she was convinced everything could be perfect again, that she could make it all up to you and be the wife you deserved."

"No way you're putting this on him!" Liz pointed an angry finger at Marrisett. "Don't you *dare* defend that bitch!"

"I'm not defending—"

"Why did you even come down here? She's dead. Your patient's dead, Doctor. And now you're looking to soothe your conscious, tell us you made all these great breakthroughs. I don't think so." Liz grabbed Griffin's arm and stood. "Come on."

He touched Liz's hand. "It's all right."

"No, Jimmy, it's not."

Dr. Marrisett apologized, "I'm sorry. This is not what I intended. I feel horrible." Some edge came into her voice addressing Liz. "And I *know* Carla was my patient. I *know* she's dead, and that is the *ultimate* failure of a physician. You don't have to lecture me on that. I'm just trying to explain what Carla couldn't. Don't you think he deserves that much? At least to know that his wife was sorry for what she did? So maybe the rest of his life, when he looks at his daughter and sees a resemblance to Carla, he won't be reminded of a woman who hated him but of a woman who was sick and—yes—self-indulgent but who ultimately realized what she had done was terrible and would have changed it all if she could? But she knew time couldn't be undone."

Liz didn't want Dr. Marrisett to be right. For her own selfish reasons, she wanted Carla no longer to stand between her and Griffin, separated or not, divorced or not, hell, even dead or not. Liz wanted Carla out of Griffin's mind, but knew that was impossible. If she was going to love Griffin, she was going to have to live with the imprint Carla had left on him. Her anger somewhat diffused, she sat back down next to Griffin and held his hand.

A moment of quiet, then Griffin said, "What about Cassie?"

"She's fine. I checked with the emergency room staff before coming up here. All her vital signs are very good. I know she's been a very healthy baby. I've been in touch with her pediatrician because a primary concern with a depressive single parent is whether they're taking proper care of their child. And even with her work and personal habits suffering from her disease, Carla took very good care of Cassie. She had good help. A nanny came to the apartment three days a week."

Griffin was nodding, glad about that, but said, "So where does she go now?"

"She's free to leave the hospital. You can pick her up when you're ready."

"Me?"

"Yes." Dr. Marrisett appeared perplexed. "Is there a problem?"

"Well, what am I supposed to do with her? Mickey Blane's in jail."

"Now I don't understand. What does Mickey Blane have to do with this?"

"He's her father."

Dr. Marrisett was stunned. "Who told you that?"

"Carla."

"When?"

"Last summer,when she took Cassie and moved out."

"Mr. Griffin, I don't know what to say. Carla was very frank with me about every aspect of her life and she never mentioned Cassie being Mickey Blane's or anyone's child but yours."

"She said it," Liz advised. "I was there."

"She said Cassie was Mickey Blane's child?"

"No," Griffin replied, able to recall the scene exactly, having recalled it every day since it happened. "She said there was no way I could win a custody battle. She said it was impossible."

"That's all?" Dr. Marrisett inquired, looking between Griffin and Liz. "I'm sure if Cassie was someone else's child, Carla would have told me. I'm positive of it."

Griffin didn't move. He didn't blink. Tears welled in his eyes and came flowing out. He slumped forward, sliding off the bench, onto his knees, sobbing. The crown of his head was warmed by sunshine glowing through the skylights. So much agony suffered because of this. What he'd thought was punishment for killing two men: his daughter being taken away from him, that she wasn't his daughter but created by the semen of the man his wife was having an affair with. But it had only been Carla's diabolical lie to keep him away from Cassie, drive him from their lives. Cassie was his daughter!

The first person to see it was twenty-three-year-old Billy Mullins, who was looking at ten years to finish college at the rate he was going. Changing majors. Dropping classes. Smoking lots and lots of grass, and drinking beer.

In his room at the frat house on Sunday afternoon, big-time hungover, keeping an eye on the line to the bathroom in case he had to throw up again, Billy slouched in front of his computer wearing three-day-old boxer shorts and nothing else.

His parents had bought him the PC super-powered enough to handle the engineering assignments he'd actually thought he could handle (no way, dude), and now this primo bit of hardware was one of the sleekest, fastest Internet-browsing machines on campus. So cool. Downloading triple-X action shots and printing them on the color laser jet.

He was also into images of death, and there was a really cool Web site that had color pictures of car wrecks, a special section on decapitation. That stuff was fucked up, but it was cool, too.

Now, on Sunday, Billy was browsing for new Internet pages that incorporated the word *death*, and he came across a whopper of a file. File said it came with a video driver, one of those mini-movies on the Net. You got the file over the phone by modem, it landed in your computer, decompressed, and played a short video. Check it out.

Billy Mullins got the download, started watching, started yelling, "Hey, hey, come check this out! Wicked shit on the Internet!" Broadcasting it to the whole frat house.

Guys came stumbling in, unshaven, uncombed, one guy and his girlfriend wrapped in a bed sheet.

"Shit!" one of them exclaimed, seeing the video. "You think this is real?"

"Sure looks it."

It was Randy Arminger's home movie. Randy's point of view, filmed from the mini-camera taped to the bill of his cap, recorded on 8mm videocassette. Randy in his sister's room, a nightstand lamp glaring harsh light across the pretty girl's face. Randy nudging her awake . . .

Claire's eyes open. She takes a few seconds, blinking

against the light. But sees the gun. The video freezes on that moment. The split second of horror. And then, super slo-mo, the girl's mouth about to open with a scream when a puff from the end of the gun held inches from her forehead sends a bullet into her brain.

Guys in the frat house cringed, "Oh, shit."

"Shit, shit, wicked!"

"Oh, fuck. What's he doing now?"

The girlfriend screamed, "Oh, my God, I can't watch this! Jon, come on. Let's get out of here."

"No, babe, let's stay. Watch this fucked-up shit."

Within two hours, Randy's kill-spree video, posted on Internet sites all across the country and headed overseas, was getting fifteen hits a minute. Fifteen computers downloading the video every sixty seconds. Nine hundred computers an hour. And the number was growing.

Internet servers scrambled to pull the file off their systems, but as fast as they erased it, Randy had it back on.

In Ocean City, Maryland, Randy was out for a drive, once again checking out the apartment where his Centennial High classmate and fellow 4.0 student was supposed to arrive sometime tomorrow. Monday.

Meanwhile, back in the oceanfront condo, Randy's computers were busy at work. Randy had programmed them to keep his video on the Internet, finding servers who'd pulled it off and putting it right back on again. Like an automated propagandist restapling posters on telephone poles after the authorities tore them down.

Randy turned the rental car onto the bayside street. A half-mile-long road of townhouses and single homes built along canals that led into Assawoman Bay. Randy slowed for the radar trap he knew was set up from listening to cops on the police scanner.

He paused in front of the cottage apartments where Leanna would be staying and filmed it on 8mm videocassette. Doing a little advance work for his next Internet kill video.

He laughed, reminding himself, "You're only as good as your last picture."

20

Griffin was adrift in disbelief. Dazed. Shocked.

His daughter. *His* daughter. His. Cassie. The little girl he'd tried to forget for the past ten months, because he didn't know how else to handle what had happened. But he'd never been able to forget her. And now here she was in his arms, Griffin holding her securely in the front seat of the Camry, Liz driving them back to Carla's apartment.

Liz gestured to the building with a covered front entrance. "This is the place?"

"Yeah."

One of the city's last remaining doormen was posted in the shade of a blue awning, wearing a starched white shirt, black pants, and uniform cap. The same man who'd brought the ambulance crew to Carla's apartment, the crew having pronounced her dead at the scene. The doorman opened Griffin's door and solemnly greeted Cassie, "Hello sweetheart." His fingertip touched her smooth cheek. "I'm sorry about your mom."

Liz dropped Griffin and Cassie and headed back to the hotel, Griffin saying he'd meet her there soon. Get a ride out somehow. Use Carla's car if she still owned one, or call a cab. Liz reminded him about expense account receipts.

The doorman followed Griffin inside. "The police were here. I stayed with them in the apartment, because I didn't want anyone to be inside alone. Police or not, valuables have a way of disappearing."

"Thanks."

"A detective left his card." The doorman handed it to Griffin. "He said he knows you."

Griffin saw the name: Alfonso Washburn, a good street-smart cop raised in the since-demolished high-rise projects on Mulberry Street. He'd been undercover narcotics when Griffin was in the city attorney's office last summer; now he was homicide.

Griffin put Washburn's card in his pocket.

The doorman held the elevator for him while Griffin one-handed him a five-dollar tip from his wallet, balancing Cassie in his other arm.

The doorman adding, "I jury-rigged a piece of wood on the inside of the door so the lock will have something to hold against. Until we call a contractor on it tomorrow."

Griffin nodded. "Okay, thanks again."

"If there's anything else . . ."

The elevator doors closed. Griffin and Cassie were alone, Griffin taking a deep breath, reassuring her and himself. "Have you missed me as much as I missed you? It's been such a long, long time. I was just starting to get the dad thing down—the food, the diapers—and then you went away. So you're going to have to show me, okay?"

It was hard to imagine. They'd known one another so long, Griffin, Mickey, and Carla, since high school. Back then the three of them were inseparable, but they were separated now. Mickey Blane was in prison and Carla was dead.

It had all been so innocent eighteen years ago, and it had gone so badly.

But Griffin had Cassie again—imagine—as though being given another chance. As he went through the condo, collecting enough of her belongings to make do, he couldn't help projecting ten, twenty years into the future, wondering how it would turn out. His mind began to race, almost overwhelmed with responsibilities to consider. It had been much the same when Carla told him she was pregnant, only that news was delivered lukewarm. Carla had considered an abortion, because they'd been having marital problems, and what kind of world was this to bring a child into anyway? So dangerous and violent. Crime was getting worse every year and the legal system failed to deter or control it.

Cassie, whom Griffin had so much hope for, would now grow up without her mother. She wouldn't have much family at all. Griffin's parents were in good health, in their late fifties, hopefully with plenty of time left, but Carla's parents were both dead. Carla had been an only child. Griffin's only sibling, a sister he talked to once or twice a year but never visited, had left the family at seventeen, unable to take any more of her father's drunken rages.

Griffin was happy to have Cassie back but sad for the circumstances. He'd loved Carla from the beginning—since high school. He'd been faithful to her, suffering with her through the early years of depression. It wasn't until her adultery that he felt any shred of hatred, but if she'd asked his forgiveness, he would have given it to her. He would have gone back to her in a second. He only pretended to hate her because that made it easier.

The one chance they might have had to talk, when she phoned him about his proceeds from the sale of their condo, he'd been brisk, because she'd sounded cool to him. If she'd have made the first overture to heal the wounds, he would have responded. But she hadn't. According to Dr. Marrisett, that was about the time Carla was feeling upbeat: hoping she could make things better. But her voice hadn't sounded that way on the phone, so Griffin had remained cold to her.

Holding his daughter, Griffin stood in Carla's bedroom. The bed was unmade, expensive linens turned down and rumpled. Carla seemed to have died peacefully, swallowing the sleeping pills in the bottle on her nightstand. A New Age CD had played out in the shelf system next to the TV.

It was a beautiful bedroom. Griffin wondered what it would have been like to live here with Carla. Even smelling stuffy and closed-up, the room was sumptuous. Carla always loved flowing window treatments and plush bedding, creature comforts like those shown in home decorating magazines.

Carla was always redoing something, and had a flair for it. Her eye could tell what would work together, and she didn't fall victim to the amateur decorator's need to make everything symmetrical. A marble-top table served as one nightstand while a slipcovered table acted as the other. Mismatched, and yet in balance: maybe that's what Carla had been trying to achieve with her life, being married to Griffin while having an affair with rich boy Mickey Blane.

So hard to say. Griffin would never know what Carla had been thinking, what drove her to suicide, because Carla took her secrets with her. She left no note.

Maybe someday, someone would tell him something

that would give a clue to what had pushed Carla so far beyond despair as to find death an alternative. Or maybe it was more chemical than psychological. Maybe, like Griffin, Carla found herself not knowing what her life was about anymore, only she'd given up hope while Griffin was determined to keep searching.

Back at the Marriott, the message light was flashing.

Liz McKinley returned the call of her state police mole—Mitch Thompson earning his $200 under-the-table per diem yet again.

The FBI had a break. They knew where Randy Arminger had a base of operations to get his video on the Internet.

Liz asking, "What video?"

Mitch Thompson quickly explained what Randy had done—taped his murders and made a video of it for the Internet—then told Liz to bust ass if she wanted her scoop.

21

Two black sedans were parked side by side behind Centennial High. Liz pulled the Camry alongside them, then walked to the side entrance to the school. One of three sets of double doors was unlocked.

Inside, concrete walls were painted in school colors: red, white, and blue, celebrating the bicentennial year in which the facility opened. The gymnasium doors were locked, lights off. Liz continued through the sprawling building, listening.

Up ahead, footsteps clicked on tile floors. An anxious man hurried past in a perpendicular hallway. He didn't see Liz, who recognized him as the school's principal, Sam Reese.

A door opened and a man in a dark blue suit stuck his head into the hall, calling for the principal he couldn't see. "Mr. Reese. Mr. Reese!" The door remained opened, but the man ducked back into the room, advising someone else. "I'll go get him," before he started down the hall. His expression was humorless and undercut with urgency.

Liz ducked into an alcove and whispered to herself, "Fed."

* * *

The Angel was kneeling before his computer, praying, when the system's hard drive was accessed. The Angel opened his eyes and saw that a program placed into his system by Randy Arminger was bringing up an image on the screen.

A sentence: FLUSHING COMMUNICATIONS PORT.

Diodes on the computer's modem flashed indication of operation.

Then: INITIALIZING MODEM.

Followed by: DIALING . . .

The modem sounded ten digits, dialing a number that was not displayed on the screen.

The phone line rang and was answered with the handshake static and signal bongs of two computers "talking."

The screen displayed a new status message: NETWORK ACCESSED.

Then: COMMUNICATING.

CONNECTED! With an exclamation point, as though worthy of celebration.

The screen went black, but the communications line remained connected.

A fresh message: VIDEO DRIVER BEING DOWNLOADED.

The modem diodes flashed between send and receive indicators. Files comprising a computer program were sent over phone lines into the Angel's computer. The devil was invading heaven yet again.

A message: FILES BEING RECEIVED . . . EXPANDING.

Files sent in compressed form to save download time were "unpacked" and placed on the system's hard drive for operation.

The FILES RECEIVED/EXPANDING message played back and forth a few times, then:

FINISHED.

VIDEO DRIVER LOADED.

OPENING VIDEO DRIVER.

A white square appeared in the middle of the computer screen. The status message line moved to the bottom right corner:

AWAITING SIGNAL.

SIGNAL INCOMING.

The white box filled with horizontal lines of static. Then an image of a test pattern that was a bit grainy but clearly displayed a circle cut into colorful pie shapes.

A voice said, "Testing, testing, testing" sounding a bit muffled and cluttered with white noise but audible.

The words being spoken were also displayed along the bottom of the screen as though subtitled.

"This is Randy. This is Randy." There were occasional dropoffs in the sound and image, but Randy Arminger's voice came through with energetic precision, like NASA Ground Control communicating with the space shuttle. "Can you hear me, Angel? Echo signals tell me you are receiving video and audio. Please confirm by hitting the spacebar on your keyboard."

The Angel rose from his knees and felt the ache in his joints. He pressed the spacebar.

Randy announced through the computer. "Very good. Confirming audio and video connection. Hello, Angel. At last we move beyond anonymity. Not that there was ever any doubt who I was. Unlike you, I haven't hid my identity. And bear with me, in a few seconds, I won't be hiding my image, either."

The video view moved from the test pattern (what The Angel now saw was a piece of paper lying on a carpeted section of floor).

Randy was hand-holding the video camera. He panned it quickly across the floor, giving fast looks at the room in which he was working: a sliding glass door, partially opened curtains; the camera lens trying to adjust to light and focal point changes, giving a glimpse of a body of water. An ocean? Then a lopsided rapid pan across the living room wall. Some framed artwork. A lamp. Portable computers set up on a table. And then another window view. The ocean again? No, Randy hadn't turned a full circle. A different body of water. And a big sign shaped like a bowling pin.

The image centered somewhat as Randy placed the camera on a tripod. The sound of it being screwed into place came through the line along with Randy whistling the tune played for Warner Brothers cartoons, "Overture . . . dim the lights . . ."

The sign screwed into the threshold above the door said Computer Lab.

Liz peeked into the room through double doors with glass insets. Three men in suits and short haircuts—more feds, she guessed—and a fourth man, a young Asian in jeans and a T-shirt, worked on computers set up in cubicles.

The Asian calmly reported, "I pull it off and it's right back on the system."

"Shit." An agent pounded the desk.

Another asked, "And there's no way to tell where this is coming from?"

The first agent swore, "Goddammit, Jack, he told you. It's *in* the system. *On* the whole goddamned network. He's programmed it in like a virus."

"A bot," the T-shirted man corrected.

"A bot! A virus! A hidden program! *Whatever!* It's in the whole goddamned network." The agent swept his arm across the room of computers. "Fucking kid. Swear to God, why they can't take all this ingenuity and put it toward something productive. I swear to fucking Christ!" The man's face was red. A tall, gaunt man of forty-five under a lot of pressure. He rubbed his hand along the back of his neck where the stubble of shaved hairs poked into his shirt collar.

The Asian, a Centennial teacher, asked quietly, "What do you want me to do?"

"Take it down. Take the *whole* fucking network down."

"Wes, are you sure you want to do that? This might be the best link we've got to him. We could put a tap on the line and see if he calls in to maintain the system from outside."

The lead agent pointed at the teacher. "Your opinion: would Arminger do something that obvious?"

"No way."

"Okay, Jack?" Wes demanded of his fellow agent.

"But he might want to get back into the system . . . to update his . . . material."

"Material! It's home movies of a kill spree, Jack. It's on the Internet getting over a thousand hits an hour. There's servers all across the country taking it off their system and this network puts it right back on again. Now how many more ten-years-olds with computer know-how do you want to see this sicko's home movie? Tell me, Jack. How many?" He didn't wait for an answer. He yelled at the computer science teacher, waving his arms like a demonic conductor. "Take the whole goddamned network down."

Moments later, he burst out of the room, shouting expletives that echoed into the hall. He moved past Liz, as though she wasn't there.

Liz hustled up beside him. "Can I ask you some questions?"

"I got one for you: where's the goddamned principal?" Shouting, "Reese!"

"Do you have any leads on the whereabouts of Randy Arminger?"

"Reese!"

"Do you know where he is?"

The special agent in charge, Wes McGovern, pivoted on his heels and headed back to the computer lab, yanked the door open by its handle, and hollered, "Jack, I got a goddamned reporter here. Throw her out and secure the fucking building." He turned back around and smacked into Liz. Forcing an apologetic smile, he said, "Sorry, but you've hit me at a real rotten fucking time."

"Because you can't find Randy Arminger? Is this a federal case now? Has Randy committed any more murders?" Liz ran beside him as SAIC McGovern walked sharply toward the principal's office.

McGovern shouting, "Reese, where the hell are you? This ain't no PTA meeting. I've got a lunatic killer violating the Telecommunications Act and I want answers. I want every teacher who's taught this scary little punk in this school by nine p.m. tonight!" Yelling this even though Sam Reese was nowhere in sight. Muttering, "Goddamned teacher's union bullshit's gonna destroy the education system yet. That baldheaded G. Gordon Liddy's got that much right."

Liz said, "Can I quote you on that?"

"Absolutely. We got parents can't parent and teachers can't teach. We are at the footsteps of Armageddon and Nero ain't the only one playing the fiddle. Reese!" he shouted.

A hand grabbed Liz's arm from behind. It was one of

the other FBI men. "Sorry, miss." He had a firm grip but a soft voice. "I've got to ask you to leave."

"Don't *ask* her anything, Jack," McGovern yelled, walking away. "Tell her. *Tell* her. Everybody's too polite to give orders any more. People need direction."

Special Agent Jack Kilmer urged Liz toward the exit. "This way."

Liz responded, "I'll go, I'll go."

Kilmer released her arm and walked beside her.

Back down the hall, McGovern shouted, "There you are, Reese, you sorry little sap. You got his student file?"

A tentative voice said something to which McGovern shouted:

"The next person says word one to me about a search warrant gets his balls run up a flagpole. Gimme that goddamned file!"

Liz commented to Special Agent Kilmer, "He's going to have a heart attack."

"He already has."

"No wonder." Liz slowed her pace, wanting a few extra minutes inside the building in case there was something else worth overhearing, but S.A. Kilmer urged her along. Liz asked, "So what's going on with the computers? Has Randy Arminger been here?"

"I can't say."

"How about Agent Ravlite? Is he here?"

"Who?"

"Ravlite."

"Ravlite? Nobody by that name in our office."

Randy Arminger stood in front of the tripod-mounted video camera, holding a remote control in one hand and a newspaper in the other, broadcasting his image to the Angel.

The Angel had refused to come to Randy, so Randy went to the Angel and didn't even need to know where the Angel lived to find him. He just needed a computer and a phone line. Helloooo, Angel.

The Angel sat on a chair and stared at the boy with whom he had been engaged in fierce philosophical debate for months. The boy who was so rebellious, so anti-God, anti-faith. Randy Arminger was no longer mere words across a computer screen, espousing agnostic dogma in chat rooms on The Angel Pages but was showing himself, having remotely set up the Angel's computer to handle a live, one-way video conference.

The Angel wondered if his was the only computer receiving this broadcast. It was possible this way for Randy to reach thousands of people simultaneously. Millions.

There were already strip clubs on the Internet where, for a fee, you could sit home in Boise and watch strippers on your PC while they performed sex shows in New York or Las Vegas. The technology was available, inexpensive, and comparatively easy to use.

This display barely taxed Randy's formidable expertise.

Randy said, "Just so you know this is live, nothing phony, here's a copy of today's . . ." Randy checked the banner.

". . . *Beachcomber.*" A weekly paper for the tourist trade. Using the remote, Randy zoomed the camera in on the paper. "See the date." Randy ran his finger under it. "Today. And here's another paper. *Sunday Sun*. Hey, lookit, lookit. 'Teenage Killer Remains At Large.' That's me. 'Police Continue Search. Airport Interviews

Net No Leads.' They can't find me, and yet here I am. How about that?"

Randy did not know whom he was antagonizing. The Angel didn't advertise the results of his pilgrimages other than to report how prayers of punishment had been answered. The Angel preached as though these were the result of prayer, not his hand.

Randy Arminger, no doubt, assumed he was dealing with some weak pulpit preacher who *spoke* fire and brimstone, but was backed only by faith, not violence. Randy had no way to know the Angel could be a furious man.

And now, Randy Arminger had made a mistake. For he had already shown the Angel too much. Views from windows. A local newspaper. The Angel would need little more to find the boy. He could get there swiftly.

His rage gathering like the dark clouds of a storm, the Angel watched Randy Arminger's live broadcast, seeking more clues that might expedite his seizure of this boy.

Randy was folding the tripod, carefully carrying the video camera down the hall, giving a lopsided, dizzying perspective of his short walk. Randy proceeded carefully, many wires running along the floor, his camera connected to one of his computers.

Plain walls were broadcast now. Randy set the camera in a corner of the room and widened out the lens so that most of a ten-by-ten room was within the video frame.

There wasn't any furniture in the room. No pictures on pale walls. A single window had been boarded over as though in anticipation of a hurricane.

Randy leaned into the picture, said, "Be right back," and left the room.

The Angel's breathing intensified.

On the screen, a shadow came into the room. A person. The chubby girl whose parents the boy had killed. The Angel recognized her from the kill-spree video. She was naked, blindfolded, and gagged. Her hands were tied behind her back. Her ankles were shackled by rope so that no stride could stretch longer than eighteen inches.

Randy stood her in front of the camera. He hugged her from behind, stroking her breasts and feeling between her legs. The girl didn't resist him. She made humming sounds, apparently enjoying this.

Dear God.

Randy asked her, "Feels good?

The girl responded into her gag, "Mmm-hmm."

Randy slapped her ass.

"Mmmm!" She quivered.

"Feels *real*-real good?"

She squealed pleasurably.

Randy roughly grabbed her left breast and shook it. He remained standing behind her. His one hand disappeared from view, and when it came back, Randy was holding a long, shiny knife.

The Angel jumped up, screamed, "You bastard!"

Randy slashed her throat, the knife so sharp, the cut so clean, at first she didn't realize what had happened. Her warm blood gushed from her body and ran onto the floor, and then she knew. She screamed into the gag and tried to run from the room, a frantic skipping stride with her feet tied together. She banged into the walls, smearing them with her blood, struggling desperately to free her hands, to put pressure somehow to her neck to stop her bleeding.

Pale walls became splattered with red blood.

The girl collapsed to the floor, blood pulsing from her

neck in ever-diminishing thrusts as the final ounces of life drained from her body.

Randy stood before the camera, proud, radiant with pleasure. Holding a knife streaked with blood, he said, "Oh, damn, that's right. I said I was going to give you the chance to stop me from doing some evil little *thang* like this, didn't I?" He shrugged. "Oh, well, maybe next time."

And the screen went black.

22

When Liz walked into her hotel suite, Griffin was getting Cassie settled in a crib.

"Just putting her down for a nap."

A bottle of formula was on the desk beside Liz's laptop along with a hand towel from the bathroom.

"Griff, I've gotta do some work in here. Can we put her in the other room?"

"Yeah, sure. This thing's got wheels. Help me out—not exactly rack-and-pinion steering."

Liz felt as though a pressure were radiating from the crib, pushing back at her, keeping her away. Nothing psychic, just cause for hesitation, maybe even—did she dare admit it?—resentment. The little girl's presence was a sudden test of all those idle fantasies Liz had experienced the past few Griffin months—the picket fence, small dog, and children. Thoughts she interpreted as her life's last gasp effort at talking her into motherhood; vague impressions pecking at the shell of her career world like a tiny chick incubating under warm light.

Liz set down her bag and helped Griffin steer the squeaking-wheeled crib through the doorway into the adjoining room. The bedroom was cool and dark, with a vague musky smell that reminded Liz of their sex last night, and how she'd watched Griffin shave that morning, his strong thighs touching the sink, his bare ass so firm and defined. Liz had caught the reflection of his penis in the mirror. And now the smell of Cassie came into their room, the fresh scent of powder Griffin had used a little too much of changing her. Liz said, "Hello, sweetie. Hi, Cassie." Talking to the baby not for Cassie's sake but Griffin's, and feeling very awkward about it.

Griffin touched Cassie's cheek once they got the crib in place, smoothing his hand over her fine, dark hair. "Everything's going to be okay," he reassured. "Everything's going to be just fine. You'll see."

Words Liz would have liked to have heard herself, but Griffin was talking to Cassie.

Sunday afternoon a lot of people were leaving Ocean City. In season, weekend traffic was murder with folks driving to the beach from Baltimore and D.C. suburbs on Friday and heading back to the rat race on Sunday.

Randy Arminger wasn't leaving. He still had plans. Standing now on the public beach parking lot just north of Fenwick Island and the Maryland-Delaware line. A pleasant breeze swirled over the sand dunes, rustling through sea oats.

Randy had parked the rental car at the far end of the lot, away from the beachgoers who'd taken spots nearer to the walkway that traversed dunes and went down to the beach.

Now and then the cry of a sea gull or sound of a small child's glee joined the steady echo of breakers tumbling onto the shore. A good day for waves, or so said wetsuited surfers and bodyboarders who trudged back across the dunes, dripping wet, colorful boards secured under their arms.

Randy wouldn't know about that. He'd never been athletic in a team-sport way, finding it tiresome and boring. Randy hated to be bored. Loved the edge. Craved it. His senses were starved for input. To have the brilliant colors of his imagination flowing through his mind. Hungry not just for knowledge but to use that knowledge as leverage and power over others, and to create images that could feed his cravings. Always looking for more, bigger, brighter, faster, more *spectacular*! That's what Randy had in mind now. Spectacular.

So here he was, breathing deeply of his desires and the thrill of fulfillment. Living in a world where most people moved along like somnambulistic drones, not realizing the entire planet was on the brink of a new era. That old beliefs and rules were no more valid than superstition.

It was *all* falling apart, on a crash course with chaos and bankruptcy, and yet people still tried to play the new world with old rules. Mankind was about to enter an era when only the brilliant and powerful would survive, thrive, and prosper, while all the rest would become slaves. Modern-day monarchies were about to create a new ruling class.

The technocrats and instantaires (billionaires created overnight by their technical discoveries) would be the new kings and queens, and their armies would maintain order with weaponry so advanced few would realize they were weapons at all. *All* of the old rules were gone. God was gone.

Randy was sure of that, plugged into his portable CD player, heavy metal zooming through his head as the buzz of his radio-controlled car's engine carried the red plastic toy across the macadam parking lot. Its rubber wheels bounded across pebbles, skidding turns on thin patches of windblown sand. Randy was testing the battery-powered car bought at Radio Shack, wanting to see how far away he could stand from the car and still get it to operate. That distance was a key factor for the equation.

"Shut it off," Griffin said, his voice hard.

Liz disconnected her laptop from *America Exposed*'s link to the Internet and a copy of Randy Arminger's no-rules kill-spree video.

Liz was shaken by the sheer, extreme violence, knowing it was real even though it looked less authentic than some of what was on television. But there was no sensitivity to images of death anymore. It all was becoming a blur: real death and make believe.

Liz knew she was a victim herself; this morning, leaving the hotel, driving through the intersection where the car thieves had caused that terrible accident yesterday, Liz saw pieces of glass swept into the gutter and pictured the mangled cars again in her mind. Then, later, taking the cab downtown to the hospital, having gotten a call from Griffin, she thought about the accident when the cab driver turned at the corner, but only for a few moments. Coming back from the city, stopped at the light, actually stopped at the scene where the family van had been smashed by the truck, Liz hadn't thought about what had taken place at all. She'd been thinking about Griffin and Cassie—how Cassie would change things between them. Those concerns displaced the accident from her mind.

Now she'd just witnessed Randy Arminger's killings.

The grainy video intercut with images of Randy's face. Randy proclaiming "No rules." Spray painting the word, ANGEL, across his sister's abused and murdered body. Holly Haskins using that same can of paint to torture the teacher's wife. Holly Haskins looking as sick as Randy, and even more out of control. Like an animal starved for flesh, she tore at Mrs. Mitzner the way she'd choked her own mother.

Griffin muttered angrily, "He's a goddamned madman."

Liz got up from the computer and went out onto the balcony, wanting to feel sunshine—the heat of real light—on her face instead of the glow of a computer screen.

When she'd first heard about this story, the murders had been horrible enough, sensational enough for Liz to know she could sell a lot of papers writing about them. The words she'd written hadn't seemed this grotesque. Printed words were easier for the mind to cleanse of horror. Pictures, especially turned into a movie as Arminger had done—like entertainment—were stark and unrefutable.

But Griffin wasn't repulsed. Griffin was outraged, his own hunger for justice running strong. Griffin didn't lose control in the face of atrocity. He concentrated on stopping it.

Liz heard Griffin inside, talking. "He's got a larger agenda." Restating the theory he'd put forth yesterday. "He's going to do it again. And he's going to do it with a purpose, at least what *he* sees as a purpose."

Liz thought Griffin was talking to her, but she went inside and saw he'd gone into the bedroom and had Cassie in his arms. But Griffin wasn't talking to Cassie, either. He was thinking out loud, walking slowly with his daughter cradled in his arms and speaking very determined words.

After a moment, he stopped and looked at Liz. "I need someone to watch her." Talking about Cassie.

Liz replied quickly, "I can't do it. I've got—"

"I know."

"Oh, okay." Liz was relieved. She didn't want that duty and had spoken without taking time to phrase her concern more diplomatically. "What about your parents? Would they fly up here? I'll get the paper to pay for—"

"I don't want to drop this bombshell on them. They don't even know *I'm* up here."

"Griff, you should have told them. The paper—my story—comes out tomorrow, and your name's in it."

"I need to see them in person to tell them about Cassie. Not over the phone. They took it so hard losing her. My father, especially."

"A day care place?" Liz suggested, not at all versed in children's needs. "A babysitter?"

"I was thinking about Janice."

"Janice?" A name Liz didn't want to hear right now—Griffin's "other woman"—someone Liz wasn't supposed to be jealous of, but she was.

"She'd probably come up."

"Why don't we find out who Carla used. Or the hotel might be able to recommend someone."

"I don't want her with a stranger."

"What's Janice, then? I mean, to Cassie? She doesn't know her."

Cassie squirmed in Griffin's arms, wanting to get down and explore.

Griffin set her on the floor and Cassie immediately started walking, little hands reaching for everything and anything. Griffin followed her, guiding her, saying, "Here, honey, back over here."

Liz picked her bag off the floor, out of Cassie's reach. She was trying hard to be objective. "You really think Janice would do this? Does she have kids?"

"She's the eldest of five. All girls. She's had a lot of experience with diapers."

"Well, I . . . hell . . ." Liz threw out her arms. "Why not? Call Janice." She didn't believe she had said that, muttering, "Janice . . ."

For Randy Arminger, "life" wasn't a narrowly defined term. Life was not limited to living, breathing organisms. Life was anything that moved. In fact, the more and faster it moved, the more alive it was. Computers moved very, very fast, were very much alive. Turn them off and they stopped moving, but they weren't dead. They were just dormant, waiting for a zot of wattage to juice them back to life.

People didn't move too fast, especially their minds. People moved slowly. They only *seemed* more alive than computers. People were no more to Randy than images drawn on a different palette. Textures for him to enjoy, explore, abuse, exploit.

All life was energy, and if energy could be neither created nor destroyed, how was taking life really so bad? The energy—neither created nor destroyed—was merely distributed in some other way in the universe. How arrogant for people to think the energy that powered their body was theirs. That was old rules thinking. And as Randy was proving, those rules were no longer in effect.

Snuff out a life, like watching the blood pulse out of

chubby Holly's throat, and her energy was merely disbursed from her overweight, very-screwed-up-in-the-head shell to a less obvious form. The atoms imprisoned in her body were released into the air, some of that energy charging into Randy's body, hitting his pleasure cells. Quite a rush.

He'd always found great pleasure in dominating other people, either mentally or physically, so it wasn't that great a surprise to learn how satisfying it was to kill them. But the real bonus was how the media was responding to him. All this attention in the newspaper! Randy becoming quite the celeb. He was one of the best students in the country, one of the brightest, and now it looked as if he was one of the better killers, too. And he was young yet.

But you were only as good as your last movie, your last song. The entertainment industry was brutal. Always demanding better, bigger. Something different but not too different.

Randy was fully aware of his responsibilities to do better. And what sounded like a good idea for his next killing suddenly seemed second-rate to what was now swirling around in his head.

Randy was on the boardwalk in Ocean City. Hundreds of people strolling arcades and trinket shops. Not the throngs of a summer crowd, but he'd still had to wait ten minutes to get a container of french fries from Thrasher's—a place that sold only fries. Often imitated, never duplicated. Great fries. Dash on some salt and a little vinegar. Yum-yum.

Randy sat on a bench eating french fries and watched the game arcade, briefly wondering if there was some way he could get his kill-spree video playing on all those screens simultaneously. But such an idle thought.

More academic than anything. That video was yesterday's release. He needed something fresh, new, exciting, something that would really grab 'em.

And what a nice idea came to mind. Oh, how sweet.

Randy did all he could to keep from smiling and jumping up and down in celebration. He kept that inside.

On the outside, he was just another guy on the boardwalk watching girls go by. Sitting there in his jeans and pressed Polo shirt, walking shoes, turbo-cool sunglasses, earplugs to his police scanner/CD player firing a surreal mix of music and voices into his head. Randy looking both damned respectable and hip, his two days of stubble notwithstanding, barely resembling the photograph of a long-haired teenager printed in all the papers. Sure, there was a resemblance, and Randy was keeping his eye out for kids from Centennial High, having seen one or two, but who would really think it was him?

Of course, within thirty-six hours—forty-eight, tops—they'd know. Mmm, humdinger, they'd all know.

23

Cassie was restless in the high chair, looking almost as anxious as Liz, who fed the little girl crackers, knowing she was only buying time until impatient whimpers turned into blood-curdling screams and shot across the restaurant.

Liz hadn't wanted to go out for dinner, figuring on calling for pizza or even the take-out taxi that delivered from local restaurants, but Griffin had wanted to do this, so here they were in a small Indian restaurant at seven-thirty on a Sunday night. Less than half of the twenty tables were occupied, and the atmosphere was quiet save for the occasional outburst of piped-in ethnic music that, to Liz, sounded like angry buzzing flies.

As soon as they'd come in, Liz measured certain diners' aggravation, expressions scolding, *God, look at this, they've brought an infant in here.* People tensing, not wanting their meal ruined by a kid seated too close. At least that's how Liz perceived it, because many times she'd been on the opposite end of the situation, dreading a brat making faces at her, starved for attention, while take-kids-everywhere parents pretended their offspring weren't misbehaving.

Liz was beginning to feel a knot in her stomach that

was only partially eased by a Tanqueray and tonic, so she thought about ordering another.

Cassie was a cute baby, but she was still a baby. Liz felt badly cast as mommy, offering a corner of a saltine, urging, "Here, sweetie, here you go," as Cassie banged her palms on the high chair, made "gah" noises, and looked around as if the world were her playpen.

Griffin came back from the pay phone and slid into the booth. "Janice'll do it. She'll fly up."

"Good." Liz managed to smile. Why not fake one more response?

"There's a nine o'clock flight that arrives at eleven-fifteen tomorrow morning."

"You gave her my expense-account charge card number?"

"You don't have to do that."

"Overhead for the story. Find Arminger, Jimmy, and it'll be worth every penny." Liz handed off cracker duty to Griffin, and was amazed how easily he shifted into the role of dad. He was definitely meant to have children. Liz sipped her drink. "I'm going to try to interview Arminger's mother. A stringer in South Carolina has gotten me some background on her. I'll stake her out. Who knows, maybe Arminger will show there."

"I doubt it. He's not going there, and if he had intentions of killing her he'd have done it already. He knows it's an obvious place to go."

"So maybe she knows something else. Maybe I can get to him through her."

"Maybe."

Cassie settled down with Griffin tending to her. He alternated bites of crackers with sips from a plastic cup fitted with a no-spill top.

Griffin had done an efficient job packing Cassie

necessities from Carla's apartment. Liz respected that, admired that, but couldn't help feeling a sudden awkwardness between them, as though they both knew Cassie changed everything but couldn't talk about it. But they'd never really talked about their relationship—never defined it. Maybe that was because they both knew, deep down inside where brutal honesty was sometimes suppressed, they weren't ultimately right for one another. Griffin's life wouldn't be full without a family, and not only couldn't Liz have a child medically, but, face it, Liz, she confronted herself—she didn't want to be a mother.

Liz finished her drink.

The waiter brought their meals.

Cassie started bawling.

Griffin carried her outside and walked her up and down the sidewalk while his chicken korma got cold.

Liz ate alone.

Randy Arminger told the clerk at the storage facility his friend's parents' station wagon had broken down. Randy shaking his head, "Piece of shit car, you believe that," as he filled out the rental application.

"Tough break." Charlie, the man behind the counter, didn't much care. The Orioles were on TV and Mussina had pitched his way six innings toward a perfect game. Charlie was a big O's fan, loving the Orioles more than his wife and her dog put together. Not that Charlie figured that much of a compliment to the ball club, seeing as he'd been married twenty years and had started fooling around on his wife with this gal he took fishing, only now his prostrate was acting up and, well, baseball was a safer mistress.

"So because of that," Randy complained, signing his

Joseph Cotton alias to the agreement, "I've got to drive up to Jersey, pick him and all his crap up, and drive back here. I still got stuff of my own to get unpacked. And with the summer season about to start . . . my boss isn't going to be too happy about my missing work."

"Oh, Jesus!" The man flinched as the batter hit a liner to left, looking like it was going to drop in when Brady Anderson stretched into an outright dive and snagged the ball about eight inches off the grass. "Oh, what a catch! You see that? Holy Mother of God!"

Randy thinking, pathetic, this fat old slob's superdo psyched about baseball. Pah-thetico grande! "Here you go." Randy spun the rental agreement around, plopped down his fake credit card and driver's license.

Charlie scribbled in his portion of the contract, reached under the counter for keys without even looking, and plopped them on the counter. "Parked out back. Just bring it back full of gas."

"What about the handcart?" Randy asked.

"Two of 'em alongside the building. Take your pick."

"Thanks a lot. See you in a few days." Randy went out the door and cowbells rang his departure. He walked down the side of the concrete block building to where two rental trucks and three vans were parked under a big halogen light. Beyond that, a chain-link fence enclosed four rows of U-Store-It units.

Randy grabbed a rusty handcart and pulled it out of a patch of uncut grass growing through the tar and chip. He pushed it ahead of him, wheels squeaking maddeningly, to the van he'd just rented for thirty-two dollars a day plus mileage. The enclosed rear of the van measured about eight by fifteen by seven feet high—the whole deal about the size of a UPS parcel truck. Plus there was a pull-out ramp. Beautiful.

Randy slid shut the rear door, locked it, and headed across the Route 50 bridge back into Ocean City.

Randy was extremely cautious driving the oversized vehicle, wary of its width as he turned onto Baltimore Avenue, where cars parked along the street left little room for error in judging lanes.

Randy kept his eye on traffic and never once glanced up at the sky. He had no idea the Angel was above him.

Liz couldn't fall asleep. She lay in bed beside Griffin, her bare leg brushing his, and the contact of his body was uneasy temptation. She wanted to have him inside her, to make mad, unrestrained love with Griffin turning her from one position to another, changing the pace from slow to frantic as their pleasure intensified. But Griffin hadn't shown any signs of interest tonight, as though it couldn't or shouldn't happen with Cassie in the other room.

Liz had been undressing in one room while Griffin was holding Cassie in the other, and Griffin closed the door when Liz unhooked her bra.

They'd talked when Griffin came to bed, but it was idle conversation. Griffin fell asleep quickly, his breathing becoming steady, as though he'd found his peace just as Liz was losing hers.

Now it was two in the morning, and Liz was tired enough, inhibitions falling enough away; she considered being bold. To reach over and slip a hand inside his boxers, stroke him hard, and whisper that things didn't have to change between them, that they could make this work . . .

Griffin started twitching. At first Liz thought he was turning toward her, but he was dreaming. His body shuddered, legs and arms jerking.

"Jimmy . . ." She touched his powerful arm. "Jim . . ." Jostling him easily. "Wake up, lover."

He lurched out of sleep and sat upright, throwing back the sheet and hurrying into the adjoining room.

"Jimmy?" Liz got out of bed and found Griffin leaning over Cassie's crib.

The little girl was sound asleep.

Liz rubbed Griffin's wide back, whispering, "Are you okay?"

Griffin watched Cassie. "I had the goddamned dream again." He was short of breath, taking gulps of air. "Kids crying. I thought it was Cassie."

"She's okay. Come back to bed. Come on, it's okay." Gently urging him.

Griffin was unnerved by the dream. The dream had been disturbing before, but now, having Cassie back, it was worse. The crying was louder. More desperate. Closing in on him. Or was he closing in on *it*? Moving closer to where the dream was turning into a reality about to occur?

He couldn't go back to sleep. He turned toward Liz, who was looking at him in the darkness. He said to her, "What if she really isn't mine? What if Carla never told Dr. Marrisett about Cassie being Mickey Blane's daughter?"

For one brief, horribly selfish moment, Liz hoped that was so: that Cassie was the responsibility of Mickey Blane, and Liz would have Griffin to herself. She thought back to the glance Dr. Marrisett had cast her way at the hospital, Liz thinking at the time that Marrisett was trying to tell her something, and maybe that something was that Marrisett was lying to Griffin about Mickey Blane. Maybe Marrisett wanted what was best for Cassie, which would be for her to be with Griffin. But such a lie would be morally and legally unconscionable for a physician.

Liz said, "Jimmy . . . she's your daughter. Cassie is *yours*. Carla was just being a bitch, lying to you." Liz touched his face. "She's yours and you've got her back. You're going to be a fantastic father."

"I'm afraid something's going to happen to her. That something . . . someone's going to harm her and I won't be there to protect her."

In his mind, Griffin saw Angie Hanes being stalked by Drew Millundra, how he'd watched as Millundra squirted lighter fluid on Angie's car, about to set it on fire. He saw Janice, a pretty, naive young girl, kept sheltered by her parents, who was now innocent and blind to the dangers of the world. He saw Randy Arminger's younger sister—digital images of her from the sick video Arminger had put on the Internet—awakened in the middle of the night to find her brother holding a gun to her head, waiting until the horror and fear seized her before he killed her, brutalized her. He saw Arminger's teacher, the one they'd interviewed, and pictured her torment and also that of the young girl the teacher believed Arminger had raped. Most of all, however, Griffin saw Randy Arminger. The immense, intolerable evil of him.

24

Monday morning, Griffin drove his late wife's Honda. He'd found the Prelude's keys in Carla's pocketbook yesterday and had used it to drive Cassie to the hotel.

Cassie was riding up front in the car seat with him again today. A square of sun-darkening film attached to the passenger window by suction cups kept the morning sun off her face. She was a good rider, alternating her attention between soft plastic toys attached to the car seat and the sights outside.

Cassie took certain interest in red lights, pointing to them like familiar characters on TV, and saying something that, to Griffin, sounded like, "Dahlites, dahlites." Griffin wondered if Cassie had picked up her impatient mother's habit of swearing at traffic signals. Damn lights! Damn lights!

Carla always hated stopping for red lights. Carla had to be moving, as though whatever she was afraid of, whatever made her anxious, would catch up to her if she wasn't in motion.

Griffin knew he should make some type of funeral arrangements for her, but he couldn't just yet. A funeral would make her death real, and he wasn't ready for that. Maybe in a couple of days.

He thought being in the car might make him feel some renewed connection to his wife, but he couldn't imagine her that well anymore. As though he were forgetting what she'd been like, except for the memory of one of the last times he'd seen her in person: catching her in a luxurious condo, screwing his best friend.

And so the car wasn't a connection, it was just transportation. It had little over 14,000 miles on it. Carla, apparently, had been doing a fair amount of driving over the last ten months (or however long she'd been leasing the car; this Honda replaced the one she'd been driving the summer before).

Griffin turned the vehicle into the exclusive neighborhood where Randy Arminger had lived with—and murdered—his father and sister.

A plain, four-door car was parked across the street. The county police were on a none-too-subtle stakeout. Griffin pulled up alongside the sedan.

A uniformed officer reached over and hand-cranked his window down. "Help you?"

"My name's Jim Griffin. I'm an investigator working with a reporter on the Arminger story."

"That right?" The policeman saw Cassie. "She your assistant?"

"The boss."

"Know how that is. Got two kids myself. Hang on a sec." The officer got out of his car and walked around to Griffin's door. They shook hands. He waved at Cassie. "You helping dad?"

She played with a soft plastic square, putting a corner of it in her mouth.

Griffin saying, "Don't do that, Cassie." Taking it from her.

"She's a cutie pie."

"Thanks, yeah, I haven't seen her for a few months. She's been with her mother."

"Tough being away from them."

Griffin gestured to the house. "Any word on this kid?"

"He's a sick one."

"But no leads?"

"Nada. Which is why I'm sitting here, because we've got nothing else. Fibbies are running the show. We're backup."

"I was by here the other night, talked to a fed named Ravlite."

"Ravlite?"

"Yeah, only now he's like the fed who disappeared. No one on the case now seems to know who he is."

"Sorry, can't help you."

"He's a white guy about five-seven, white hair. Forty-five, fifty. Wore a pretty expensive-looking seersucker suit."

"Lead agent's a tall, thin guy. McGovern. Maniac, but they tell me he's good."

"He find Arminger yet?"

"Nope."

"Then he's not that good, is he?"

The Angel rented a motel room across the street from the big bowling pin sign he'd seen through the window in Randy Arminger's videoconference killing. The boy's thrill at evil was making him reckless. He'd used a local newspaper to establish the date, and let the camera stray to window views that helped pinpoint his location.

Before sending those live video images into the Angel's computer, Arminger had managed to keep his whereabouts a mystery. Now, the Angel was in Ocean

City, having flown his single-engine prop plane into the little municipal airport and rented a compact car.

Now the Angel stood on the side street and looked at the big bowling pin sign across the highway, seeing it at the same approximate angle that the boy had revealed in his broadcast. Only Arminger's viewpoint had appeared four or five stories off the ground, which narrowed the possible buildings to three.

One of those buildings was the L-shaped motel where the Angel was staying, a location directly on Coastal Highway—six lanes running north and south through the narrow island's approximate center. But the boy had been in a much larger space—multiple rooms and a hallway—than offered by a motel.

Of the two remaining buildings tall enough to provide a four-to-five story view, both were condominiums, and both had units with east and west facing windows. The Angel couldn't differentiate any other characteristics, but his task had been reduced to a matter of patience. The beach houses, cottages, and townhouses that filled every open square of sand were of little importance to him, as were the countless high-rise condos, motels, marinas, shopping centers, and T-shirt shops. Of all the places in the world the boy could be, the Angel had found him.

The Angel went back into his corner room, where he'd positioned the bed nearer to a sliding glass door and balcony view of both buildings where the boy might be.

The Angel knelt beside the bed, and as he moved into that position his right knee made a cracking sound, warning of aging bones and arthritis that was how many years away?

The Angel prayed for continued strength while

keeping vigil, waiting for Randy Arminger to show himself.

"Oh, isn't she cute."

"What's her name?"

Three girls stopped to talk with Cassie, whom Griffin held by the hand on the front walk of Centennial High.

Griffin said, "This is Cassie."

"Aww."

"Hey, Cassie." A slender girl in jeans and a softball uniform shirt bent down. "Do you want to come to class with us today?"

Cassie reached for the girl's earrings—diamond studs that sparkled in the sun.

The girl tilted her head to the side, pushing silky blond hair over her shoulder to show her earrings. "Do you like those? Aren't they shiny!"

Cassie made a sound—maybe trying a word—and smiled broadly.

"She's *so* adorable."

Behind them, school buses delivered students for what was the start of the next-to-last week of class. Other students arrived in their own cars, some driving Mom's Beamer or a used Benz. The kids' moods were light and breezy as the weather in anticipation of summer vacation. Any dark notoriety the school had taken on in the wake of Randy Arminger's spree killings had no apparent effect on them.

Not so with the teachers, who appeared gravely concerned, some noticeably apprehensive. Despite the presence of uniformed county police at the doors, and FBI agents failing to look inconspicuous in the parking lot, there was distress among teachers that Arminger might target more of them than Bill Mitzner.

Griffin overheard two substitute teachers talking about a rash of "sickness"; teachers calling in ill and remaining ill until Arminger was caught. A vice-principal tried to calm a staff member who'd been led to believe metal detectors would be set up at the school entrance today, the staffer complaining loudly, "Reese told me yesterday there'd be *full* security. Full security!"

"Everything's fine," the vice-principal assured, toting the spin-doctored line.

Griffin let go of Cassie's hand so she could touch the girl's earrings, telling his daughter, "Just be gentle. Don't pull."

The girl didn't mind Cassie's little fingers on her ear. Cassie seemed mesmerized by the reflections of light off the diamonds.

"I think she likes these. Are her ears pierced?"

"I don't know. She's been living with her mother."

"Well, let's see, Cassie. Do you have little holes in your ears?"

The three girls bent down around Cassie, one examining her ears, the other brushing her hair with her hand, complimenting, "Cassie, you have lovely, lovely hair."

Cassie was fascinated by the attention.

Griffin continued his casual stakeout for Paul Demmis, Randy Arminger's computer club friend.

A group of sophomores walked behind them, three boys and two girls, one of the girls saying, "I hear they've got these like, you know, stress-coping people coming in in case anybody feels traumatized about it."

"Traumatized about what?"

"What Randy did."

"I don't know what the big deal is. People get shot every day! Jeez."

One of the boys adjusted his backpack, asked, "*Anybody* can go to one of these stress people?"

"Yeah."

"Does it get you out of class?"

"I'm pretty sure."

"Cool."

The kids went inside.

Griffin touched Cassie's shoulder, "We'd better go."

Cassie reached for Griffin's hand.

"Okay, Cassie," the diamond girl said, " 'bye-bye."

"See you 'round."

The girls picked up their stuff and headed into the building.

Griffin led Cassie toward the parking lot, where Paul Demmis was heading for the side entrance. Demmis carried a heavy backpack, the nylon sides bulging with the stack of textbooks he was lugging.

Demmis's head was down, watching the toes of his hiking boots kick macadam pebbles. The short, curly-headed boy appeared deep in his own thoughts, eyes not blinking, the sort who'd grow a beard once he reached college and spend hours a day stroking it while his mind wandered between academic exercises and idle reflections.

Demmis walked forward on such auto-pilot he didn't realize Griffin was coming toward him, didn't even glance Griffin's way until he heard someone call his name. Looking up, Demmis's mind shifted back into the world around him. He first saw Cassie, then Griffin, and reality snapped in.

Griffin said, "Talk to you a second?"

"Uhm, I gotta . . ." Demmis glanced nervously, not looking for a place to run, but suddenly worried. "I should get inside."

"My car's parked back near the basketball court. A white Honda Prelude. Come outside after school starts. Say you need to see one of the special stress counselors and they'll let you out of class."

Demmis's legs wanted to keep walking even though he was standing in place.

"Anybody asks who I am, tell them I'm your crazy Uncle Jimmy, and this is your cousin, Cassie. And Uncle Jim's here because you need to borrow a couple hundred dollars from him." Griffin took two folded hundreds from his pocket. "Uncle Jim's here to help you out of a jam. Uncle Jim's not a computer genius, but he's a pretty bright guy in his own right. Okay?"

As Paul Demmis considered Griffin, that look Griffin recognized was in the young man's eyes again: something he was burdened with and wanted to get out. Something troubling his soul.

"Go ahead inside . . . but be back out here within half an hour. And don't leave school grounds without permission. Okay? You're a good kid, Paul. Keep being a good kid. Don't get fucked up in this mess, okay?"

"I, I—um, I'm not sure they'll let me out . . ." Demmis wasn't quite ready to confess yet, not sure he needed redemption.

"They don't let you out in half an hour, I'll come get you. Me and two of those guys in the dark suits over there. Federal agents." Griffin pointed to a pair of FBI men across the parking lot.

The fibbies weren't paying any attention to Griffin. Tall, lanky SAIC McGovern paced manically back and forth. But no Ravlite.

Griffin put his strong hand on Demmis's shoulder, squeezing. "Half an hour, Paul."

Paul Demmis began to experience the anxiety of a

closing trap. But sometimes a lack of options could be very freeing.

Randy Arminger awakened early Monday morning with a hard-on, thought about screwing Holly, then remembered. Well, there were bound to be some inconveniences along the way.

In the master bedroom of the expensive condo, Randy sat up and shook his head side to side, throwing off residual cobwebs of sleep. He was still surprised to not have his long hair thrashing around when he did that. He'd gotten to like all that hair. Maybe he would start growing it back once he got to Amsterdam.

Out of bed, he pulled open the front of his baggy boxers and checked out his erection, gave a few seconds' thought to masturbation, then decided, "Mr. Johnson, you just gotta wait, my friend."

He padded barefooted down the hall into the dining room, yawning as he sat before the computers. The police scanner he'd been keeping hooked to his belt had spent the night plugged into one of the computers, the scanner's audio output being monitored by a voice recognition program Randy had written. If the words "Randy," "Arminger," or the phrase "Straight-A Killer" were "heard" by the computer, the program began a careful screening process—one designed to weed out false alarms, because there were other Randys and Armingers in the world—but if it appeared likely that Randy was the subject of police communications, the computer would send out an alarm piercing enough to awaken Randy in the bedroom down the hall.

He hadn't heard any alarm through the night, and now, scrolling back through seven hours of police communications transcribed to disk by his program since

1:00 A.M., Randy confirmed his name had not gone out across the local police band.

Randy smiled, stretched, said to himself, "Well, let's go then. Get this diggity dog of a day going."

He connected the CD player/police scanner to portable speakers and carried the set-up into the bathroom. He shaved, showered, and, after considerable deliberation, masturbated. That hard-on just wasn't fading. So he leaned back against the tile wall, got his hand soapy, and let it ride. Raging youth hormones.

Showered and spent, he dressed in a new Eddie Bauer T-shirt and jean shorts, socks, and Sperry Topsiders. He unplugged the refrigerator, put some umph behind getting it away from the wall, and ran out an entire roll of duct tape around it, sealing the doors shut. He loaded the fridge on the handcart from the van rental place, and struggled like hell getting it out the condo door, but managed.

An older man heading for his morning beach walk held the elevator for him.

Randy, polite and breathing heavily from exertion, said, "Thanks."

"Quit on you?" the man asked of the fridge as the elevator started down.

"Only four years old. You believe that?"

"Sure." The man shook his head sourly. "*Nothing* lasts any more. Not like it used to be."

"The rules are changing."

"You can say that again." The man was still shaking his head, then got a whiff of something. A rotten smell.

Randy said, "Had fish in the freezer when it conked out."

"Oh, that'll stink up a place."

"Yeah. Tell me about it."

* * *

The Angel rose slowly from his knees and went closer to the window, shading his eyes against a glare of sun peeking over the right side of the two buildings he was watching. There: easing a handcart down three steps, hauling a taped-shut refrigerator across the parking lot, pulling it up a slide-out ramp into a rental van. It was him! Randy Arminger.

The Angel felt calm vibrations in his muscles. God giving him strength yet again.

25

Griffin was changing Cassie's diaper when Paul Demmis came outside looking for him. Griffin, in the back seat of the Honda, called, "Hey. Paul. This way."

Demmis's hands were stuffed deep in the pockets of well-worn jeans, his slender arms like sticks pressed to his sides. Head tilted down, he gave sideways glances to see who might be watching as he came toward the car.

Griffin said, "Get in up front. Driver's side," he clarified, when the child constraint strapped to the passenger seat proved an obvious obstacle.

Demmis circled the front of the car and got in, flinching from the smell.

"Just be another second here," Griffin said, putting Cassie's disposable diaper in a plastic bag and tying it shut. Diaper changing had become a whole new olfactory adventure from ten months ago. Griffin slid a new diaper up Cassie's sturdy legs.

Demmis was used to living in computer worlds of artificial intelligence; he wasn't at all accustomed to the natural—and strong—smells of real life.

Griffin said, "I take it you never had little brothers or sisters."

"I'm an only child."

"Good parents?"

"Yes, sir."

"What do they do?"

"Sir?" Demmis asked uneasily.

"Your mom and dad: what do they do for a living?"

"My mom sells real estate, and my father works at a bank."

"Probably not a teller."

"No. He's senior vice-president of the commercial loan division."

Griffin fitted a cooperative Cassie back into her overalls. "And what do you want to do once you graduate from some fine Ivy League college?"

"I'm hoping to have a joint major, electrical engineering and business."

"Be a shame to let Randy Arminger keep you from realizing that dream, wouldn't it? And being an only child . . . your parents have a lot of time invested in you, Paul. Lot of hopes and dreams of their own. It's a long way from this age . . ." Referring to Cassie. ". . . to where you are now. Lot of roadblocks and worries. Lot more time yet to go, too. What could be very good years, assuming you don't have to waste any time recovering from something stupid you got *caught* at."

Paul sat sideways in the driver's seat. He was old enough to have a license, but still looked so young behind the wheel. So damned smart, but inexperienced.

Griffin held Cassie in his lap, waiting for Paul Demmis.

Demmis said, "I saw the story about you in the newspaper yesterday. That you chased one of the guys who stole that jeep and caught him."

"I was just there."

"You didn't hurt him. The article said people were screaming for you to hurt him, but you didn't."

Griffin didn't respond.

Paul Demmis was quiet for a while, then: "Randy's messed up. He's gotten worse the past two years. I've known him since we were ten, and he's gotten scary."

"He is that."

"When his parents divorced is when it started going bad for him. He couldn't handle it. He was very close to his mother, but she had some kind of nervous breakdown." Paul Demmis was one of the rare young articulate, his conversation not potholed with *um, you know,* and *like*. He spoke clearly and at an even clip, neither rushing his thoughts nor slowed by them. "I don't think Randy's mom went crazy, but I don't know what it really was. At least that's what I've heard my parents say to their friends. Someone else said she was having an affair with some guy and Mr. Arminger found out and threw her out of the house. Randy's father was a very cold person. He'd barely even say hello when I was at the house, and as smart as Randy is, his father would never say anything positive to him. He always picked on little things, telling Randy how something he'd done was stupid—not stupid in terms of knowledge, I guess, but common sense. Like putting something in the garbage disposal that jammed it. Or putting something wet in the trash can that would leave a mess. Mr. Arminger had this thing about trash. He was obsessive about it. What was put in the trash versus what went in the disposal versus what was recycled. It was crazy."

"Are you going to tell me that's why Randy killed his father?"

"No. There's no excuse for it." Paul was clear on that

point. "He's gone over the edge. Randy's always been very hot-headed, very revengeful—is that a word?"

"Your SATs were probably a lot better than mine." Back to the point, Griffin said, "So he's revengeful."

"And competitive. Randy has to be the best. He's as obsessed with that as his father was organizing trash."

Griffin reached for a soft plastic dinosaur for Cassie, who was starting to squirm. "But his father was a bright man, too?"

"A genius. But he was so hard to get to. *Very* impatient. Randy felt like his father hated him, and that's when he started talking about getting out of the house. He felt like his father was always punishing him, calling him down and never praising him. And I think more than anything, Randy wanted his father's praise. He just never got it. His mom was different. She thought Randy could do no wrong. She didn't think any of us could do anything wrong. She thought we all pushed ourselves too hard. So a year or so ago, when things were really horrible between Randy and his father, Randy wanted to move in with his mom, only his father refused to let him. And I don't know why Randy didn't just go, unless maybe his mother still wasn't that well—whatever was wrong with her—and Randy was going crazy in the house with his father. He started acting very weird. He was brewing all kinds of chemicals and trying them. It started messing with his head. He got very aggressive, but in this slick kind of way. He'd have it in for someone and wouldn't want to just get them, he'd draw it out into this long process, like a game. Like . . . torture. Not necessarily physical, though. He'd work something on someone and do it anonymously or in a way he couldn't get caught even if he might be suspected."

Cassie threw her soft toy onto the floor of the car and

Griffin picked it up, wiped it on his shirt, and handed it back. "He didn't kill his father and sister anonymously. He videotaped it and put it on the damned Internet."

"I know," Paul stressed, "that's because he's been getting *worse*. He started with this really crazy idea. He's *talked* about killing his father, but I never, never thought he'd do it. But it came to that extreme. Whoever Randy saw as getting in his way, he wanted to wipe them out *completely*. It used to be he was just satisfied goofing on someone. Crashing their computer. Sending anonymous notes or presents."

"Like lingerie to a teacher?"

Demmis acknowledged, "Yes," confirming his role as an Arminger confident, which Griffin had suspected. Arminger would want someone to report his successes to, and who better than the friend in that computer club photograph—Randy having positioned himself as though he was Demmis's mentor.

Cassie wanted down, legs kicking.

Griffin said, "In a minute, Cass. One minute." He held up a single finger, then said to Demmis, "But didn't Randy also rape another student? A younger girl?"

Demmis was surprised, not that Randy might have done such a thing, but that Griffin knew about it. Demmis put his head down. "It was pretty terrible."

"Randy told you about it?"

"I . . . um . . . I was there when it happened. I was there." Demmis spoke faster, wanting to get this out. "Randy told a couple of us—we were all tight—to meet him in the auditorium, this dressing room back behind the stage. He said he was going to have a surprise. So we were there, and I don't know how he got the girl there, but he had her on the floor, with her hands tied together over her head with duct tape, and had tape around each of her ankles, tied to the floor so her legs were open. And her mouth was gagged and he'd just about ripped her out of her clothes. And Randy was naked too, and he said we should join him. That we were starting a new club and we were going to call it the Gang Bangers."

"So did you?"

"No way! I was out of there. Henry, too. But Jerry stayed. And for a couple of days, Randy and Jerry ragged on Henry and me pretty bad. Called us pussies. Faggots. They started excluding us. Randy said no more Craming for us, and that went on for about a week, until Randy needed me to help him with some programs he was writing. He was getting impatient debugging, and knew I'd do it for him, so all was forgiven, I guess."

"When was this?"

"Last fall. October. When Randy started going out there. The talk about killing his father began after that, and I think getting away with hurting that girl is what got him going in that direction. Randy was always into violent sex stuff on the Internet or on video, and he talked about gang-banging stuff a couple months before he and Jerry did that. Once he did it, and nothing happened to him, it was like he could do any scam and pull it off. There were no walls any more. No rules. He became obsessed with that idea. No rules. No rules. He'd get like a mynah bird about it. And then this religion stuff started. Or anti-religion. Randy got involved in this no-censorship-on-the-Internet kick, and started going after people who were posting messages about wanting pornography off the Net. He really locked in on this one address. A place called The Angel Pages."

"Angel?"

"Angel *Pages*. It's maintained by someone, a preacher, who talks about praying to punish people who escape the police or get off on some technicality. The Angel became Randy's latest obsession. Randy would be up all night on Cram arguing religion and punishment with this guy."

"On the Internet?"

"Yes. The guy wouldn't talk to Randy over the phone, which pissed Randy off."

"You know Randy spray-painted the word ANGEL on his sister's body?"

"Yes . . ."

"You didn't say anything Saturday when I asked—"

"The other guys were right there! I'm telling you now and taking a chance."

"What's the chance?"

"Maybe Randy finds out. Maybe one of the other guys sees me and tells Randy."

"They're talking to him? They know where he is?"

Paul didn't answer.

"Do *you* know where he is?"

Leanna Landy, Randy Arminger's valedictorian competition at Centennial High, was eating breakfast when her mother came home from her power walk around Centennial Lake.

Leanna, chewing a spoonful of cereal in her mouth, complained, "Mom, you let me oversleep." A dribble of skim milk ran down her chin, which she wiped with a cloth napkin.

"I thought you deserved a treat. You were up late last night." Chris Landy kissed her daughter's head of curly chestnut hair. "I'm guessing you got your paper finished."

"And modemed it into school. So I am *off* to the beach. Thanks to you."

"Your father's just concerned. It has nothing to do with not trusting you." Chris pulled out a chair and sat across from her daughter. The spacious eat-in kitchen served as frequent site of Landy girl gatherings, all closely supervised by Chris and Wilton Landy, mom and dad. Plenty of snacks, no drinking, no smoking.

"Dad just makes things so impossible sometimes."

"Not really."

Leanna gulped more cereal: Grape Nuts mixed with Corn Flakes. She was seated on the three-sided padded bench seat built into the huge bay window. Just outside, trellises of clematis and trumpet vines screened morning sunshine and lured hummingbirds seeking sweet nectar.

"Well, Dad didn't even want me *doing* the seminar."

"He was just concerned about you being away from home for so long."

"I'm going to be with Mallory."

"Your sister's starting college next year. She spent a semester in Paraguay. She's had more experience living away from home." Chris Landy didn't want to come right out and say that Mallory, just fifteen months older, was much more mature, but there was quite a difference between the two girls.

Mallory, the sociable athlete-scholar, was bright and outgoing, while Leanna was outright brilliant but sometimes moody, conniving, insistent on having her way, and anxious about her schoolwork. Leanna tended toward tantrums when the slightest thing went wrong, while Mallory was a self-described Ms. Go with the Flow. Stand them side by side, however, and the resemblance was clear. Cute girls with thick, wavy hair and pretty skin. The same height, but Mallory was developing a curvaceous shape like her mother, while Leanna was more slender.

Charging through her cereal, Leanna said, "It's going to be *so* cool at the beach. A *whole* month. *So* cool."

"Don't get carried away. You're just going down for two nights right now. Orientation for Habitat for Humanity tomorrow, then home Wednesday before dark. Back to school for finals next week."

"I know, I know. I'll be back, and I'll ace them all. And next year at this time, I'll be working on my commencement speech. The *only* commencement speech. That crazy Randy Arminger will be *long* gone by then. He *and* that spazoid Holly Haskins. What a perfect pair."

"Leanna—I wish you wouldn't sound so . . . pleased about what's happened. It's a horrible, horrible tragedy." This reaction of Leanna's was precisely why Chris Landy had made excuses to the police and a reporter to delay their talking to her daughter. Lingering spasms of Leanna's immaturity could pop up at embarrassingly inconvenient moments. "The boy killed his father, his sister, Mr. Mitzner, and—"

"Mom, hey, hell*ooo*. Who's been telling everyone he's a wacked-out drug fiend for the past year and a half? But no one wanted to listen because it was *sour grapes*. Because Randy was off at Hopkins and I wasn't admitted to their program. That Randy should be sole valedictorian next year because he not only had a four-oh but college credits *and* perfect SATs. I'll have college credits next year, too."

"Leanna, that's not what I mean. Just don't sound so pleased about what's happened. That's all. People might misunderstand."

"Okay, Mom, okay," Leanna laughed the fake laugh she used to hide her tension. She wasn't going to push this into a debate that might get permission for her two-night trip to the beach taken away. Not after her mom talked her father into letting her go, *and* gotten him to lend her the Acura for the drive, leaving Mr. Landy driving Leanna's old Corolla clunker to work for the next two days. But the truth was, Leanna was glad Randy Arminger had done what he'd done. She was thrilled. Exhilarated. She'd been telling everyone he was insane and a loser, but no one had listened. Except Mr. Mitzner. And if Mr. Mitzner had called the police right away when he found those crazy drugs Randy made and gave to his friends instead of waiting to discuss the situation with Sam Reese, Mr. Don't Smudge My School's Reputation, well, Mr. Mitzner might have had a better Friday night.

Leanna finished her cereal, spoon clanking into her bowl as she jumped up. "Take me to . . . *the beach*!" Leanna saying that like Tom Hanks in *Joe Versus the Volcano,* telling the Woos he was ready to jump in the bubbling lava of the Big Woo. Leanna loved Tom Hanks movies and didn't know why talk-show hosts always ragged on him about the Volcano movie. Especially that goofy David Letterman, who wasn't funny any more at all but had turned into a bitter, spoiled brat. A loser who got beat out for the *Tonight Show* job by Jay Leno and had never gotten over it. Too bad, Dave. Too bad.

Leanna rushed upstairs, getting her stuff together.

Chris Landy called after her, "You better slow down if you expect to drive the car."

Leanna sighed, but responded cheerily, "Yes, Mom. I'll go forty the whole trip."

"Fifty-five is fine. But it's a three-hour drive, which means three hours."

Leanna furrowed her brow, thinking, Whatever that

means, but said, "Okay." She wasn't as good as Mallory at playing her parents, but she did fine in a pinch.

Just outside Ocean City, Randy Arminger put the refrigerator in the landfill, having kicked and dented the hell out of it in back of the van lest some dump picker consider salvaging it. He dusted off his hands, put the handcart back in the van, pulled down the sliding back door, and checked his watch.

Pretty much on schedule.

Once again in the van, Randy headed back to Ocean City. Plugged into his CD player/police scanner, he glanced in the sideview mirror, then glanced again.

Small white car. Small white car . . .

A small white car had followed him out of Ocean City. Was this *another* small white car?

Randy switched on the van's turn signal and pulled onto the shoulder, tires churning up dust out of crushed rock as he braked to a stop.

The white car, a little compact, drove by. Randy tried to see inside the car, but the van's seat was too high above the road, the car too low; his angle of sight to the driver was blocked by the car's roof. He could only tell, once the little car drove by, that from behind, the driver's silhouette looked like that of a man.

26

Once at BWI airport, Liz changed her early flight to Myrtle Beach and Randy Arminger's mother to an afternoon departure.

At a newsstand, she picked up the just-printed edition of *America Exposed,* her paper having outdone itself with a boldly graphic headline, huge block letters surrounding last year's high school photo of Randy Arminger: STRAIGHT-A KILLER SLAUGHTERS FAMILY, TEACHER'S FAMILY, GIRLFRIEND'S PARENTS. The first words of the headline contained small trickles of red ink drawn like blood.

The paper was selling rather briskly. Someone commented, "Disgusting," but plunked down the quarters to buy.

Finding an empty row of chairs near a jetway, Liz read her article, pleased to find it had only been gently edited—"massaged" as the senior editor referred to it. Her byline appeared boldly. And substantial room had been given a sidebar about Griffin being attached to the story, including background about his rise to notoriety as the cop who twice tracked down Bright Eyes.

Liz was almost through reading her article when the plane taxied up to the gate. Her stomach tightened despite her telling herself this was nothing to be nervous about. But her hands were cold, too. Her emotions were overruling attempts at logic.

Passengers came off the plane just in from Florida: a mix of business people wearing suits and toting briefcases, casual travelers in shorts and T-shirts, and the requisite super-saver retirees coming up from West Palm Beach to see relatives in Maryland.

Liz had never met Janice—never even seen a picture of her—but was sure she'd know her upon sight. She thought this was her: a petite blond in jean shorts, sandals, and T-shirt; and Liz felt relieved Janice wasn't as pretty as she'd imagined. Only then a taller, thinner young woman came through the gate wearing a conservative yellow dress.

She had lustrous, long hair. Naturally blond. A complexion of roses and peaches. Clear, innocent eyes. She politely asked an airline employee the direction to baggage claim. And Liz knew *this* was Janice.

She was beautiful. Young. Chaste in a way Liz believed drove men crazy. A take-home-to-mom girl all the way. Liz had only been taken home to meet a few moms, and her boyfriends had always coached her extensively before the big meeting, making sure Liz didn't say this or that, didn't wear *that,* didn't do a lot of things that might cause Mom to faint.

Janice would sail through those mom meetings. Kids? Love them. Hope to have a houseful. Cooking? Oh, yes, let's share recipes. Church? We'll come over to pick you up every Sunday, then go out to a nice brunch afterward.

Liz watched Janice walk toward the terminal. Just about every man passing her offered a smile. Janice was probably smiling back, having little clue what thoughts lurked behind those married-man grins.

"Oh, Liz," she mumbled to herself, "stop being such a

cynic." She folded her paper into her bag, zipped it shut, and jogged after Janice. She'd changed flights in order to be here when Janice arrived—to meet her—so there was no sense in chickening out now.

Paul Demmis stalled out the Prelude pulling onto Centennial Lane. He glanced in the rearview mirror, apologized to Griffin, who sat in back with Cassie in his lap.

Not moving from his diaper-changing seat, letting Demmis drive, Griffin said, "Don't worry about it."

Demmis restarted the Honda and waited for a short line of cars to pass. He pressed on the gas and tentatively released the clutch, the car drifting backwards until the clutch engaged and the car jerked forward, wheels spinning, leaving a little rubber on the school parking lot.

The sudden momentum thrust Cassie back against Griffin's chest, surprising her at first, then she laughed a big, "Yahhh!" Liking it. Griffin figured he had a future roller coaster devotee on his hands.

Demmis didn't live far from school—lived close enough, in fact, to walk, which was what he'd been doing half an hour ago when Griffin saw him crossing the parking lot.

Now Demmis drove less than a quarter mile north on Centennial Lane, and did an adequate downshifted turn into a small development of Tudor-style homes set in the woods.

The Demmis house was at the end of a cul-de-sac situated on a "flag" lot with a long driveway the developer had managed to squeeze between two other homes.

A lawn placard along the driveway advertised the security system that protected the house. Demmis disarmed the alarm via keypad once he unlocked the side door.

The air inside the house was cool and clean-smelling, circulated through a quietly humming duct system that included an allergen, dust, and whatever-ails-you filtration system.

Griffin held Cassie's hand, leading her through a gourmet kitchen with Jenn-Air stove over which hung an army of copper pots and pans.

For the elaborate kitchen set-up, Griffin was surprised to see the side of a Scandinavian-made refrigerator looking like a bulletin board with countless take-out menus fixed to the stainless steel surface by magnets. Full-time working mom and dad were probably too busy to cook.

Demmis went up the stairs, saying, "My folks are at work, so it's cool. They usually don't get home until seven, seven-thirty."

Cassie came to the stairs and immediately looked up at Griffin, raising her arms to be carried.

Griffin picked her up, saying, "Legs too short for that, huh?" Or maybe Cassie hadn't come across many steps before, the downtown apartment being on one level and having an elevator. Then again, maybe Carla hadn't taken time to help her learn.

Griffin and Cassie followed Paul Demmis into his room, which, after the master suite, was the larger of three remaining bedrooms. Demmis's decor was far more orderly than Randy Arminger's. His room was sectioned by purpose for sleep, study, and entertainment, with a queen-sized bed, sectional desk and wall shelves, and stereo/TV cabinet. The only wall art was a framed poster of Einstein and a collection of computer-generated art matted behind pieces of glass.

Demmis's computer was already on, a screen-saver

program moving a nude-though-tame Elle Macpherson image slowly across the monitor.

Demmis's hand lightly grasped the computer's mouse as though his fingers were programmed to that shape. The nude Elle disappeared into electronic ether, and the operating system came up.

Demmis moved the mouse, finger clicking its left button with amazing speed and dexterity, images appearing on the screen and disappearing like flashes of lightning as Demmis made his way through what to Griffin was a digital maze.

Cassie was fascinated by the screen's colors and movement. She wanted to touch it, but Griffin kept her away.

Opening the program screen he wanted, Demmis began using the keyboard as well as the mouse. Printed text appeared in sections of the screen. Demmis saying, "This is from Randy." Using the mouse, he moved an electronic arrow across the screen as a pointer. "This message. This. This." He clicked on each entry in a log, and that line expanded into a fuller section of text. "This is what came in Friday night. A message attached to a program. It's the bot Randy wanted me to put on the network at school."

"A bot is—?"

"A type of program. This one was designed to hide on a computer system. It operates unseen in the background, looking to do a certain task."

"How did Randy send this to you?"

"Attached to e-mail over the Internet."

"And where'd he send it from?"

"I don't know. He could have been anywhere—"

"There's a phone," Griffin said, learning.

"Right."

"So how did you get the bot from here to school?"

Demmis picked up a floppy disk. "I copy the bot from my hard drive onto this, take the floppy to school, put it on the network."

"How long does it take?"

"To copy a program this size from floppy to hard drive? About five seconds."

"Not something you have to worry about getting caught doing. Not like walking into a bank with a gun and holding the place up."

"Hardly."

Cassie reached for the screen again, and Griffin kept her from it. She tried touching the mouse, and Griffin said, "Dangerous. No, no." Cassie didn't like hearing that, and made a noise of protest. Struggling with Cassie's increasing restlessness, Griffin said, "And Randy couldn't have gotten this bot on the school computer over the Internet?"

"He could have, but Mr. Wo, the sys-op, checks all files that come in over a modem line before letting them on the system. Randy could have designed the program to look like something else, but that would have taken more time, and this was easy."

"Because he knew you'd do it for him?"

"I didn't know what he'd done," Paul defended. "I wasn't in school on Friday. I didn't know about the shootings."

"How did you know the program—the bot—wasn't destructive before you put it on the school's system?"

"Like I told you Saturday, Randy did some hacking, but it was never malicious."

"So you were assuming this would be no different?"

"Right."

Griffin didn't press the illogic of such trust, knowing

it was often de rigeur among friends, especially in high school: a fact of which Randy Arminger was also likely aware and willing to exploit. "And the whole purpose of this bot was to keep Randy's video on the Internet?"

"If an Internet server took it off its system, the bot put it right back."

Griffin tried not to look too amazed of or terrified by the impact of abused computer power. The best and the brightest fighting a war of minds trying to dominate the latest highway of commerce, only it wasn't like laying railroad tracks across virgin land, but spawning a battlefield in the mist.

"And Randy's been in touch with you since Friday," Griffin confirmed.

"Yes." Demmis used the screen arrow to indicate new messages, and displayed them.

Randy's notes appeared in the order in which they were received:

Sent Thursday afternoon, received Friday night: LOAD THIS ON THE SCHOOL NET FOR ME BY 1800 SATURDAY. IT'LL BE A KICKER. THANKS A MIL.

Sent Saturday night, received Saturday night: THANKS FOR HANDLING THE ERRAND FOR ME. BTW HAVE YOU HEARD? THIS IS ALL PRETTY COOL HUH? SHOWED THE OLD MAN DIDN'T I? THE FUCKER. THE BASTARD! AND MR. MITZNER. ARROGANT ASSHOLE. MR. AUTHORITY RULE ENFORCER. THOSE WHO CAN'T DO TEACH. YOU SHOULD'VE SEEN THE LOOK ON HIS FACE. KIND OF AD-LIBBED HOLLY'S PARENTS, THE MULTIPLE SUPERDO LOSERS WHO ARE NO GREAT LOSS. BLEW AWAY HER OLD MAN WHILE DICK DEEP INSIDE HOLLY. TALK ABOUT RUSHA-RUSHA. HOLLY DID HER MOM HERSELF. REALLY WAILED ON HER. WELL, BE WELL. THE QUEST CONTINUES.

"So Arminger knew Mr. Mitzner was about to bust him for Cram?"

"Yes."

"Does Randy know how Mitzner found out about it?"

"I'm not sure."

"Saturday at the basketball court, everyone seemed to think it was Leanna Landy—it that the right name?—who was the one who pointed the finger at Randy."

"I think that's just a rumor. Randy sometimes called Leanna the Fly, because she was always buzzing around doing something to try to get him. And it was like a game to him, fending her off." Demmis pointed to his screen. "This came yesterday morning from Randy."

SEE THE SHOW! SEE THE SHOW! STEP RIGHT UP. INSERT CIRCUS MUSIC: YAHT-DAT-DATTA-DAT-DAT-DAT-DAT-DAH! IT'S GONNA GET BETTER. NEED YOUR HELP, THOUGH. STAY TUNED!

"And this came last night."

ANOTHER ATTACHMENT. MUST BE ON THE SCHOOL NET BY MONDAY 1800. HOTCHACHACHACHA. BTW HOLLY SAYS GOODBYE.

Griffin asked, "What's BTW?" having seen those initials twice.

"E-mail shorthand for *by the way*."

Griffin picked Cassie up. "What about 'Holly says goodbye?' "

Paul shrugged.

"You don't know what that means?"

"No."

"It means he's killed her."

"Oh, shit." Demmis bent forward with a wave of nausea and clutched his head in his hands. "Oh, shit, shit, shit."

"Have you been sending messages back to Arminger?"

Demmis winced in pain, his head started to throb along with anxiety gripping his stomach. "No."

"Why not?"

"What would I say?" Demmis asked desperately. "One of my best friends goes completely berserk . . . ? I'm scared for him. I'm scared for *me*. I put that bot on the school system for him. I helped him keep that video on the Internet."

"Get me where he is, Paul. Find him for me. Come on," Griffin urged, leaning forward, rapping the monitor with his knuckles, "make this thing sing."

Demmis rubbed his temples, a nasty headache coming on, fearing he was about to slip into one of those auras that signaled the start of a migraine.

"Come on, Paul. He's liable to kill someone else if I don't find him!"

Demmis felt the intense pressure of an important exam, this one in real life, not academics. "He's not going to tell me where he is."

"So trick him into telling you."

"You don't trick Randy!"

"Send him a message."

"And say what?"

"Tell him whatever it is he wants you to do by six o'clock today you can't do."

"I can't tell him that."

"Not because you don't want to, tell him it's because the FBI's involved. Make up some computer stuff he'll believe."

Paul rubbed his temples and thought. "If the computer lab's been closed, I wouldn't be able to load the program . . ."

"Tell him that."

Demmis took a breath. He started typing, fingers flying like the best of secretaries, then he stopped.

"What?"

Demmis looked up at Griffin. Another confession. "There's something else I can try."

"What?"

Demmis erased his message and started retyping, explaining to Griffin, "I'm going to attach a bot to this message." Demmis laughed sadly, ironically. "Actually, it's one of Randy's bots."

"What's it do?"

"Simple answer or long answer?"

"A clear answer. Think like a real person, not an engineer."

"The bot tries to determine the phone number of the line the computer's connected to."

"You can get me Randy's phone number? Where he is now?"

"I've got about a fifty-fifty shot. Depending on how updated the local phone system is. Randy came up with the idea after going on line in sex chat rooms."

"Sex chat rooms?"

"Yeah—you write dirty conversation with other people on line. Only lots of times people cross gender, guys pretending to be girls and vice versa. Randy didn't like the idea of having hot chat with some girl who was actually a guy, so he'd send them this bot via e-mail, and once he had their phone number, he'd call to make sure a girl answered."

Griffin wondered how all this had ever become possible. A long way from *Watson, come here. I need you.*

Paul Demmis sent his message to Randy Arminger over the Net, then rubbed his eyes with the palms of his hands. "I need to take care of this headache. It's gonna be a killer." Demmis staggered to the bathroom, closing the door.

Griffin no sooner heard Demmis open a medicine cabinet than a message appeared on the computer screen's upper corner:

YOU HAVE MAIL FROM MINDGAME.

"Paul," Griffin called. "Hey, Paul!" Griffin carried Cassie to the bathroom door and knocked. "Paul?"

The poor kid was grunting in there.

"You okay?"

"Yeah." Straining.

"Paul there's something on your screen, says you have mail from Mindgame."

"What?"

Griffin heard Demmis pulling his pants on, zipping up, buckling his belt. Demmis came out with his shirttail partially untucked.

Griffin glanced into the bathroom and saw the opened prescription container on the sink: pain-relief suppositories the poor kid needed for his migraines.

Demmis peered at his monitor. "Shit."

"What?" Griffin and Cassie stood beside him. "Arminger?"

"Yeah?"

"He got your message that fast?"

"No. No way. But I'm getting something from him."

27

Randy Arminger no sooner sent e-mail to Paul Demmis and was walking away from his computers, about to look out the window for that white car again, when his computer sounded a warning alarm: a Randy-programmed alarm, like a fire station signal calling in volunteers.

Randy hurried back to the computers, muttering, "What the hell? This better be a false alarm. This better *fucking* be a false alarm!"

The monitor was going crazy, like an electronic beehive with activity, displaying output.

"Son of a bitch!" Randy swore.

He was under attack.

The alarm was attached to his virus detection system, a part of his computer that constantly scanned for electronic "disease," prevention against bots, Trojan horses, and other constantly mutating infections that flew across the Internet looking to sneak into unknowing computers and steal, corrupt, or destroy.

And he was being hit. He was definitely being hit.

His anti-virus software was safely packing away the infected data coming into his system, putting it into quarantine and analyzing it. Randy, furious as hell, immediately considered revenge. That someone dare come after him! He'd find who was doing this and launch a counterattack that would completely wipe out his assailant's system. Nuke it. And if they were on a network of machines, the whole net was coming down.

Randy stared at data coming across his screen, hard copy being put to paper by his portable printer. The system had diagnosed the invader. It was one of his own programs. A phone-number-verification bot. Attached to e-mail coming in from Paul Demmis.

"You little fuck," Randy muttered, staring in disbelief at the machine. Paul? Someone Randy had taught, brought along, given Cram to for exams. This was gratitude? A fucking insurrection?

Paul?

No, no, no, not Paul. Not Paulie. Something was going on here. Why would Paul want his phone number. Want to know where he was? Paulie wouldn't care. Paulie wouldn't want him caught.

And Paul would know that Randy would have his system immunized against one of his own bots. Or would he?

Randy had given other computer club members virus-protection programs for their computers, but those programs were specifically designed *not* to prevent Randy's viruses from being detected. Always needed a way to check on the troops. So maybe Paul *did* think he was slipping this in unseen. Or was Paul sending him a warning of some kind? Or maybe both.

That would be like Paulie. Try to play both ends against the middle, keep everybody happy. A trait gleaned from that phony-faced real estate saleswoman mother of his. Lie to everyone and be everyone's friend.

Well, it couldn't be that way, Paulie. Could not be.

* * *

Paul Demmis was relieved, reading e-mail from Randy Arminger, telling Griffin, "He's wondering why he hasn't heard from me. He wants to make sure I'm going to put the program on the school's system for him."

Griffin read Arminger's paragraph-long message along with Paul.

Cassie was over Griffin's shoulder, sucking her thumb and letting out the occasional sigh. Bored but being good, although Griffin figured he was pressing his luck without more to keep her occupied. Maybe it was time to get her back to the hotel. Janice should be arriving soon.

And then Demmis got another e-mail alert:

YOU HAVE MAIL FROM MINDGAME.

Demmis said, "He must be at his machine." Demmis opened his e-mail, holding his own against the headache thanks to those embarrassing but effective suppositories.

Arminger's new message read: LET'S CHAT, and included the chat address where Arminger wanted to "meet."

Demmis keyed in the Internet address, his system taking him there, and as soon as he was "in the door," got a live message from Arminger.

PAULPAULPAULPAULPAUL, just like the message sent the other night GODISDEADGODISDEADGODISDEAD, words packed together without spaces.

Griffin stared at the screen, frustrated that at the other end of this "conversation" was someone he couldn't locate other than in this ghostly electronic world. Arminger, as he had Friday night with Ravlite, was appearing only as electronic letters on a computer screen.

WHAT'S GOING ON PAUL?

Demmis looked at Griffin. "What do I say?"

"Ask if he got your e-mail."

Paul: YOU GOT MY E-MAIL?

SURE DID. There was a pause, then: TROUBLE AT SCHOOL?

Griffin said, "Tell him it's the FBI."

Paul: COPS HAVE GOT THE SCHOOL NET COVERED. THEY'RE SUSPICIOUS SOMEONE IN SCHOOL'S HELPED YOU.

COPS HUH? Another pause.

Demmis saying, "He knows something's up. Shit, he may have caught the bot I sent. If he did, I'm fucked. He'll take my system down. He could be injecting me right now." Demmis glanced at the tape backup of his data on his shelf, wondering how long it would take him to get his system back up if Randy crashed him. And with finals coming next week, two term papers due . . .

Randy sent: IS THERE A COP WITH YOU NOW PAUL?

"Shit." Demmis pushed his chair back as though surrendering. "He knows."

"Tell him an *ex*-cop's with you."

"What!"

"Go on, tell him."

Demmis typed: EX-COP.

WHAT'S THAT MEAN PAUL? EXCOP?

"I used to be a cop, now I'm a reporter."

Demmis sent what Griffin dictated.

Adrenalin surged through Griffin, making contact with Arminger himself.

WHAT'S EXCOP'S NAME?

"James Griffin. Ex of Baltimore City now working for America Exposed."

There was no immediate response, which left Paul Demmis fretting. "He's nuking me. I just know it." He stared at send and receive diodes lighting on his external modem, the device that sent signals over the phone line. "I just know it."

Randy: I LIKE THAT PAPER. THAT AMERICA EXPOSED.

Griffin dictated and Demmis typed. "Did you see today's edition? You're in it."

OH YEAH. MAYBE I'LL CHECK IT OUT.

"So what's next?"

NEXT?

"Who gets it next?"

WHAT MAKES YOU THINK SOMEONE'S GOING TO GET IT?

"Seems like you're having fun, and fun's hard to quit."

FUN?

Griffin didn't dictate a response to Demmis, who looked at him. Griffin shook his head, waiting.

Randy: YEAH IT'S A RUSH.

Demmis sighed sadly, "God, Randy . . ."

"Can we meet?"

NOW WHY WOULD I WANT TO DO THAT?

"To get your story in the newspaper. Whatever you want to say. However you want to say it."

I DON'T NEED YOUR NEWSPAPER. I'VE GOT THE INTERNET. BESIDES, IT'S A LONG TRIP FOR YOU TO PHOENIX.

"You drove all the way to Arizona since Friday? Have you been on Cram all that while?"

A pause, then: MAYBE I TOOK A PLANE.

"You drove. Wherever you are, it's not that far away. You've got too much going on to be on the run. You're someplace you're familiar enough with to know how to get around. Somewhere you've been before to scope out."

No response.

Griffin said, "And you cut your hair short."

As Demmis typed, his expression registered that Griffin was putting forth a good theory.

Griffin continued, "You've been letting your hair grow long the last year or so, knowing you'd want to change your looks and this would be the easiest way. A short haircut. Tell me I'm wrong."

No response.

Griffin didn't want to lose Arminger. He needed something to work as an angle and felt an intellectual challenge might be the only way to intrigue the boy. "Who's the Angel?"

No response.

Griffin asked Demmis, "Is he still there?"

Demmis hit a single key and his last message was repeated: WHO'S THE ANGEL?

Arminger: ANGELS ARE EVERYWHERE. AREN'T THEY SUPPOSED TO BE?

"The Angel you argue religion with on the Internet. Friday night you told him God was dead. Who's that Angel?"

I'M TRYING TO FIND THAT OUT MYSELF. THE CHICKENSHIT BASTARD WON'T SHOW HIMSELF.

"Why do you care if he shows himself?"

SO HE CAN SEE FOR HIMSELF THAT GOD IS DEAD.

"Is God dead?"

OH YEAH. LONG GONE. TAKE A LOOK AROUND EXCOP. MORE AND MORE PEOPLE REALIZE IT EVERYDAY. Randy's words appeared quickly. Like Demmis, he knew the keyboard, typing with very few mistakes. GOD IS DEAD. THE ONLY ONES WHO THINK HE'S STILL ALIVE ARE LIVING SOME WORN OUT DREAM. Pause. LIKE PEOPLE ON THE BEACH GETTING THEIR FEET WET FROM A WAVE THAT'S JUST COME ASHORE ONLY THE WATER'S

PULLING BACK TIDE'S EBBING AND THERE ARE NO MORE WAVES COMING.

"Don't be so sure."

YOU A BELIEVER EXCOP? YOU BELIEVE IN GOD?

"I don't know."

SEE? YOU'RE A DOUBTER. THAT'S WHAT I'M TALKING ABOUT. BECAUSE THERE'S NO SIGN GOD'S STILL ALIVE. IT'S ALL FICTION. MAKE BELIEVE. A WAY TO INSTILL ORDER AND RULES. BUT IT'S A LIE. AND PEOPLE NEED TO KNOW THEY'RE LIVING LIES. THAT GOD IS DEAD.

"And this is why you want to find the Angel? Sounds pretty lame. All this trouble just to have a debate."

WHO SAID ANYTHING ABOUT A DEBATE. I WAS THINKING MORE ABOUT A MORALITY PLAY. OR SHOULD I SAY AMORALITY PLAY.

"The same kind of play you put on Thursday night?"

No response.

Griffin urged Demmis to type, "The same kind of play you acted out on Holly? You did kill her, didn't you? 'Holly says goodbye?' "

No response.

"Is he still there?"

Demmis sent the last message again.

No response.

No response.

Then: YOU'LL SEE.

Griffin demanding, "When?" yelling as though Arminger were right there.

SOON. It looked as though Arminger disconnected after that, but then: SAY BYE-BYE TO YOUR COMPUTER, PAUL.

Demmis crying, "Oh, no!" as his screen filled with violent flashes of color. "He's nuking me!"

Randy Arminger had indeed sent a very destructive virus through the phone line, a virus that was now inside Paul Demmis's computer, tearing at its memory, erasing files from the hard drive even as Demmis jerked the electric cord from the wall.

Randy Arminger hustled down the stairs, bypassing the elevator. He emerged from the enclosed stairwell into bright sunshine. A warm day that was going to be a hot one if Randy had his way. And Randy *was* going to have his way.

Plugged into his CD player/police scanner, music and cop band bouncing in his head, Randy was calmer now, but he'd been rattled by that excop who'd used Paul Demmis to get to him. Randy wasn't sure he was buying the reporter line. The excop—Griffin—had been accurate as hell about Randy's plan. Not accurate enough to know just where Randy was, but if the guy was following the theory that Randy was somewhere familiar, the world was suddenly a smaller place to search. Besides his mom's new place in South Carolina, an uncle's place in Louisville, Randy hadn't traveled much beyond Ocean City and Amsterdam—a month spent there last summer arranged through AFS. Single trips to New York, D.C., Pittsburgh hadn't been long enough to give him the orientation the excop theorized.

Randy began to rethink Amsterdam as his next destination. Maybe it was too obvious.

He walked quickly down the side street, away from the beach, cutting between two cottages across their small sandy "lawns."

The beach town was quiet at ten o'clock; all the high school kids in town for June Bug Week were still asleep, about to wake up with vicious hangovers and other anxieties about what they'd done the night before. Randy figured most warm nights in Ocean City you could almost hear girls losing their virginity, like cherries dropping off a tree.

Randy ran across Ocean Highway, beating a few cars coming off a red light. He went into a convenience store and found the small newspaper rack, skipped over the major metropolitan dailies, past the freebie advertisers, and—bingo-dingo—*America Exposed.*

Hey, look, that's me! Front fucking cover. Not bad, not bad! Look at that longhair. Straight-A Killer. A-fucking right.

Randy grabbed a paper and tossed it on the counter along with a quart of orange juice. Got out his money for the college dropout beachcomber/manager running the register. "How's it going?" Talking too loudly because of the music blaring in his earphones.

"Same sand, different day." The guy gave Randy change, which Randy deposited into a small box labelled EMPLOYEE BEER FUND. "Thanks, man. You have a good day."

"Planning on it," Randy said, out the door. He was about to walk into the deli two doors down, get a bagel when—son of a bitch—there was that white car again. Parked in the motel lot across the street, pulled in beside a dumpster: a spot Randy couldn't see from his building. But Randy wasn't in the condo now, was he?

Randy entered the deli and ordered two bagels with lox—better stock up, might not have time for lunch.

Janice was sitting by the window, washed in sunshine when Griffin and Cassie came into the hotel room. Janice's face lit up seeing the little girl holding Griffin's hand. "Jimmy, she's beautiful." Janice seemed overjoyed and looked as though she might cry.

Cassie peered up at Janice, her expression revealing attempts to recognize a new face, turning to Griffin when she didn't. Not fearful but seeking explanation.

Griffin bent down. "Cassie, this is Janice." He picked her up.

"Hello, Cassie." Janice touched the soft skin of Cassie's arm. "Jimmy, she's so pretty. This is incredible. She's perfect."

"Thanks for coming up here. I really appreciate it. I apologize for dumping this situation on you. It's so damned strange—it's as if I'm half in a dream."

"Can I hold you?" Janice asked Cassie. "Would that be okay?"

Cassie wasn't sure.

"Come here, honey," Janice urged Cassie. "It's okay. I'll take good care of you."

Cassie's weight shifted away from Griffin's chest, leaning toward Janice.

Janice held Cassie, who looked like she might give crying a thought, but Janice hummed sweetly against her ear, telling Griffin, "She's a good girl. Have you fed her this morning?"

"Just some milk and baby food. There's some jars—"

"Jimmy, she's too old for baby food. You need real food, don't you honey?"

Janice's presence meant more to Griffin now than ever. But that security—Janice's goodness, her peacefulness and calm—was for Cassie, because Janice would not be Griffin's antidote today.

Griffin went into the bedroom, but came directly back. "All Liz's stuff's gone. Her clothes."

"She said she'd call you from South Carolina. I thought you knew she was going."

"I did, but—you saw her?" Griffin wondered how that was possible given that Liz's flight was supposed to have left *before* Janice's arrived.

"She was waiting for me at the airport. She drove me back here. We talked. She told me what's been happening."

"Why did she pack all her stuff? She left this morning with just an overnight bag. Now everything's gone."

"I don't know."

"Did she say—what did you talk about?"

"Everything." Janice sat beside Cassie on the floor, letting her play in the sunshine. "It's all happening for a reason, Jimmy. It's just like I said Saturday on the way to the airport. Your coming back to Baltimore. Your wife. Cassie. This young man you're looking for. These aren't random events. They're your sign. I can feel it. You're getting your mission."

28

The Angel watched from his window and saw the boy come out the enclosed stairwell into the parking lot. He lost sight of him cutting between buildings, then picked him up again on the side street, then lost him, then saw him crossing the highway.

It was difficult to follow someone covertly in this beach town, especially by car. On Coastal Highway, numbered side streets came at approximate fifty-yard intervals, with frequent red lights, and just enough traffic to require staying close to keep from losing the boy. Once out of town via either of two bridges across the bay, the open roads—long and straight—made it impossible to stay close at all without being obvious.

The Angel was experienced in tracking people, watching them, learning their habits in order to find their weak points, but the surroundings Arminger had chosen were unique. And the Angel's previous targets, for the most part, were unsuspecting. The boy seemed wary, and with good reason. He was the subject of an intensive yet fruitless search. Law enforcement seemed to have handicapped itself by taking the boy too lightly at first, thinking him unworldly and perhaps crazed; assuming he'd make a mistake or be easy to find.

The boy was none of that. He was brilliant. Deranged. Also arrogant, and *that* would be his failing.

But just as Randy Arminger would foolishly fall victim to his own arrogance, the Angel couldn't assume his own success in this battle against evil. He would need to be sharp, to strike against the boy and make his escape.

Maybe he would have to kill the boy less artfully, less symbolically than he had the others. Maybe he should do it now. Right now!

The boy was coming back across the street. A newspaper folded under his arm. A paper bag in his hand.

The Angel's weapon was loaded. He was a fine shot. He could shoot the boy right here, from the window. At less than thirty yards, a slight downward angle from the second floor. The railing would be a concern—he would have to shoot through it—but he'd have his aim.

He wanted to do it that way, but couldn't.

The boy must have a chance to ask for redemption. Before his death, he had to be given one last chance to accept God and ask forgiveness. It was this burden—this cross—that the Angel had to bear.

And so the boy passed beneath the Angel's window. The Angel watching, gun in his hand.

Griffin stopped back at Centennial High School. To gain access past a county police officer posted at the side doors, Griffin asked, "How do I get to the front office? I'm from the University of Miami, scouting a baseball player up here."

The cop figured that explained Griffin's tan. It was too early in the season for that kind of beach look around here. Barely past Memorial Day. "Down the hall, take a left."

"Thanks a lot." Griffin started in, then stopped, seemingly concerned, asking the officer, "Some trouble here today?"

"Oh, no sir. Just routine." The cop covering up, playing the game as instructed, whenever there was a call to a county school to deal with drugs or violence. Don't let reality upset the taxpayers.

Griffin went inside, down the hall past the gymnasium. He turned left as directed, then scouted a new path, finding his way to the library and some studious girls who seemed to be juniors or seniors, asking them, "Can you help me out? I'm trying to find Leanna Landy."

"She's hooking," a girl with thick-braided hair replied, willing to play the rat.

"Don't tell me she's getting another scholarship?" A slender girl in a Ralph Lauren shirt muttered and rolled her eyes. "Just what she needs."

Griffin said, "Hooking?"

"But not like that," a third girl replied, coming to Leanna's defense. "She's got permission. She's going to orientation for Habitat for Humanity. They help build low-income housing. It's usually just for graduating seniors, but Leanna got accepted. She's been looking forward to this for weeks."

"Bragging about it, you mean," the envious Lauren girl cut in.

"She'll be home Wednesday night."

"Wednesday night? Orientation's not around here?" Griffin asked.

"The beach. You believe that luck? And the weather's gorgeous."

"It never rains on Leanna," the Lauren girl snipped. "It wouldn't dare."

"Shut up. I get so sick of you whining about her."

"Excuse me, then." She slapped shut a calculus text and stomped off to another table, muttering about life not being fair.

"She's a dork," Leanna's friend apologized.

"Leanna's at the beach?" Griffin asked.

"O.C. Left last night, or this morning, she wasn't sure which. Her mom was still working on her pops to let Leanna go. Leanna figured it would work out, but Mr. Landy's not much of a free thinker so there was this poco chance she'd get stuck home."

"Habitat for Humanity?"

"That's it."

"Thanks."

"Any time." The girl smiled politely, went back to her calc problems, then, when Griffin was out of earshot, commented to her friend, "Nice butt."

Liz sat in the car for a long while, watching planes taxi down the runway and take off. At least a dozen jets streaked into the hazy blue sky before she started to cry. And then she cried for a long while, resting her forehead on arms crossed over the steering wheel.

It had been a long, long time since she'd fallen in love with someone. Long enough she'd forgotten why she didn't ever want to do it again. But she hadn't expected to fall in love with Griffin. Even after her feelings had come so strongly for him, she'd denied them. But there was no denying it now, just as there was no denying a relationship couldn't happen between them. Griffin needed someone like Janice. Someone to take care of him *and* Cassie.

Janice made Liz feel old, and tired, and—admit it, Liz—used up. Too much time spent irreverently, hedonistically, years gone by walking down a path that was too long and unforgiving to double back on.

Driving Janice to the hotel from the airport, Janice had spoken of Griffin in terms of adoration. She thought he was a guardian angel. She talked of life having meaning and purpose, that a divine power—what Liz would call fate or dumb luck—was always at work. Liz found Janice naive, but sweetly so. And she knew that Janice was also in love with Griffin.

Griffin may have been sincere when he told her Janice was just a friend, but in a few more weeks, maybe months, he'd begin to forget the difference in their ages, and especially when it came to Cassie, he'd see how well they'd fit together. How much better than Liz Janice would be for Cassie.

Janice would blossom in his presence. Griffin would pull her into maturity while she tempered his rough edges and provided the comforts he'd never known in his life. The girl was sweet—my God, she might even be a virgin—and it would be a whole new start for Griffin. Someone who came to him without any link to his past, and washed away his painful history like a baptism.

Liz did not have that advantage. She was a part of his past, a reminder of it, and just when Griffin was trying to escape all that had been wrong with his life, Liz brought him back here, and he was right in it again.

So Liz's bags were packed. She was going to Myrtle Beach to interview Randy Arminger's mother, then she was going back to Atlanta. She'd let the story break—let Arminger be found—and go to him from there.

She'd already scooped all the other papers with the Randy Arminger details she'd uncovered. Amidst all the hype and sensationalism, score a few more points of legitimacy for *America Exposed*. And let Griffin go.

She held a little hope that she was overreacting, and maybe a life for her with Griffin could work out after all, but that hope was the kind reserved for fairy tales, for dreaming of what might be so in a far-off land where the stars were angel dust dancing across the sky. Liz could not deny whom she really was and what she really wanted in life. A husband? Yes. A career? Yes. But both on her terms. Which wouldn't be right for Griffin, not now that he had Cassie again.

Liz sat up and wiped her eyes. She started the car and pulled back onto the road, turned in her rental car, and checked in for her flight to Myrtle Beach.

When her cell phone rang, she didn't answer it. She knew it would be Griffin. It was "his ring." And if she heard his voice right now, she'd just start crying again.

"Goddammit, where the hell are you?" Griffin checked his watch as his phone call rang unanswered. Eleven-thirty. The airline said the next flight to Myrtle Beach didn't leave until one o'clock. Liz wouldn't be in the air yet.

Griffin got the cellular message service after the third ring. "Liz, it's Jimmy. What the hell's going on? Why'd you move your stuff out of the hotel? I'm at a convenience store a couple of minutes from Centennial High. I've been back there twice this morning. One of the basketball kids got me in contact with Arminger on the Internet. I talked to him, Liz! Chat, whatever you call it. Arminger says he's got something else planned and it's happening soon. And it might be happening nearby. Leanna Landy, Arminger's valedictorian competition, the girl Arminger's friends think ratted him out about Cram, has gone to Ocean City for a couple days. She's there for an orientation that's been planned—known about for some time. Arminger could have heard her talking about it at school. Ocean City's a beach resort a few hours east of here. *A few hours.* Someplace Arminger could have driven Friday morning. Consider this: Arminger likely killed his teacher because Mitzner had evidence Randy was using drugs and was going to have him expelled. Rumor is—and Randy might believe—Mitzner got this information because of Leanna Landy. Which might be enough for Arminger to act on. If he is after this girl, he might not have had time to fit her into his schedule Thursday night, or maybe he figured she'd be an easier target away from home. The location makes sense, Liz. I'm thinking, wherever Arminger is, it's somewhere he's familiar with, someplace he knows. And *every* kid around here knows Ocean City. It's a shot, is what I figure. It's a shot. I'm headed down there in an hour or so. I'll try you again before I leave." He started to hang up, then added: "Don't get on that plane."

Griffin drove back roads to Route 1, one of the original highways that linked Baltimore to D.C. It was a mostly commercial area of trailer parks and light industry, where Griffin knew a guy who ran a shop not far from the city line. It was a place that took care of cops.

The owner was a former cop and gunsmith. A guy who always seemed to be running afoul of the Alcohol, Tobacco, and Firearms boys for this, that, or the other thing. A guy who was a bit of an anti-government nut and threatened to change his name to Waco Texas, but a guy who knew how to keep his mouth shut—even under pressure.

The front door of the gun shop was painted with a silhouette body target, the "body" wearing an ATF cap.

(Targets were also for sale with IRS initials on the chest).

Griffin walked in and Ted Lyle aka Waco Texas let out a hale and hearty, "Jesus Christ, if it ain't Jimmy Griffin! Somabitch, hon, how you doing? Where you been hidin' at since them rat bastards downtown done you wrong? That prick Mickey Blane's some big homey's bitch by now, and serves him right."

Ted Lyle's only customer at the moment was a fellow government-hater, the two men having been angrily bashing the governor's proposed limit to restrict handgun purchases to one a month.

Griffin nodded Lyle toward the back room, a dark windowless square of concrete built back into the hillside. The low-ceilinged chamber smelled of dirt and gunpowder. Bare bulbs supplied minimal light overhead.

"You need somethin'," Lyle anticipated, "you know it's yours, Jim. Anything."

Ted Lyle had made a small cash fortune over the years supplying boys in blue with untraceable "throw-down" weapons—a little something to keep handy in case that suspect you just shot, thinking he'd drawn down on you, was unarmed. Or if you needed a little probable cause for that car you knew was cruising up I–95 full of coke—reach down between the driver's feet and come out with a Ted Lyle piece. Manufacture a little evidence in an effort to tip the scales of justice away from 1970s-approved Supreme Court insanity.

"You got a dependable nine millie you can let go for a couple hundred?"

"Numbers?" Meaning serial numbers.

"Preferably not."

Lyle knew this was no throwdown gun, no Saturday

night special to be planted. This was a gun to be fired and tossed. Lyle had supplied Griffin with one years ago, and Griffin had killed a man with it in the middle of the night. A lunatic killer known as Bright Eyes.

Lyle picked up a piece of floorboard and reached down into a hole it took a man not fearful of snakes to attempt. He petted the rattler sleeping in its cool hole and came out with a burlap-wrapped oiled and ready Beretta. Displaying it for Griffin. "She's a sweet one, James."

Griffin checked it out, pulled back the slide, gave it one dry fire. There were two clips already loaded.

"Packed 'em myself," Lyle said of the ammo. "You hit a small elephant, it ain't gettin' up. Recoil'll knock your jock off."

The weapon felt strange in his hand. So many years he'd strapped a similar gun under his arm, but the past ten civilian months had been spent unarmed save a .38 his father gave him to keep under the bed—Florida being Florida. Griffin thought back to the last time he'd fired a weapon, killing the second man he'd ever shot. Flash images of it came to him, as did the feeling that had haunted him afterward. The odd sense of justification. A complete lack of remorse. The feeling he'd do it again if circumstances dictated.

Randy Arminger had asked Griffin two hours ago what Griffin had asked himself so many times since he'd killed those two men: Did he believe in God? Griffin didn't know. He didn't know which he feared more: the sin of killing, or that there was no God to judge him. At least in the former case, others—Cassie, Liz, Janice, his parents—would have a chance at heaven, even if he was doomed.

Griffin took three hundreds out of his wallet, asked

Ted Lyle, "This cover it?" He knew Lyle would have given it to him for nothing, because Lyle operated this portion of his business for principal, not profit.

Lyle took the cash as a donation and said, "Good not seeing you again." Meaning if anyone asked, Griffin hadn't been there. Ted hadn't seen him in years.

Griffin left the store knowing what he'd so often told Liz was true: he wasn't a reporter. He couldn't just observe and comment. He needed the sense of closure that only justice could provide.

Not that it was his intention to kill Randy Arminger. He wasn't an assassin. He was just—well, he was just prepared. That's all. He was just getting prepared. His finger might never have to touch that trigger. He might not even find Arminger. He might be all wrong about this.

Arminger might be in some friend's basement right in the backyard of Centennial High, laughing his ass off, plotting his next move. Maybe Griffin was driving to the beach for nothing. But maybe not.

29

When Leanna Landy wheeled her father's Acura into Amy Tran's driveway, Amy jumped up from the front porch bench with a whoop, calling, "Yeah, Leanna. The Acura. We got wheels. We're stylin'!"

Leanna had the radio cranked and the windows rolled down. Amy came running to the car with a pair of backpacks, one jammed with clothes, the other with clanking bottles. Tossing the clothes in the back seat, she unzipped the second bag for display. Announcing of the cool sweating beer bottles, "Little Sam Adams courtesy of Billy Taylor."

"All right, Amy."

"Want one now?"

"Let's at least get out of the county."

"Okay." Amy zipped shut the bag and got in up front. "Nice car."

The two girls talked over the music, WHFS pounding out modern rock.

"So cool of you to let me come along," Amy said. "And thanks for the Habitat thing brochure. My 'rents bought it. They think I'm turning over a new leaf."

"You gotta play to win," Leanna said, backing out of the driveway fast.

"I got other stuff, too." Amy reached for her backpack.

Amy was an attractive though easily called astray sixteen-year-old, straight blond hair pulled back in a ponytail that somehow made her look older. Smart but unmotivated, she and her two-years-younger brother had been latchkey kids for the past seven years when mom went back to work. Amy got good enough grades to keep her parents from worrying, hitting the occasional honor roll, which got her treated to dinner—not that dinner out with the 'rents was much of a treat—and managing successfully to sneak experiments with sex and drugs.

Amy dug around in her bag, retrieving a few items as she settled in the passenger seat. "Show and tell," she said to Leanna. "First, matching sunglasses."

"Oh, cool." Leanna took her pair of the latest and hottest shades and put them on.

Amy slipped hers on. "These are also courtesy of Billy Taylor, who is a really, really good shoplifter. I watched him the other day pull *ten* CDs out of this store in the mall. Razor blades them out of the cases, security strip comes off. He's so quick—like that Japanese guy that cooked at the table at my birthday party, remember him? The one who asked Janine for a date?"

"He was so, so gross."

"And . . ." Amy produced two more matching items. "Fake I.D.s. Not driver's licenses, but student I.D.s. Best I could do. Look, we're sisters."

Leanna drove and checked out the laminated card. "This's incredible. It looks so real."

"You're Carly and I'm Marissa. We're juniors at the University of Delaware."

"These are the pictures we had taken at the mall!"

"It's why I told you not to goof for them."

"Where'd you get the I.D.s?"

"Billy Taylor from a friend."

"So, so cool. Put it in my wallet, will you?" Leanna shifted positions so Amy could get her wallet out of her pocket.

"And here are some of those Billy Taylor boosted CD's." She put a stack on the dash. "And . . ." Amy had something between her hands, something small and flat enough to hide in her palms, opening her hands as if spreading a clam shell.

Leanna shrieked amazement.

Amy laughed, "Ribbed for her pleasure," reading from the wrapper.

"My God!" Leanna smiled broadly at the two condoms. "Did you buy those?"

"Nope. Billy Taylor brought them over last night. But there *were* three."

"Three!" Leanna was interested. "You did him?"

"On the sofa."

"My God, my God. Oh, my God!"

Amy screamed in joyous celebration.

"I can't believe you did it. Tell me, tell me. Did it hurt? Did you come? What was it like?"

Pretending to be serious, Amy said, "Let's see, that would be: A little. No. And quick."

They both laughed.

"But it doesn't feel as good as making yourself come."

"Amy!"

"What? Like you don't." Amy reached into the back seat. "I'm having one of these beers. You want one?"

"Not yet."

Amy clanked bottles looking for the opener. Back in

her seat, popping the Samuel Adams cap, she said, "Yeah, last night I got it over with. Got that first time down. Don't have to sweat that anymore."

"I can't believe you did it." Leanna was almost at I–70 and hoping no one her parents knew saw Amy drinking beer in the car.

"It's about like we thought. Like a bigger tampon that moves in and out kind of fast. Nothing to be afraid of."

"Not the Big Bad . . ."

". . . Dick!"

They both laughed.

Nestling the beer bottle in the crotch of her shorts, Amy tore the remaining two sleeves of condoms apart. "One for you," she said, placing it on Amy's thigh, "and one for me. Who knows Lee, by this time tomorrow . . ."

Leanna smiled and let out a whoop, but she kept the anxiety inside. Lots of her friends were doing it, some on a regular basis. She knew her older sister Mallory used to have sex all the time with one of the AFS guys she went to Paraguay with, a guy Mallory didn't see anymore, and it wasn't the end of the world the first guy she'd done it with wasn't in the picture now. It was just sex. Still, Leanna was scared about it. But she was also determined. Like the commercials encouraged: Just do it.

Alfonso Washburn always felt a little out of place leaving Baltimore City and coming to the suburbs. Probably it was some leftover feelings from his being raised in the projects on Mulberry Street. Growing up living with his mother and aunt—father's location unknown—he imagined all the white folks thinking, wasn't that typical, poor little nigger boy being raised by mama while papa's nowhere in sight, probably in jail or busting into some good white folks' house to steal and support his heroin habit.

Alfonso still lived with that every day, out of the projects for fifteen years but not really. Even after they tore the old high rise down it remained in Alfonso's mind's eye when he drove down the block and thought how he and other kids used to climb the chain link fence that enclosed all the balconies, having no idea white people driving in and out of the city were making comments about them being just like monkeys. "Look at them little nigger kids, hon, just like little apes. Cute as hell until they get older."

Alfonso worked hard not to be bitter, and it still wasn't easy, not even now—making pretty good money as a homicide detective—because there was so much equal rights/affirmative action backlash. So much resentment of blacks supposedly getting ahead because of their being black, not qualified. Forget that Alfonso literally risked his life, getting shot twice and stabbed another time working undercover narcotics. That he made a name for himself going after kingpins, not little street hustlers. Despite all that, to some it was still because he was black that he'd been moved up to homicide. Goddamn . . . what could you do?

Alfonso drove south on I–95 out of the city. He exited onto 175 in Howard County and found the Marriott Courtyard, looking for Jimmy Griffin. Alfonso had been assigned Carla Griffin's death to verify it as a suicide.

He parked the city-issue car near the entrance and went inside, badge-identifying himself to a desk clerk. The clerk asked if he should contact hotel security. Alfonso advised that was unnecessary, he just needed Mr. Griffin's room number. The clerk obliged and Alfonso was on his way.

He strode down the carpeted hall to the stairwell and went up to the third floor two steps at a time. He emerged into another hall and began checking room numbers and was almost to Griffin's when a man called him from behind.

A very friendly tone asking, "Can I speak with you for a minute."

Alfonso turned and saw a stocky man with white hair, wearing a starched white dress shirt with french cuffs, and flashing a shield of his own. "Special Agent Ravlite. FBI. Just take a minute of your time."

Cassie and Janice were playing on the floor when Griffin got back to the hotel. Janice was reading to Cassie, who was more interested in turning—twisting, really—pages to get to the next colorful scene than in hearing the story.

Janice announced, "Here's dad."

Cassie looked up and, seeing Griffin, smiled broadly and gave out a "Yah!" She made her way to her feet, wobbled a moment, then came toward Griffin. "Yah-yah-yah!"

Griffin swept her into his arms. "You being a good girl?"

"She's perfect," Janice said, kissing Griffin on the cheek. "Just like her father."

Griffin was glad he'd left the gun in the car. Holding it and Cassie would have left him feeling anything but perfect.

"Forty-eight hours, maybe seventy-two," Agent Ravlite said. "That's all I'm asking. He shouldn't be distracted right now. Called away."

Alfonso Washburn was in a room not that far from Griffin's, hearing the Fibbies spiel. Ravlite sat comfortably at a desk, where a laptop computer was set up. A room service tray was on the floor.

Alfonso clarified, "Jimmy Grif's working for you?"

"Yes. I take it you know him. Jimmy *Grif*? Is that what you used to call him?"

"Grif, yeah, sure. Short for Griffin." As though that wasn't obvious.

"How long have you known him?"

"Long time. Going on ten years. Why?"

"Just curious," Ravlite said, sounding just so. "He seems upstanding, but any time you haven't worked with someone before, there's always a little anxiety. You worry about them being there for you in the clutch."

Washburn laughed.

Ravlite smiled. "What's so funny?"

"You worryin' about Jimmy Grif watching your back. I was him, I'd be worryin' about you, champ. You look pretty pressed and pampered to be working the streets."

"Well, looks can be deceiving."

"I guess that's true."

"My concern with your friend—is he your friend?"

"We don't socialize, but we worked together."

"My concern is that he's been involved in a shooting, killed someone, and sometimes that weighs on a man. I've seen it take many a law enforcement officer down. They don't fully recover from the trauma. They think they do, they try to play it tough, but it's a heart-wrenching act, killing another human being. And if circumstances arise again, dangerous circumstances where it might have to happen again—to kill someone—there can be a moment's hesitation, or worse. The hand holding the gun starts to shake instead of pulling the trigger."

"You don't worry about that."

"Are you sure? When's the last time you saw him? Spoke to him?"

" 'Bout a year ago, I guess."

"Before the shooting?" Ravlite almost said before the *last* shooting, which would have given away all he knew.

"Yeah, that's right."

"But you still wouldn't have any hesitation working with him?"

"Absolutely none."

"Well, that puts my mind at ease. Thanks for your time, and for agreeing to let whatever you need to speak about to Griffin—Grif—wait a few days."

"It's no problem."

"And if you happen to see him, please don't mention our conversation. I don't want him to think I was questioning his abilities."

Ravlite shook Alfonso's hand, matching strong grip for grip, and showed the city detective out.

30

Randy Arminger had to run an errand.

He left the condo around 2:00 P.M., walking with quick purpose along the sidewalk, crossing behind a row of townhouses, not looking to be elusive, just taking a shortcut. He wore a clean T-shirt, shorts, hiking boots with socks, shades, and surf-logo baseball cap, like any other college kid moving to town for the summer season.

Headed south, he strayed from the ninety-degree layout of streets and sidewalks, making his route in zigzag fashion between cottages and small motels, hurdling low fences, tramping on little lawns and patios, ducking the occasional clothesline, and smiling at girls lounging by a tiny motel pool filled with greenish water Randy wouldn't swim in on a bet.

He never looked behind him until he stepped into the super-sized hardware store, even then just giving the street a surveying glance.

"Help you?" asked an employee.

"Sure can," Randy replied, taking off his sunglasses and reciting his list from memory. "I need some two-by-fours, a hand saw, power drill with half-inch bits for wood and metal, half-inch diameter bolts about eight inches long, a hundred feet of extension cord, triple-A batteries, kerosene, bag of clean-up rags, acetylene torch, two-foot section of lead pipe, electrical tape, duct tape, and what's the biggest hot water heater you've got in stock?"

"Sounds like some project you've got going, young man."

"It's a doozy." Always ready with an endearing tale, Randy lied, "The damned place is a wreck after the winter. My parents made the mistake of renting it out. Guys made a mess of things and skipped on the last two months' rent. But at least I get to stay for free this summer while I'm fixing it up. Last summer they charged me and some buddies rent."

"Very enterprising of you. You'll save a bundle doing it yourself."

"And if you want it done right . . ." Randy said, following the helpful man down the aisles.

Except for the time he was moving the refrigerator in the handcart, Arminger always took the stairs, not just walking down from the fifth floor, but walking up as well.

And so the Angel inspected the stairwell. It was a completely enclosed concrete structure, with solid steel exit doors on each of five floors.

The Angel was coming close to the moment that defined him: the clash between good and evil in his own soul. It was only God's forgiveness of his sins, God's approval, anointing him as an angel, that kept him from going completely insane.

When Arminger drove the van from the condominium parking lot, the Angel followed him.

Arminger drove the van to the rear of the large home-center store and backed to a two-bay loading dock. He hopped down out of the driver's cab and went inside.

Within five minutes, Arminger and a store employee were loading the van with supplies, the exact nature of which the Angel couldn't determine because the van was backed so closely to the building.

After fifteen minutes, the van was loaded and Arminger pulled away, driving back to the condo, where he ran an extension cord to the building's outdoor power supply and commenced what sounded like building something inside the van. Sawing and drilling. But the rear door was pulled down so that when the Angel walked by he couldn't see in.

Phonebook opened on the bed, door closed, Griffin placed a call that a woman answered.

"Mrs. Landy?"

"Yes."

"This is James Griffin from Habitat for Humanity. I'm calling for Leanna."

"She left for the beach this morning. Is there a problem?"

"Oh, no, not at all, we've just had a schedule change and are trying to get notice to everyone. Do you know where she'll be staying? Do you have an address or phone number for her?"

"Hold on, let me get them for you." Mrs. Landy put down the phone and came back a moment later, asking, "Will they still be finished Wednesday? Leanna has to study for finals next week."

"Not a problem."

"Good." She gave Griffin the phone number and address for her daughters in Ocean City.

That call completed, Griffin dialed the FBI's Baltimore office and asked to speak with the agent in charge of the Randy Arminger case.

Janice assured Griffin she and Cassie would be fine, so Griffin packed his few remaining clean clothes into a suitcase. He kissed Cassie goodbye. Kissed Janice goodbye. Said he'd call later with the phone number of whatever motel he found, and if Liz called, to please tell her how urgent it was that she get in touch with him.

Griffin was outside, walking to his late wife's car, when he noticed someone out of the corner of his eye. Someone about to get into a familiar car: the car that had been parked at Randy Arminger's house Friday night. "Agent Ravlite?"

Ravlite looked up and appeared surprised. "Mr. Griffin, isn't it? Staying here, too? Small world."

"Actually, it's fairly large." Griffin walked to the white-haired FBI man, suitcase in hand.

Ravlite wore another seersucker suit, another long-sleeved shirt even on this warm day, french cuffs showing. He offered his hand. "How's your story going?"

"I just got off the phone with your Baltimore office. They don't know you."

"I work out of Washington."

"Can I see that shield again?"

"Sure." Very accommodating, Ravlite produced his I.D. and card, pointing out his office address. "FBI headquarters. Washington, D.C."

Griffin read aloud, "Assistant Director, VICAP."

"Violent Criminal Apprehension Program."

"I know what it means. Assistant Director?"

Ravlite put away his I.D. "Behavioral scientist, actually."

"So your interest in Randy Arminger is—?"

"Very high."

"I was going to say academic."

"*You* could say."

Griffin considered this. "Any whereabouts on him? Arminger?"

"I was about to ask you the same."

"He might be in Ocean City. There's a girl he goes to school with, Leanna Landy, who's on her way down there. Should be there in an hour or so. Arminger might have reason to make her his next target. I tried to get word to McGovern, the special agent in charge, but he's out in the field. I left a message. I'll try him later, but maybe you could get word to him as well."

"Sure," Ravlite responded, then considered, "Ocean City . . ." He gestured to the suitcase. "Is that where you're off to?"

"Yeah."

"Go where the story takes you."

"Right."

Ravlite gestured to his business card, which Griffin held in his hand. "May I?"

Griffin handed it back, and Ravlite added a phone number, writing with a polished gold pen. "My cellular," he explained. "Let me know how it goes."

"All right." Griffin put the card in his jeans pocket, turned to walk away, offering, "Talk to you later, then."

Ravlite checked his watch, the face of which was inlaid with mother of pearl. When Griffin was two paces away, Ravlite said, "I'm very sorry about your wife."

Griffin stopped, unsure how Ravlite knew about that or if it mattered. "We were separated."

"I know. Still, it's tragic."

"Yes . . . yes it is." Griffin squinted against sunlight

that shone behind Ravlite. "She suffered from depression for a long time."

Ravlite opened his car door. "It's a terrible disease." Got in the sedan. "Again, though, my sympathies. For you and your daughter." Ravlite closed the door and started the engine.

Griffin stared at him, wondering how Ravlite knew so much about him and trying not to be unsettled about it.

Ravlite pulled from the parking space, waved goodbye, and drove off.

"Leanna's here!" One of Mallory Landy's friends shouted inside through the screen door.

Another girl, slouched on the broken down living room sofa watching *Jenny Jones,* relayed down the hall, "Hey, Mal, Superbrain's here."

Mallory Landy came out of the bedroom in her new bathing suit. Having just finished lunch ten minutes earlier, she was set to get in another hour or two of sun. She slapped the foot of her sofa-slouching compatriot. "Be nice to my baby sister."

"Yeah, right."

Mallory opened the screen door to the second-floor balcony and screamed, "Leanna! Yah!"

Leanna screamed back, "Mallory! Yah!"

The girl on the porch covered her ears, laughing, "It's so obnoxious when you two do that."

Mallory went down wood steps, peeling paint coming loose under her bare feet. "Leanna!"

"Mallory!" Leanna opened her arms for what they called their mock-Hollywood sister hug, a satire gesture of sicky-sweetness. Hugs followed by faked cheek kisses, delivered with a chorus of "Mmm-mmm-mmm."

Mallory smiled as she whispered in her sister's ear, "Who said you could bring Amy?"

"She's my friend," Leanna whispered back, between mmm-mmm-mmm kisses.

Mallory warned, "The alkie pukes, you clean it up."

Amy, getting her backpack of bottles out of the car, greeted, "Hi, guys. I got beer." Expectant of accolades.

"Yes, you do," Mallory said coolly. She and Leanna went up to the second floor of the four-unit apartment house.

Leanna asked, "So how's the place?"

"A dump but fabulous, because . . ."

"No mom and dad," the sisters said in unison.

Leanna was flying high, her first unsupervised trip away from the 'rents. "This is going to be great."

T-shirt striped off, Randy Arminger was sweating fiercely by the time he stood back to admire his handiwork. It may not have been as efficiently built as could have been done by those brain-defunct losers who spent half their high school day at vo-tech, but it was definitely going to do the job.

Everything was coming together so nicely. And the concept of utilizing the van this way hadn't occurred to him until he'd needed to dump chubby-thighed Holly at the landfill. There was so much less exposure this way. Like the old traveling preachers used to say, *If you can't get people to the altar, take the altar to the people.*

The Angel was growing anxious. Arminger was very active today, moving about in mysterious ways as though planning something imminent.

Now, just after 5:00 P.M., he was settled in the condominium and had been for almost an hour.

Dressed in khaki workman's pants, a white T-shirt, and well-worn work boots, the Angel left his motel room. His T-shirt was oversized on his taut frame, allowing for the belt holster to conceal the .22 caliber handgun under his untucked shirttail.

The .22 was his weapon of preference for shootings conducted in more populated areas; the sound was more of a crack, and it lacked the deep resonance of higher-powered explosions of gunpowder that could reverberate in your chest. Three quick shots of the .22 at close range—where the Angel worked—sounded like firecrackers, or the little snap caps kids flicked onto the sidewalk. And three shots would do damage. Unlike larger caliber bullets, a .22 didn't necessary shoot straight through its target but could deflect off bone and bounce around inside the body. Especially for headshots. The .22 would pierce the back of the skull but not necessarily come out the front.

On the outdoor walkway of his motel, the Angel kept watch, wary of Arminger's sudden reappearance.

People were leaving the beach, coming across the snow-fence-barricaded path through dunes planted with sea grass. They carried umbrellas, coolers, and blankets. Beyond the dunes, a lifeguard whistled swimmers in from deep water. Two blocks south, an ice cream truck played its monotonous jingle, a tune the Angel had quickly grown to despise.

The Angel made his way down the final stairs to the parking lot, where the worn soles of his boots kicked loose pebbles. He stuffed his hands in his pockets, trying to look casual but knowing he stood out here, as he stood out many places. Even at his age, there was an intensity about him people noticed. He tried to avoid their eyes, but could feel them looking at him.

His brown and gray hair was tied back in a thick ponytail, his beard untrimmed, his color surprisingly pale for such leathery skin. His look was more appropriate to the isolated cabin where he spent most of his time.

With full faith in his purpose, the Angel walked to the rear of Arminger's van. He glanced up to the fifth floor of the building, where white stucco was washed with the orange sunlight of late afternoon. The boy was not in sight, so the Angel tried the lever that sprang the van's rear door. Locked.

The Angel didn't linger. He moved on, walking toward the enclosed stairwell the boy always used. As he entered it, the ground-floor door snapped closed behind him. He started up the stairs that turned at every landing between floors.

Each landing had a trash chute, and the chute doors were not a snug fit, allowing the stale, wet smell of garbage to permeate the concrete walls.

When he was between the second and third floors, the Angel heard a door open above him. Someone came in, whistling. The step was quick upon the stairs, just as Arminger's gait had been swift today.

The Angel breathed steadily. The whistler had already descended a single flight of stairs, hand skimming the metal railing, rubber soled shoes squeaking as he turned at the landing.

The Angel slipped a hand inside his shirt onto cool gun metal. If it was Arminger, he would shoot him—not a fatal shot but a wounding one. Then give the boy a chance to ask forgiveness. One chance. And then, no matter what his answer, he would drill three shots into his head.

Such powerful feelings when the kill time arrived. His calm thoughtfulness was often swept into a rush of urgency. A certain taste in his mouth. A taste he used to associate with the crude violence of hunting and killing until God told him it was the sweetness of redemption.

The whistler was closer. On the floor above him. The Angel glanced up between the narrow gap of poured concrete steps. He saw a hand on the railing, someone wearing a shirt and shorts. Arminger.

The Angel slid the gun from his holster and held it concealed in his pants' baggy pocket. He started up the stairs again. They were just steps away. The Angel visualized it: he'd see the boy, perhaps smile, but wouldn't meet his eyes, then, one step past him, gun out, turn, fire, shoot him in the lower back, and if the shot didn't drop him, shoot him again. It wouldn't matter if he screamed or cried for help. It would all end quickly.

The Angel came to the landing and the whistler was there, too. The Angel saw him. Yes! Arminger was right there, passing beside him *now,* wearing earplugs hooked to a CD player, jerking with surprise at the sight of the Angel because he hadn't heard him. Had likely been so intent on his own thoughts they'd nearly collided. But Arminger politely moved to the outside of the stairs, gave a brief smile, and continued down the stairs.

The Angel started to bring out the gun, only the stairwell door opened right beside him. A middle-aged woman struggled to turn the knob with one hand while carrying a soggy grocery bag stuffed with trash in the other. The woman muttered, "Oh, hell," as liquid seeping through the bag ran down her leg.

The Angel stuffed his hand and the gun deep into his pocket and continued up the stairs.

Arminger came back up the steps two at a time, taking the trash bag from the woman, offering, "Here, let me get that." He put it down the garbage chute for her.

The woman thought, what a nice young man, and good-looking. Why couldn't more college-aged boys be like him instead of the drug-using, beer-bottle-bashing rowdies who rented the ramshackle cottage across the street?

As the elevator door closed, the Angel took a deep breath. He closed his eyes, reliving how he'd been that close. Within inches of taking Arminger's life until the woman opened the door. Why? If this was his mission, why was it being made so difficult?

Was that light—God's presence—that he felt growing ever weaker and more distant, providing less guidance? In moments when the Angel felt so alone, he could only summon his faith and move forward. If he was meant to carry this burden alone, he would do so, though his prayers for God to help him lasted longer each day. This was such a difficult task to perform without help. So much unpunished evil to sentence.

Without his pushing a button, the elevator began to move downward, called by laughing children in wet bathing suits who'd just come back from the beach.

On the ground floor, the doors opened and the children started to pile in, then pulled back, a bit wary of him.

"Hello," he greeted, friendly and calm.

"Hi," one of the three managed to reply. The children smelled the earthy scent of him spawned by adrenalin and perspiration.

The Angel started across the parking lot, then stopped, realizing: the boy was gone. The van was still there, but Arminger had driven off in his car. And the Angel knew not where he'd gone.

31

Randy Arminger drove slowly past the little apartment house, checking the second-floor unit on the right. A few colorful towels were tossed over the wood railing. Someone on a lounge chair read a magazine, plugged into her Walkman, but a blond, not Leanna.

Leanna was here now, though, he knew it, because there was her father's car, parked right in front. He popped out his CD/police-band-tuned earplugs and heard music pumping out of the second-floor unit. Girls laughing.

He drove down the block, hung a U-turn, and came back just as the apartment's screen door banged open and out came Mallory Landy. Oh, and look at that bikini. Definitely no mom and dad seal of approval on how much cute ass was showing out of that suit. And behind Mallory, looking not nearly as hot, tanned, or curvy, was the lying, manipulative bitch herself. The pesky fly. Leanna. Wearing a yawn of a two-piece no self-respecting guy would give a second look. With big sis, Leanna tried to act hip, but she was nowhere so cool as Mallory.

Randy thought, Welcome to the beach, fly. Tonight we party.

* * *

Randy Arminger returned to the condo by bus.

Ocean City's Coastal Highway and other larger side roads were serviced by pollution-belching city buses just like downtown Baltimore. The big, hulking, lane-hogging chunks of metal looked as un-beach as it got, but with the highway already at maximum width, and evening traffic often bumper to bumper from Seventy-third Street to the inlet, there was a need to reduce the congestion no matter how vile the solution.

Leaving the bus, Randy walked quickly along the sidewalk, angling across the street to his building. He opened the stairwell door and started up the steps two at a time.

The boy was back. But where was his car? The Angel watched Arminger cross the side street, surprised to see him on foot. What had he done with the car?

He watched Arminger enter the stairwell and regretted not being there to greet him, kill him. But the Angel felt that element of surprise was gone now. Arminger had seen his face once, and that made a difference. Besides, not knowing when—even if—the boy would return had made it implausible to stake out the stairs.

Yet as anxious as the Angel felt, there was also relief because Arminger had come back so soon. Not enough time for him to cause more mayhem.

The end was coming.

The Ocean City skyline appeared to Griffin shortly before dusk.

The last of the deep-sea fishing charters returned to inlet marinas over which sea gulls hovered lazily.

Beyond the calm bay, low buildings cut a silhouette across a watercolor sky lit with neon reflections from the arcades and thrill rides of the boardwalk.

Griffin knew the town, having spent many summers there from the time he was a kid until a few years ago. It was hard to imagine it was the same place.

When Griffin was a boy, the tallest building was five levels high, and there were only a handful of them. The early seventies real estate boom took care of that, and high rises appeared at an alarming rate. The maintenance man at the motel where Griffin's family stayed every summer said he was moving off the island for fear it was going to sink.

The town didn't sink, but real estate prices did, boom turning to bust in the mid-seventies. The high rises came far and few between after that, but they were now threatening to start up again. Older motels on the boardwalk were falling to the wrecking ball to make way for monstrosities that would shade the beach from sun by mid-afternoon.

In early June, the island was full of kids on their own—Senior Week seeming to last longer every season—which made it a great place for someone Randy's age to hide, blend in. Everyone was loose, having fun, slacking, not looking for fugitives.

Griffin pulled into a convenience-store parking lot and used the outdoor pay phone to dial Ravlite's cell phone.

Across the street, parents played putt-putt golf with their kids, looking to win free games by putting a colorful ball into a clown's mouth.

Ravlite answered on the third ring.

"James Griffin."

"Jimmy Grif, how are you?"

"In Ocean City," Griffin replied, wondering where Ravlite got the Jimmy Grif moniker—what friends on the city police force used to call him.

"You find Arminger?"

"No. Did you talk to McGovern? I was thinking if you could get an agent to watch this girl—I know you've got a Salisbury office—"

"McGovern's not too enthused about your theory, especially in lieu of some breaking activity up here."

"Dammit—what?" Griffin was upset at the prospect of having driven three hours for nothing.

"Another former teacher of Arminger's: she received a box from Federal Express today that contained some very risqué lingerie."

"Nancy Marler," Griffin said, more to himself than Ravlite.

"Yes. Do you know her?"

"Interviewed her Saturday." Griffin banged the plexiglass side of the wall phone frame. "Dammit."

"The lingerie was direct-shipped from Frederick's of Hollywood. An order placed through an Internet shopping source yesterday that requested overnight delivery. McGovern's running the credit card information on the purchaser, but all indications are it was Randy Arminger using an alias. The gift note said, 'Wear this tonight for me.' Apparently Arminger has sent her this sort of thing in the past, which was news to us. At any rate, manpower's being directed toward the teacher."

"No, no, no, wait," Griffin said, analyzing the development. "He's never warned anybody else, he just showed up and killed them. And he's got no reason to kill her."

"No? She didn't reject him?"

"I don't think it was a matter of rejection, or love, or a

crush, I think it was sadism. He liked manipulating and scaring her."

"Sounds like you're getting to know him pretty well."

"Maybe I do, maybe I don't. Maybe Arminger's halfway around the world. Who the hell knows? But something's going to happen soon, and it might happen to this girl down here."

"You say something's going to happen soon?"

"Yes."

"Another theory?"

"No. Arminger told me."

"When?" Ravlite sounded excited.

"Earlier today. On the Internet. We had a chat."

"Fantastic. I'll tell McGovern."

"Get an agent down here, Ravlite. Your Salisbury office's half an hour away."

"Keep in touch."

"Hey, wait a minute. Don't—" Griffin looked at the phone. "—hang up." But Ravlite was gone. Griffin slammed the receiver into its cradle. "Goddamned feds."

Randy Arminger was packing up his computers and readying a few other little gizmos he'd worked on this afternoon. He checked the length of iron pipe and found the cement mix hardening nicely inside its tube. He had his duct tape. The kerosene was already in the van, along with the acetylene torch.

Randy was starting to feel a little concerned about the details—keeping them straight, not wanting to forget anything, because unlike the other night, this hadn't been so long in the planning that he'd had the chance to live it out in his mind before actually doing it. Thursday night had been more of an exam. This was along the lines of a pop quiz. Still, a little Cram would do wonders for keeping him focused. He tore off a square and did a hit that would keep him going all wild night long.

At Mackey's open-air restaurant on the bay, dinner and bar patrons sang a rowdy though respectful rendition of "God Bless America" as the sun dropped slowly behind the tree line on the other side of Isle of Wight Bay. The end of another day. Start of another night, and as wonderful as Ocean City was while the sun was up, the town could really come undone under the moon.

Not far from Mackey's, the Angel left his motel room with no plans to return.

32

Arminger had come out to the van twice now. The first time, getting to the driver's side door and reaching into his pocket, he realized he didn't have his keys. He seemed to have cursed under his breath before returning to the building, going up the stairs.

He came down a second time. Had his keys, but was no sooner behind the wheel of the van, turning over the engine, than he shut it off.

Again, he appeared to curse his memory, as though he'd forgotten something else. Arminger exited the van and went back up the stairwell again, slamming the ground-floor door. Impatient with himself, it seemed.

He would come out of the condominium again soon, was the Angel's appraisal. Back down the stairs. And the Angel would be waiting for him.

This one had been maddening. Luck and timing were often factors, but the sheer energy level of the boy, all the coming and going, was making the Angel anxious to get it done.

Randy Arminger's heart was beating strongly after two trips up and down the stairs, and about to take a third trip down. He was all set now. Going over the plan again in his mind as he turned the doorknob and went into the stairwell. His thoughts were fine-tuned on Cram, but he wished he was plugged into his CD player, wanting that soundtrack pounding in his ears.

He started down the steps quickly, almost at a run.

The boy was coming, sounding to be skipping down the stairs. Not whistling this time but breathing audibly. Shoes squeaking as he turned at each landing.

The Angel wedged a triangular block of wood along the bottom edge of the ground-floor door so no one would be able to enter from outside. A precaution.

He took the gun from his pocket. As soon as Arminger came face to face with him, the Angel would shoot. Not a fatal shot, not at first, for there had to be chance for redemption.

The Angel waited just inside the ground-floor door. He'd shoot the boy on the landing.

The Angel glanced up the narrow gap between the stairs, seeing Arminger almost down to the third floor.

Waiting.

A door opened. A door?

Suddenly, there were no more footsteps. The stairwell was quiet. The door that was opened drew closed on its mechanism.

The Angel glanced up between the stairs. What happened? Where had he gone? Had Arminger gone onto the third floor walkway? Why?

The Angel started up the stairs, listening, expecting him to come back into the stairwell, but he didn't. The Angel went up the steps quietly, the gun still out.

He reached the third floor and listened. The stairwell remained quiet.

He opened the door to the third floor. The carpeted

walkway was lit by floodlights mounted in corner roof eaves and light fixtures on the stucco walls.

Arminger wasn't there.

The Angel slipped the gun into his pocket and stepped out of the stairwell. He looked over the railing down to the parking lot.

The van was still there, its lights off. No one was crossing the parking lot. Where was he?

The Angel retreated to the stairwell and started urgently back down the steps. He had to get to a spot from which to watch the building again. Find Arminger. Start over. *Damn him!*

The Angel's breathing came harshly. He felt himself fighting fatigue. His heartbeat seemed too fast, not the steady, strong pulse of years past. A brief moment of lightheadedness came and went. He had to ignore it.

At the ground floor he tugged on the door handle, forgetting the triangle of wood he'd used to wedge it shut. He bent down, feeling a twinge in his lower back as he grabbed for the door stop. Old age was gnawing at his spine. He threw aside the wedge and was moving to stand upright when he gasped with surprise.

Someone was behind him! The Angel turned quickly.

Arminger—his arm raised above his head, holding something—letting out a menacing grunt as he moved to strike.

The Angel raised his arm to deflect the blow. A hard, dense object struck his elbow, shattering it. The Angel was about to cry out when Arminger struck swiftly again. A length of iron pipe filled with concrete crashed against the back of his head.

The Angel felt as though he were falling forever, twisting round and round, spiraling ever deeper into darkness. The heat of his blood was all over his head, his face, his eyes. Angel blood being spilled. The devils had invaded heaven.

Randy was exhilarated, working quickly, efficiently. The Cram running through his system had his senses on ultimate superdo edge. The adrenalin rush from violence burned in even deeper, like staring into the hot sun with dilated pupils. Flash bursts charged through him as though injected sweetly by syringe.

Randy went to the van, opened the back door, lowered the ramp, and went inside the trailer for the handcart and large, sturdy box the 120–gallon hot water heater had been in. The box was now empty; Randy set it on the handcart and wheeled it to the stairwell, where the bearded man lay unconscious and bleeding under a section of stairs.

Randy positioned the box against the concrete wall and opened the front flap he'd razor-cut to take out the water heater hours earlier. The box was manufactured with a cardboard "skin" around a frame of one-by-two slats of wood and maintained its size with the one side dropped open.

Randy grabbed under the man's arms—the man he'd seen following him—and hefted him to his feet. The man's 175 pounds gave little strain to Randy's muscles. Randy hauled him upright into the box and let him drop. The man's knees cracked hard against the floor, his feet pushing against one side of the box as his bloodied, battered head and shoulders fell against the other.

Randy raised the lowered flap of the box and whipped it shut with duct tape. He was reaching for the handcart when he realized he had blood all over the front of his shirt and on his hands.

He took off his baseball cap and pulled his shirt off,

wiping his hands clean on it and throwing it under the stairs. Cap back on, he slid the base of the handcart under the box.

He backed toward the door, opened it, got his leg in place to hold the door open and shuttled the big box out of the stairwell.

He wheeled his freight across the parking lot, having to keep the cart tilted back so the man's weight leaned into him, not side to side, which would wobble the box off the handcart.

With a slight running start, Randy started the ramp into the van, but the angle was too steep, the box too heavy. He was within a foot of the trailer bed but couldn't get it all the way in when a car pulled into the parking lot.

Randy glanced around, feeling a twinge of panic. On the side street, a handholding couple walked toward the beach for a moonlit stroll. Witnesses, dammit!

But they didn't seem to take note of him. Randy kept in mind their perspective: he likely seemed no more than a shirtless worker hauling a hot water heater. The brand name of the heater was right there on the side of the box. Why would anyone suspect it to contain anything else?

The car that had driven into the lot pulled into a parking space within fifty feet of the van. Four people got out: mom, dad, and two pre-school-age kids. The kids ran toward the building. Mom shouted warning about watching for cars. Dad slunked behind, looking beat, too much of his day having been spent drooling over young girls in bikinis he couldn't do anything about because he had to trail after his kids, throw money after them while mom tried to get a little suntan on her cellulite and varicose veins. That's how Randy saw them, anyway, thinking it pathetic. All this parent-kid stuff these days, parents fooled thinking how wonderful and important and blessed their kids were. Sanctimonious bullshit!

Randy backed down the ramp and turned the handcart around. The man shifted position inside the box and groaned, but the sound was easily covered by the handcart's squeaky wheels.

Randy took a deep breath and started up the ramp again, this time pulling the handcart after him. He jerked his boxed victim the final eighteen inches and wheeled him to the center of the trailer.

Randy pulled in the ramp, sliding it into place under the floor bed. He lowered the back door and turned on the camping-style flashlight.

Stark illumination shone across the box and threw a long angled shadow along the inner walls of the van. Blue tarpaulins covered the two large objects Randy had built.

Randy went at the box with the razor knife, slashing through the duct tape until the front flap fell open. He reached in and grabbed the man by the bloody collar of his shirt.

The man's blood was sticky as it began to congeal. His one arm was twisted horribly from where Randy had shattered bone with the iron pipe.

The man groaned, barely conscious. Randy silenced him with a strap of duct tape drawn tightly across his opened mouth, wrapping the man's head with tape; three, four, five revolutions of tape into his mouth and behind his head, the tape pulling the man's long, gray-brown hair.

Randy stared at the man, and when the man wouldn't or couldn't open his eyes, Randy put his thumb on his eyelid and drew it wide open, shining the flashlight inches from his face, Randy breathing sharply, smirked, "Could it be . . . ? I think maybe it is. Maybe you *are*. Who else knows I'm here?" Randy's eyes were inches from the man's face. "It never dawned on you, not once, that I *wanted* you to find me."

The Angel suffered excruciating pain and shock. In and out of consciousness. Something was very wrong with his head, as though a chunk of it had been broken off. His concentration was frazzled by what seemed like jolting spikes of electricity. His arm felt snapped in two. He was cold, about to shiver, when he saw the bright light and believed he was in heaven. He expected the pain to stop and the cold shock to be washed away with quiet warmth.

Someone touched his hand and the Angel anticipated comfort, but his broken arm was wrenched horrendously. The Angel screamed, or tried to, but his mouth was immobilized. His jaws were held open by something that completely sealed his mouth. His tortured groan howled no further than his throat before he blacked out again.

When the Angel next came to, vague impressions of motion reverberated the daggers of agony that stuck deeply inside him. His body was vibrating.

Though he was enclosed by darkness, he sensed from how his head dangled uselessly on his neck that he was upright and somehow held in that position. His legs were immobilized at the ankles. Yet the soles of his feet weren't pressing against anything. So how could he be upright?

His broken arm was outstretched, both wrists grasped, but not by another hand. He tried desperately to fend off the pain, to concentrate on what was happening to him.

Searing agony refused to release him for longer than quick blips of thought, allowing him outside of his body for seconds at a time before pulling him back into its wracked grasp.

He heard an engine . . . felt wheels turning under him . . . remembered the boy . . . the van. Arminger had been building something inside the back of the van . . . that's where the Angel was now. Arminger had captured him . . . lain in wait . . . oh, God . . . he'd been trapped . . . the arrogant, insane boy had trapped him! The Angel realized that now.

In the moments of thought his shattered mind allowed, these realizations came to him, as did the full sense of the position of his body. A realization that had the Angel screaming silently into the tape that bound his mouth. He was upright, his arms outstretched, his legs tied together at the ankles, his feet off the ground. Arminger had affixed him to a cross. That's what he'd built in the back of the van. A cross.

33

"Is Cassie doing okay?" Griffin asked, calling Janice from a pay phone.

"Perfect," Janice replied, her voice reassuring, leaving no doubt Cassie was just that: perfect.

"I really appreciate—"

"Stop worrying, okay? I'm happy to do this. I'm *really* happy." Janice sweetly enunciated that point, speaking in a manner Griffin was beginning to realize meant she was telling him more than the mere words she spoke.

Griffin wondered if he hadn't recognized just how strongly his own feelings may have been for her because of the circumstances under which they'd met. Along with the age difference. Lifestyle differences. But he'd been thinking about her differently since the other morning, admitting to himself—and not without guilt—his attraction toward her. At the same time his relationship with Liz complicated his emotions.

Griffin leaned an arm against the pay-phone ledge, watching the apartment house where Leanna Landy was staying with a group of other girls. Lights were on inside the apartment, and he could see four of them moving around, Leanna included. Windows were open and music that he could hear a hundred yards away was blaring.

Janice assured, "We're fine here, Jimmy. You do what you have to do." It was almost an order of understanding.

"I'm not sure I'll check into a motel. I'll probably sleep in the car so I can stay close to the girl."

"Okay." Again, her response was not just a reply but an echo of agreement that he was doing the right thing.

"Did you hear from Liz?"

"No. Nothing. But I'm sure she's okay." Unlike Liz, there was no animosity in Janice's voice when talking about the other woman in Griffin's life.

How could Janice seem so sheltered and naive yet appear so knowing? Perhaps faith was a wonderful, necessary element to a peaceful, pure life.

Griffin wouldn't know.

"I'll call you in the morning."

"Whenever you get the chance. Stop worrying, honey. Everything's fine here."

"Okay. Thanks."

"Jim . . ."

"Yeah?"

"Be careful." As though she knew something was going to happen.

A hundred yards away, the apartment door opened; Leanna and her friends piled down the steps. The girls were whooping it up, wearing splashy print sundresses with pleated skirts. Four of them were outfitted similarly, almost as if in uniform. One girl drank beer from a bottle.

Griffin told Janice, "I'll be careful." He was putting down the phone when he heard Janice say quietly:

"Love you."

* * *

Leanna expected her sister to be right behind her, but Mallory was headed in the opposite direction with her friend. Leanna called, "You're not coming with us?"

"No way, chickie. Bev's got the Miata."

"Oh, cool. Can we get in with you?"

"Sorry," Mallory sang, boy-catching-cute in her sundress. "Not this time. See you at Wild Whales." Mallory cast a quick glance at Leanna's friend, Amy, the unspoken comment being if Leanna hadn't brought along the drunk . . .

Leanna was having second thoughts about Amy as well. Mallory's friends had been cutting on her all day and dissing Leanna about her, too. Amy was so used to rejection from her parents, she took the razzing as good-natured sisterly fun, while Leanna was frustrated by her friend's drinking, which had been almost non-stop.

Amy had gone through the six beers in her backpack, then gotten another six-pack on her fake I.D. at the 7-Eleven and polished that off, too. The scariest part was she hadn't started showing signs of all the drinking until two beers ago. Talk about Tolerance City.

Now, Amy was having trouble walking a straight line to the car. A shoulder strap to her sundress slipped down and she didn't realize it.

Leanna fixed that as they got into the Acura.

Amy replied, "You're just making more work for some hunk to get me out of this dress."

"Don't talk like that," Leanna snapped, tired of Amy's incessant sex talk.

"You're just jealous 'cause I did Billy Taylor last night."

"No. No, I'm not. Not at all." Leanna started her

father's car. So far, this trip to the beach wasn't turning out the way she'd hoped.

"First good-looking guy I see," Amy announced, "I'm going for him."

Leanna thought, Good for you, go home with him so I won't have to worry with you. She backed the car off the stone parking pad and drove to catch up to Mallory and Bev in the Miata.

The other two girls rode with the top down, hair blowing in the breeze.

Leanna was envious of Mallory's looks and how she fit in with the crowd. Guys were crazy about Mallory, and great guys, too, not the thieves and druggies like Billy Taylor that Amy hung with.

As they neared the intersection, Amy grabbed Leanna's arm, causing her to jerk the car to the right. "Stop here, stop here! I wanna get some more Sam Adams."

Leanna shook Amy's grip from her elbow. "God, Amy. They've got beer at the bar." Leanna looked up, saw the light had gone red and slammed on the brakes.

Amy, not wearing a seat belt, jerked forward into the dash and jarred her wrist against it, yelping "Ow!" then started laughing. "Nice driving, Lee. Think it's time for a driver's ed refresher course."

"Shut up." Leanna watched her sister and Bev speed up the highway, looking so cool in that little sports car. Guys beeped their horns and flashed headlights, and Leanna was stuck here with the drunk.

When the light changed green, she peeled through the intersection.

Amy whooped, "Go girl, go!" Rolling down her window, she shouted, "Here comes Speed Racer!"

Leanna wanted to get to the bar, which she hoped was

crowded enough so she could ditch Amy and be with Mallory and her friends. Try to act like Mallory, learn from her. Maybe loosen up a little like Mallory always encouraged. Stop being such a straight-A anxiety attack.

Mallory didn't understand that the same competitiveness she experienced on the volleyball court or lacrosse field—wanting to be the absolute best—was what Leanna felt in class. And the lacrosse season was two and a half months, same for volleyball. Making straight A's was year-'round, full-time work. There was no off-season, not even in the summer, which was spent reading and studying, and doing more SAT prep.

Mallory might be able to ride her athletic scholarship to a great school, but to make Ivy League Leanna would need perfect grades, perfect SATs, and tons of extracurricular activities. There were articles all the time in newspapers and magazines about the great universities being harder and harder to get into, turning down students who would have been easy admissions years ago.

Leanna was in serious competition with the likes of Randy Arminger and his crowd. Leanna was as envious of Randy as she was of Mallory—success came so easily to them and was such hard work for her. At least she wouldn't have Randy Arminger to worry about anymore.

Leanna sped through a light as it clicked red. Competitiveness charged through her, filling her with the urge to catch Mallory and Bev in the Miata, pass them, beat them to the bar.

The girl drove the Acura crazily, cutting in and out of lanes, going through a red light.

Griffin winced, anticipating a possible accident, but Leanna cleared the intersection. And she wasn't even the last vehicle to ignore the signal. Some maniac in a small moving van—Griffin couldn't see his face—cut into the bus lane and blew through the light without even touching his brakes.

34

Griffin knew the name of the bar one of the other girls had called out to Leanna—Wild Whales—so he didn't have to worry about keeping up with her in traffic.

Ten years and numerous liquor law violations earlier, the bar had been called Beach Babes, then Bikini Bombers, now Wild Whales, giving cause for wonder if there was some requirement that all tenants use repetitive initials to name their business.

Wild Whales was a shopping center bar, occupying the corner unit of a strip center on Coastal Highway. The front lot was jammed full of college-kid cars, from rust-and-dent junkers to sleek two-seaters.

Griffin pulled down the side street and parked the Honda beside a chain fence that lined a thousand yards of manmade canal. Leanna Landy had gotten a better parking space on the other side of the street and was already inside the bar.

Like the parking lot, Wild Whales was packed.

The front door was open, allowing DJ-spun alternative rock to blast out into the night. A bouncer worked the entrance, perched on a stool in thigh-hugging jeans and a sleeveless denim jacket that showed massive biceps. He checked I.D.'s and collected a two-dollar cover.

Griffin walked up, bypassing three young guys being screened by the bouncer. He handed the bouncer a five and got a nod inside while the big man spun one of the kid's very bad and bogus I.D.'s across the parking lot.

The kid protested, "Hey man, what're you doin! That's legit. You can't do that." He was yelling but backing away and growing braver the further from arm's reach he got. "I'll sue your ass."

Griffin went inside, and was immediately shoulder to shoulder with college kids who crowded the left half of the long and narrow hangout. They drank bottled beers and shouted happy conversation. A four-bartender bar lined most of the right wall, with the back section of Wild Whales set up to handle the DJ and a cramped dance floor.

Leanna and her three friends had made their way halfway to the dance floor and were presently stalking a good-looking trio of college guys, business major types with "pre-banker" haircuts and prestige-logo shirts.

Griffin leaned back against the window wall and watched. The group's body language indicated a certain jockeying for position, like thoroughbreds rounding the clubhouse turn and heading down the stretch.

All three guys paid most attention to the best-looking girl, Mallory. Leanna was forcing it, trying to belong, and it was an awkward fit, just as she didn't look quite right in that dress, the way it hung on her slender frame. Griffin was unsure if the garment was simply the wrong size or if her discomfort in wearing it made for a gangly appearance.

While not stunning, Mallory had a certain natural flair

that intensified her attractiveness, and she moved with an athletic grace. Leanna more resembled a baby giraffe still unsure of her legs.

Mallory took a liking to one of the guys, touching his arm as she laughed at something he said. One of the other guys immediately went for Mallory's blond friend, Bev. The third guy stayed in the contest for Mallory only to soon find himself aiming for the second runner-up: Amy, another blond, who was obviously drunk.

Which left Leanna as the odd one out. She kept trying to blend into the conversation, but the others formed a standing circle that blocked her out. Mallory and her new friend hit the dance floor. Bev and her impromptu date elbowed their way to the bar for strawberry daiquiris. Amy was simply hanging all over the guy she'd met, and the guy suddenly didn't think she was that bad, especially the way her shoulder strap dropped down and she didn't seem too intent on fixing it.

As though watching water drain out of a tub, Leanna was suddenly alone in a crowd of people, looking anxiously for the good time she thought would surely be here.

Griffin felt badly for her. She didn't know where to go: the bar for a drink; the perimeter of the dance floor, move a little and hope someone asked her to dance; or saunter toward the small group of younger guys and girls beside Griffin, wondering if she could introduce herself. The situation was a multiple-choice question and the right answer wasn't one of the options; she had to choose the best *wrong* answer.

Meanwhile, Mallory was into a second dance, Bev enjoyed a strawberry daiquiri, and Amy—well, where the hell had she gone? Griffin kept casual check on the whole group, though he was mainly concerned with Leanna.

Amy suddenly reappeared through a forest of bodies, leading her boyfriend by the hand to Leanna. Griffin thought they were going to include her, then Amy stuck out her hand and said something at which Leanna smirked. Leanna shook her head no, and Amy responded with a come-on-lighten-up look, so Leanna went into her little satchel purse and gave Amy the car keys with a warning of some kind.

Griffin watched Amy—God save her—as she and her date went out the side exit-only door and crossed the street to the Acura. The guy had his arm around her. She leaned against him while searching through Leanna's keys, trying two before one fit the passenger door.

The guy looked around, checking out the street for conspicuousness, likely deciding it was worth the risk, because he and Leanna got in the back seat and fell into almost instant embrace.

Griffin could make out the silhouettes of their heads as they kissed a while, then the guy leaned back, one hand on Amy's head, urging her down to his lap. She didn't object to the invitation.

Griffin thought this was a strange generation; faced with more deadly perils and risks than any other group in recent history, they seemed intent on ignoring the odds and going for the very immediate moment in terms of pleasure, while also being intensely concerned about their futures.

Maybe it was simple cause and effect, that worrying about their future—what the world was going to be like by the time they reached fifty—was what made them live for the moment. Not that any generation hadn't done that to some extent, but the results were getting exponentially wilder.

Wilder. Sure, why not? In a bar called Wild Whales, where the logo was a seafaring whale named Spermy equipped with impressively sized goods, the kind of bold mascot designed to offend those over forty and keep them out.

Griffin peered not that many years into the future and pictured Cassie in a place like this. She'd want to go, and he'd have to make the decision whether or not to let her. Or maybe it wouldn't be his decision. Maybe she'd just go.

He was worrying about that when there was a sudden motion inside the Acura. Amy's date jerked about, arms pushing away the girl as he scrambled out of the car, pulling up his pants.

Kids on the street noticed and started pointing and laughing.

The front of the guy's pants were wet, smeared with something. He flicked his hands, looking to dry them somewhere. He still wasn't quite back into his pants and didn't know what to do about it. He finally pulled off his shirt, cleaned himself with it, then came into the bar. He didn't get far when people started making noise about the smell.

The guy shouted, "Danny, Danny, get over here, man!"

The bouncer was hauling the smelly, shirtless guy back outside.

The guy shouted angrily, "She barfed on me, man! Look at this! She puked all over me!"

Kids waving hands in front of their faces laughed hysterically and applauded the bouncer for getting the guy outside.

Griffin looked across the street and saw Leanna hurrying to the car and her friend, having gone out the side door. Griffin made his way through bodies to follow her. He was about thirty feet from the door when he got a profile glimpse of a young guy also going toward the exit.

The guy had on a baseball cap and wraparound sunglasses. A way to be cool—sunglasses at night—but it was also a way to hide his face. He wore an untucked button-down shirt and jeans, dock shoes.

The guy went out the door, and Griffin pushed his way after him.

When Griffin reached the door, Baseball Cap was already on the street.

Leanna was at the opened back door to the Acura, kneeling down, talking to Amy.

Baseball Cap didn't appear to be looking toward Leanna. He was walking down the street, away from her.

Positioned behind him, Griffin couldn't see his face.

Baseball Cap had a purpose to his walk, as if he wanted to run but didn't want to be noticed, staying on the street, but angling across it.

Griffin broke into a quick jog after him, wanting to come up alongside him, get a better look.

Baseball Cap glanced back.

Griffin couldn't see much of his face, but there, right there: that move. Like Drew Millundra in the Palm County courthouse looking at Angie Hanes. A purpose to it. Not looking over his shoulder to check for traffic as he crossed the street—looking *at* Leanna. Then, seeing Griffin, he pivoted toward him. He saw Griffin coming at him.

And Griffin saw his face. A band of light from a street lamp slipped alongside the curved brim of the baseball cap, reflected off a sunglasses lens, and showed his cheek and mouth. The expression—mouth upturned with a knowing sneer—was all Griffin needed to see.

Arminger.

The fugitive teenager broke into a sprint.

Griffin was after him. "Arminger! Right there! Don't move!" Griffin shouted warning as though he had a gun, but it was back in the car, about a football field away. One hell of a reach from there.

Arminger cut between parked cars, striding onto the sidewalk, sprinting alongside a row of low-rise condo buildings.

The small string of similar three-story units shared a swimming pool, bay views, private docking facilities—

There he went! Arminger threw off his sunglasses and cap and darted between two buildings.

35

Randy Arminger's legs pumped hard and fast, working almost as rapidly as his mind turned. He'd been made! Motherfucker! He'd been made!

Randy didn't recognize the voice shouting his name, but it was authoritative, like a cop's.

Randy emerged between the two buildings and saw—shit!—the bay. Goddamned water. He turned and ran along a narrow sidewalk, shirttail flapping around his waist, cursing his decision not to take the gun into the bar. Should've had the gun. But it was too difficult to conceal.

"Randy!" The guy shouted his name again, having made the turn after him.

Arminger had a lead, but not much. Fifty yards max. Almost to the end of another building, he hurdled two landscaping ties onto a soft patch of grass. He had to lose this guy. Outrunning him on a straightaway probably wouldn't work. The guy shouting his name didn't sound out of breath.

Randy was between two buildings now. A dark and narrow passageway. His feet splashed shallow puddles of collected water.

Hurdling a hose wound into a snake curl, he came out one end just as the guy chasing him went in the other.

Shouts of "Randy!" echoed against concrete walls.

A group of four kids sneaking cigarettes across the street saw him. Two other kids skateboarding the sidewalk stopped and looked.

Arminger wanted to get back to the van—turn right—but the guy was too close. Randy cut left, running along the street side of the building.

A car came slowly down the road, windows down, music blaring. Kids looking for a parking space for the bar? Someone he could hijack? No. Pass. Not enough time. No weapon. Randy sprinted ahead, cutting back between the final two buildings of the bayside condo complex. Another narrow passageway. He sprinted harder, faster—with all he had—back to the bayside of the buildings again.

Brief consideration: dive into the water? No. Too restricting.

He turned right, but not on the sidewalk by the water. Randy stayed on the grass, farther from pole lamps that illuminated the little piers.

He ran past first-level balconies. People inside watching TV. Older couples playing cards. Two young girls outside with their feet up on a picnic table, drinking Cokes, being cool.

Take them as hostages? Human shields? No. Keep running. Lose the guy!

Randy was halfway to the end of the building before he heard his name shouted again. Randy breathed tensely. His eyes scanned buildings up ahead. Individual cottages and small houses with private yards. Just beyond that: a five-story condo at the end of the point.

Randy rounded the turn and was briefly out of sight of his pursuer. This was time he had to make use of. The next ten seconds. Hide. Throw the guy. Randy searched for opportunity to exploit.

Arminger could run.

Griffin hadn't been able to close on him. The kid used the buildings well, making quick turns that caused Griffin to lose him for seconds at a time.

Arminger had gone between two buildings and come out the other end before Griffin had gone in after him. Griffin didn't know which way Arminger had turned once he'd reached the bay. Griffin guessed left—that Arminger would head back toward the bar, figuring he had a car there—so Griffin made that turn only to discover his quarry had gone the other way. A brief couple of seconds caused by a wrong guess and Arminger almost doubled his lead.

Griffin was back running hard after him. Arminger turned at the far end of the buildings and was out of sight again. Seventy yards away. Griffin hoped like hell the kid stayed on the street and tried to outrun him, but when Griffin cleared the buildings and ran out to the street, looked left and right: no Arminger. "Dammit!"

Arminger couldn't have gotten that far. He was hiding somewhere. Griffin bent down as he ran along, looking under parked cars. Griffin stayed on the street where he had the widest field of vision, wanting to flush the kid out. He shouted, "Call the police! Anyone near a telephone, call the police. We've got a wanted criminal on the street. Stay inside. Lock your doors."

The kids with skateboards glared at Griffin as if he were drunk.

Griffin yelled at them, "Call the cops. This is no joke."

They weren't sure.

"Do it!"

A man in his forties appeared at the doorway of an A-frame house. Alerted by Griffin's shouts, he turned on his porch light.

"Sir, call the police. Tell them Randy Arminger is right here. On this street. He's wanted for murder! Call the police and lock your doors."

The man slammed his door shut and was, Griffin hoped, going for a phone.

Griffin walked rapidly along the street, scanning left and right, glancing under parked cars. "Come on, you little son of a bitch. Where are you?"

Griffin stopped when he heard glass break, then ran toward the sound, where three Cape Cod homes shared a single driveway. Two were dark. Griffin figured Arminger had picked one of them, looking to get inside and hide.

Griffin quickly circled the first house, his pants legs scrapping bayberry hedges planted around the raised foundation. He checked windows: all intact.

At the second house, he crossed a front walk lined with salt-sprayed junipers. The front windows were okay. He went around the side, three steps up to a door. Individual window panes were inset in the door, and the rectangle of glass closest to the doorknob was shattered.

Griffin pressed himself to the wall, listening. Quiet inside. He tried the knob. It turned freely. He started to ease open the door, but it caught. Deadbolted.

Griffin felt inside for the bolt, but the key had been removed from the cylinder.

Randy Arminger moved quietly into the kitchen. The room was dark except for a small night light glowing through a plastic sea shell. Down the hall, changing colors of a TV screen glowed against the wall. Someone was watching reruns of an old sitcom.

Randy breathed deeply, but quietly, feeling his head pulsing from the exertion of his run. Blood rushing his veins carried the potent, focusing effects of Cram.

He was on the verge of euphoria, having been confronted with a true panic situation and come through it. Within seconds of being apprehended, and still able to escape. He'd never been under that intense physical strain before, had often wondered how he would respond, and now wondered how he'd ever doubted himself. He was so perfect in every other way, why should anything be different now that he was being pursued instead of being the pursuer? It was actually fairly easy to escape, just like it was easy to get away with all sorts of wonderful mischief if you were smart enough. Resourceful enough. Brilliant.

Randy's eyes grew accustomed to the low light. His breathing returned to near normal. And he saw, on the wall, held in place by magnetic strips fixed into a wood frame: carving knives.

The police car came slowly down the street, door mounted floodlight being directed across the walls of the bayside condo buildings around which Griffin had chased Randy Arminger.

Griffin moved into the street and waved for the car, but the officer was too intent on following his light's beam and didn't see Griffin until Griffin hollered for him.

The policeman's approach was wary. The flood was shone directly in Griffin's face.

Griffin shielded his eyes, keeping his hands in plain view and not moving as urgently as the situation dictated lest the officer misinterpret his actions. Griffin kept watch on the house with the broken side window, muttering, "Come on, come on," as the police car crept along the street.

When the car was within fifty feet, Griffin shouted, "I'm trailing Randy Arminger, wanted for multiple homicide in Howard County. He's here."

The cop car came alongside Griffin, and the fellow in uniform behind the wheel looked about as old as Randy Arminger, yet not nearly as confident.

Griffin said, "He might be in this house," and pointed.

The young cop didn't know what to do. Most of his training had been in arresting drunks and obtaining consent searches to go through kids' cars or apartments for drugs.

"You watch the door," Griffin suggested, "and I'll go in. All right? Come on, let's go."

"Sir, I can't let you be involved. This is a police matter." He was reciting from some training session.

"Then goddamned do some police work. Search the goddamned house!"

"Another car is en route to the scene." The young cop was so intent on his jargon, he didn't know why Griffin took off running.

Griffin wasn't sprinting toward the house with the broken window, but the condominiums built on the point. Where a woman was screaming.

36

On the second-floor balcony, her nightgown covered with blood, a woman screamed hysterically for help. "My husband's been stabbed!"

Griffin ran up the stairs, shouting, "Where is he! Where is he!"

The woman, in her mid-forties, shook violently. "In here!" Pointing to the nearest doorway, but unable to move toward it.

Griffin jerked open the storm door and ran inside, down a short, narrow hallway.

A man's desperate, weak moans. "Oh God . . . Oh God." He lay in a puddle of his own blood on the linoleum floor. His hands were at his throat, trying to stave off a profuse flow of blood, but too weak to apply necessary pressure.

Griffin grabbed a kitchen towel and knelt beside the man, the knees of his pants immediately soaking up blood.

"I'm dying." The man's hands were cold as Griffin pressed the towel to his neck. Other cuts on his hands and arms had resulted from trying to fend off the attack. A sturdy man in his mid-sixties, he hadn't stood a chance against surprise and had been slashed horribly.

"Tell Charlene how much I love her, will you? She knows, but tell her that for me."

Griffin turned toward the front hall, shouting, "In here. We need an ambulance.

Within moments, someone rushed in. Not paramedics, but a neighbor. A gray-haired man about the age of his friend on the floor, he was intense but in control. "Max, my God!" He turned on lights and knelt beside Griffin. "What the hell happened here?"

"He's been stabbed."

"Christ Almighty!" The man's hands took Griffin's place with confidence. "I'm a doctor. There's a phone on the counter, right there . . ." Nodding with his head. ". . . get nine-one-one and have them put you through to the paramedics. I'm going to relay some instructions."

Griffin did as told, bloodied hand clutching the phone, clearly relaying the doctor's orders as a paramedic crew and twenty-four-hour emergency center were informed of the wounded man's condition.

Griffin established clear communications while noticing the balcony door. The screen had been forced open. From the volume of the TV set in the bedroom, Max and his wife had probably been watching TV in bed when Arminger snapped the cheap lock on the screen and gained entry. With his physical abilities, Arminger would have no trouble climbing onto the second-floor balcony. Once inside, Arminger probably stood about where Griffin was now, regaining his bearings after the chase, figuring his next move.

Griffin observed the knife set on the wall, and figured that two knives were missing. His eyes picked up one of them, covered with blood, on the living-room floor.

Beside that, a partial bloody footprint led back to the

door. Arminger looked to have cut the man and escaped the same way he'd entered. His diversion created, Randy fled the scene.

The doctor assured Griffin there was nothing more he could do to help, the doctor working to stabilize his wounded friend. Two other neighbors were there now to help.

Griffin hurried out of the condo, down the steps, and got a look at the police who'd arrived at the scene: a picture of complete disarray. No one in uniform was over the age of twenty-five, and *everyone* was waiting for a supervisor.

Considering his blood-stained hands and pants, Griffin evaluated what he'd have to explain to the police—how long it would take—and decided against it. No time.

He wiped his hands on the seat of his pants and took off running around the far side of the building. He climbed a fence into a neighboring yard and sprinted along the sidewalk where he'd chased Arminger. An occasional red-brown footprint told Griffin that Arminger had come this way, too.

People drawn outside by multiple flashes of emergency lights didn't pay attention to much besides the police. One guy did see Griffin, hollered, "Hey," in a tone of protest, but by the time he thought beyond that single syllable, Griffin was past him, a blur in the night.

Griffin slipped into the Honda as another cop car and ambulance turned down the street, sirens and lights on full. Griffin started the engine and pulled a U-turn out of the parking spot, got on Coastal Highway and sped south.

It was about twenty blocks to Leanna Landy's. Griffin drove the entire distance in the bus lane, where there was little traffic ahead of him. He cautiously ran red lights but didn't push the accelerator too hard. There were too many pedestrians, especially kids on the street. The June bugs leaned on bus stop poles and twirled half into the street. When Griffin blew the horn at them, they replied with their middle finger and nasty shouts.

He turned down the side street where Leanna was staying with her sister. Leanna's car was in front of the building. Lights were on inside. Lights *and* music blared out of the apartment next door.

Griffin went into the trunk and unwrapped the Beretta from its burlap. He noticed his hands were still red with blood and tried to wipe them clean on the rough-hewn fabric. He slid a clip into the handgun, clicked off the safety. Tucked the gun in the waist of his blood-stained pants and started across the street.

He went up the stairs as laughter barked from the apartment next door. Four college guys in there were drinking it up, shouting debate about what club they should go to as they clanked empty bottles into a trash can.

One guy screamed, "I don't understand women! Can you tell me please, *please,* what it is with women." Drunk out of his mind. His buddies laughed at him.

No one was in the living room at Leanna's. There were lights on, but no TV or stereo.

Griffin knocked on the cheap screen door and the contact of his knuckles pushed it from the paint-peeling frame. A "safety" hook, the only means of keeping the door closed, dangled unlatched.

Griffin called, "Leanna. Leanna!"

If she was back in one of the bedrooms, she wouldn't be able to hear him over the music next door. He went inside, footsteps falling upon aged shag carpeting beaten down by years of wet, sandy feet. "Leanna!"

The walls were panelled in the yellow knotty pine that had been de rigeur in the 'sixties when the apartments were built. Worn kitchen appliances were of mismatched colors from bygone times: avocado, mustard, and beige.

"Leanna!" Griffin went down the center hall, which accessed three small bedrooms, two baths.

Water was running in one of the bathrooms.

Griffin had one hand on the gun in his belt as his other hand rapped a fisted warning on the wall. "Leanna! Leanna, I'm a police officer." A lie, but it would put her at ease, as opposed to any other explanation for why he was smeared with blood. "Leanna."

Griffin approached the bathroom where water was running. A strong odor from in there. Vomit.

"Lee—"

Griffin peered into the bathroom. Observed a shod foot on the floor. A leg. Someone lying there, face down. No, kneeling.

Amy Tran was pitched forward over the toilet to throw up, which was what she'd been doing when she'd been shot twice in the back of the head and once in the neck.

Arminger. Griffin pulled out the Beretta. He aimed the gun for the hall as he stood over Amy Tran and checked for her pulse. She was dead, slumped lifelessly over the john.

"Leanna!" Griffin ran through the apartment. One bedroom was a mess, bed covers thrown about, a hand mirror broken. In the middle of the bed was a long section of duct tape pulled off the roll, ready to be used but left behind.

Griffin pounded the wall with his fist. "God*dammit*!"

He tucked away the gun, ran to the front porch, and went over the low wall that sectioned off the apartment next door.

The boys were partying.

Griffin went in without knocking.

One guy saw the blood on Griffin and yelled, "Holy fuck!"

"I'm a cop. A girl next door's been shot."

"What!"

"No shit!" One kid was fascinated, wanting to see. "She dead?"

"You see anything? There was another girl over there. Seventeen. Dark hair. Thin."

One of the boys, sprawled across a chair, too drunk to be certain if anything happening around him was real, said, "Yeah. She was passed out. Her boyfriend carried her out."

"Boyfriend? When?"

He shrugged. "Ten, fifteen minutes ago. Drove off in some moving van."

"What kind of moving van?"

"From Bayside Rent-All. One of those jobbie kind of deals." The guy slurred his words, grinning. "Yeah, her boyfriend said she'd had too much to drink and he had to get her to the hospital. Way she looked with him carryin' her in that sundress, it was all hitched up showing her panties, I said he should bring her on over here and we'd all take a turn."

Griffin took three steps to the kid and punched him hard on the cheekbone, sent him flying out of the chair.

"Jesus!" Another kid jumped up, stumbling over the table leg.

The drunk who didn't understand women was on his

feet as if he'd fight Griffin for his friend, but Griffin took one step toward him and the guy held up his hands. Didn't want any of that.

The most sober of the bunch also held up his hands. Truce. "It's cool." Of his friend on the floor, accepting, "He had it coming. He's an asshole."

Griffin left the apartment. He was running down the stairs, heading for the pay phone on the corner to call the police, when he saw the car.

A man got out of the vehicle smoking a hand-rolled cigarette. White-haired Ravlite in his seersucker suit, looking cool, collected, professorial.

Griffin charged at him, shouting, "He's here, goddammit. Why didn't you fucking send someone?"

Ravlite remained silent.

Griffin yelled into his face, "He's got Leanna."

Ravlite took half a step back and made a quarter turn to the side. He calmly raised his cigarette to his mouth and took an easy puff, exhaling cool white smoke that rose into the air like a thin cloud. He looked at Griffin, who was enraged, then gestured at his car. "Get in."

37

"Tell me what happened at the bar." Ravlite spoke while driving, having radioed information about Randy Arminger's apparent abduction of Leanna Landy and the death of Amy Tran.

Ravlite's police radio, tuned to Ocean City's communications band, squawked with activity. The search being mobilized for Arminger sounded in frightening disarray. A dispatcher reported problems coordinating a helicopter with Maryland State Police.

Griffin shook his head. Arminger *was* more organized than the police.

Ravlite asked again, "What happened at the bar?"

"At the bar?" Griffin confirmed.

"Yes."

They were on Coastal Highway. Ravlite didn't drive with any sense of urgency, not at all driving like Griffin felt. They hadn't waited for police and the M.E. to arrive for Amy Tran's body, because Griffin wanted to be looking for Arminger—having no idea where he might be, only that Griffin had to look. Arminger was moving forward. Griffin wanted to be doing the same, trying to intersect Arminger's path, not clean up debris in his wake.

Griffin said, "Turn here," directing Ravlite down a

random side street. They were going to check *every* block, ocean side and bay side. Do the resort town from one end to the other and back again until Arminger was found.

Ravlite steered as Griffin instructed.

Griffin looked across a condominium parking lot, knowing full well this was a hopeless way to search, but it was the only way he had.

Ravlite again asked, "What happened at the bar?"

Griffin snapped, "If you know I was there, you know what happened."

"I don't know what happened."

Griffin noticed Ravlite didn't deny being there. "What the *hell's* going on with you?" Griffin demanded.

"How did Arminger get away?" Ravlite asked politely but firmly.

"We were outside before I knew it was him. He *saw* me before I knew it was him. He took off running and I couldn't catch him."

"Why did he run?"

"Because he saw me."

"Does he know you?"

"No." Griffin looked over his shoulder, double-checking what could have been a van but was a pickup truck with a cap.

"So why did he run?"

"Because he saw me following him and got spooked."

"How did he know you were following him? You could have just both been heading in the same—"

"He turned around and saw me. That's all there is to it. What the hell does this have to do with where he is *now*?" Griffin pointed. "Turn here."

Ravlite did as told, then asked, "When you *were* a

police officer, and you were about to apprehend a suspect, at what point would you announce who you were?"

"What difference does it make?" Griffin snapped.

"I'm very interested in knowing," Ravlite said pleasantly.

Griffin was more concerned with Arminger than with past history.

Ravlite asked, "Would you always wait until you had a suspect in custody before saying you were a cop? Or would it happen simultaneously? Or a few seconds before?"

Ravlite interchanged the words "cop" and "policeman" in the manner of someone who was neither, and not just in the way federal agents differentiated themselves from state and local police but as though he weren't law enforcement at all. Ravlite spoke like the designation on his card: behavioral scientist—or a shrink.

"When would you tell them you were arresting them?" Ravlite probed.

Despite impatience, Griffin answered, "It depended on the situation."

"Did it depend on your personal feelings for a suspect?"

"My personal feelings?"

"Yes."

"No, it didn't have to do with that."

"If there was a suspect with whom you wouldn't have minded a physical confrontation, someone who'd been rubbing you the wrong way, who'd been particularly elusive—?"

"Would I give them a chance to run so I could chase them down and fight them?"

"Something like that?"

"No."

Ravlite said nothing.

Griffin amended his answer, thinking about it honestly: "Maybe."

"Your father," Ravlite pointed out, "when he was a policeman, used to beat suspects with a nightstick, didn't he? To get their attention."

Griffin demanded, "How do you know about my father? I'm not like my father. I didn't do things the way he did."

"Your father never killed anyone."

"Why do you care about all this?"

"Your father was indiscriminate in his violence. He was a frustrated man, usually controlled by alcohol, either its direct influence or a want of it. You, on the other hand, drink hardly at all. The now-and-then beer. And your physical confrontations are more focused, more reasoned. Justified."

"What the hell are you . . . are you suggesting I *wanted* Arminger to run from me?"

"Possibly."

"So I could chase him? Catch him? Then what? Fight him?"

"I'm not suggesting—"

"Like hell you aren't."

"I'm just curious what you would have done had you caught Arminger."

"What do you think I'd've done?"

"I don't know. You didn't catch him."

"I'm still looking. Drive the car." Griffin pointed at the intersection. "Light's green."

Leanna Landy had never known or even conceived this degree of fear. Her body was charged with panic, nearly overdosed on fight or flight reflexes. Her legs and arms wanted to flail, but her mind—as though thrown into an icy sea—had gone blank.

She'd tried to fight him in the bedroom, not knowing who he was at first, just some guy walking in. Leanna had even smiled at first, a little nervously, but he'd looked okay enough. Then she realized the red on his shirt was blood and recognized the arrogant upturn of his mouth just as he said, "It's Randy." And pounced on her as she screamed.

No one heard her cry for help for the blaring music next door, not even Amy, who was probably still in the bathroom throwing up.

Leanna threw a hand mirror at him and tried to crawl away over the bed, but he got her around the neck and squeezed, cutting off blood flow to her brain, singing—My God, he'd been singing!—"Go to sleep, go to sleep, go to sleep, little fly bitch." Fly bitch? Like a nursery rhyme.

And she'd blacked out, had some recollection of coming to at some point, that it was dark, her eyes unable to focus light beyond a state of fuzzy glow, but a hand, Randy's hand, had been back on the side of her neck, pressing. He'd sung again. "Go to sleep . . ." And her world had gone back to black.

Now she was coming to, slowly, groggily, her brain still iced with fear and reacting slowly, as though left drugged from impeded blood flow that had rendered her unconscious. Leanna's first thought was that her brain had been permanently damaged. Then she realized: she couldn't see!

Waves of panic raced through her. She tried to prove to herself she could still think and actually calculated a trigonometry problem as a test, fearing, Dear God, don't leave me incapacitated like that poor boy on the football team who'd suffered brain injury when his helmet had split.

Leanna was able to do the trig problem and felt relief, then thought: What a strange way to react. Simultaneously, a voice in her head said, *What difference does it make? He's going to kill you. Randy Arminger is going to kill you.*

That instant, Randy's hands were on her, fixing her into position. Leanna was standing and could feel the weight of her body pressing down to her feet, yet was unable to move her legs. Her feet were secured apart just beyond shoulder width by something around her ankles. Her left arm was also immobilized, and Randy had her right arm in his grasp. Tying her? No, her brain filtered the ripping sound: tape being pulled off a roll. Duct tape. He'd had a roll of it in his hand in the apartment. He was taping her arm in an outstretched position.

Leanna tried to determine where they were. Moving her head side to side, she saw threads of light. Light! She was blindfolded, not blind. Another relief. Yet that voice in her head again reminded, *What difference does it make? He's going to kill you.*

The reason she couldn't talk was that her mouth was taped.

What difference does it make? He's going to kill you.

Some determined part of her, some seed of confidence residing deep inside her sent an internal response along a faint though clear channel. *He's going to kill me? Not if I can help it.*

Leanna focused on that slender line of hope even when Randy Arminger began tearing at her clothes. His hands pawed her savagely like a madman.

Leanna could not fight him, so instead she fought the

swelling panic rushing through her, struggling to stay sane as the world went insane, as her taped shut mouth screamed with Randy Arminger abusing her.

He's not going to kill me! Not if I can help it, not if I can help it! Small internal voice of encouragement.

Leanna wanted to split herself in two: her mind and spirit would leave her body, shutting down any reaction to physical humiliation and pain.

Her thoughts became defiant despite his horrible assault. Thinking, *I'm smarter than you, Randy Arminger. I am so much smarter than you. I'm going to get you.*

Leanna mentally battled to hold onto her faculties, block out the pain and fear, while Randy Arminger seethed, "Time for your confession, fly bitch."

He took his hands from her and Leanna's tensed body slumped with relief. She whimpered as he stomped across what sounded to her like a hollow metal floor. Randy demanded, "Time for your confession, too, Angel."

Over the rush of her own fear, Leanna heard a man's tortured groans.

Randy shrieked, "Look at her. Here, smell her. Right here on my hand. Smells wonderful, doesn't it, you pious fraud!"

Randy's crazed screams intensified the fear icing through her veins. Leanna's heart palpitating.

He's going to kill you.

No. No. No! No, he's not! Leanna struggled against her wrist and leg straps.

"You want to do her, don't you?" Randy screamed at whoever sounded those horrendous groans. "Don't lie to me. You want to do her and you'd like to kill her, too. You're a killer, aren't you? How many people have you killed? All those people you said to pray for so they'd be punished, and, hey, look at that, now that person's dead! But not by God, you lying hypocrite. By you! You killed them, didn't you? Admit it! You might have fooled those other poor bastards, hiding behind your pseudo-religious bullshit! But not me. Confess it! You killed them, didn't you? Killed them because you *liked* to kill them!"

The man Randy called Angel screamed horribly.

Randy had lights. Had cameras. And God bless it, he had action. Action a-plenty. Better than he'd imagined. Superdo rush. Both his evil enemies here together: the Angel and the Fly Bitch. Two sad stories of folks who thought they were smarter than him, thought they could lecture him, antagonize him, beat him. But Randy was not a student, he was a teacher. Not a follower but a leader. So far above and beyond the common intellect it was immeasurable. He was smarter than every single teacher in that high school. Smarter than half his professors at Hopkins, and fast catching those who had some gray cells up on him.

Leanna Landy thought she could manipulate and nag and rat him out of her way and get that meaningless little valedictorian trophy all to herself.

The Angel had come here to kill him, drawn here, lured here by Randy. Brilliant, genius Randy had not only deduced that the Angel was a killer but trapped him into exposing himself and captured him.

The Angel Exposed. Live, next Ricki Lake. Too bad that chubby Holly Haskins wasn't around to see it happen, but Holly had been turned into bait, chum, to draw the Angel. Randy was in the white marlin capital of the world doing his own kind of fishing.

Now the videotape was rolling. Halogen lights on.

The Angel was all bloody and broken up, strapped to one homemade cross, and Leanna was "crossed" naked on the opposite wall, her pose altered by a little bar that held her ankles open.

Randy had always wondered what she'd look like naked. Knowing her tits were small and she was a little gangly, but the thought of her nipples and what kind of bush she'd have had been intriguing him for months. Now he knew. Cool. So very cool.

Randy went back to Leanna, giving her little pink nipple a bite to make it hard. Leanna twisted her shoulders but wasn't squealing or screaming anymore. She moaned, as if she was wearing out, wearing down.

Randy got it all on video. Coming soon to an Internet site on your desk.

Randy took two long strides back to the Angel. He grabbed a support bar on the truck wall and hoisted himself up, putting his face to the Angel's, screaming, "How many people have you killed? How many?"

The Angel screamed back at him, but not words, twisted sounds, as though his soul had been cleaved open and was spilling evil.

Randy hopped down to the bed of the van, his weight shaking the floor. He grabbed the container of kerosene and poured it over the screaming Angel's head.

The Angel gagged, spitting it out, and screamed louder with kerosene searing into his opened wounds.

Randy thought, Leanna should see this. So he hurried to her and ripped down her blindfold.

Leanna blinked unfocused eyes but looked toward the screams. She saw the mutilated man, his head caked with dried blood, his broken arm twisted unnaturally. Leanna's screams expanded her throat, trapped behind her gag.

Randy laughed, "Flip out!" as Leanna wickedly kicked and pulled at her wrist and ankle ties, banging the walls of the van.

No problem, they were in the middle of fucking nowhere.

Randy grabbed the kerosene and doused Leanna. Flammable liquid soaked into her hair.

Leanna pressed shut her eyes to keep out burning liquid. She kept trying to kick her legs and flail her arms. Skinny girl with spunk, her white skin shining with oily liquid. Randy decided that this was very, very sexy. Hot.

He slid his fingers over her slicked flesh. Finger-painting swirls around her tiny breasts, down her stomach, trailing streaks along her slender thighs.

Leanna kicked and twisted. Like a dance.

The Angel groaned, "Let her go."

Randy jumped over to him, wired by this. "He speaks! Tell me more. *Why* should I let her go? So temptation will be out of your sight? So you can ignore the desire you have to kill her?"

The Angel's cries were snarled by pain, like vines tangled around barbed wire. "I don't want to kill her! Let her go! Don't hurt her because of me!"

"Because of *you*? No, no, no. It's because of *her*. She's no innocent, are you, Leanna?"

Leanna wailed uncontrollably. Tears streaming from her eyes couldn't rinse away the sharp sting of kerosene. The entire truck smelled of it.

Randy grabbed a corner of Leanna's taped gag. "You're no innocent, are you?" He ripped off the tape with one hard pull and Leanna's piercing screams made mad escape.

Randy screamed, "Tell him how you plotted against

me. Tell him how your father cozied up to Ms. Stark to get you an A in calculus two quarters ago. To keep your straight A's going. Keep that four-oh. Keep you in contention with me. Tell him!"

Leanna shrieked violently.

"Tell him how your father conned Ms. Stark into *loaning* you some percentage points, Leanna. How your eighty-seven, *B-plus,* was turned into a ninety, *A,* with the understanding you'd have to get a ninety-three next quarter to get an A. That you *borrowed* three points, you pesky fly, you bitch, so you could pretend to be as smart as me. Tell him!"

"Let her go!" the Angel bellowed.

"No! *No!* I will not let her go. She pays for her sins like you pay for yours." Randy grabbed a pile of rags and threw them at Leanna's feet, doused them with kerosene, then dropped a small metal box onto the rags: a little square contraption with wires protruding from it.

Randy dug into a bag and retrieved a remote control unit to a child's toy car, which he stuck in the Angel's face. Announcing of the remote, "*This* will set off *that.*" Pointing to the metal box at Leanna's feet. "Push *this* button," Randy said of the switch below a plastic steering wheel, "and *that* ignites. She burns. She dies." Randy stuck the remote in the Angel's good hand. "Go ahead. Do it. You know you want to kill her. You love killing people. I know you do. It's power. Superdo power. Control. A rush. Admit it. Confess it! You've killed lots and lots and lots of people, haven't you?"

The Angel howled, "Yes!"

"And not all of them deserved to die, did they?"

The Angel stared at the device in his hand.

Leanna, fully aware of what was happening, frantically struggled to free her taped ankles, desperate to kick away the saturated rags. More kerosene dripped down her body. Her flesh was primed to burn.

"Did they all *deserve* to die?" Randy demanded.

The Angel pressed shut his eyes.

"Did they—?"

"No!" The Angel yowled, sounding more like a devil than a man of God.

"They died because you wanted them to die. Because you wanted to kill them!"

"Yes!"

"You like the killing!"

"Yes!"

"It thrills you. Satiates you!"

"Yes."

"You just use God as an excuse. Punishment as reason to kill, but the plain truth, the *real* truth, is you enjoy it. You love to kill!"

"Yes!"

"So kill her now. Kill her! Push that button!"

The Angel's pain far surpassed that of his wounds. The insane boy somehow knew. Somehow had deduced, had reasoned . . .

For years, the Angel had stalked victims, killing indiscriminately. Not as a madman, but at random. His job, back when he could maintain employment, caused him to travel a great deal. It was when he was on the road, in cities and towns filled with strangers, that the appetite gnawed at him: the hunger to snuff out life. Something unspeakable inside him created these urges. Devil-born desires. But God had saved him, come to him. A voice, a pale, fading light in a room of white walls covered with the blood of angels. God saved him from the insanity of killing, absolving him, then enlisting him to fight the very devils that had come to claim heaven. Only now one of the devil's men had come to reclaim him as one of their own. Bring him back into the dark fold.

Now, undeniably, even through the agony of his physical wounds, the hunger for killing that had never faded but had for a short sweet time been justified, was back in its stark form. The girl with her arms bound to a cross, her legs braced open. The way she struggled, the way many of them struggled against the face of death, the cold fear of being pushed into the unknown afterlife, where lifelessness turned thoughts to dust and blew them away on dark winds.

The insane boy—one of the devil's own—was here to reenlist him for battles against goodness, to restore his desires of evil.

He—the Angel—and the brilliant, insane boy would cross the landscape by night, streaking terror. Watching, breeding death together.

Yes, the Angel wanted her to die. The Angel had wanted to watch death. He wanted to writhe in its power. The Angel felt as though falling, a sense that made him think the boy had released him from the cross.

He was falling back into the devil's flock. And so the angel pushed the switch on the remote control. The angel waited to see fire erupt at the girl's feet, to engulf her. He heard her scream.

But there was no fire. The remote was grabbed from his hand.

Randy Arminger screamed with celebration, "I love when I'm right! Loveitloveitloveit."

The Angel had been tricked again.

Leanna's muscles strained from exhaustion. Energy was sapped from her. Yet the very stress that tired her muscles managed to keep her mind from going insane. She felt as though at the brink of a deranged abyss, but she managed to pull herself back. That small voice in her encouraged survival. She was absolutely powerless, yet fought on.

When the badly beaten man pushed that switch, Leanna felt heat, anticipating a rush of fire swirling around her like lightning wrapping its hot lick around a tree. She tried to kick at the kerosene-soaked rags and screamed, but while she felt heat, there was no fire.

She'd imagined the hot temperature. Nothing was burning.

Randy Arminger was in front of her, showing her the red plastic toy: the remote control. He opened the back of it and smiled at her, said, "No batteries." Mock smacking his head with the palm of his hand, he smiled, "Oops. I forgot." But he was putting batteries in the unit now and speaking with constrained rage, words barely audible over the other man's fierce howls.

Randy demanded, "Tell me about that calculus grade, Leanna. How Daddy Landy got that B-plus changed to an A. Let's hear about that. Let's hear all about it." Randy retreated to the videocamera set on a tripod near the closed back door of the van. He looked through the viewfinder, focusing, zooming in on her.

The courageous voice inside Leanna told herself, *You are not going to kill me.* Leanna managed to draw breath to speak, words coming weakly. "The grade was changed."

"B-plus to an A?" Randy cross-examined.

"Yes."

"Now say it louder."

Leanna took a deep breath, heart pounding, battling

fear as it raced through her. "The B-plus was changed to an A."

"Because your father talked to Ms. Stark?"

"Yes."

"Louder!"

"Yes."

"You only deserved a B-plus?"

Loudly: "Yes!"

"But you got an A?"

Screaming: "Yes!"

"That's cheating."

Leanna whispered something.

"What's that?" Randy moved closer.

Leanna whispered, "I had to keep up with you."

"Mission impossible."

The other man no longer screamed but whimpered weakly. A pause between torments.

"I know . . . I just hated losing to you . . . I envied you . . . I could have . . ."

"Could have what?" Randy was intrigued.

Leanna's lips moved. A whisper of sound.

"Could have what?" Randy prompted.

And Leanna, that little voice inside her head telling her to survive, said, "I can't say it."

"*Lee-annie* . . . sure you can. You envied me. You could have . . . ?"

She whispered, "Been in love with you."

"Ahhhh," Randy exhaled as though having drawn a breath of clean spring air, not air filled with adrenaline-fear, sweat, and kerosene. "The thin line between love and hate."

"Yes," Leanna gasped confession like a bad soap-opera actress, those shows Mallory and her friends loved to watch.

Randy smiled at her, looked at her, turning thoughts in his mind. "Brains turn me on. You had your moments."

"I wanted to be part of your group." Leanna was amazed she was able to say it.

Randy checked his watch. He'd been off the CD player/scanner for thirty minutes now. Risky. Cops would be looking for him. He was falling behind schedule. But this interesting development.

Leanna had actually finagled a bit of a confession from *him*. In a competitive way, he *was* attracted to her. Had even masturbated thinking about her a couple times, hadn't he? And now, after all this, roughing her up like this, treating her like shit, she couldn't hide her feelings for him. Amazing.

Randy got a knife, fine piece of German cutlery taken from the condo of that old man he'd sliced up, and went to Leanna with it.

Leanna gasped, "What are you doing?"

Randy cut her loose, slicing the sharp knife through the tape but leaving it wrapped around her wrists and ankles instead of tearing it off.

Standing naked, coated with kerosene, Leanna rubbed circulation back into her hands.

Randy was taking the videocamera off the tripod. "Help me get this shit together. Bring me that Halliburton." Randy pointed, ordering.

Leanna brought him the hard-sided case.

Randy opened it and started packing up the camera gear. He looked up at Leanna standing naked and obedient beside him. "Pretty weird, huh, you and me?"

He was so insane, but Leanna managed to respond, "Yeah," as though wasn't this kinky-romantic.

The man he'd called Angel was barely conscious. The only sounds now seeping from his mouth conveyed utter defeat. Leanna wasn't sure, but she thought the man might have been praying.

Randy grabbed clean rags and wiped Leanna's body, roughly removing kerosene, but most had seeped into her skin, making her oily. Randy seemed to like having his hands on her, said, "Nice."

Leanna tried not to think about it. She had to escape, but only when she was sure she'd be successful. One chance was all she figured she'd get.

Randy said, "Let's go." He raised the rear door of the van.

Leanna hoped to see somewhere to run to, but there was only darkness beyond the halogen light spilling from the rear of the van. The smell was horrible, worse than the kerosene—a dank, humid odor, like excrement and death.

Randy hopped out of the van and helped her down. "Come on, sexy."

She stood on a floor of dirt and decaying straw inside a long, decrepit wood building with lots of small windows, wire mesh cages, and a walkway up on the second level. Moonlight shone through square windows and broken roof slats. "Where are we?"

"An old chicken coop." Randy started toward a car at the far end of the long building.

Leanna followed him, crossing an arm over her breasts and working every second to suppress panic.

At the car, Randy went into the trunk and opened a small suitcase, handing her a polo shirt and shorts.

Leanna pulled the shirt over her head, which hung on her slender frame like a trash bag.

"Get in," Randy told Leanna. "Can't take the chance of anyone seeing you in the car." He wanted her in the trunk.

Leanna climbed in. If he was going to kill her, it would be terrible not to go down fighting him, but she had the sense she was gaining an edge by being compliant.

After he shut the trunk, she had second thoughts. Randy didn't get into the car.

The man Randy had called Angel was screaming again, and along with the smell of chicken feces and kerosene, Leanna smelled smoke.

38

Turning down yet another side street, Ravlite asked Griffin, "What are you thinking?"

The two men had been silent for a few minutes—Griffin surveying the streets while listening to the police radio and grateful that Ravlite had ceased his queries as to Griffin's methods of apprehending suspects.

A helicopter had finally arrived, but it was a medivac unit and could be called away for a medical emergency. Police reported no sight of the van, no sight of Arminger. Checkpoints were setting up on the main routes out of Ocean City.

"I'm thinking," Griffin said, "that Arminger's anticipated this. He's probably ditched the van by now. It's too noticeable. He's probably got a car."

"A stolen car?"

"No." Griffin relayed his theory of Arminger renting a car back at BWI airport under an alias.

Ravlite didn't comment on that proposition. He fell into silence for another moment, then asked, "What other thoughts are you having right now? Are you thinking only about Arminger or do other images come to mind?"

"Some other thoughts," Griffin answered.

"Such as?"

Griffin sighed, thinking, here we go again.

"You don't have to answer if you don't want. I'm just making conversation."

"I'm thinking about my daughter."

"Ah . . ." A pause, then: "Are you afraid she's not really your daughter?"

Griffin's eyes snapped over to Ravlite, who said:

"I'm assuming the thought crossed your mind at some point. Your wife was having an affair. Once you and your wife separated, you didn't see your daughter for almost a year. The separation agreement filed with your divorce papers proposed to give your wife full custody, and some judge had been enticed to sign a waiver—what was under Maryland law an illegal waiver—releasing you from ever having to pay child support." Ravlite looked at Griffin. "It's public record."

Griffin's glare released Ravlite and resumed searching the streets for Arminger. "I think about it . . . but mainly I worry about her being safe. And if I'll be a good father for her."

"Would it make a difference if she wasn't your daughter?"

Griffin started to ask Ravlite what he knew about *that,* but changed his mind.

Ravlite said, "You're very good with things that have to be done."

Griffin didn't comment.

Ravlite proposed, "I have another question."

"What a surprise."

Ravlite chuckled, "Yes, I suppose so. But tell me, the first time you fired a gun at a man, did you hit him?" There was a knowing expression on Ravlite's face. He repeated, "The *first* time."

There was only one reference in Griffin's police

folder about a shooting, because he'd fired his gun only once in the line of duty. The other time, the *first* time, he'd shot a man, killed a man, had been anything but official. Until tonight, Griffin thought only one other person knew about that. If Ravlite knew, that made two.

A six-year-old secret was burning inside Griffin. The only other person who had known was his best friend—the best friend Griffin hadn't known was having an affair with his wife—and now that man, Mickey Blane, was not his friend anymore. And Griffin had no one to talk to about what he'd done. So he answered Ravlite's question. The first time he fired a weapon at a man: Did he hit him?

"Yes."

"That's very unusual, you know. Not as uncommon as it used to be, but still unusual. We've found that most men, *if* they even fire their weapon in their first battle, aim over the heads of their enemy. Even if that enemy is looking to kill them. There is a natural inclination *not* to kill. Even men who are hunters and kill animals are hesitant to kill another man. The percentages are staggering. It's estimated that less than one in twenty men in the Revolutionary War had the ability to kill in their first conflict using firearms. Even with battles fought where two armies came straight across the field, not hiding but shooting at one another, getting closer and closer, the combat ended up hand to hand. And you think logically how could that be? Even given the slowness of reloading more primitive weapons.

"By World War One, our training techniques had improved. World War Two had us better still, but only twenty percent of soldiers shot to kill in their first fight. It wasn't until Vietnam we really had the conditioning streamlined, depersonalizing the enemy and the violence. The problem was it made civilians almost as easy to kill as the enemy, and once those poor boys came home . . . well, it was horrible. We'd conditioned them to kill so well we never thought about unconditioning them. You see, the problem is, for most people, the taking of human life eventually drives them—to put it simply—insane. Fortunately, we're good enough now at picking up the early warning signs to establish treatment, and those indicators generally arise within a couple years after a killing. But the real study—my study—is of those men who kill and *don't* suffer or show the usual syndromes of post-traumatic stress."

"And this is why you're interested in Randy Arminger?"

The police band crackled with new information. The dispatcher was unable to keep emotion from his voice, alerting that Delaware police had information on Arminger.

Leanna Landy couldn't keep from crying. Locked in the trunk of the car, she was bounced around as the Halliburton cases shifted and knocked against her. It was too much to take. Having time to think about what happened the past hour, she was being pushed by those images toward shock.

She no longer smelled smoke or chicken feces—they were out of the old, abandoned coop—but she was still in Randy Arminger's grasp, vulnerable and helpless.

The roads were rutted and crimped with tight turns. Leanna feared an even more desolate and horrible place than the chicken house, where Randy would torture her before killing her.

She cried in the trunk, at first trying to keep quiet, not wanting Randy to be able to hear, but then the defiant inner voice that had given her hope faded, and Leanna figured it didn't matter if he knew she was crying, that her going along with him was an act—God! To pretend to be attracted to him. This insanity!

She began to feel her body's aches from his torments, and every shift of position reminded how he'd hurt her. She thought about her parents, her sister—that she might never see them again. Her school, her teachers, all the things she'd wanted to do in her life, with her life . . . they were never going to happen, because she'd be dead.

Oh, God, dead. She didn't want to die. Was scared to die. But was scared to live, too, at the hands of Randy Arminger. What more would he do to her before he killed her? There was no doubt in her mind that's what he'd do, because Leanna had time to think about Holly Haskins.

Wasn't she supposed to have run off with Randy? So where was she now? A girl everyone at school knew Randy was screwing. He'd probably killed her.

Oh, God, please don't let him kill me. Please don't let me die.

The little voice reappeared inside her. *So don't let him kill you. Stop crying. Think, think, think. You're smarter than him. Outsmart him.*

Griffin got out of the car and was running before Ravlite had braked the sedan to a complete stop.

Fire engines were hosing down the ground around the abandoned chicken coop, one hose drawing water out of a marshy pond to spray the dilapidated roof. The coop didn't seem to have been on fire, yet white smoke billowed out of breaches in its roof and hung heavily in the humid sky as though about to rain.

The stench of the fire was horrible. Burned excrement.

Five Sussex County police officers were on the scene. They were small-town career cops, save the sergeant, who was a veteran import from New Jersey. He directed local-born-and-raised officers while looking very out of place with his slicked-back black hair and strong South Jersey accent.

Griffin ran through snaking firehoses into the coop, the Jersey cop calling after him. "Get dah fuck oudda dere. Who's dis guy! Kermit, get day guy oudda dere."

Griffin was inside, running down the narrow center. Wire caged walls were on both sides of him. Water dripped through gaps in the roof.

The paramedics had backed their vehicle inside once the fire was extinguished. A rental van was charred black from the blaze. A man and woman in white jumpsuits worked frantically to free a man inside the van.

Cops shouted after Griffin, chased after him, and their voices echoed inside the coop's curved ceiling.

The smell was worse here. Stronger. Pungent. Not only burned feces but flesh.

Griffin looked inside the van. Two-by-fours secured to its walls formed a cross, and someone was attached to that cross. His skin was charred black. Clothes were seared to his body. The man's head, hair burned away, hung limply. Dead, Griffin assumed, but the man's eyelids opened, like crinkled parchment paper peeled from his skin. Slowly, weakly the whites of his eyes appeared, seemingly the only part of him not scorched by the fire. He looked right at Griffin—right at him—and his ruined lips moved to speak.

Griffin couldn't hear him over the cops rushing him from behind. Two of them grabbed Griffin's arms, twisting them behind his back as they forced him against the back of the van. One of the cops shouted, "Gun, partner," pulling the Beretta out of Griffin's belt.

More footsteps ran in behind them: The Jersey cop and Ravlite.

Ravlite was getting mud on the legs of his seersucker pants. Seeing inside the van, he swore, "Damit. No—*no*!"

One of the cops who held Griffin moved to seize Ravlite when their sergeant said, "Let him in. He's FBI."

Ravlite pulled himself up into the van, scrambling agily to his feet and asking the paramedics, "Is he alive?"

The burned man's eyes, practically his sole form of expression, focused upon Ravlite, and Griffin detected recognition. Whoever this horribly injured man was, he knew Ravlite. And Ravlite knew him.

Ravlite tried to reassure the man, who fought intense pain as paramedics gingerly released him from the cross. The man was so badly burned it looked as though his arms and legs were stiff and brittle and would crumble like pieces of charred wood under the slightest pressure.

The fire had not spread beyond the van, and had followed a strange pattern, consuming only certain portions of the floor and walls.

Griffin, still pinned to the van by two police officers, saw a can of kerosene and realized it had been the accelerant, laid as flammable river to catch fire. A good bit had apparently been poured over the man, and once it burned off, the fire had begun to extinguish itself. The rest of the van's interior, primarily metal, resisted further damage. Still, it was nothing short of miraculous the man was alive.

The sound of a helicopter neared, the loud chop of its blades whipping the night sky. The medivac unit that had been dispatched to search for Arminger was being called to its primary duty.

The chopper's powerful floodlights scanned the landscape for a safe place to set down, its bright beams of light cutting inside the coop.

The sergeant from Jersey shouted, "Kermit, Jones, go 'head, let him go. Get outside and help the chopper. Get 'em in here."

The two uniforms released Griffin and backed from him warily. The one who'd disarmed Griffin handed Griffin's weapon to his sergeant, who saw that the serial numbers had been obliterated.

The sergeant waited until his two men were outside, then walked to Griffin and handed back the gun. "Here yah go, buddy."

Inside the van, Ravlite talked to the burned man as he was secured to a stretcher. The man began to shiver, body going into spasms.

The helicopter made landing close by and the power of its chopping blades blew off dilapidated pieces of roof with a deafening sound, like a twister setting down.

Paramedics wheeled the burned man down the ramp. Passing Griffin, the man was racked by intense pain, yet his eyes showed—there was no other way Griffin could put it—relief. His crinkled, scarred lips moved to speak.

Griffin was unable to hear what he said, so he walked along with the paramedics and leaned closer, so close to the man he could smell his burned flesh.

Even his breath smelled of fire as he repeated to Griffin what he'd tried to say before. The man's words were spoken weakly, but with strange clarity. Telling Griffin, "I knew you'd come." Thanking him.

Paramedics carried the man away.

Griffin watched him, then turned quickly when he felt a hand on his shoulder, but no one was there.

The ex-Jersey sergeant was outside the coop. Ravlite was still in the van, looking badly shaken.

Griffin shouted at Ravlite over the hacking whirl of the helicopter, "Who is he?"

Leanna was out of the car, standing in the middle of a packed dirt driveway. Randy Arminger was beside her. Dark fields surrounded them; some type of low crop grew across the flat earth for acres and acres.

A reflection of lights along the distant treeline pointed to Ocean City. Leanna estimated it was ten or fifteen miles away.

Mosquitoes buzzed loudly in the dark sky. Leanna, feeling one on her arm, hit it with her hand and its death smeared a trail of blood over her flesh. She was glad it was dark. She didn't want to see any more blood. It might push her back toward the edge again just when she felt some hint of control coming back. A slender ray of hope—a ray of light she could hold onto a little longer, even out here with no one else around for miles.

Randy was looking at her but not talking. He was plugged into a CD Walkman. Leanna heard the jarring tin and bass of the music from plugs jammed into Randy's ears.

Randy moved a little, as if he was dancing.

Leanna stayed by the rear of the car. The trunk was still open in case Randy wanted to shove her back in. She stuffed her hands in the baggy shorts pockets and waited for Randy, as if they were on a date. Leanna didn't know how else to act, and this seemed to be working.

She wondered how Randy had gotten this crazy this fast, as if it had all been inside him, distracted in some way, and now it was exploding. But she didn't want to think about that because it made her think he might explode on *her* next. Kill her, and she couldn't think that way.

She swatted at another mosquito that landed on her neck but didn't get it. She didn't want to have its blood all over her.

Randy took the earplugs out and hooked them around his belt, where the CD player was attached. He looked around, then smiled at her with approval. "You want to take off?"

"Take off?"

"Yeah."

Was he offering to let her go? Why phrase it like that? Leanna wondered, then knew: a test. Questions to be answered carefully. "Do *you* want to?"

"No," he laughed. "I mean you. Just you. You can split. Take off."

Leanna thought, No way, too easy. "What're *you* gonna do?"

He leaned against the bumper beside her, very casual, as if they were hanging in the halls at school. Randy tilted his head forward and glanced sideways at her. "You're a lot cooler than I thought."

Trick, Leanna thought. Trick. She said, "I always knew you were cool. No rules."

"Yeah." He inhaled deeply. "You gotta hate rules, especially rules made and imposed by people who're so damned stupid. The crap people believe. Unreal."

"I know . . ." Leanna tried to fall into his rap, as if she were right there with him. "My parents . . . they're so rigid about everything. They didn't want to let me come down here. They thought something bad might happen to me." Leanna, looking at Randy, managed a smile, managed to laugh when he did.

Randy laughing, "Shit, shit . . ."

Leanna said, "Boy, were they wrong, huh?"

Randy laughed louder and when his cackles ebbed, muttered, "Parents . . ."

"Yeah."

"Quite a world they've got us living in. Like giving someone a really fabulous book to read, only it's due back in the library in five minutes."

"And half the pages are missing anyway."

"Right . . ." Randy shook his head.

Leanna smacked her knee—another mosquito.

Randy said, "They like you because you're sweet."

"Sure."

He touched her face very lovingly. Less than an hour ago he was pouring kerosene on her, about to set her on fire. Now he stroked her face. A gentle, kind touch, but so insane.

Leanna did her best not to shudder. Part of her was going completely mad, but she had to soldier on.

Randy withdrew his hand and crossed his arms. He looked over the dark fields. "Really, you want to split, you can. I just need some time before you see anyone else. You'll have to tell them about the car, the van back there, and Amy."

Leanna thought: Amy? Then, comprehending: He'd killed her. Oh, dear God. A wave of nausea rushed over her. Her head began to feel light. Her pulse beat rapidly with panic.

"So if you want to go . . ." Randy offered, "go on." He gestured across the field, inferring she could walk away from him. "An hour or two, max, you'll come across a house or a car. Enough time for me to split."

Leanna managed to stay in character. Managed to *think.* "You *want* me to go?"

He hesitated, as though her response had caught him off guard. "Doesn't matter. If you want . . . go on and go."

And she knew if she started walking across that field away from him, he'd kill her. She hadn't seen a gun, but he was talking about Amy. Leanna assumed he'd killed her, and even though she hadn't heard any gunshot at the apartment, maybe she wouldn't have because of the music that had been coming from next door. And even without a gun he could chase her, kill her with his hands. Or run her down with the car. Leanna looked at him, right at him, unblinking into his eyes. "I don't want to go." Estimating her next line quickly, she added, "This's fun."

He laughed again, touched her again on her face and throat. His fingers traced down the button line of the shirt she was wearing, looking for her small breasts in the baggy top.

Leanna, feeling as if she might be sick, trembled—damn, trembled—a giveaway.

But Randy read her reaction another way: "Never done it before?"

Think, Leanna, think! She looked down, shook her head. It was okay to be nervous about *this.*

"It's fun. Feels good." He fondled her breasts.

Think, think! "I . . . I don't want to . . . not here. I always wanted the first time to be someplace nice."

"We don't have that kind of time." He was being patient—pretending to be, anyway—but it was clear what he was after.

"I really wanted the first time to be nice."

He pinched her nipple through the shirt and said, "Tell you what." He started unzipping his pants. "I really want to be with you, do something with you, but I understand." He took out his erection. His penis, engorged with the flow of his blood, was big and full of veins.

"His name," Ravlite said, "is Evan Ritterhauf." Ravlite was answering Griffin's question as to the identity of the burned man. "I first interviewed him five years ago in Louisville. He'd been arrested for the killing of a businessman who was found murdered in a hotel elevator. Shot to death. The evidence was circumstantial, and there was no motive whatsoever. No link between Ritterhauf and the victim. Ritterhauf was tried and acquitted. But I knew he'd killed that man."

"How?"

Griffin and Ravlite were outside the chicken coop. Only one firehose was in use now, saturating the ground, making sure to eliminate potential hot spots where an ember could jump and ignite.

"He was showing the signs—what I was talking about before. Ritterhauf was beginning to go crazy from the killings."

"Killings? More than one?"

"Yes. There had been a series of killings in the Midwest. Chicago, Indianapolis, Cincinnati, Columbus, Lexington. Unsolved murders. All of the victims were from out of town, traveling through the city. Most were killed in their hotel or in a rental car. Usually it happened late at night and always during the week. I was investigating Ritterhauf for those murders and had subpoenaed his travel records from his employer.

"Ritterhauf was on the road half the year. He scouted shopping center developments for a real estate investment trust. He was very successful, made an excellent living. He even owned a few small shopping centers himself. He was unmarried. His parents were both dead and he had little contact with his brothers or sister. And he was either in the city or within driving distance of almost every one of the unsolved murders I was investigating.

"I started watching Ritterhauf after the Louisville incident, but he disappeared. He quit his job without notice and signed his property management over to a real estate company under the arrangement that they forward monies to him in an overseas account.

"I figured Ritterhauf was gone. Then, just over a year ago, there was a very strange incident in Vermont. A prosecutor named Terry Moore lived in a farmhouse. Secluded area. He was up late at night and was disturbed, because he'd just lost a very big trial. A child killer had gone free. A man named Raymond Jarvis, an onion farmer who enjoyed smothering young girls with his hands. Terry Moore, the prosecutor, had an unannounced visitor that night. A man broke into his house and accused him of having mishandled the trial. The man asked Terry Moore to pray with him."

"Pray?"

"That's right. Which Terry Moore did. He was so distraught over losing that case, feeling responsible for that girl's killer going free, that he got on his knees and prayed. And after Terry Moore finished praying, he opened his eyes, and the man was gone. But he'd left behind a satchel, and in the satchel were the hands of Raymond Jarvis. The rest of Jarvis's body was never found."

"My God."

"Other incidents began to occur, and with increasing frequency, and every event was noted on this religious home page on the Internet. The Angel Pages."

"I began to investigate and met Terry Moore, who is a very nice young man and not a bad trial lawyer, either. In describing the man who broke into his house that night, Moore said he thought the man was an angel. He also described someone who looked very much like Ritterhauf, five years older than when I last saw him in Louisville. I believed Ritterhauf had come back and reinvented himself. I made some contact with him through The Angel Pages. And while he knew who I was, he denied he was Ritterhauf. He said he was an angel and that he had been dispatched to earth to fight demons. That he was trying to keep God from dying. It's what I was talking about before. The killings had driven him insane. And yet he couldn't stop killing, so his mind created this illusion that he was working for God. Killing for God."

Griffin looked across the dark landscape. The conversation of firemen sounded very distant though they were nearby, calling routine orders to one another, securing the scene.

Ravlite said, "Randy Arminger also found The Angel Pages. He began posting messages that were very derisive of the belief in God. He and Ritterhauf got into intensive electronic arguments, and Arminger was getting the better of the exchange. He's truly brilliant . . . but insane. It annoyed Arminger that Ritterhauf wouldn't identify himself by his real name or include an image of himself on The Angel Pages. So Arminger's torments continued and intensified."

Ravlite sighed sadly, "Somehow Randy got Ritterhauf

here. I imagine Ritterhauf's intent was to kill Randy. Randy, apparently, was expecting him. I'm sure the image of Ritterhauf—the Angel—burning on a cross won't take long to find its way to the Internet and The Angel Pages."

"As if there weren't enough motives for people to kill one another before, now we've got this whole other dimension of sickness flying across the phone lines."

"It's not as bad as you make it sound. Randy Arminger was going to turn killer with or without a computer and the Internet. Evan Ritterhauf was a serial killer before he ever owned his first PC." Ravlite considered Griffin. "And you hate computers."

Griffin let Ravlite's unspoken implication vanish into the night air. He was not about to be drawn into Ravlite's circus. "If you knew Ritterhauf was killing people again, why didn't you stop him?"

"I'm a behavioral scientist. I study people. I don't arrest them." Again, Ravlite communicated an unspoken message. He reached into his suit jacket for his cigarette case, lighting one of his own-rolled unfiltered smokes. Ravlite was calmer than immediately after his discovery of Ritterhauf burned on a cross. "Besides," he said, puffing smoke, "and this is very far off the record, but on his latest spree, Ritterhauf didn't seem to be killing anyone who didn't deserve to die." Ravlite hesitated, waiting for Griffin to comment.

"Why'd that cop give me my gun back?"

"I told him you were with me."

"That I'm an FBI agent?"

"No. That would have been lying. *I* just said you were with me. *He* assumed that meant you were an FBI agent."

"If I *were* an FBI agent," Griffin bit off, "I

wouldn't sit idly by and let someone like Ritterhauf—or Arminger—kill people."

"I know you wouldn't."

"You don't study someone like that." Griffin angrily pointed a finger into Ravlite's chest. "You stop them."

39

Don't think back about what's happened, Leanna coached herself, think ahead. Don't think about the horrid taste of him. Think ahead. *Ahead!* Next move, closer to escaping.

Leanna was locked in the trunk of the car again, and those hard-sided cases bashed against her whenever Arminger steered around a corner. But she detected other cars nearby now, and heard the deep whirling sound made by tires passing over road grates at regular intervals; Leanna recognized the sound as that made driving into Ocean City via the Route 90 bridge.

They were going *back* into Ocean City. Leanna heard horns, car doors, music, people's voices. Thank God! Voices.

Leanna tried not to feel too optimistic. The test wasn't over. Arminger still had her. She was not free yet.

A few anxious minutes later, she heard the heavy gears of a thrill ride drawing riders up a steep incline, and the deep bellow of a foghorn.

She knew the sounds because she'd heard them since childhood. The inlet of Ocean City. The end of the boardwalk, where neon-lit block after block was jammed with arcades, games, ice cream stalls, food booths, and the junk and trinket shops where Leanna used to beg her mother to buy her cheap jewelry.

Randy parked the car, got out, slammed the door, and walked away.

Leanna listened. Other voices: a man and woman talking to one another as they pushed a squeaky-wheeled stroller. The man had a nice voice, saying, "He's really bushed." The woman replied, "It's late. He's had a big day." They were talking about their baby.

Leanna's instinct was to pound on the trunk and scream for help, for the police, but reminded herself, *Test, test, test,* it could still be a test. Randy might be close by, waiting to see if she'd holler and scream. He'd know she *was* trying to escape. And what might he do? He could drive off in the car, take her somewhere and kill her. Or kill her right there. Shoot her—she was more and more convinced he had a gun—and maybe he'd shoot the couple, too, and their baby. He was capable of anything.

So Leanna stayed quiet, waiting for the right moment, again hoping she wasn't passing up an opportunity that might prove her last.

The man and woman closed the doors to their vehicle, sliding one door shut. A minivan, Leanna guessed. The engine started. She couldn't bring herself to make noise to alert them. She told herself to wait. Listen.

More footsteps, coming closer. Keys jingled, went into the trunk, unlocked it.

Randy opened the trunk. Leanna saw him backlit by the thrill rides on the pier. Randy had a brand-new baseball cap on, the stiff brim folded the way he liked it, and a baggy windbreaker. "Come on, let's go." He took her hand and helped her out of the trunk, warily checking their surroundings.

He'd parked at the section of the big lot nearest the pier and beach. Only a few other cars were parked nearby, and all were vacant.

They were three hundred yards from the boardwalk, where thinning crowds of people played carnival games before places closed for the night. Mostly the revelers were high school kids—a lot of June bugs—and families keeping their kids up past bedtime.

The fishing pier was beside and above them, creosote-stained boards creaking with the footsteps of two couples walking out to where they could stand over the ocean and look down at waves breaking against the pilings.

Leanna dusted herself off. A surge of euphoria charged through her that she'd come this far. Her plan was working, so she stayed with it, asking, "Want to get on some rides?" As though this were the continuation of the most bizarre, mad date ever.

Randy put his arm around her and drew her close, face to face. The brim of his cap touched her forehead. He spoke urgently. "Look, we can't fuck around. We're going to get in and get out, and we've got to be careful we don't get caught." His voice was charged full of malicious intent. There was no more gentle stroking to get her in the mood like back in the field. All hard-edged now, Randy advised, "If anything happens, someone recognizes me, or you, if shit hits the fan, run back here. *Right back here.* I'm going to start shooting. Make sure no one gets us."

Shooting! He did have a gun. Randy showed her, flashing open the windbreaker to reveal a handgun holstered under his armpit; its steel grip dangled downward, barrel pointing up.

Leanna sustained another rush of panic, but rode it

out. Telling herself to keep playing the girlfriend, she asked Randy, "What're we doing?" Sounding as though she was excited about it.

"Open that case." Randy pointed to one of the Halliburtons in the trunk and watched Leanna from the corner of his eye while paying more attention to the parking lot.

A few rows away, a cop wrote parking tickets. Little Chamber of Commerce greeting card for the tourists.

Leanna opened the case. The left half contained a videocam packed in custom-cut sections of protective padding. The other half held a small metal-sided box with quarter-sized holes; protruding from the box was a small, pliable wire affixed with a red cap. Leanna identified the wire as a cheap antenna, the sort most commonly seen attached to a child's remote control car.

"Take out the box—carefully."

Leanna did as she was told, fingers slipping between the pillow-foam packing and warm sides of the metal box. The contents weighed a few pounds. "What's this?"

Randy flipped open a brown paper grocery bag and gestured for Leanna to set the box inside. He rolled over the top of the bag and fixed it in his grip. He shut the trunk. He put his arm around Leanna and led her toward the boardwalk, telling her, "It's sort of like a bomb."

Leanna knew what she should say, and managed to say it without too much hesitation. "Cool."

"Most fun you can have without a prescription."

Leanna put her arm around Randy while her mind was racing. A bomb! God! She couldn't let this happen. She had to make her move. Get away from him. Get someone to stop him.

They walked along the outer lane of the parking lot, away from the ticket-writing patrolman. Cars leaving the inlet lot passed by. Leanna prayed someone would recognize Randy. His picture had been in the newspaper. Someone, please, look under the brim of the cap and see his face.

As they neared the boardwalk, smells became more pronounced. French fries cooking in peanut oil. Soft-shelled crabs and crab cakes frying on a grill.

Leanna and Randy mixed with the relaxed crowd on the boardwalk, hearing snippets of conversation of people on vacation.

An older couple on a bench sat close together, seeming to be thinking back to years past and seeing that vision, not the present-moment image of tattooed and pierced teenagers sauntering by smoking cigarettes and shouting obscenities at one another.

A young mother and father held their son's hand and swung him into the air as they walked along, delighting the child until mom said that was enough, it might not be good for him.

A seventeen-year-old boy was proud of the huge stuffed pink ape draped over his shoulders: a prize won for the stringy-haired, gum-chomping girl laughing beside him.

Randy Arminger muttered, "I hate this place. You find me one person who passed algebra two, I'll give you a hundred bucks. This's why the whole country's going to hell, Leanna. Why the world's going to be bankrupt by the time we're thirty. These assholes. Grease-eating, overweight ignorant procreating blue-collar assholes like an anchor dragging us down. Fucking look at them. Work their measly hour-wage jobs for health care benefits so they can get two-dollar prescriptions and free eyeglasses. Go to church on

Sunday and believe in God like that's going to be their salvation. Fucking ignoramuses."

Leanna wondered what drove him to such enraged diatribes.

Randy kept on. "Check out this group." Slightly changing the direction they were walking, he angled Leanna toward a small stand-alone building that served homemade ice cream.

Four teenage boys hung around a painted bench, acting look-at-me cool. Dressed in the current parental-dread fashion, one boy sat on the top rail of the chair back, his ripped-tennis-shoed feet tapping the seat. Another slouched beside him, catcalling at a trio of thirteen-year-old girls whose parents didn't know they were out. A third member of their group jogged over to harass the girls playfully.

Randy commented, "Yeah, guys, that really turns them on."

Leanna couldn't help thinking the kid's approach was nothing at all like tying a girl up and dousing her with kerosene. Talk about romance.

Randy said, "Yeah, they're it. Perfect. Kind of morons the school system teaches to now. Why we don't have any decent teachers any more, because you've got to teach to losers like this. Design courses to reach the lowest common denominator. Losers who'll never make it."

Deciding she'd better say something, Leanna muttered, "Creeps."

Randy instructed, "Go in my pocket. No, not pants—jacket."

Leanna reached across their bodies and slipped her hand into his windbreaker, feeling an oblong plastic object.

Randy said, "That's it."

She took it out: the same remote control he'd had in the van, what he'd pretended he was going to use to let that man set her on fire, then acting as though he'd forgotten batteries. But batteries were in it now; Leanna could tell from its weight. She held the controller as though afraid of it.

"It's okay," Randy assured, "safety pin's out."

Leanna turned the device over and saw a small hole into which a paper-clip "key," fit. The key dangled from the remote by a small length of string; its absence interrupted the source of power from the batteries to the miniature signal-sending device. Until the key was inserted, the remote wasn't functional.

Randy and Leanna walked toward the boys on the bench. Leanna looked around, longing to see a familiar face, someone else from school, someone who'd recognize Randy. Didn't anyone know who he was? Couldn't they see him? Look at him!

Even those whose eyes did fall over Randy didn't identify him. Who would think a wanted mass murderer would be strolling along the boardwalk? Even someone seeing a resemblance would likely think it no more than a lookalike. But maybe that was better. If Randy thought they were in trouble and started shooting . . .

Come on, Leanna, think.

When the bench boys saw Randy and Leanna coming toward them, one of them puffed up his chest like a little bird in mating season, as though there might be a confrontation for a seat.

Randy nodded, said, "How ya doing?" and set his paper bag in the trash can beside the bench. He led Leanna past the boys, taking her on a wide circle around the ice cream place back into the parking lot. Randy stepped off deliberate paces, measuring their distance from the bomb, telling Leanna, "Get ready."

"What?"

"Get ready to put in the pin. Blow those little fuckers up. Once it goes off, we're running like everyone else. Back to the car, and get out of town."

Oh, God.

"Couple more seconds . . ." Randy alerted. "Countdown. Five . . . four . . . three . . . two . . ."

With all the strength she had, Leanna pivoted in place. She threw her weight behind the swing of her arm, doing it suddenly, determinedly—this was it, *the moment*. She mashed the remote into Randy's face, catching him completely off guard.

He was thinking about the countdown, anticipating the explosion, no longer holding her so tightly.

He yelped as the plastic device smacked his nose, part of it scraping his eyelid, missing his eye by only a fraction of an inch. Groaning, "Bitch!" as Leanna jerked out of his grasp.

She was away from him. Running.

Randy swiped an arm for her but missed, reeling slightly from being hit.

Leanna screamed, "Police! Police! He's going to kill me! He's got a gun! Police!" She ran on legs weak with anxiety, feeling she'd collapse any second. Breathing frantically, already short of breath, she sensed him right behind her. Telling herself, keep running, run, run!

On the boardwalk, people stared at her.

Leanna screamed, "Help me! Help me!" and wondered why no one would—like in a nightmare.

Leanna ran toward a cop who'd heard screams and was looking for the source. A big guy with a nightstick in his grip, he grabbed her by the arms, holding her upright as her legs gave out.

Leanna covered her head because Randy would be close behind, shooting at them. "He's got a gun!"

The big officer held her upright in one arm. In control. "Who's got a gun? Where is he?"

Leanna sputtered, "What?" and looked back. An informal circle of onlookers gawked at her. No one seemed afraid. Leanna gasped, "He's got a gun! He's going to kill me. Randy Arminger!"

"Arminger?" The patrolman knew the name; it had been all over the radio.

"He was chasing me." She fought for breath. "I thought—he was right back there. In the parking lot."

"What's your name?"

For a moment, she didn't know. "Um . . ." My God, what was her—? "Landy. Leanna. Leanna Landy!"

"Where is he? Do you see him?" He held her so she faced toward the end of the boardwalk. "What's he wearing?"

"A baseball cap, long pants, a windbreaker."

The officer used the compact walkie-talkie attached to his uniform jersey. He gave his location and advised a sighting of Randy Arminger.

Leanna was more scared now than since Randy cut her down from the cross, because now she didn't know where he was, only that he was going to want her dead in the worst way when he found her.

Standing between two vans, the parking-ticket officer heard the call and radioed in, "This is five-six. Ten-twenty inlet parking lot. Repeat subject description. Repeat—" His sentence was interrupted—ended—by his harsh grunt.

The officer's body slumped over the car parked at an expired meter, two shots at close range punched into the back of his head.

Four-year-old Michael Trey had white skin like paste and dark circles under his eyes. He'd been wearing the same T-shirt for two days now, and it smelled like cigarettes and beer because his nineteen-year-old mother and twenty-two-year-old father, Lisa Su (no "e") and Bart, made it their charming practice to cart their son to the saloons they frequented. Mikey's folks commonly sat his butt on the bar, sometimes using it to wipe sweat rings left by their frosted mugs.

At the moment, Bart and Lisa Su weren't paying a whole lot of attention to Mikey because of a fight they were having about an ex-boyfriend of Lisa Su's, Bart having just scraped his knuckles on her ex's face in an alley because the guy had made a crack about Lisa Su being a good lay.

Lisa Su screamed at Bart, "You didn't hafta go off and bust 'm Bart. Jesus mother and fucking Christ."

"Guy talks like 'at deserves it. What'm I apposed to do, agree with him?"

"Christ, you're ignorant!" Lisa Su crossed her arms in disgust, and stopped suddenly with alarm. "Where's the fuckin' kid!"

Bart looked around the inlet parking lot. "Fuck! I dunno. I thought youse was watchin' him."

Little Mikey appeared just then between two parked cars, having been attracted by something red, which he put in his mouth.

Lisa Su scolded, "Don't eat that, honey!" She went toward Mikey, but Bart got there first and banged the back of Mikey's head with the butt of his palm.

"Youse hear your mother, squirt! Don' eat dat. 'S got germs and shit on it."

Lisa Su slapped Bart's face. "I told you, asshole, *don't hit him no more like 'at.* He'll get brain damage."

Lisa Su and Bart started arguing again, no longer debating ex-boyfriends but the fine points of parenting.

Mikey tagged along, intrigued by his new red toy, especially the key that dangled from it. In a few more years, the current pattern of abuse and malnutrition Mikey was subjected to would reduce him to a state of clinical disfunction, but for the time being, he was pretty clever. The dehydrated state of the gene pool from which he'd been reared notwithstanding, Mikey was able to make a correlation between the key on the string and the hole in the back of the plastic toy.

About twenty feet from where Randy Arminger's sort of bomb sat in a metal trash can, Mikey made a sound, and tried to get the key to fit in that hole.

40

Recoil from the handgun still reverberating up his arm, Randy Arminger ran hunched over between parked cars. He stood upright once the cars thinned out toward the edge of the parking lot near the pier.

His gun back in its holster, Randy took a quick glance back. No one had found the dead cop yet. No one had seen him do it. Randy wasn't sure why he'd killed the cop. No immediate tactical reason except the guy was a cop and he was close by and bottom line, Randy guessed, he felt like shooting him. Take out his frustration over Leanna Landy getting away. Fly Bitch.

Opening the trunk of the rental car, Randy dug into a suitcase and pulled out the first clothes he came to: dark shirt and jeans. He balled them in his hand and closed the trunk. He reached into the front seat and grabbed his CD player, bunching earplug cords with his clothes, then ran onto the beach beneath the pier.

In the dark shadows of creosote-stained pilings, concealed from view, Randy stripped off his jacket, holster, shirt, pants, and shoes. As he slipped on the jeans, his sandy feet stuck in the legs so he had to kick his way into them, getting sand in his pants. It didn't matter. He pulled on the new shirt, whipped the belt out of his discarded pants and fed it through loops in the jeans. He hooked up his CD player to the police band.

The cops were going crazy. A sighting of him, but that was all. Dispatcher was trying to contact a cop—"Five-six"—no doubt the one Randy popped, because Five-six wasn't responding.

Randy breathed hard. His nose stung like hell. He took the shirt he'd pulled off and pressed it to his nose. There was a little bit of blood, but not much. Leanna Fly Bitch! She hadn't really tricked him—not that he didn't *expect* something out of her, at least that's what Randy told himself now, not wanting to blame himself for the lapse that had allowed her escape. He was even smiling, thinking about her. It had been fun dueling mentally with someone closer his equal than anyone else he'd come across since Thursday night.

And if she escaped death at his hand tonight, well, was that really so bad? Maybe it was better, because she'd *know* he'd be after her. Would dread every minute of every day of the rest of her life that the next corner she turned would find him standing there.

So go on, Leanna Fly Bitch, Randy thought with amusement. Run, run, run, run away. Try keeping up that straight-A average next year knowing I'm looking for you, that I might find you, and if you thought tonight was fun, well, just wait . . .

Randy smiled and checked his watch. He was back on schedule. Even had some time to kill.

"Five-six?" the dispatcher called again, trying to keep desperation from his voice. "Five-six, respond."

Officer Five-six was face down dead in the inlet parking lot, but no one knew that except Randy Arminger. Although Griffin had suspicions.

Griffin was in the passenger seat beside Ravlite, speeding to the inlet. Griffin warned, "Tight turn here."

Ravlite didn't know the road, that Coastal Highway snaked into an "S" before running out at the Oceanic Motel. Three lanes abruptly fed a single 45-degree right.

Ravlite laid on the brakes and the tail end of the FBI sedan fishtailed as he cut the wheel. The left rear tire jumped the curb. The undercarriage scraped concrete.

Griffin said, "Close enough." He was out of the car, running down the block, cutting into the street where a group of kids awaiting the bus clogged the sidewalk. Griffin's palms smacked the hood of a car that braked to avoid hitting him, the driver shouting at Griffin.

Griffin ran hard and fast, cutting up a side street closed to traffic. The wide avenue dissected small scale thrill rides and arcade booths: the tilt-a-whirl, baseball throw, and others about to close for the night. More groups of kids hanging out.

Griffin sprinted to the boardwalk and passed through the outdoor tram station—a length of open "cars" pulled by jeep was readying to take passengers north to hotels and condos.

Griffin reached the parking lot and kept running. Cut through the center of long aisles of cars parked parallel to the boardwalk, looking up and down each row for Arminger, having heard the description over the radio: that Arminger wore a dark jacket, baseball cap, and light-colored pants.

Griffin reached the end of the parking lot farthest from the boardwalk—only a long stretch of sand and the ocean beyond—but no sign of Arminger. Griffin turned a slow circle, looking, scanning, running up and down each aisle now instead of cutting across them.

He was sixty seconds into that effort when he saw the feet.

Bart Trey fired up the Z-28, engine roaring and stereo blaring. One helluva car. Too bad the repo man was looking for it, Bart having only made one payment before his financial priorities got rearranged.

His wife Lisa Su cried, "Love this song! Oh, yeah!" She started dancing in the front seat, gyrating her butt against faux-fur seat covers and swaying her arms in front of her.

Little Mikey was in back, still enthralled by his new red toy.

Bart peeled wheels out of the parking space. Loved peeling wheels, often forgetting it might cause a cop to notice. Forgot he was driving on a suspended license, Motor Vehicles having yanked his driving privilege for forty-five days for a .18 breathalyzer test; the administrative judge having gone on and on about how Bart was halfway to a coma with a blood alcohol reading like that, and Bart's lawyer—who looked a lot younger on those late-night TV ads—just sat there and did nothing. Which Bart figured justified his driving on a suspended license. A lousy lawyer and the system were taking advantage of a hardworking man yet again.

Little Mikey's neck snapped when the car shot back in reverse, and he lost his grip on his red toy just when he was about to get that key in the slot. Mikey made a sound of protest that sounded like "Poop," and went crawling on the floor for that red toy.

Mikey was free to roam because no child seat was going to hold any kid of Lisa Su and Bart's in place like a damned straitjacket. No sir. "Cops don't like it," Bart always bragged, "they can kiss my ass."

* * *

"You've got an officer down," Griffin reported, using the fallen policeman's walkie-talkie. "Inlet parking lot. Between the fourth and fifth rows of cars."

"Identify yourself," the dispatcher replied sharply.

"Concerned citizen," Griffin replied, unhooking the officer's portable communications unit where it snapped on his uniform shirt. "Your man's dead. Head shots." Half of the man's face was on the parking lot: wounds generated by a substantial-caliber weapon. Griffin wondered why the body hadn't been found sooner—hadn't anyone heard the shots?

The dispatcher radioed for an ambulance and put out an all-units call, requesting the nearest officer respond to the scene, then advised, "Sir . . ." Unsure how to address Griffin. ". . . whoever found Officer Kent, are you there? Sir? Whoever called in Officer Kent, please respond."

"What?" Griffin demanded, moving away from the dead policeman, taking the man's radio. Griffin renewed his foot search for Arminger, outrage flowing through him.

"Identify yourself," the dispatcher insisted.

"You've got one entrance to this parking lot and I suggest you secure it now!"

"Identify yourself."

Another voice came on the air. "This is Special Agent Ravlite, FBI. You are communicating with an undercover operative who has full authority as re: fugitive Randy Arminger."

"Special Agent, please confirm identify."

Ravlite began rattling off a series of identifying monikers when Griffin talked over him:

"Secure the parking lot exit! Let's go! Let's go! And

advise if the girl Arminger kidnapped is now in police custody."

A police officer responded: "Affirmative. She's with me in my cruiser at Wicomico and the boardwalk."

"Goddammit, I didn't ask *where* she was, I asked if she was in custody. Get her out of there now. Get her somewhere secure and do not—repeat, do not—announce your next location."

The officer hesitated, called in, "Dispatch, please contact Lieutenant Krauss to confirm instructions."

"Get the fuck out of there!" Griffin yelled. Considering all possibilities: "If Arminger's got police band access, he's got your twenty. Get the girl somewhere safe and do it now!"

Officer, after a pause: "Dispatch, we're going to await Lieutenant Krauss until we secure I.D. on this caller. Do we know this isn't Arminger using Kent's radio?"

"This is Special Agent Ravlite. Please do as instructed." Ravlite maintained a cool authoritative edge.

"Dispatch, can you confirm these identities?"

"Stand by."

Griffin, frustrated, radioed, "Ravlite, use some of that goddamned federal authority and get these yokels moving."

"On my way to local police station now. ETA five minutes."

Sirens neared the inlet parking lot, two cars wheeling in at the opposite end from Griffin.

Griffin, on the radio, demanded, "Ask the girl what kind of vehicle Arminger's driving."

Dispatch authorized, "Five-fifteen, please advise on that."

Griffin wondered when someone was going to get

around to considering that Arminger might just drive away.

The officer with Leanna replied, "Beige four-door sedan. Unsure of make and model, but she believes American-made."

Griffin: "Where's it parked?"

"Stand by."

Griffin muttering, "Standby . . . like Arminger's hanging around with a thumb up his ass." Griffin looked for a pale sedan and saw two possibilities.

Arriving police cars located Officer Kent's body. One stayed with him, the other car began speeding through the lot, searching.

The officer with Leanna radioed, "Twenty on that beige sedan is inlet parking lot at the corner near the pier and beach."

Griffin, just about there, saw the car. He pulled his gun from his waist and approached the sedan but maintained a peripheral scan as well.

He wanted Arminger. No other thoughts in his mind. End this. Not that long ago, outside the bar, he'd been within fifty yards of him. Griffin wanted him that close again and made no apology for that desire—not to anyone, anything.

Maybe what he'd done in the past was a sin—twice taking human life—and maybe he'd rot in hell for eternity. One thing eternity had going for it: once you were there, you were there. No such thing as consecutive sentences to eternal damnation.

The beige sedan looked empty, but someone could be hiding along the seats. Not likely, though. Arminger didn't hide. He moved.

Still, Griffin had to check. He didn't know how

Leanna had gotten away from Arminger; maybe she'd called out to the police officer who Arminger then shot.

Griffin was at the car, handgun aimed on it. No one inside.

A woman shouted from the pier, pointing down at Griffin: "Some guy's got a gun! There's a guy with a gun!"

Griffin shouted, "I'm a cop. Get out of here!"

A panicked voice came through the radio. "Shots fired! Shots fired! We're being shot at!" It was the officer who was protecting Leanna. The sound of glass breaking, an engine unwinding. Leanna was screaming.

Randy had been content to let Leanna go, to let her worry about him for the rest of her life. But when the cop came on the radio and said where she was—about two blocks away—Randy figured, hell, fishing in a barrel was still fishing.

He made the trip on foot, and there was the cop car, parked halfway down the side street. A few people walked around, but there were no other cops. Randy strolled down the ramp off the boardwalk, stayed close to the buildings, checked out the car, saw two heads inside.

Randy no longer wore the windbreaker but had it balled up in his hand, wrapped around the gun, concealing it. Coming up on the driver's side, his fingers slid along the handgun's trigger.

Thirty yards.

Cop didn't see him.

Leanna looked straight ahead.

Twenty yards.

The cop's window was open. Randy watched the

sideview mirror, seeing the cop's reflection, the cop looking at Leanna, talking to her.

Ten yards. Out comes Mr. Gun.

Randy pulled off shots at close range. One, two, three. Just missing the cop's head. Bullet slicing through the front window.

Leanna, unsure what was happening and why the glass was being pierced, saw him and screamed.

Randy moved parallel to them. Wanting a shot past the cop at Leanna. Still ten yards away.

Leanna ducked down, screaming louder.

The cop saw Randy as bullets flew past his face. He reacted fast enough to get the car in gear and drive off.

Randy shot through the rear window.

The next bullet came through glass quietly, a thud of impact immediately followed by the splintering of spider web cracks, like ice cubes snapping when dropped in warm liquid.

The bullet after that hardly made a sound at all going into the policeman's neck. A direct, soft punch. That was all. Blood erupted over the windshield. The officer grunted and slumped sideways against his door. His hands fell off the wheel. The cruiser smashed into a phone pole near the intersection.

Leanna was thrown forward into the dash. She hit her head on the windshield and was vaguely aware of her skin breaching open from impact. Warm blood oozed into her right eye. Her vision was blurred, she was light-headed, but she got out of the car, staggering, running—again. Wanting to get away. *Get away.* She ran into the street without realizing there was traffic. She heard another thump and didn't understand it was the sound of a car hitting her torso, throwing her into the air.

* * *

Randy Arminger liked that. Hey, Leanna can fly. Fly, Fly Bitch, fly. Her rail of a body bounded off the hood of that car, then sailed about fifteen feet in the air before landing.

Randy smiled as he ducked into an alley. He glanced at his watch, said, "Now that didn't take long at all."

Griffin got there in four minutes and ran into the melee. Cop car piled into a pole. Fifty people in the street screaming, panicking for an ambulance. Someone had been hit by a car. A cop was shot.

Griffin pushed through the spectators and saw Leanna's slender body. Blood on her head. Her eyes were open and she blinked. Her hand twitched.

A woman, an off-duty nurse, knelt beside her and warned that Leanna shouldn't be touched. "We need something to cover her and keep her warm!" Someone offered a beach blanket.

Two more police cruisers tried to get through, but traffic was at a standstill. Everyone was out of their car. One officer abandoned his cruiser and made the final fifty yards on foot, getting to the wounded officer and administering first aid.

Griffin estimated half the on-duty police were here now. People didn't get shot in Ocean City. Maybe one all year. Not two in one night. And never, ever a policeman.

Griffin's gun was back in the waist of his trousers with everyone becoming very edgy, cops and citizens alike. Rumors were flying around. Griffin had heard it on the boardwalk. People acting scared. A policeman had been shot. Some lunatic running around with a gun.

Griffin had the gut feeling Arminger was liking this: all the chaos he'd caused. No Rules working a little bit of Armageddon.

Griffin heard a young guy tell a cop, "Guy with a gun went down there." He pointed to a paved alley between two buildings.

Griffin started down the alley before the cop reacted to the witness's statement. He stayed wide of a dumpster and other hiding places where Arminger could lay in wait.

On Griffin's right: a six-unit apartment house, windows open, lights on. Solid concrete wall left. A small grassy parking lot ahead. Three cars there. A clothes line. An old lawnmower.

A door closed just ahead. Metal screen door. Griffin hurried forward, around the edge of the little apartment house, and saw a ramshackle cottage with a For Rent sign screwed to a porch railing. Motorcycle on the porch. Ripped window screens flapped open.

Inside, college kids watched ESPN, drank beer, and laughed. Guys in shorts. Two girls in sundresses looked let's-go-somewhere bored. The guy who'd just walked in announced urgently, "A cop just got shot right outside!"

"Ho, fuck!"

They came piling out to see for themselves.

Griffin reached the next side street; there and on the boardwalk was a strange feel of urgency. News and rumor rippling like a tidal wave. On Baltimore Avenue, traffic was backing up. Nothing moving. Cops on loudspeakers ordered people to stay in their cars and be on the lookout for a man with a gun.

Griffin thought, Damned good advice.

* * *

Arminger looked around in wonder, awed by his latest accomplishment. Look at this. Panic and fear running strongly. Oh, yeah, baby, yeah. Arminger was actually on a high. What a rush. Better than any drug. He was immersed in the complete and total terror of others. Thrilling on it. Better than he imagined. And it was so easy.

The sense of order that held people's lives together, held society together, was just dangling like a long thread on a cheap suit, waiting to be pulled so the whole mess would unravel.

Arminger was in the middle of the street, walking through a line of stopped cars. Cops were running around like blue-suited chickens looking for their heads.

Plugged in, Arminger heard the dispatcher going nuts on the police band. Randy wanted to make sure he knew if someone got a glimpse of him. Not that he needed to hide.

One cop was running right at him, right now, but not seeing who he was. The cop breathed hard. Rushed by gasping for breath.

Randy called after him, "Don't have a heart attack." He continued across the street, coming up behind a van with a family inside: mom, dad, two young kids. Mom and Dad looked edgy. Kids in the back seat were confused about what was going on.

Randy had a sudden urge. An impulse to pop mom in the passenger seat. Hey kids, wanna see mom's brains?

"Whewwwee," Bart Trey exhaled, sitting upright in the Camaro, watching two cop cars speed across the inlet parking lot. "Man, I thought for sure dem cops wuz comin' for me."

Still spoiling for a fight, Lisa Su said, "I tole youse you oughta lemme do the drivin'." Lisa Su sat up and untwisted the front of her shirt. "S'stupid's whadditis."

Bart refired the Camaro's big engine with a roaring vengeance.

The smartest one of the group, Mikey, offered a celebratory "Nnnnyah," and proudly held up the toy he'd found. Showing his folks he'd gotten that key in the hole of the remote control. A little red light went on. Nothing else happened.

At least not until Bart drove closer to the boardwalk. Bart and Lisa Su were wondering what people were running around about. All the cops. And an ambulance.

Bart cruised alongside a guy driving a new Mustang 5.0. Bart rolled down his window and called over, "Hey youse. What dah hell's goin' on?" Bart coasted beside the Mustang at about five mph because traffic was backed up leaving the inlet.

The two cars were in the double exit lane, nearing the ice cream stand.

The Mustang driver said, "Cop was shot." He pointed toward the ambulance and people milling around. "Right over there. Gruesome."

Bart looked over and said, "Huh." Coasting closer to Dumser's.

Little Mikey was still trying to show his parents what he'd done. Got that key in.

Lisa Su finally saw, said, "Hey, honey, that's great."

Mikey was beaming, "Nnnnyahhh!" when the remote's signal found Randy's bomb.

A deep, hard explosion burst red-orange globs of fire into the air. The ground rumbled. People were thrown off their feet. Demonic fireworks filled the night sky.

Chunks of flammable jelly blasted out of Randy's bomb, sticking to whatever they landed on and burning it.

The fire jelly melted from the heat and spread, setting old wooden roofs and walls ablaze. People's clothes were on fire. A young woman ran screaming, her long blond hair ablaze like a streaking comet.

Randy was about to shoot the mother riding in the van when he heard the explosion. Was a quarter mile from it and not only heard the blast but felt it. And the screams. The wonderful, horrified screams as reflections of red-orange light filled the sky.

His bomb! Somehow, some way, it had been set off. He'd assumed Leanna had run off with the remote after hitting him with it. But no. Detonation! Fan-fucking-tastic!

New calls of panic flew over the police radio.

"Something just blew up!" a cop shouted. "Jesus Christ, it's raining goddamned fire. Get the fire department down here now, now, now!" The guy sounding as though he was running while screaming.

Randy *had* to check this out. He sprinted toward the melee. A regular apocalyptic carnival going now. Randy's three-ring circus of hell. Welcome to reality, morons, Randy thought. Come on in. Enjoy the show!

Griffin ran toward the explosion. Coming to the boardwalk to see—God, a small war zone. Fire and panic. Griffin avoided people who ran blindly.

A girl screamed. Her hair was on fire and she couldn't get it out. She slapped at her head with her hands, only the blaze spread to her palms, sticking to her skin, burning flesh.

Griffin grabbed her and tackled her easily to the

ground. Flames jumping around his face, he lay on top of her head, shouting for her to be still, forcing her to be still, feeling fire's heat attaching to his shirt, flame twisting hot around him. Some slimy substance was burning the girl, like napalm.

Griffin worried the fire wasn't going out as he tried to smother it with his body—that he was going to burn with her. The smell of her scorched hair was horrible.

All around, people ran or staggered about, dazed, in shock.

The blast had gone off near the ice cream store, where a trash can was now on its side, peeled open and on fire. Two bodies lay still, dead, burning. Children were screaming, crying.

Griffin had never seen anything like it. Dozens of small fires were spreading across old, wooden buildings—timber boxes ready to ignite. Flames licked the night like evil, mocking tongues.

Kids cried loudly, screaming for their parents. Kids lost in the confusion. Their cries were like Griffin's nightmares, but the vision was so much worse.

A little boy walked into a puddle of burning jelly and his shoe caught fire, but he didn't notice. He was disoriented, crying, calling for his mother.

Griffin got up from the girl, having smothered the fire from her hair. The front of his shirt was black and smoking. The skin around his throat was burned. He ran to the boy and picked him up, flame swirling around the rubber sole of his little shoe; Griffin wrapped the tail of his shirt around the fire's slick, oozing heat and put it out.

Griffin was soothing the boy, telling him he'd find his mother, when he looked across the boardwalk, through black chemical smoke and fire, and saw Arminger.

Arminger. Standing there. Beaming. Surrounded by his creation. Arminger, at the top of his lungs, over all the noise and confusion, screamed a possessed, "Yeah!" He walked away, fist held high above his head in victory as he turned down the side street.

Secure that the pandemonium he'd created would conceal him, Arminger didn't look back. He didn't see Griffin.

41

People ran either toward the boardwalk to help, or away from it in fear, except Arminger, who proceeded slowly with his own purpose, king amidst the ruins.

On the only road leading from the inlet, police struggled to control the situation, to get people back in their cars and out of Ocean City's old town section, needing to clear gridlock from the streets so fire personnel and equipment could get to the scene before blocks of aged, wooden structures—decades of history—burned to the ground.

Unrecognized, Arminger crossed the dual lane road between stopped cars and policemen shouting orders. He continued down the next block, past small taverns and cottages where people watched in stunned disbelief as fire spread and the sky turned brighter orange.

That this chaos had been created by one person was unthinkable. And yet there he was, half a block ahead of Griffin, with something dark and thick wrapped around his hand.

Had Arminger been hurt? No, Griffin estimated. That wasn't a bandage—he was hiding the gun in his hand.

Griffin followed cautiously, not wanting Arminger to glance back and see him. It was easier for Griffin to conceal himself here than outside Wild Whales, ducking between small buildings, staying in the shadows.

Arminger jogged across the four southbound lanes of Coastal Highway, his athletic frame caught in the red swirling light of a fire engine's emergency signals. The big truck bore down the highway, gears grinding out, siren blasting, escorted by a police cruiser with one officer driving, another running alongside the car to direct stopped cars out of the way.

Arminger slipped around the corner of a small apartment house and proceeded toward the bay.

Griffin ran forward. He had to close the distance. Griffin stayed close to the buildings, shoes slapping lightly upon the sidewalk. Sirens rang his ears. His throat hurt and stung from being burned.

He paused at the corner, quick-glanced around the side.

Arminger was less than twenty yards away, walking toward the marinas. Alone. No one else on the street. The curious had gone to the boardwalk. The scared were inside. The oblivious had somehow managed to stay asleep in bed.

Blocks from the boardwalk, the air smelled less of fire and more of the bay's salty aroma. Ahead were small marinas: piers of oceangoing yachts and for-hire deep-sea fishing boats.

Arminger left the sidewalk and cut between a bait shop and cottage, as though aiming for the shortest distance to the northernmost marina.

Griffin thought, a boat. The police had set up checkpoints on the highways and Arminger was going to make his escape by boat.

On a course parallel to Arminger, Griffin sprinted down a short driveway. He hurdled a little picket fence into the side yard of a small house. Behind the house, he ran between a storage building and marine engine repair shop. A real mixed bag of development in this old section of town.

Griffin stopped fifteen feet from where the concrete block building met the sidewalk. Hidden, he held his breath, listening.

If Arminger was headed to that far marina—the apparent direction he'd started out on—he'd walk past this spot.

Griffin waited, hearing gulls over the bay and water soft slapping the hulls of oceanworthy boats. A slight smell of diesel fuel bit the air. Then: footsteps to his left. Approaching. Arminger?

Griffin watched the pavement and street. Overhead lights cast shadows. Griffin waited for a silhouette to appear. Footsteps came closer.

A head materialized as shadow on the sidewalk. The rest of the shadow body followed, walking at a brisk pace. A foot kicked a small oyster shell, skidding it across the sidewalk. The walker was just about to the corner of the building. Would be less than five feet from where Griffin stood—

Now. The person emerged. Arminger. Looking forward, not to the side. Not seeing Griffin in the shadows.

Griffin stepped forward and shot him three times in the side and back of the head. Bang-bang-bang. Loud shots. Griffin pressed forward the whole time, each shot closer to Arminger's head than the last. Blood, bone, tissue erupting. Griffin said—thought he said, anyway—"Enough." Or maybe he just thought it. Enough.

Griffin ducked back between buildings before Arminger hit the street. He tucked the gun in his pants and kept his head down, walking quickly but not running.

He turned the corner, stayed to the sidewalk. In the open now, eyes checking side to side, and taking quick glances behind him. Not thinking anyone had seen him, but not sure. He'd been too focused on Arminger to let any more than his peripheral vision watch for witnesses.

So far no one was pointing at him, calling after him.

Griffin doubled back toward the marinas but by a different route. Two blocks from where Arminger lay dead, Griffin broke into an easy run. He covered the side streets quickly, until the sound of sirens and police bullhorns grew distant.

Bay waters lapped against bulkheads near the big concrete pilings of the Route 50 bridge. Secure he was alone, Griffin stood on loose gravel packed against the bulkheads. He slipped the gun from his waist, wiped it on his charred shirt, and hurled it into the bay. It landed with a quiet splash and began a slow descent into deep briny water around the pilings.

It was the second time in his life he'd thrown a gun into water after killing someone. And he wasn't in hell yet.

Griffin walked away from the bridge, back toward the street, taking deep breaths, waiting for the dread to wash over him. For some sort of tortured anxiety to take hold. For lightning to strike.

Adrenaline gripped frantic hold on him. His heart pumped wildly. His mind raced. And yet he experienced a most unusual—how could he describe it?—Calm. Relief. Or was it satisfaction?

There were certain passages into which his mind would not allow him to venture.

Griffin walked into the open, and found a line of the city's transit buses assembled by police to get people back to their motels and condos.

A lot of high school kids stood there. They had been down at the ocean for Senior Week. Some maintained images of cool; others were visibly shaken by what had happened.

Griffin got on one of the buses, squeezing in a seat between two kids. It was strangely quiet. None of the usual antics. A couple of them talked quietly. One boy started crying, the girl beside him offering a hug and assurance Beth would be all right, their friend having been burned and taken to the hospital by ambulance. Others looked around, afraid the next disaster might get them. It had all been so horrible, no one questioned Griffin's appearance. The blood on his pants. His burned shirt.

Griffin thought about Liz, how she'd claimed that night in the movie theater parking lot that at this age, kids felt immortal, indestructible. Seeing these kids here, right now, Griffin was pretty sure Liz was wrong. There was no such age any more that allowed for such cocky security. These kids were a lot more aware than previous generations; they knew there was a lot to be afraid of. They probably also knew—or at least guessed—that the people and institutions who were supposed to be protecting them were becoming increasingly outnumbered and ineffective.

42

Smelling of smoke and sweat, Griffin got into his ex-wife's car and drove out of Ocean City.

He looked toward the inlet a few miles away, and was relieved to see the sky was dark with night, not orange with fire.

Just across the Route 90 bridge, a short line of cars was stopped at the police checkpoint. Police officers required drivers to open their trunks, and most people complied, but others who didn't know what was going on yelled and screamed about their rights.

The way the country was headed, Griffin wasn't sure how much longer those rights would be around. How much more insanity could be sustained before periods of martial law were imposed? Most people had no idea how much violence was prevented by the FBI and the police—thwarted attempts that didn't get into the newspapers because of the covert nature of the operations.

But for how much longer? Criminal sophistication was increasing. Schematics for bombs were freely available on the Internet. Law enforcement felt its hold slipping, its efforts leading to more frustration than prosecution. Morale was sinking fast in police departments across the country, so much so it was getting tough to recruit good cops anymore.

Griffin watched the young guys searching the cars just ahead of him. They were barely trained and made tactical mistakes. If Arminger had been in one of the cars, he could have shot all four of them before they knew what happened. Because Arminger had fired a gun at someone before—he liked it—and these guys didn't look to have aimed at anything more than a paper target, or maybe—raised around here—geese or deer. A big difference.

Griffin pulled up to the checkpoint, his window already rolled down. "Evening," he said to the young officer, and released the trunk latch from inside the car.

The policeman shined his flashlight over the interior of the Honda, considered Griffin's burned shirt, but didn't say anything; Griffin wasn't Arminger, and that's what he was concerned about. He checked the trunk, shut it, and passed Griffin through.

Griffin pulled away slowly but was soon driving fifteen miles over the speed limit, passing other cars. Halfway to Salisbury, he was practically alone on the road. All the windows were down. Warm air rushed through the small car's interior. The highway was dark and straight.

He slowed through small towns, stopping for the occasional traffic light, then was back over the speed limit again once outside of populated areas. Corn and soy fields and stands of pines stretched across the flat horizon.

His sense of calm remained. Had he not been here before, experiencing the moments of life after causing death, he'd have believed it might be shock. A false sense of nonreaction keeping away the anxiety that was sure to engulf him. But he knew that wasn't the case.

Still, he struggled against the urge to truly gauge his

emotions, not wanting to look that deeply inside himself for fear revelation would cause the shock that shooting someone did not.

He wasn't ready to admit what he felt—wasn't going to define it—although ninety minutes from Ocean City and Randy Arminger, driving across the Chesapeake Bay Bridge, the water looking so peaceful and dark, lights of tankers reflecting off her still waters, Griffin felt a warm surge press through him. The sensation was at once tranquil and disturbing, for he saw a glimpse of what he was and what he was capable of.

The impression left him longing for solace, which he found an hour later at the hotel, arriving after three in the morning.

Cassie was sleeping peacefully, but Janice was still awake, watching news bulletins about Ocean City.

Janice was scared, but not for him. As though there was no doubt in her mind Griffin would be fine—for she had her own vision of what she believed him to be. She wrapped her arms around him. Kissed him.

Griffin said, "It's over."

Janice took him to the bathroom, ran the shower, undressed him. She undressed herself and got in under warm water with him. She never asked about his burned shirt or commented what the news reporters were saying: that Arminger was still on the loose. As though she knew Griffin would not have come back if that were the case. As though somehow she knew everything.

And yet they didn't speak of it. Not one word.

She took Griffin to bed, and while he felt completely awake—was sure he wouldn't sleep at all—with her arms around him, he was asleep within minutes, and slept as though dead until well past noon, when there was a knock on the door.

* * *

The knock sounded again, and Griffin awakened. The bedroom was dark and cool, and he had no sense of time until seeing illuminated numerals on the clock.

He remembered where he was, what had happened, and waited to see if sleep changed his perception. It didn't.

Another knock on the door.

Where was Janice? He didn't hear Cassie either.

From out in the hall, a voice called, "Maid service."

"Yeah . . . okay . . ." Griffin reached for his boxers and tugged them on. "In a minute." His body ached. The skin across his throat was tender from the burn.

He went into the sunny living-room half of the suite. Cassie and Janice weren't there.

Griffin opened the door to the young woman in the maid's uniform.

She asked, "Checking out today?"

"Yes, but we need a little more time. Okay?"

"Sure."

"Thanks." Griffin started to close the door, but stopped. "My . . . friend . . ." Unsure how to describe Janice. ". . . and daughter aren't here, have you seen them?"

"No. But maybe the pool, or there's a little play yard around the far side of the building."

Griffin thanked her again, shut the door, and began organizing the day in his mind. Looking over Cassie's things, he estimated there was enough to make do. He wasn't going back to his wife's apartment. He didn't want to see any more reminders of the past. And while he supposed he should do something about a funeral for Carla, he still had no idea what.

He thought about that while staring at Cassie's clothes

and the few toys he'd brought with her, beginning to feel the thrill and apprehension of a new beginning starting right now. This very moment.

But then there was another knock at the door.

Griffin, anticipating Janice had forgotten her key, opened it.

"Sleep well?" It was Ravlite, asking that question like a bed-and-breakfast owner greeting his guest for Sunday brunch. His appearance was neat as always. His white hair was washed, combed, and nary a strand out of place. No seersucker suit today but linen pants and a crisp long-sleeved shirt, french cuffs, and beautiful silk tie. "Did you sleep well?" he asked again, really wanting an answer to that question, not making rhetorical comment.

"Yes."

Ravlite nodded, then: "Sorry we got separated last night. Very hectic."

"Don't worry about it." Griffin looked down the hall for Janice and Cassie.

"They're taking a walk. The young woman is very good with her. She likes children."

"I know."

Ravlite's eyes maintained surveillance of Griffin's expression and posture. "How did you find him? How did you know where he'd be?"

Griffin looked at Ravlite, then glanced away. "I've got a lot to do today. We're going back to Florida. And it's a long drive."

"Yes, it is."

"That's not a problem, is it? My leaving for Florida?"

"Of course not. Why should it be a problem?" Realizing what Griffin meant, Ravlite added. "Oh, I see. You think—well, whatever you think, I told you, my interest is strictly academic. I just study events and people and publish findings for other field agents to utilize. Analyzing and predicting behavior is becoming more and more critical. You know, a former colleague of mine has packaged a software program that evaluates seemingly innocent habits of parolees and can determine with remarkable odds which of them are going to be repeat offenders. You wouldn't think such small details as eating schedules, sleep habits, and what TV shows someone watches would be so telling, but they are. There are many other factors, too—all tiny little insignificant 'tells.' "

"That's good work, then."

"Yes, it is . . . but tell me, would you, how it happened. Did he see you? Was he running from you? It doesn't look like it. Not from the trajectory of the bullets and how his body fell. It looks as if you were waiting for him, and when he got there . . . well, let's see . . . he would have been walking by you, like this . . ." Ravlite prepared to re-create the scene, using where Griffin stood in the doorway as the spot from which he'd ambushed Randy Arminger. "Arminger was headed for the marina. You know, he'd hired a boat to take him to South Carolina. Possibly he was going there to kill his mother, or maybe it was just a launch pad for wherever he was going next. It was somewhere he was familiar with, anyway . . ." Ravlite returned his conversation to point. "Arminger was probably somewhat anxious about the boat—maybe worrying if all the evening's commotion had jeopardized the charter captain's availability—so he would have been looking straight ahead, not looking around the corner of that building."

Ravlite walked down the carpeted hall toward Griffin, watching Griffin for reaction, as though re-enacting this event would cause telling response. Ravlite, approaching the doorway, aimed his hand straight ahead. "Arminger's looking out there, even a bit left of center, I believe, given the location of the marina. And as he comes by here . . . you're right there . . . probably a step or two back, though, where he wouldn't notice you. So he walks by . . ." Ravlite did as he described ". . . and then you step out. Put the gun right to his head." Ravlite stopped, glanced sideways at Griffin. "He'd have been right about here when you stepped out."

Griffin hadn't moved from the doorway. He just watched, expressionless.

Ravlite's eyes looked frankly at him. "Did you say anything to him? Anything at all?" Ravlite was unable to conceal how desperately he wanted to know.

"Enough," Griffin said.

"Wait, don't close the door. I don't know what I can tell you to assure you I'm not at all interested in making an arrest. I don't care that Arminger is dead. It's just fascinating—"

"Enough," Griffin repeated, and his eyes met Ravlite's.

Ravlite had thought Griffin was saying that about him. *Enough.* Now Ravlite understood. And he smiled. His body relaxed as though eased into warm water. "Thank you."

Griffin didn't nod, just stepped back to close the door, saying, "You'll waste your time keeping tabs on me. I'm not picking up a gun anymore, let alone putting my finger on the trigger."

Ravlite nodded as though in agreement but said, "We'll see."

43

It was hot in Juno Beach, an almost oppressive heat.

Still, Griffin was sitting outside on the porch. There was shade and the humid breeze off the ocean was made slightly more comfortable by the Casablanca fan he'd gotten the owners' okay to wire into the ceiling.

After running three miles—half on the beach, half on the road—Griffin didn't bother to dry off after his shower, just slipped on shorts and a T-shirt, grabbed his Gatorade, and sat on an Adirondack chair on the porch.

The air stirred and rustled palm fronds like wind chimes. The ocean was bright blue. The beach was mostly empty, because not only were the snowbirds gone, but even local residents were packing up to spend summer vacations where it was less humid.

Liz arrived on time, having flown in from Atlanta and rented a car in West Palm Beach. She waved and smiled tentatively as she steered the mid-sized sedan into the driveway.

Griffin walked to the side of the house to greet her.

Liz said, "Don't you look sexy," hugging him. But her hug, like the tone of her voice, was without the intensity of just three weeks ago.

Liz hadn't seen Griffin since the morning she left Baltimore for Myrtle Beach, flying south to interview

Randy Arminger's mother. Liz had been with her when FBI agents came to the door, advising that Randy had been killed—shot in the head. Randy's mother collapsed hearing the news. Her last words Liz recorded were, "He was such a good boy."

The FBI said there was no information on who shot Randy Arminger. Twenty days later, there was still no information on the shooter. No suspects. No witnesses.

From Myrtle Beach, Liz had flown back to Baltimore, but Griffin, Janice, and Cassie had already left for Florida. It had been then that Liz decided with finality, whatever she and Griffin had shared was over. Not because she didn't love him, not that she wouldn't yearn for him, miss him, just that it was different now.

She'd written her story from Baltimore and back home in Atlanta, getting information from Griffin by phone only—conversations she wouldn't let stray from Arminger even when Griffin wanted to talk about *them.* Liz having told him, "Don't. It'll just make it harder."

From the beginning of their relationship, Griffin had let Liz make the decisions, as though he were treading as softly with her as he had his late wife, who'd psychologically manipulated him into a reactionary role: be there when I need you, and don't ask anything in return. It took Liz all this while to realize that's why Griffin seemed to hold back emotionally. It wasn't that he was unwilling or incapable, he was just suffering a little post-marital shell shock.

Now Griffin was a father again, and Liz—idle fantasies aside—had no interest in being a mom. And that wouldn't be fair to Griffin or Cassie or herself.

It was better this way—friends—although Liz found it hard to tell herself that as Griffin walked her to the front porch with his arm around her.

In her wilder, younger days, Liz would have reacted to the urge inside her right now to seduce him, make wild love to him—on the front porch, and who cared if somebody saw them. But she was changing, too.

"I'm seeing someone," she said, wanting to get that out of the way.

Griffin nodded.

"Nothing serious," Liz added, compelled to say that. "He lives in the city. He's a stockbroker. Now that I don't blow my whole paycheck, I have some money to invest. I went to a seminar he gave. . . . He's nice."

Griffin opened the door and they went inside.

The cottage had taken on new life since Liz was last here. Cassie's influence, pop-up books and playthings, were scattered about. A big box of disposable diapers sat on the kitchen floor.

"Where's Cassie . . . and Janice?"

"Janice took her to the store. They'll be gone for a while."

"You told her I was coming?"

"Yes." Griffin poured himself more Gatorade. "Want some?"

"No." Liz sat at the kitchen counter, flopping her saddle bag on the stool beside her. She watched him. She'd missed him. "You look good."

"So do you."

"You seem more—I don't know, settled. Relaxed. Less restless."

"I feel less restless. Still don't know what the hell I'm going to do, though."

"Law school?"

"No." As though that was far out of the running.

"I guess working with me . . ." Liz began nervously, having told herself she wasn't going to bring that up and here she was saying it only five minutes after pulling into the driveway.

"I don't want to chase people anymore. I don't want to see the bad in people." He leaned against the counter beside her. "I don't watch the news anymore. I don't read the newspaper." He gestured to the porch. "I like to watch the sunrise. I love being on the beach. I'm swimming a couple of miles a day. And I've never had this experience before—just living a life. I've always been a cop or around cops—and crime. From the time I was a kid with my father. It's a relief to pretend none of that's out there . . . because if I know it's out there, I'm compelled to do something about it. Now I don't want to know."

Liz smiled, but had to point out, "Innocence lost is tough to recapture."

"I've done tougher."

"Yes, you have," Liz admitted. "You have." Still, she couldn't help thinking he was trying to fool himself. "Well . . ." She reached into her bag for an envelope. "I brought your check, so at least you'll be able to eat for a while." She slid it across the counter. "It's sixty grand. I got the paper to cough up a little extra since you gave us so much detail no one else had. I'm also getting a nice wire-service check, so I'll cut you in."

"This is way more than enough."

"You can be innocent again if you want, Grif, but don't be naive. You've got a kid. You need money. I'll send the check."

He nodded.

The silence that fell around them was familiar for a few moments, then suddenly felt awkward, as though they'd already run out of things to say. Or maybe it was anxiety about what needed to be said.

Liz asked, "How's Cassie?"

"She's doing really well." Griffin smiled proudly. "I think she likes it here. She loves my parents. We see them a lot."

Liz smiled and forced herself to hold that smile, asking, "And Janice?"

"She's fine."

Liz was jealous and couldn't keep from wanting to know, "Are you sleeping with her?" She dreaded the answer.

"No."

"No?" Liz wondered if she and Griffin were over as a couple, why was such passionate relief flowing through her? "Nothing? Not even a little—?"

"We're just friends. She watches Cassie for me to help out."

"She loves you. You should marry her, Grif. You really should."

"We have feelings for one another but not like that. It looked like it for a week or so, but . . ." Griffin shook his head. "We're just going to be friends."

"She's better for you than I could have ever been. She's . . ." Liz felt as if she might start to cry, so she picked up her bag and started for the door.

"Liz, wait." He caught up to her.

Liz, sniffling, said, "This is embarrassing. *God-dammit.*" Scolding herself.

"It's okay." He held her and, after a few minutes, said, "I miss you."

"Don't say that. It'll just make us both believe things can happen that shouldn't. That can't. That won't."

Griffin held her firmly, whispered, "A lot's happened. A lot to adjust to. It's strange, but it's good."

"It's too painful now. You and me. It could never work."

Griffin held onto her, not ready to let her go. He said, "We'll see." Hugging her closely. "We'll see."